SABRINA JEFFRIES

Let Sleeping Rogues Lie

Pocket Books

New York   London   Toronto   Sydney   New Delhi

Pocket Books
An Imprint of Simon & Schuster, Inc.
1230 Avenue of the Americas
New York, NY 10020

This book is a work of fiction. Any references to historical events, real people, or real places are used fictitiously. Other names, characters, places, and events are products of the author's imagination, and any resemblance to actual events or places or persons, living or dead, is entirely coincidental.

This Pocket Books paperback edition January 2018

POCKET and colophon are registered trademarks of Simon & Schuster, Inc.

For information about special discounts for bulk purchases, please contact Simon & Schuster Special Sales at 1-866-506-1949 or business@simonandschuster.com.

The Simon & Schuster Speakers Bureau can bring authors to your live event. For more information or to book an event, contact the Simon & Schuster Speakers Bureau at 1-866-248-3049 or visit our website at www.simonspeakers.com.

Manufactured in the United States of America

10 9 8 7 6 5 4 3 2

ISBN 978-1-4391-4019-2
ISBN 978-1-4165-6506-2 (ebook)

For my husband and my parents,
who together taught me what genuine morality is.

Let Sleeping Rogues Lie

Prologue

"Your father is ready to see you, Master Dalton." With a nod, the maid at Norcourt Hall stood aside to let Anthony pass into the viscount's study.

She was a pretty maid, with large bosoms that fascinated the eleven-year-old Anthony. And when she smiled at him, the naughty thoughts those bosoms sent running through his head made him blush scarlet.

Mumbling a thank-you, he hurried inside. Aunt Eunice was right. He was the wickedest boy in England. No matter how often he told himself that he shouldn't notice the maids' bosoms or wish to touch them, he still did. Lately, the urge to see women naked was a sickness inside him. Father must never guess. Never.

When his father removed his spectacles to fix him with a stern gaze, Anthony blushed again, half-afraid Father had already read his wicked mind.

"I understand that you have something to discuss with me," Father said.

Anthony swallowed. Father's blue eyes and thick black eyebrows might mirror Anthony's own, but when those eyes were set in a scowl and those brows topped stone-sharp features, the effect was terrifying.

Thrusting out his chest, Anthony tried to appear un-cowed. "Father, I wish to go to Eton."

His father's stern look softened a fraction as he folded his spectacles. "And you will, my boy, you will. You will go at twelve as your brother did."

Another year. He couldn't bear another year living with Uncle Randolph and Aunt Eunice Bickham in Telford. He would prefer any caning at Eton to that.

"I wish to go when Wallace returns for the Michaelmas term." At Father's silence, Anthony went on hastily, "He says half his classmates began at eight."

"They probably knew their Latin well enough to gain admission so young."

"I do, too." He prayed he did, anyway. He detested Latin. It wasn't like maths, which he could do in his sleep. Latin made no sense.

His father lifted an eyebrow. "Your uncle says you can't even read Cicero."

"Because Cicero is thicker than Wallace's head," he said under his breath.

When Father's gaze iced over, Anthony wanted to die. Why couldn't he ever govern his tongue? "Beg pardon, Father, I didn't mean that Wallace—"

"Is a fool? Indeed you did. But I suppose some impudence from the younger brother to the elder is to be expected." Father tapped his spectacles on the shiny mahogany of his desk. "Unfortunately, proficiency in Latin is required, and your uncle says you haven't attained that since you came home last Easter."

How could he? It was hard to learn Latin while also

memorizing the precepts contained in *The Youth's Guide and Instructor to Virtue and Religion* for Aunt Eunice. "If you would only test me, you'll see that I know Latin well enough."

"I do not need to test you. Your uncle's word is sufficient."

A sweat broke out on Anthony's forehead. He would never escape the Bickhams, never! After Mother's death, Father had sent him to live with them as a "temporary" measure, yet Anthony had been there three years already.

He'd learned not to cry for his mother after the third time Aunt Eunice had smacked his face for it, but he couldn't seem to learn to stifle his bad thoughts and hold his tongue.

"If I can't go to Eton, might I come home? With you overseeing my studies, I know I'll be reading even the hardest Latin in a short time."

The sharp gaze his father leveled on him made him uneasy, but he kept his countenance. Father despised any sign of weakness.

"Is there a reason you do not wish to live with your uncle anymore?"

Had Aunt Eunice told Father of the countless mortifying punishments she'd had to administer because of Anthony's bad character? He would die if she had. But she'd promised not to if he swore to be better. So he'd sworn and begged and done whatever she asked, knowing he would never escape the Bickham household if Father learned the full extent of his wicked nature.

Anthony had initially been banished to his aunt's because, as Father had said, "A boy coddled by his mother needs a strict environment." Why should Father change his mind just because Anthony was too wicked to benefit from it?

He managed a shrug. "Uncle Randolph's house isn't like here, that's all. I wish to be home with you."

His father flashed him a thin smile. "Sometimes you remind me so much of . . ." The smile vanished. "I'm sorry, lad. I do not think it wise for you to live at Norcourt Hall just now. You're better off with your aunt and uncle."

Despair clutched at him. So he had another year of kneeling on the marble floor during long afternoons while Aunt Eunice read to him from *Wesley's Sermons*. Another year of ice baths while she attempted to freeze his naughty urges into oblivion. Another year trapped for hours alone in the dark—

No!

"Father, I *promise* to be good. You'll hardly know I'm here. I'll study hard and do as I'm told. I'll never say a word unless I'm bidden."

Father laughed mirthlessly. "I fear you are incapable of that, Anthony. Besides, it has naught to do with goodness. I'm off to a friend's estate in the north to observe his new irrigation system, which I hope to implement here. I cannot take you with me, and I've no time to engage a tutor. Nor shall I leave you to the indifferent attentions of the servants. No, you must return to Telford until you can enter Eton at twelve, and that's an end to it."

His father settled his spectacles atop his nose and returned to reading his newspaper, his signal that the discussion was over.

In that moment, Anthony hated his father horribly, which only further proved his bad character.

Yet he'd offered to be good, and it hadn't mattered.

Father didn't care how hard Anthony tried. Father didn't care *what* Anthony did, so long as it was well away from Norcourt Hall. And the thought of returning to Telford to his aunt's . . .

The sharp pang to Anthony's chest made tears start in his eyes. He suppressed them ruthlessly. He mustn't cry! He wasn't a little boy anymore. He was nearly grown now, or would be very soon. He ought to be able to go to Eton if he wanted. He ought to be able to do as he pleased without everyone railing at him.

And he did *try* to please his aunt and Father. What good did it do? He still burst out with the wrong words all the time, and the bad boy in his breeches still got randy whenever he saw a pretty girl, so he still got punished.

Fine. If he must suffer either way, he might as well give them something to punish him for.

So when he left his father's study to find the attractive maidservant still outside, he didn't hide his admiring glance at her ample bosoms.

She laughed. "Master Dalton, you're incorrigible!"

Incorrigible. He liked the sound of that. Because he was—or would be from now on. That would show them. "Yes," he said with a thrust of his chin, "and don't you forget it."

Then he strutted off, burying his conscience so deeply it would never trouble him again.

Chapter One

Dear Charlotte,

I'm glad you are finally giving greater responsibility to your teachers, instead of taking everything upon yourself. Miss Prescott in particular sounds like an asset, given her penchant for bookkeeping. I know how much you despise numbers—this way you can keep your hand in without having to submit to the tortures of doing sums.

Your friend and cousin,
Michael

Miss Madeline Prescott stared at the sealed envelope for the fifth time that day. *Refused* was written across it in a bold hand.

She couldn't believe it. Though she'd received no answer to her previous correspondence, she'd still hoped that Sir Humphry Davy might one day read one of her letters. If they were being refused entirely, she hadn't the smallest hope of making her case in person to the famous chemist.

Tears stung her eyes. Now what? She didn't know where to turn, and Papa got worse by the day. If she didn't find a solution soon—

"Ah, there you are," said Mrs. Charlotte Harris, owner and headmistress of Mrs. Harris's School for Young Ladies, as she entered the school's office. "I thought I might find you here."

Shoving the letter into her apron pocket, Madeline forced a smile. "I'm still balancing the accounts."

Mrs. Harris took a seat on the other side of the partner's desk, her red curls jiggling. "I don't envy you. I am so grateful you took those duties over."

Her employer wouldn't be nearly so grateful if she knew about the scandal clinging to the Prescott name in Shropshire. Mrs. Harris expected her teachers to be above reproach.

A footman appeared in the doorway to the office and said to Mrs. Harris, "A Lord Norcourt has come to call on you, ma'am."

Madeline's throat went dry. Sir Randolph Bickham's nephew, *here*? Could the Viscount Norcourt be seeking her out because of his uncle's wicked plot against Papa? Had Sir Randolph actually hunted them down here in Richmond?

That made no sense. Not only had the viscount never met her, but he and Sir Randolph were rumored to be estranged. Would Lord Norcourt even realize her family's connection to his?

Even if he did, he couldn't know she taught here. She hadn't told anyone at home in Telford. And she'd certainly kept her former life secret from Mrs. Harris.

Mrs. Harris looked perplexed. "But I don't know Lord Norcourt."

"He's here about a prospective pupil, I believe," the footman said.

Madeline slumped in relief. So this was a chance occurrence. Thank heaven.

"I have no openings for this term," Mrs. Harris said.

"I told him, ma'am. But he still wishes to speak with you."

Mrs. Harris turned to Madeline. "Do you know anything about Lord Norcourt?"

"A little," she said evasively. "He only inherited the title from his elder brother last month. Before then, you would have known him as the Honorable Anthony Dalton."

Mrs. Harris blinked. "The rakehell with a fondness for widows?"

"So they say."

"I wonder why he's here. He has no children to enroll." With a glance at the waiting footman, Mrs. Harris rose and touched one slender hand to her temple. "The gossips say he has seduced half the widows in London."

"That's impossible." Madeline did a swift calculation in her head. "Given a population of over one million, if even one-twentieth are widows, he'd have had to bed a woman every four hours over the past ten years to achieve such a feat. That would scarcely leave him time for gaming hells and wild parties."

Mrs. Harris's arch glance showed that she didn't particularly appreciate Madeline's practical perspective. But then, few people did. "I've heard about those parties," Mrs. Harris said tartly. "Cousin Michael even described one."

"Cousin Michael" was the school's original benefactor, a reclusive fellow who wrote Mrs. Harris of any intelligence he thought would aid the heiresses who attended. Privately, Madeline wondered if Cousin Michael was as removed from social affairs as he implied. But she wasn't likely to find out, since the man's identity had never been revealed to anyone, even Mrs. Harris.

"You don't think Lord Norcourt has come because *I*

am a widow, do you?" the headmistress asked as she paced before the window that overlooked the school's extensive gardens.

"I hardly think it likely."

"Nonetheless, I want nothing to do with the man." Mrs. Harris whirled on Madeline. "Perhaps *you* should speak to him. It's time you learned to deal with this sort of thing, and you're more likely to be tactful than I, given his reputation."

"But—"

"Why should you be limited to teaching classes and doing the school's accounts? You've amply proved you can handle weightier responsibilities. So go explain to Lord Norcourt that we have no openings."

Madeline hesitated. What if the man recognized her surname as Papa's?

No, that was silly. Prescott was a common enough name. And he'd hardly be familiar with the physicians in his uncle's town.

Rising from her seat, Madeline nodded. "I'll take care of it at once."

The more she ingratiated herself with Mrs. Harris, the more solid her standing at the school and the less likely she'd be to lose her position if the scandal surrounding Papa ever caught up with her here.

As she followed the footman into the hall, something else occurred to her. Though she'd heard much about his rakish reputation, the viscount had connections among men of science and learning. According to reports, he knew Sir Humphry Davy himself! She had to use this opportunity to her advantage to save Papa and get her former life back.

But how, if she had to turn his lordship away?

As she and the footman neared the foyer, she halted him in the shadow of the stairs, wanting first to study the man who paced the marble floor with spare, quick strides, his hands clasped behind his back.

Lord Norcourt was considerably taller and more handsome than his loathsome uncle. In his coat, waistcoat, and trousers of black superfine, with his equally black hair tumbling fashionably about his white collar, he was as glorious a creature as any wild fallow buck she'd described in her work of natural history.

She assessed his features in the mirror beyond him—the noble brow, the aquiline nose jutting above a full, sensual mouth, the square-cut jaw. But nothing compared to his well-knit figure, which bespoke many hours engaged in fencing or boxing or some other gentlemanly sport.

Yes, a splendid beast indeed.

Then he halted before the mirror with his head cocked, like a stag scenting danger, and she had only a second to prepare herself before he pivoted to fix her with amazing blue eyes, the exact hue of the azurite crystals she kept in a jar on her desk. And twice as sharp, not to mention unnerving. It seemed quite at odds with the outrageous fellow described by the gossips.

"Mrs. Harris, I presume?" he said, his brief bow every bit as haughty as one his uncle might have managed.

Heart thundering, she stepped forward. "No, my lord. I'm Miss Prescott." As she curtsied, she held her breath, waiting to see if he recognized her surname.

He merely shot her the same dismissive glance he would give any underling. "I wish to speak to the headmistress."

"She's busy, so she sent me." When Lord Norcourt frowned his annoyance, she dismissed the footman with what she hoped sounded like authority. Then she smiled coolly. "I handle the school's finances. I also teach mathematics. And natural history, when I can fit it in."

The viscount's chiseled features softened. "A naturalist? That is excellent. There should be more of that in schools for young ladies."

The casual compliment struck Madeline dumb. No one but Mrs. Harris viewed her interest in maths and natural history as an advantage. Certainly no man other than Papa ever had. How extraordinary.

But when he followed the compliment with a measured assessment of her, one that ended in a breathtaking smile, all white teeth and ingratiating appeal, she regarded him more cynically. He was very good at charming women, wasn't he? No wonder they fell into his bed so eagerly.

"I suppose you're wondering why I'm here," he went on. Abruptly, his smile vanished. "You see, my elder brother and his wife died in an inn fire last month."

"I'm very sorry for your loss," she murmured.

His nod of acknowledgment dropped a wave of silky raven hair over his brow. He shoved it back with a swiftness that hinted it was an oft-repeated gesture. "They were survived by a twelve-year-old daughter, the Honorable Miss Teresa Ann Dalton. That's why I've come. To enroll my niece in your academy."

"Surely the footman told you we have no openings at present."

He arched one brow. "Such matters can generally be got round for a price."

Thank heaven Mrs. Harris hadn't handled this—the implication that her goodwill could be bought would have ended this discussion. But Madeline refused to banish the viscount until she figured out if he could help Papa.

"As it happens," she said, softening her words with an amiable tone, "my employer need not take whoever offers her the most money. She will require some weightier reason before considering your request."

"Your employer's discriminating taste does her credit, as does her unusual curriculum. But surely neither of you would let some arbitrary limit on the number of pupils persuade you to turn away a girl of superior intelligence who might bring credit to your institution."

"There are other schools—"

"I wouldn't enroll my horse in them, much less an impressionable young woman. They're badly run, providing an indifferent and frivolous education."

Well, well, he'd certainly investigated the matter thoroughly. And surely Mrs. Harris could make room for another girl, with some adjustments. Besides, if Madeline could do this favor for Lord Norcourt . . .

But first she'd have to convince Mrs. Harris to allow it, and for that she must learn more. "Why have you been given charge of your niece? Isn't it unusual to name a bachelor as a guardian?"

"The married man that my brother named died a few years ago, and Wallace never took the trouble to change his will." An edge entered his voice. "Negligence was his particular talent."

So she'd heard. In Telford, Wallace Dalton was known as an extravagant dullard who'd neglected his Surrey estate in his pursuit of high living. Madeline wouldn't be surprised to learn that he'd left his younger brother a mountain of debt.

"Fortunately," the viscount continued, "my niece is to

inherit a substantial sum through her mother's marriage settlement, which my brother couldn't touch. So if you're worried that her legacy can't cover the fees—"

"I'm simply trying to understand your legal standing. Are you Miss Dalton's guardian or not?"

For the first time since she'd greeted him, the viscount's confident manner faltered. "I am not," he admitted, then added quickly, "But I hope to be soon. The court must appoint someone and I've petitioned for guardianship. I fully expect to have my petition granted."

With *his* reputation? Madeline didn't know much about the courts, but she doubted they'd assign a bachelor rakehell as guardian to a young girl.

Still, he was a viscount. And would he be here if he weren't certain of the outcome? "Your niece has no other relations interested in serving as guardian?"

A muscle flicked in his jaw. "My maternal uncle and aunt have also petitioned the court for guardianship."

Did he mean the Bickhams? But their daughter, Jane, was grown. Why would they take on a young relation at their age? Unless . . .

"Your brother's estate must offer a nice sum to the guardian," she said.

Any vestige of his charm vanished. "It's not my niece's money I seek."

"Oh, I didn't mean that *you*—"

"Tessa has been living with my Aunt Eunice and Uncle Randolph since her parents died, and they make her more miserable by the day."

Madeline could well believe *that*. The Bickhams would make anyone miserable, especially a grieving girl who needed comfort, not moralizing.

Poor Miss Dalton. When Madeline had lost her mother to consumption a few years ago, she'd at least had time to prepare herself. Nor had she been caught in a battle between her relations afterward.

"Misery is one thing," she said, "but surely your relations wouldn't actually mistreat her."

"That's precisely what I fear." His features grew shuttered. "They've done it before."

To whom? Surely not him. If she remembered correctly, he'd lived with the Bickhams for a brief while as a child, but his father had been alive then, and even the Bickhams weren't so arrogant as to mistreat a viscount's son.

Perhaps Lord Norcourt referred to his cousin Jane. She'd married and settled in Telford, yet noticeably avoided her parents. That gave Madeline pause.

"I must get Tessa out of that unspeakable place," he went on. "Neither of those two is fit to raise a child, especially my aunt."

"I understand your concern," she said softly, "but I don't know how enrolling your niece here can help."

"The Bickhams cultivate a façade of cozy domesticity. They're a high-ranking, respectable family in a stolid country town. In the eyes of the court, their advantages outweigh the disadvantages of my being a bachelor with an unsavory reputation, even a titled one. The only way to tip the balance is to show I can offer her other advantages—the refinements of town, exposure to a society more fitting her rank, and an exemplary education, the sort she couldn't possibly receive in the country. That's why it's so important that you accept her."

"I see."

She saw a great deal. His niece's situation was almost

as desperate as her own. But they could both be helped if Madeline could do this favor for the viscount.

"Very well, my lord, I shall speak to Mrs. Harris on your behalf. Wait here until I return, if you please."

She walked off, tamping down the pain roused by the viscount's clear affection for his niece. Papa had been just as protective of her own future, until Sir Randolph had ripped his reputation and livelihood from him.

A sob rose in her throat. These days, Papa couldn't drag himself from the bed, much less defend her. His melancholy overwhelmed him too much to fight, and without the income from his practice, they would soon run out of funds, despite her modest position here.

She *must* restore Papa to his former life—even if that meant begging a favor from the viscount. But she could only do that if she convinced her employer to enroll Miss Dalton.

That proved more difficult than expected. Even after Madeline explained Miss Dalton's dire situation, Mrs. Harris still wavered.

"He's a scoundrel, for heaven's sake," Mrs. Harris bit out. "He shouldn't be raising a young lady."

"He wouldn't be," Madeline pointed out. "*We* would. Besides, you know how the gossips exaggerate. His reputation can't be nearly as bad as reported."

"You think not?" She snorted. "Then you haven't heard what I have. What about those debauched social affairs that his lordship throws, the ones they're always writing about in the papers?"

"If you're speaking of my nitrous oxide parties, madam," came a taut male voice from the doorway, "those are held for the sake of intellectual enquiry."

Madeline groaned. She should have known that the viscount wouldn't leave this to her. He was the sort of man to take charge.

As Lord Norcourt entered, anger flared in his finely carved features. "My parties are attended by some of the leading minds of science and the arts."

Which was precisely why Madeline was trying to help him. But right now, with his temper up, the arrogant fool was sealing his fate with Mrs. Harris. "Lord Norcourt, this is my employer," she said hastily, determined to regain control. "Mrs. Harris, may I introduce—"

"No need to introduce a man whose reputation precedes him," said Mrs. Harris, her own temper high as she turned to the viscount. "And your 'leading minds' aren't the only guests, sir. What about the half-dressed females who cavort about while the young men 'of science and the arts' puff on their bladders and ogle the women for sport? According to my very reliable sources, your parties aren't always given for the 'sake of intellectual enquiry.'"

Irritation glittered in his eyes. "You must have very interesting sources. And yes, I am aware I will have to be more discreet with a young woman in my household. There will be no more parties for bachelors at my lodgings, and no women except a respectable lady's companion to attend Tessa. When my niece isn't here, she will live the same life as any young daughter of a lord."

"So you mean to give up your mistresses and your long nights at the clubs?"

"She'll never hear or see aught to shame or corrupt her," he said evasively. "I doubt you'd get more than that from any married man whose daughter attends here, blissfully ignorant of her papa's . . . activities."

Mrs. Harris knew better than to claim that her pupils' fathers didn't engage in such behaviors; many men of fashion did. "If I thought your lordship capable of discretion, I might make a place for your niece this term, but given your reputation for flaunting your wickedness, I rather doubt—"

"Do you question my word, madam?" He spoke the words softly, which only made their quiet menace more chilling.

And Mrs. Harris had always despised being threatened. "Let's just say that through the years, I've grown cynical about a man's ability to change his habits."

The viscount stalked up to plant his hands on the desk. "Cynical is one thing, cruel and heartless another. I *swear* that if my niece is raised in the household of my harsh relatives, her spirit will be scarred for life."

Though Mrs. Harris flinched, she didn't relent. "Then you will have to enroll her in another school for ladies."

"I can't!" He grimaced, then shoved away from the desk with an oath, as if he hadn't meant to admit that. "I can't enroll her anywhere else."

"Why not?" Mrs. Harris demanded.

"They won't take her."

"I thought you said that *you* did not want *them*," Madeline put in.

"I don't. But they also refuse to promise her a place until I gain guardianship. They don't want to become embroiled in my fight."

"Neither do I," Mrs. Harris said.

"Yes, but you have the reputation to pull it off. They don't. Unfortunately, unless I find a reputable school to enroll her, so I can prove that being raised by me is an advantage, I won't be approved as her guardian. That is my dilemma."

Mrs. Harris tipped up her chin. "Your dilemma is that headmistresses aren't as easily charmed into betraying their principles as your usual female companions."

He clenched his jaw. "I see that even a woman as forward-thinking as you can be exceedingly small-minded when it comes to men. I didn't approach you until the end of my search because I suspected that your well-known 'principles' would keep you from helping me. Apparently I was right. Good day, ladies."

As he stalked away, Madeline panicked. She couldn't let Mrs. Harris drive the viscount away. He might be her only chance to help Papa!

"Perhaps his lordship could *prove* that he would make an acceptable guardian to a young female," Madeline burst out.

As the viscount halted, a wary hope flickering in his face, Mrs. Harris glowered at her. Oh, dear. Madeline had to handle this delicately. She couldn't afford to lose her position in her zeal to gain her favor from the viscount.

"If his lordship demonstrates he can keep his private activities discreet," Madeline went on, "wouldn't it benefit the school to enroll his niece? Think of the cachet of having a student who is a previous viscount's daughter and a current viscount's niece. We have few noblemen's daughters as pupils."

"True," Mrs. Harris said, "but by agreeing to take her, I'd be showing approval of his lordship's petition for guardianship, which makes me uneasy."

"You wouldn't commit to anything until you're satisfied that Lord Norcourt is capable of being a good guardian."

"I cannot twiddle my thumbs waiting for some overly

high-minded headmistress to decide my fate," he growled. "I have my brother's debts to settle, an estate to put to rights—"

"I understand. But proving your suitability shouldn't take more than a couple of weeks. My proposal would enable you to be useful to the school . . . and in the long run, to your niece."

"Really, Madeline, this is pointless," Mrs. Harris put in. "What could his lordship possibly offer of use to the school?"

Madeline focused her persuasive power on her skittish employer. She wouldn't let this chance slip through her fingers! "How often have you bemoaned the girls' lack of practical experience in dealing with fortune hunters and scoundrels? No matter how much you warn them, the minute they're in the presence of a handsome gentleman spouting compliments, they forget everything."

"What is your point?" Mrs. Harris said irritably, not denying Madeline's claim. They often despaired over the foolishness of impressionable young girls.

"If the girls could hear warnings from an expert in such manipulations, they might actually heed them." Squaring her shoulders, she faced her employer down. "I think the viscount should give our girls lessons."

Mrs. Harris gaped at her. "What kind of lessons could he possibly—"

"He can teach them how to avoid the machinations of scoundrels and rogues." Madeline smiled. "Rakehell lessons."

Chapter Two

Dear Cousin,
  I don't remember ever telling you that I hate numbers. How did you know that I would rather scour washbasins than do the school's accounts?

> *Your curious relation,*
> *Charlotte*

Anthony gaped at Miss Prescott, unsure what to make of her proposal. What the bloody devil was a rakehell lesson, anyway?

"You suggest that I let the fox into the henhouse to corrupt our girls?" Mrs. Harris retorted.

Oh, for God's sake— "I don't 'corrupt' children. Why should I, with plenty of already corrupted grown women to choose from? Virginal schoolgirls with pistol-packing papas and childish insecurities are far too much trouble. I prefer women who know what they want and aren't ashamed to take it." He scowled down at Miss Prescott. "Which is why I'd have nothing of use to teach your pupils."

"Surely the techniques of seduction are the same for any woman," the petite teacher persisted. "You're rumored to have enjoyed the . . . er . . . favors of several widows.

You must have used *some* tricks to entice them, the sort a less scrupulous man might use to seduce an innocent." Miss Prescott flashed him a guileless smile that made her creamy skin glow. "Unless you're claiming that women fall into your arms simply because of your dashing air."

"It's as good a reason as any," he shot back, annoyed by the teacher's clear immunity to his "air." "I have no idea why women choose me for a lover. Perhaps you should ask them."

"Give me a list, and I will." When he blinked, the woman cast her employer a quick glance, and added in a warning tone, "Though such an investigation could considerably lengthen the process of getting your niece enrolled here."

Was the woman trying to help him circumvent her employer? If so, it must be for reasons of her own. He'd met enough teachers in his endless trek through London's schools to know they were all eager to escape their miserable existence.

And yet . . .

She seemed different. For one thing, she was far prettier. For another, she dressed like someone who actually enjoyed what she did. No gray woolens for Miss Prescott. Her cheery gown of yellow spotted muslin complemented her fair coloring and skimmed her petite form in all the right places.

Some might deem Mrs. Harris the more beautiful of the two because of her exotic red hair and blue eyes, but the widow's stiffness put him off. He found Miss Prescott's open and honest manner more appealing. She reminded him of a country dairymaid, with her honey gold curls and apple cheeks.

Except for those unusual amber eyes. Cat's eyes. Temptress eyes. Yet remarkably, eyes that assessed him as one might a fascinating sculpture, without flirtation or censure. Women never looked at him like that. It made him wonder if she really *was* trying to help him and Tessa.

Not that it would do any good, given the absurdity of her proposal. "I wouldn't know how to give these lessons. I'm not conscious of using any 'tricks.' "

Miss Prescott let out the unfettered laugh of someone who'd never been coached by a society mother. "Forgive me, but didn't you once say 'where there's a widow, there's a way'? That implies a certain polished skill with women."

He tensed. The idiotic comment he'd made to his friends while foxed had dogged him for years. How clever of her to use it to make him sound like a calculated seducer. Granted, he was no saint, but he wasn't like his friend, the Marquess of Stoneville, bedding women just to prove he could. Perhaps she was more critical of his character than she let on. Perhaps she *was* like everyone else.

Deliberately, he let his gaze linger on her pretty mouth. "Touché. Although, for the sake of my pride, I hope you'll admit that *some* of my talent with women comes from my natural charms."

The chit didn't so much as blush. "Certainly. If *you* will admit that some men are better at attracting a female and keeping her interest than others, regardless of looks. Just as some women are better at attracting men."

She faced the wary Mrs. Harris. "Our young ladies know how to attract men. But if they could hear how men entice women—especially from a man who excels at it—they might learn to recognize when men who court them aren't sincere."

"Men like me, you mean," he drawled, still unsure what to make of her. "Do you think me insincere?"

"Actually, my lord, you're rather famous for shocking people with your honest and outrageous opinions." She arched an eyebrow. "Though I suspect you're more circumspect with women you wish to seduce."

He stared at her. "That depends on the woman."

"Exactly," she said. "And that alone would be a good lesson for our girls—how a rakehell can tailor his seductions to particular women."

His eyes narrowed. So that's what she meant by rakehell lessons. But why press her employer for them? Just because of the few things he'd said about Tessa?

Shoving his hand in his pocket, he suddenly encountered the papier-mâché snuffbox his niece had "specially made" for her "favorite uncle." It hadn't occurred to her that he never took snuff, and he hadn't enlightened her, especially after seeing the charmingly awful miniature of herself she'd painted on the lid.

She'd given it to him last Christmas, before Wallace's untimely death. The last time they'd all been together. The last time he'd seen her smile.

He stiffened. Miss Prescott's proposal might be odd and rather insulting, but he could put up with that if it saved Tessa from suffering.

"If his lordship were to give these lessons," the prickly Mrs. Harris asked, "how would that prove his acceptability as a guardian?"

Good question. He glanced expectantly at Miss Prescott.

"Why, it will allow us to observe how he treats them. We'll see firsthand if he can restrain his language around them and behave like a gentleman. We'll see if he can be discreet, which seems to be your main concern."

Mrs. Harris sighed. "While I admit that the idea has merit, Madeline, it also seems a little dangerous."

For *him,* perhaps. Aside from wasting his time if nothing came of it, one of their silly girls could claim he'd made untoward advances. Marriage to a virginal chit scheming to become his viscountess wasn't in his plans—especially since the ensuing scandal would scotch his chances of gaining guardianship of his niece.

"I will oversee the lessons myself," Miss Prescott told her employer. "I'll make sure his lordship adheres strictly to the rules of the school, and that—"

"Look here," he broke in, "if I'm to make a fool out of myself before your young ladies, I'll need more than some vague hope that you'll agree to my niece's enrollment. I daresay no other applicant has to go through such nonsense."

"I turned away four wealthy young ladies last week, sir," the headmistress said in a haughty voice. "As I told you, I have no openings available. To take your niece, I'd have to make room for her, no small feat during our busy Easter term. And we've just lost our cook—"

"I'm sure his lordship could help us find another." Miss Prescott shot him a sidelong glance. "Just as I'm sure Mrs. Harris will promise to write a letter supporting your petition for guardianship if she's pleased with your lessons."

He fixed his gaze on Mrs. Harris. "Would you indeed make such a promise?"

"That depends. Miss Prescott assures me that your niece will be mistreated if put into her relations' care. Do you honestly believe that?"

He nodded. "I've been sure of it ever since I watched my aunt bully the girl at my brother's funeral to make her stop crying." He'd hoped his aunt had softened with age, but her behavior to Tessa had dashed that hope. It reminded him too painfully of his own boyhood.

To his surprise, sympathy flashed over Mrs. Harris's face. "Very well," she said gruffly, "two weeks are left in this session, during which you will offer rake lessons for an hour a day under Miss Prescott's supervision. If, at the end of that time, we are satisfied with your behavior, and you've managed to avoid being discussed in the newspapers for a change, I'll enroll your niece for the Easter term and write a letter to the court supporting your petition. Are we agreed?"

He hesitated to put himself at the mercy of a woman whose high-minded notions reminded him of his detestable aunt, and he was wary of being under the "supervision" of a woman as difficult to read as Miss Prescott.

But if he told them to take their "rake lessons" and shove them into the nearest privy, Tessa would have no school. The courts would decide that she'd be better off spending her days in the home of a God-fearing couple than in the home of a profligate, and that would be the end to his being her guardian.

Tessa's last letter had chilled him, since it had so obviously been coached by Aunt Eunice. Ever since the girl could hold a pen, she'd been writing him—he knew her style. It was *not* the style of that letter. And the fact that Aunt Eunice was overseeing her correspondence terrified him, for it made him wonder what his niece might have written otherwise.

How much worse would it be if Aunt Eunice gained free

rein as Tessa's legal guardian? What sort of horrors might the old bitch inflict if she could do so unchecked? He remembered the hours his cousin Jane had spent standing with her face to the wall just for smiling at a handsome boy. And that had been an easy punishment compared to—

He shuddered, absently rubbing the ridged scar across his wrist. He would do anything to keep Tessa from enduring what he and Jane had. And he could use a letter supporting his petition from a woman as upstanding as Mrs. Harris.

Forcing a smile, he thrust out his hand. "Agreed, madam."

As Mrs. Harris shook it, the weight that had lain on his shoulders since his brother's death settled more heavily upon him. Damn Wallace for dying, and laying this responsibility at his door. *Damn* the man!

Given his brother's dim-wittedness, he'd probably set fire to the blasted inn himself with a cigar. And now Anthony, after years of fighting to ignore how the man drove the family estate into the ground, had to clean up the mess Wallace and his extravagant fool of a wife had left behind.

He ruthlessly squelched his twinge of guilt at the unkind thought. If Wallace hadn't died, he would shoot the man himself. How dared the idiot not make sure that Tessa had a suitable guardian?

Well, the poor confused child would just have to be stuck with her rogue of an uncle until she could marry. Which meant he was stuck with the superior schoolteachers, for a while anyway.

And it would be a damned trying while, judging from the rules Mrs. Harris began dictating.

Rule One: He was to arrive by horseback, so as not to rouse gossip among the locals with his carriage.

Rule Two: He must enter the school through the same door the staff used.

Rule Three: He wasn't to speak of this enterprise to anyone in society.

Speak of it—was she mad? If word got out that he'd agreed to teach young ladies how to avoid seduction, he'd be the laughingstock of London.

"And you must never contrive to be alone with the girls," Mrs. Harris said.

For God's sake, this grew more ridiculous by the moment. "Must I? Such a pity. I'd hoped to work my way through them one at a time, sullying their virtue and ruining all their hopes for the future. Are you quite sure you won't allow that?"

The startled look on Mrs. Harris's face didn't please him nearly as much as Miss Prescott's smothered sputter of laughter.

"Lord Norcourt—" Mrs. Harris began in a warning tone.

"No being alone with the girls. I understand." The wicked devil in him made him add, "What about being alone with the head of the school? Is that allowed? I could bring some champagne, a few strawberries—"

"Oh, Lord," the widow said with a roll of her eyes. "Heaven help us, Madeline, he will have the girls falling in love with him before the week is out."

"All the better to prove our lesson," Miss Prescott retorted. "That a rakehell can be charming and still not mean a word of it."

"Or that rakehells are more fun to be around," he quipped.

That gained him a scowl from both women. He must stop letting his tongue run away with him. Provoking the pompous played well at the club with his friends, but not so well with schoolmistresses.

Mrs. Harris turned to Miss Prescott. "What are we to tell the parents about this? They won't approve."

"Why tell them anything?" Miss Prescott said. "We're doing nothing wrong."

"But the girls might mention it."

"Yes, I suppose we must at least explain it to them." The teacher tapped her chin. "We'll say that Lord Norcourt's niece will soon be attending the school, so he's offering cautionary lessons as a courtesy. If his lessons don't meet with your approval, we'll simply claim he changed his mind about enrolling Miss Dalton. Either way, by the time the parents hear of it and protest—if they do—the matter will be resolved. It's hardly enough time for anyone here to connect Lord Norcourt with the notorious Mr. Anthony Dalton."

"*You* did," he pointed out.

"Exactly," Mrs. Harris said. "And the girl shares his surname, Madeline."

"The parents send their children here precisely because our curriculum is unusual. If you explain that the lessons are supervised and appropriate to a young lady, I doubt they will care." Miss Prescott slid her delicate hand in the crook of his arm. "Come, my lord, let me give you a tour of the school."

"Certainly, Miss Prescott," he said, wondering at her eagerness to hustle him from the office. "I'd be delighted."

Mrs. Harris's eyes narrowed, but she said nothing as her protégé hurried him out, then walked briskly down the hall ahead of him in full expectation that he would follow.

And follow he did, though at a more leisurely pace to allow him a good look at her small but shapely bottom, made for cupping and fondling and squeezing. No doubt *that* would rouse a blush—

Stop that, you randy arse! he told himself. *You can't seduce Miss Prescott, not if you want Tessa to attend here.*

Besides, naturalist or no, she was still a schoolteacher, which made her the marrying sort, not the take-a-tumble-with-a-rake sort. She was probably as virginal as a nun, too, which ruled her out entirely.

He'd never ruined a woman before and didn't mean to start now. It was the surest way to end up trapped into wedding some virtuous female, which could only lead to disaster. Let other men hunt that elusive creature—the happy marriage. Although he occasionally allowed himself the sweet luxury of imagining himself in one, it could never happen. Men like him didn't dare to marry.

But that didn't mean he couldn't enjoy looking at the unattainable, and his practiced gaze drank in the pretty curve of Miss Prescott's back, the small but obstinate shoulders, and the bouncing yellow curls.

As if she'd read his wicked mind, the young lady turned on him a good distance from the office. "See here, Lord Norcourt, if this is to work, you must be guided by my advice. When I tell you to wait for me, I have a reason."

"To gossip about me with Mrs. Harris? I hardly think that helped my cause."

"*You're* certainly not helping it by saying outrageous things to her. With every rash remark, you make it more difficult to persuade her to keep you."

"Keep me!" He eyed her askance. "You seem to have mistaken me for a lapdog, sweetheart."

"I am not your sweetheart, drat it!" She cast a furtive glance toward Mrs. Harris's office. "And that's precisely the sort of rash remark I'm talking about. My employer is generally amiable, but men of your kind annoy her."

"My 'kind,' " he echoed.

"Rakehells. You know what I mean."

"Forgive me, I'm still trying to imagine Mrs. Harris being 'amiable.' "

With a sigh, Miss Prescott continued down the hall. "In her youth," she explained as he kept pace with her, "she eloped with a dashing rogue who turned out to be a fortune hunter. Is it any wonder she dislikes that sort of man?"

"And how do *you* feel about rogues and rakehells, Miss Prescott?" he asked, watching to see her reaction.

"Having only met my first one today, I can hardly voice an opinion."

"That doesn't stop most people."

"Most people have seen a rakehell in his natural habitat. I have not."

"Natural habitat?" He laughed. "You *are* a lover of science." Stepping in front of her, he blocked her path. "But I know you have an opinion. Everyone does. You won't wound my feelings if you voice it." Then he'd know where he stood with her.

A sigh escaped her lips. "Very well, then."

Ah, now we get to the lecture.

"From what little I know, rakes seem a fascinating species, well deserving of study." Sidling neatly past him, she continued down the hall.

He closed his slack jaw long enough to hurry after her. A "fascinating species"? "Deserving of study"? Was she serious?

Seconds later, they emerged into the foyer where he'd earlier been admitted. Sounds of girlish chatter cascaded down the impressive central staircase. The Elizabethan-era building had apparently been a private residence before being adapted for use as a school, and the high ceilings amplified the noise.

Miss Prescott halted outside a white door. "Why don't I show you the dining room before the girls come down for afternoon tea?" She spoke as if she hadn't just made the most bizarre pronouncement he'd ever heard. "Then we can tour the classrooms while the girls aren't engaged in lessons."

"All right." He followed her into a spacious room with a mahogany dining table that easily seated twenty. "Tell me, Miss Prescott. Why in God's name would you think rakehells deserve study?"

With a shrug, she strolled along the table, straightening chairs. "Because of your reckless way of life, I suppose. I want to understand how you can stomach it."

"I want to understand why you think it reckless," he countered, not sure if she was trying to insult him.

"Don't you fight duels?"

Ah, *that* was the sort of thing she meant. "Absolutely not. You have to get up at dawn for those, you know."

Her eyes narrowed. "Don't you race your phaeton?"

His smug smile faltered. "I don't own a phaeton." But he did race his curricle from time to time. No point in mentioning that.

"And I suppose you don't drink strong spirits, either."

"Well, yes, but—"

"It isn't good for the constitution. Otherwise, it wouldn't make generally healthy men suffer from headaches the morning after or cast up their accounts in the street. Surely you see that such reactions tax the body unduly."

He held out his arms. "Do I look as if I'm teetering on the edge of death?"

Miss Prescott skimmed him with blatant nonchalance. "Not now, but I daresay you look quite different the mornings after your carousing."

"I can handle my liquor perfectly well," he remarked, unaccountably peeved by her logical observation. "I certainly wouldn't call my 'carousing' reckless."

"Fine." She strode off toward a door across the room. "Do you gamble?"

"Of course." This had to be the oddest conversation he'd ever had with a woman.

"Surely you consider *that* reckless. Given the odds of winning versus losing, any good mathematician can tell you it's rare for someone to increase their annual income by gambling. Yet rakes insist upon risking the loss of their property."

"It isn't a risk if you know the mathematical odds and play accordingly. The odds of winning at loo are about five to one. Of course, that depends on whether you're playing three- or five-card loo, but when you factor in what trump the Eldest Hand plays to start, it can vary from five to one to ten to four. According to my calculations."

Her look of shock rapidly changed to one of admiration, and that warmed him as no woman's ever had. He'd always excelled at mathematics—that's why he'd been able to supplement his small allowance so effectively with investments—but women weren't usually impressed by a man's skill with maths.

To have her look at him through new eyes full of interest roused his instincts. How easy it would be to step close and kiss that enticing, lushly proportioned mouth . . .

Now *that* would be reckless.

"The point is, Miss Prescott, I'm well aware of the odds, so I never risk more than I can afford."

Setting her hand on the door handle, she frowned. "But why risk anything at all? You don't have to gamble to enjoy playing cards."

He laughed. "My fellow club members wouldn't share your opinion, I assure you."

A thundering noise overhead made her start. "The girls are coming. Quick, through here. We don't want to be inundated by questions and curious glances."

With a nod, he followed her into a ballroom. He paid no mind to the oak floors that stretched an impressive distance beneath a crystal chandelier or the rows of simple white chairs that flanked walls covered with elegant green fabric. He was much more interested in why Miss Prescott, with her apparent disapproval of reckless rakehells, had proposed that he give lessons to her charges.

"We have dancing lessons three times a week in here," she said in the tone of the impersonal guide. "Every Saturday night we hold an assembly for the girls, and once a month we invite local young men to attend so our students can practice their skills with gentlemen."

"Do you dance, Miss Prescott?" he probed, hoping to learn more about her.

"When I can." Circling the room, she headed out through the open French doors onto a gallery that afforded a fine view of well-laid-out gardens teeming with roses and lilacs. When she halted beside the marble balustrade, the sheen of gold cast by the afternoon sun over her glorious curls made him itch to touch them.

"I'm surprised that you don't find dancing to be reckless," he said, imagining her slender hips swaying, her pert breasts pushed high in an evening gown until they rose and fell fetchingly with her exertions.

"I suppose dancing *can* be reckless." She tipped up her chin at him. "If it leads a man and woman to do other things."

At last they got to the heart of the matter. He had known she would eventually raise the subject of morality, especially in relations between men and women. The marrying sort always did.

"What 'other things,' Miss Prescott?" he drawled, the devil in him determined to force her into speaking the words aloud.

She eyed him as if he were a fool. "You know what I mean. Swiving."

"*Swiving?*" He burst into laughter. "You have an interesting vocabulary for a schoolteacher."

"The word comes from Shakespeare," she said defensively. "It's perfectly acceptable."

"Perhaps for a tavern in Spitalfields, but gentlewomen don't discuss swiving."

"Oh, but they should! Then they'd learn the dangers of it. Indiscriminate swiving is the most reckless activity of a rake. It spreads disease, it provokes characters like that Harriette Wilson with her *Memoirs* to blackmail gentlemen with the threat of ruin, and it can result in the siring of illegitimate children—"

"Disease?" he broke in, incredulous. "Blackmail and illegitimate children. *These* are what concern you about the indiscriminate swiving of rakehells?"

"Of course." She eyed him with clear surprise. "What else?"

"Virtue? Morality?"

She snorted. "Those are what make indiscriminate swiving so reckless in the first place. The woman bears the brunt of it, you know. Aside from losing her position and possibly her home, she risks finding herself with child and cast out by a society that dismisses her as 'immoral' to excuse its not protecting women from—"

"Men like me?"

"Well . . . yes."

The thinly veiled accusation unnerved him. It was true that women could plummet from respectable to disreputable in society's eyes very easily, even when the man was to blame for it, but he had never let that little inequity bother him. His lovers had either been soiled doves or widows—having fun with him was entirely their choice. Neither seemed to need much protecting.

With his young niece's future to consider, however, he couldn't look at the average woman's prospects in quite the same way. And that disturbed him. Deeply.

Then it annoyed him. It wasn't as if *he* were ruining respectable women right and left. And he was trying to do right by Tessa, damn it, even though it could mean years of long nights alone in his bed, unable to chase away the darkness with drink or whoring.

The thought of what he was giving up—the sacrifice she didn't even heed—goaded him into looming over her.

"Some people, even women, find the pleasures of 'swiving' well worth the risks, Miss Prescott."

Though she caught her breath, she didn't edge away. "I can't imagine why." Her clean, sweet scent engulfed him as she met his gaze. "You were *sincere* about behaving as a gentleman while here at the school, weren't you?"

He started to point out that he'd only agreed to be a gentleman to her pupils. But nothing had changed—she was still the wrong sort of woman to seduce.

With what he considered admirable restraint, he drew back. "I don't have much of a choice," he bit out, still chafing over that truth.

"Everyone has a choice, sir."

"Even those of us born wicked?"

"Don't be silly," she chided. "Wickedness is just a pattern of bad behavior, a habit cultivated over time. One merely has to break the habit."

"Ah, but we both know that habits are hard to break." Awareness dawned. "Is that what you're worried about? That I can't keep from exercising my bad habits around your charges?"

His bluntness brought a shadow to her wholesome features. She dropped her gaze. "What I have heard of you suggests you were telling the truth about your preference for experienced females."

"And as a naturalist, you really want to trust in that." He searched her face. "But part of you still worries that the temptation of so much young female beauty will be too much for my . . . er . . . habit of seducing women."

When she met his gaze, her answer plain in her expression, he stiffened. "Don't worry, Miss Prescott. My seductions are limited to grown women. I'm no debaucher of children. You can trust me to behave with perfect propriety around your girls."

"Good." Relief shone in her face. "I need this position, you know, and if you were to attempt to seduce even one of my pupils—"

"Or you?"

The words were out before he could stop them, and a flicker of uncertainty deepened her eyes. She masked it with a shaky laugh. "You may attempt to seduce *me* as much as you please. It would be pointless; I'm too aware of the risks. Besides, such things don't tempt me."

The bloody devil they didn't. "Then you'd best watch your step around me, sweetheart," he said softly. "Or I will prove you wrong."

To his vast satisfaction, the words finally roused a blush in her cheeks. "That wouldn't exactly show Mrs. Harris that you can be discreet, would it?"

Only the faint reproof in her voice kept him from demonstrating just how "discreetly" he could seduce her.

He leaned against the balustrade. "I have to ask—given your beliefs about rakes, and your obvious skepticism about my ability to behave, why on earth would you suggest I give your students lessons?"

With a panicked expression, she pivoted to face the gardens. "I . . . um . . . the truth is . . . well, I was hoping you'd do something for me in exchange."

The disappointment that lanced through him bore a keener edge than it ought. He hadn't expected her to be so thoroughly like everyone else.

After he'd inherited the title, near strangers had begun professing themselves his grand friends. Society matrons who'd disdained him all his life now invited him to their parties to improve their social status. Sycophants who'd dismissed him as a mere second son now clamored for his attention at balls.

The tradesmen were the worst. Suddenly he couldn't walk into a shop without having costly items thrust into his face for his perusal. That had never happened to "the young Mr. Dalton." The weight of his brother's legacy never felt so heavy as it did this moment.

"How much?" he said tersely.

Her head snapped around. "How much what?"

"How much money do you need?"

That seemed to spark her temper, for she planted her hands on her hips and eyed him coldly. "All I need is a favor. One that will cost you little, I daresay."

"I doubt that," he said dryly.

"It's nothing new for you—just those nitrous oxide parties you throw."

"*Used* to throw," he corrected her. "I won't be throwing them anymore."

"Oh, but you have to! That's the favor I want, you see. For you to invite me to a nitrous oxide party."

Chapter Three

Dear Charlotte,

*You know you need not mention anything for me
to find out about it. Before I ever began supporting
the school, I conducted research on its headmistress.
Besides, at least once a year you complain about doing
your accounts. I would have to be blind, deaf, and
dumb not to notice.*

*Your friend,
Michael*

Madeline frowned. She probably shouldn't have blurted
out her request, but she might as well make her position
known from the start.

"Are you daft?" the viscount snapped.

"Not at all," she retorted, refusing to let him cow her.

So he was angry. Well, she was angry, too—angry and
tired of staying one step ahead of creditors, of watching
Papa wander aimlessly through their tiny cottage, of worrying about the future.

Lord Norcourt leaned close, a darkly dangerous scowl
spreading over his brow. "Why the bloody devil would you
be interested in a nitrous oxide party? It's hardly the sort of
affair that a respectable young lady attends."

She tried to look impassive as she spun out the story she'd hastily cobbled together. "I told you—I'm a naturalist. I study human behavior. I've been writing a pamphlet about the effects of nitrous oxide on people, but my limited knowledge of the gas has hampered me. I need to witness its use by a variety of individuals."

"*That's* why you want to attend a nitrous oxide party?" he said incredulously. "To research some scientific article?"

"Yes." A few years ago, that might actually have been true. But once Father's use of the gas had caused his disgrace, exploring its benefits had lost its appeal.

"I can satisfy that without a party. I'll gladly get a chemist to mix some up. Then you can experiment with it on anyone you please."

"That won't work!"

His eyes narrowed. "Why not?"

Because that wouldn't enable her to meet Sir Humphry. Which she needed to do more than ever now that her last letter had been sent back.

She'd been trying to pierce his rarefied circle ever since she'd moved herself and Papa to London last year. Calling upon the famous chemist at his home and the Royal Society had proved as fruitless as writing him. She was at her wit's end trying to figure out how to get an audience with him. And without his aid, Papa would never be able to return to his practice.

The only thing that seemed to entice Sir Humphry out into society these days was a nitrous oxide party. And in such a casual atmosphere, it would be easy to gain an introduction.

"Well?" Lord Norcourt bit out. "Why can't I simply provide you with nitrous oxide?"

"How can I find people to experiment upon? I teach young ladies. If I attempt to use it on *them*, I'll lose my position."

"You're more likely to lose your position by attending one of my parties," he pointed out.

"You don't have to throw the kind with the cavorting women, for heaven's sake," she said irritably. "Just the kind held for purposes of scientific enquiry."

He snorted. "You can't be that naive. It makes no difference what kind I throw—I'd be a rakehell throwing a party. If you attend, you'll risk not only your position, but your reputation and future."

The fact that he was probably right rubbed her raw. "If the world were fair, sir, attending a party for scientific purposes wouldn't be a risk at all. Women would be accorded the same respect given male naturalists. They'd be able to attend a university like any man."

His gaze softened. "But the world isn't fair. Not yet, in any case."

The sentiment settled over her soul like a caress. Other men spouted the usual rot about women needing protection and not having the intelligence to handle such an education. But not him. Amazing. Especially for a rakehell.

He leaned back to plant his elbows on the balustrade, his muscles flexing beneath his perfectly fitted coat, and the electric pulse that seared her senses threw her off-balance. Sweet heaven, he moved like a well-bred stallion, with natural ease and confidence.

But it was more than his uncommonly handsome looks that disturbed her. She was used to observing beautiful animals, to recording their characteristics and detailing their behavior. She wasn't used to coveting them.

Coveting *him*? She must be mad. A man like him wouldn't look twice at her, when women fell into his bed with regularity. She almost wished he would, since he'd proved surprisingly intelligent.

No doubt he cultivated that impression so he could seduce women.

Careful, you are far out of your realm here. He's both an unrepentant rakehell and a lord. Never forget that.

As if he'd remembered it himself, he turned frosty again. "It's precisely because the world isn't fair that I can't give you what you want. As you've already pointed out, Tessa's enrollment here is predicated upon my showing that I can be discreet. Throwing one of my famous parties will show the opposite."

She steeled herself to be firm. "You forget, my lord, that your niece's enrollment is also predicated upon *my* approval of your lessons."

"I haven't forgotten," he bit out. "Ask anything else—"

"That's the only thing I want!" She cast about for a way to convince the stubborn wretch. "It can be private, you know. Why does everyone in society have to find out about it?"

"Because they always do."

"They wouldn't if you didn't invite people who write for the newspapers!"

A mirthless laugh escaped his lips. "I wish it worked that way. You undoubtedly spent your life in a quiet country town where the gossip is limited to what Mrs. Prattling Squire served at dinner, but in London, we like our gossip mad, bad, and scandalous to hear."

"Believe me, there's plenty of that sort of gossip in Te—" She caught herself. "In the country." Otherwise, Papa wouldn't have lost his patients. Or his reputation.

"Yes, but I doubt that people in the country bribe servants for tidbits. I doubt they pass their tales on to the press or blackmail their friends with it to gain favors." His voice dripped acid. "Gossip is the legal tender of a society that pretends to despise filthy lucre. It's hard enough to attend such a party without being talked about, but to throw one—" He shook his head. "It can't be done."

"I don't believe that," she said in despair.

"Even your employer had heard of my parties."

"Because they were mentioned in the papers!"

"Because of her 'sources.' The parties that involved scantily clad women were never mentioned in any paper. They were held in the country at a friend's hunting lodge, and still your Mrs. Harris got wind of it."

From "Cousin Michael," no doubt. How *did* that man get himself invited to so many affairs? He was supposed to be a recluse.

The viscount rubbed his wrist with a distracted air. "Surely you can be satisfied with trying out the nitrous oxide on your friends or family."

"I have no friends and little family." Besides, that wouldn't help her.

He was watching her oddly. "None?"

She caught herself. "None who would let me experiment on them."

"I'm sorry, you'll have to ask another favor." The chill in his voice deepened. "The right amount of money could buy you plenty of friends to experiment upon."

She'd put him on guard, drat it. How she wished she could tell him that his uncle was pressuring the vicar to bring criminal charges against Papa—but that would send him running for sure. His case for guardianship was already flimsy; the last thing he needed was involvement with Papa's scandal. Sir Randolph would certainly use such a sordid association to ruin Lord Norcourt's suit.

Perhaps the viscount would simply introduce her to Sir Humphry?

Right. After six months at Mrs. Harris's school, she well knew how London society worked. A lowly teacher didn't beg an introduction to a man like Sir Humphry, especially since the chemist had retired from public life. Sir Humphry's wife and friends had closed ranks around him, protecting him from every interloper. And Lord Norcourt was one of those friends.

Even if the viscount agreed to introduce her, he would speak to Sir Humphry about it first. And given her constant pursuit of the man, Sir Humphry probably thought her mad by now. He would either tell Lord Norcourt what she wanted, which would end her scheme, or he would refuse to meet with her. Either way, another door would be closed.

No, her best chance was to maneuver an introduction to him in society. Which was unlikely to happen except through one of Lord Norcourt's parties.

She'd have to force the viscount's hand. Leaving the balustrade, she headed for the ballroom. "No other favor will do. I'll tell Mrs. Harris that I've reconsidered the wisdom of my proposal; that these rake lessons won't work after all."

"You conniving little witch," he growled, as she passed through the doors.

She forced herself to face him, although the icy glitter in his eyes set her back on her heels. "Tsk, tsk, Lord Norcourt, such language won't get you into my good graces."

"I don't want to get into your good graces, madam," he snapped, then stalked past her into the ballroom.

"And your niece?" She swallowed hard, but made herself continue. "I thought you said you had to get her out of 'that unspeakable place.'"

He halted, his back stiff with rage. "A nitrous oxide party is your price for getting Tessa enrolled?"

"Yes." When he turned around and approached her, she had to resist the impulse to back away. "You throw the party. I attend."

His stare bore into her. "Would taking you to someone else's nitrous oxide party satisfy you?"

Sir Humphry did occasionally attend other parties. But it was less certain.

"It's that or nothing," he went on. "Because if I throw a nitrous oxide party, it will damage more than Tessa's chances here. It will almost certainly come up in the courts, so I would lose guardianship, too."

She blinked. "But if you attend another party—"

"That's easier to keep secret. I can sneak you in and stay out of sight."

She couldn't ignore his logic. "But you swear you will take me to one?"

A muscle worked in his jaw. "I swear."

"And a great many of your friends will be there?"

"My friends?" His eyes narrowed. "Why does that matter?"

Lord, this deceiving him was hard. "I-I just meant it must be large. I assumed you wouldn't attend any party that didn't involve your friends."

He glared at her. "Fine, I'll make sure it's large. I'll convince someone I trust to throw it."

Even if she didn't meet Sir Humphry there, she might gain entree into the circle so she could be invited to a party he *did* attend. "All right, I am satisfied."

"How reassuring," he said, a sarcastic bite to his voice. "I'm to risk everything so you can write a bloody pamphlet, while *you* risk nothing."

"I risk my reputation and my position by attending," she pointed out.

"Which doesn't seem to concern you much."

Because if she got what she needed from the party, she'd be returning to Telford.

"Besides," he went on in that same resentful tone, "since no one knows you, you won't be found out. As I said, little risk to you, much risk to me."

"I can't help it you're better known and have so much to lose." She cocked up an eyebrow. "Nor is it my fault you lead a reckless life. Other gentlemen don't generally have to prove themselves."

His scowl held a wealth of ire. "Yes, if I'd subscribed to the narrow rules passing for morality in society, I wouldn't be in this position. How careless of me."

"I said nothing about morality." His uncle had hidden behind the claims of morality to condemn Papa, and she hated being lumped in with his kind.

"You didn't have to. It lurked beneath your talk about recklessness. But because you want something from me, you fear insulting me by calling me immoral."

"Don't be absurd."

His eyes glittered that unearthly blue. "You needn't bother; by most standards of society, I *am* immoral. And if not for my niece, I'd still be living exactly as I please because I don't care what society thinks." He leaned close.

"There, I've been honest with you. The least you can do is be honest with me."

"I am! I always state exactly what I think." Which was why hiding her reasons for wanting to attend the party was so hard. "Morality has nothing to do with my opinion, I assure you."

"Really." A decidedly unholy gleam shone in his eyes. "So if I were to ask you to seal our bargain with a kiss, you would have no moral objection."

A kiss? She squelched the peculiar jolt of excitement coursing through her at the thought.

"After all," he went on coldly, "I have no diseases, I can't use it to blackmail you since no one would take my word over yours, and it would certainly not result in illegitimate children." He glanced about the deserted ballroom. "Without witnesses, there's no risk to your position or reputation, either."

The gaze he fixed on her held an unfamiliar light that made her pulse drum violently. No man had ever looked at her quite like that. The few unmarried men in Telford had avoided the peculiar physician's daughter.

"So if you have no moral objection," he continued, "I see no reason for us *not* to kiss. Especially since you already told me I could 'attempt to seduce you all I please' because such things don't 'tempt' you."

How clever of him to use her own words against her. The odd thing was she'd love to have him kiss her, if only to see why everyone made such a fuss about it. But that was unwise, for so *many* reasons. "Kissing me would hardly prove you're sincere about being discreet."

"This is as discreet as I get, my dear." He shot her a scathing glance. "Besides, you don't really care if I'm sincere. You proposed those rakehell lessons only to put me in your debt, so you could ask your favor."

Oh, Lord, he'd seen right through her. But she was *not* a "conniving witch," drat it, who would say anything to get her "favor" while secretly despising him for his morals.

"Fine," she said, attempting nonchalance. "Kiss me if you wish. But not here." Whirling on her heel, she walked into a nearby card room, where they had less chance of being seen if someone wandered by.

She turned to find him gaping at her, frozen in his tracks. Clearly, he'd expected her to protest that such behavior was immoral. Then he could smugly congratulate himself upon having unmasked her lying character.

Hah! She'd shown him, hadn't she? "Well? Are we going to kiss or not? I have things to do, you know. I can't stand here all day . . ."

The words died in her throat as he began to move, a large and splendid beast stalking its prey. Before she could back away from the dark intent in his gaze, he'd caught her head in his hands and was kissing her. His mouth showed her no mercy, covering hers so thoroughly she could hardly breathe, then softening to liquid silk as it molded and tasted hers.

A strange and unfamiliar exhilaration seized her limbs, making her knees go weak and her belly tremble. If he had no diseases, what was this fever infecting her? Her brow felt hot, her cheeks felt hot . . . everything everywhere felt hot.

She placed her hand on his chest to push him away, but the wild tempo of his heart gave her pause. Because her heart beat the same wild tempo.

Although she'd read about the mating habits of animals, her sources hadn't mentioned increased heartbeat and temperature. No wonder women spoke of swooning from a kiss. She'd thought it silly, but it grew less silly by the moment.

Until he angled his head and slipped his tongue between her teeth.

She jerked back. "Your tongue does not belong inside my mouth, sir."

For a moment, he looked stunned, as if the kiss had surprised him as much as it had her. Then he gave her lips a covetous glance that sent an odd tremor along her spine. "That's part of kissing," he said, his voice low and husky. "You've never been kissed, have you?"

Did he consider her too unappealing to attract a man? She hated having him think her some pathetic spinster he could initiate into pleasure. Even if she was.

She thrust out her chin. "I didn't say that. But you know perfectly well it's improper for you to kiss me that way."

"That only adds to the enjoyment." His rakish smile stopped short of his eyes. The contrast between its amiability and his bleak gaze fascinated her.

What was she thinking? She might not know rakehells, but she recognized a snare when she saw one. And being ensnared by the incorrigible Lord Norcourt, no matter how splendid a beast he was, could hardly serve her purpose.

"Come now, sweetheart," he said in a smooth voice that slid over her skin like satin, "it's only to seal our bargain. Let me give you a real kiss. Just one."

Though she hesitated, curiosity about his "real kiss" won out over her good sense. "Just one," she agreed.

This time when he cupped her head between his hands, he brushed his lips over hers, coaxing them apart before he plunged his tongue inside. At first the sensation was peculiar. Then he withdrew his tongue, only to drive back in, over and over in a slow, seductive motion that roused the fever again.

The play of tongues should disgust her, but it didn't. The commanding thrusts, the heat, the slide of his lips over hers . . . how amazing. Quite astonishing, really. It reminded her of something, this rhythmic in and out . . .

Oh, Lord.

She tore her mouth from his. His "real kiss" resembled swiving, but with tongues. She'd witnessed enough animals in heat to recognize that. "That's quite enough, my lord," she said, marveling at her shaky voice. "I should think our bargain is quite thoroughly sealed."

He dragged in a sharp breath, then ran his thumb over her lips. "Yes, I should think it is."

A blush rose to her cheeks as she stepped back. She never blushed. How appalling that a rake could make her do so! She could never teach the girls to avoid unwise liaisons if she fell so easily into the arms of an avowed ne'er-do-well. "This can't happen again."

The speculative gleam in his eyes made her wary. "Afraid that you might be tempted by 'such things' after all, Miss Prescott?"

"Certainly not," she lied. "But we both want something from this association that we won't get if we're caught kissing."

Fortunately, that reminder turned him chilly.

Needing to escape him, she glanced at her pocket watch. "Forgive me, but I have a class to teach. We'll have to end your tour."

"Fine." He watched her closely, as if to assess her character. "I'm dining with old friends from Eton tonight, so I'd best be leaving anyway."

"I'll show you out." His brooding gaze making her uneasy, she headed for the door. "Can you start the lessons tomorrow?"

"Certainly."

"Then I'll see you at eight. That's when I teach natural history to the girls."

"Eight?" He looked incredulous. "In the *morning*?"

"I'm sorry," she said in a syrupy voice. "Is that too early for your lordship?"

His lips tightened into a thin smile. "It's fine."

Clearly, it wasn't. And she shouldn't make this *too* hard for him. "But you're meeting friends for dinner, and there will probably be drinking." Especially considering who his friends were.

She remembered the gossip in Telford after he and some other schoolboys at Eton had landed in trouble for having a Bacchanal, complete with wine, tavern wenches, and rides upon a goat. She waved her hand. "Never mind. Arrive when you please. I can accommodate your schedule."

"I'll be here promptly at eight, Miss Prescott." He made a curt bow. "Now, if you'll excuse me, I know the way out. I'll see you in the morning."

She watched him stride off, back erect. He was a strange mix of aristocratic arrogance and barely banked fires. She had the oddest feeling that if she poked too hard at those fires, the smoldering coals would flare up to burn her.

She must be careful. He wasn't like the driven merchants and the self-important Cits who came here to see their sisters or enroll their daughters. Those gentlemen were perfectly willing to let society dictate their behavior.

Not Lord Norcourt. He didn't answer to anyone's rules. He'd already spent his life in reckless pursuits; he would seduce a schoolteacher without compunction if he thought he could get away with it. And it would mean nothing to him.

Yet even that realization didn't reduce his tantalizing appeal. Because the thought of having the virile viscount initiate her into womanhood . . .

Madeline groaned. *Now* who was reckless? With her family steeped in scandal, letting him ruin her was out of the question. It would certainly *not* help Papa.

But Lord help her, this was going to be a very long two weeks.

Chapter Four

Dear Cousin,

Speaking of your intelligence-gathering capabilities, do you happen to know the new Viscount Norcourt? I have heard (do not ask how) that he is intent upon living a more circumspect life for the sake of his young niece, who recently lost her parents. Do you know if that is true? Have you seen any evidence of it?

Anxiously awaiting your reply,
Charlotte

Leaning across the dining table, Anthony snagged a macaroon from the dish that Oliver Sharpe, Marquess of Stoneville, was hogging. But he hardly tasted it, even though the Sablonière Hotel made delicious macaroons. He could only taste Miss Prescott.

A groan escaped him. What had he been thinking, to kiss her after barely gaining Tessa a foothold in the school?

He *hadn't* been thinking. He'd been too bloody angry to think. How dared that impudent chit offer to help him with Tessa, then blackmail him into agreeing to that bloody party? How dared she prove to be just like everyone else—only out for what she could get from him?

And how dared she have a mouth so soft and sweet that

the taste of it, like citrus or cloves or another tangy spice, lingered with him for hours?

He bit back a curse. That never happened to him. Not even the most alluring demi-rep ever stayed in his thoughts more than an hour after he left her. Yet Miss Prescott, with her temptress eyes and amazing mouth . . .

His bad boy roused, and he squirmed in his seat. He always kept his flirtations casual, choosing only whores and widows of easy virtue, who knew how the game was played and never asked for more than he wanted to give, who didn't unduly tax his control over his appetites.

But Miss Prescott had caught him off guard with her tart opinions and refreshing ideas, her seeming intelligence and willingness to help him. He simply didn't know what to make of her.

Her bloody secretiveness about her reasons for wanting to attend a nitrous oxide party worried him. She was risking her position to champion his cause. Would a woman really do that just for science?

He doubted it. And before he set up a party that could endanger his getting Tessa, he meant to find out what she was up to.

The woman had suggested rake lessons for girls, of all things. Was that just the act of a practical, forward-thinking naturalist? Or a schemer who had spotted him as a means to gain her freedom from drudgery the moment he'd walked in?

She certainly hadn't balked much at his kiss. Nor had she behaved like a virginal schoolteacher. Yes, her kissing had seemed untutored at first, but sometimes that was a jade's trick for enticing a man. And it had faded once their kiss turned more ardent.

Then there was her behavior afterward. She'd shown no maidenly outrage, treating it like a necessary part of their bargain. Except for her blush.

He sat back in his chair. So the kiss *had* unnerved her.

Fine, then he would continue to do so, until he learned her real reasons for the party. He would flirt just enough to put her off-balance. He needn't even fear she'd complain to Mrs. Harris of his advances. Miss Prescott was clever enough to realize that if he revealed how she was blackmailing him, it would end *her* plans as well as his. Whatever they really were.

"What's got you so quiet this evening, Norcourt?" asked David Masters, the Viscount Kirkwood.

That dragged Anthony from his obsessive thoughts, thank God. "Nothing." He wasn't about to tell his friends what a mess he'd landed himself in.

Especially given Kirkwood's determined drinking this evening. No doubt his wife, a rich banker's daughter whom Kirkwood had married for the sake of his impoverished family, was giving him trouble again. And marital strife always turned Kirkwood cynical.

"It must be a woman," Simon Tremaine, the Duke of Foxmoor, offered. "What else makes a man pensive?"

Stoneville chuckled. "You should know better than to think any woman can do that to Norcourt. He discards women as a dandy discards cravats."

The description inexplicably irritated Anthony, even though he often said the same thing about himself. "At least I leave them with their hearts intact." Unlike Stoneville, who regularly used his gypsy-dark looks to seduce opera dancers, then ended the affair when they fell madly in love with him.

"Actually," Anthony went on, "I was thinking of a new project of mine." Perhaps his friends could help him with the rakehell lessons. "A rich acquaintance is concerned about his daughter falling prey to a fortune hunter, so I agreed to dine with his family and explain to her how to avoid being taken in. Only I'm not sure what to say."

"Is she pretty?" drawled Stoneville.

"Who?"

"The daughter, of course." Stoneville grinned. "Because a kiss is worth a thousand words."

Anthony scowled. "You may be devil enough to seduce a friend's daughter, but I'm not." He turned to the duke, the only one of his friends with a happy marriage. "Tell them, Foxmoor."

"Tell them what?" Foxmoor shot Anthony a veiled glance. "I wouldn't let you near any daughter of mine. I'm not even sure I'd let you alone with my wife, and I trust her implicitly."

"Ah, but Norcourt is a new man, didn't you hear?" Kirkwood remarked, a bitter gleam in his green eyes. "Gaining his brother's title knocked the wickedness right out of him. Now he never looks at a woman except with respect."

Silence greeted that pronouncement, followed immediately by laughter.

Anthony glowered at the group of friends he'd had since his days at Eton. "I should have known better than to ask *you* lot for advice. Your idea of a serious conversation is to debate the quality of the brandy."

"Who's debating?" Kirkwood tapped the bottle. "This brandy is dandy."

As the others laughed, Kirkwood downed what was left in his glass, then called for another bottle, their second since dinner began.

"Besides," Foxmoor added with a worried glance in Kirkwood's direction, "I have enough serious conversation at Parliament. I'd rather do without when I'm with the three of you."

"Especially if Norcourt means to be boring and respectable." Stoneville gave an exaggerated shudder.

"Don't worry," Anthony retorted. "The last thing I'll ever be is respectable."

Responsible, yes, for he fully intended to clean up the mess his brother had left behind, both with Tessa and the estate. But respectable?

Never. He would curb his outrageous tongue in public for Tessa's sake. He would even be "discreet," a word he loathed. But he refused to become a hypocrite.

"Here, Norcourt," Kirkwood said, as the second bottle arrived. "Have another glass. The trouble with you is you're not yet drunk enough to appreciate our wit."

"What wit?" Anthony shot back.

Lady Kirkwood must really be in the boughs this time. Kirkwood only numbed himself with liquor when his wife's gambling debts grew too large. He'd surely suffer for his night's indulgence in the morning.

It isn't good for the constitution.

Damnation, Miss Prescott was invading his thoughts again with her odd, bluestocking opinions. And his constitution was just fine. He thrust his glass toward Kirkwood. "Give me another, then."

"That's the spirit," Kirkwood remarked, and poured him a glass.

The liquor went down easy and smooth, for it was indeed "dandy" brandy, but Anthony took less joy in it than usual. He flashed upon an image of his niece sitting wide-eyed and innocent at his table as she watched him stumble down to breakfast, and the liquor turned to ashes in his mouth.

Damn it, Tessa wasn't even in his care yet. Why the bloody devil shouldn't he enjoy himself? He trusted his friends—they would never reveal outside this room that he was the same as he'd always been.

Draining his glass, he thrust it out to Kirkwood. "Another."

"Now see here, you fool," Foxmoor said, as Kirkwood refilled it, "we weren't daring you to get cup-shot."

"Speak for yourself," Stoneville retorted, an unholy light in his black eyes. "Give me another, too, Kirkwood." He turned to the duke. "What about you, Foxmoor? Too henpecked to have a brandy?"

"I have a brandy already, thank you." Foxmoor tapped the glass he'd been nursing for the past hour.

The duke's tone of quiet reproach didn't escape Anthony, who'd admired him ever since Foxmoor had befriended him at Eton. The older man had been the one to suggest that Anthony enroll Tessa in Mrs. Harris's school since Foxmoor's wife was connected to the place in some way.

A pity that Anthony couldn't get the duchess to put in a good word for him with the prickly Mrs. Harris. But Foxmoor's wife had taken a dislike to him ever since she'd overheard him flirting with a widow in her Ladies Association. Like most charity-minded females, she had firm ideas about proper behavior.

What would the duchess make of Miss Prescott, who claimed to have more concern for practicality than virtue? The image of the teacher debating the physical effects of strong drink with Foxmoor's wife had him chuckling to himself until he realized the others were staring.

God save him, couldn't he get that chit out of his mind?

He shot to his feet and held up his glass. "A toast, gentlemen!" He would banish the vexing female from his thoughts, even if he had to drink himself into a stupor. "To wine, wenches, and wickedness!"

All except Foxmoor echoed the toast, with the duke only sipping some liquor. Now that the man had married, he was turning into a prig.

As Anthony dropped back into the chair, Stoneville lifted his glass. "To brandy, brothels, and bad behavior!"

Kirkwood arched an eyebrow. "That's only a variation on Norcourt's toast."

"Good enough for me," Anthony mumbled, already slurring his words.

Not that he cared, by God. He repeated the toast, then drained his glass.

Raising his own glass, Kirkwood cried, "To spirits, soiled doves, and sin!"

"And you called mine unoriginal?" Stoneville complained. "At least it flowed off the tongue."

"The only thing flowing off your tongue is bad breath," Kirkwood shot back.

Foxmoor rose abruptly. "I'm off, gentlemen. Thank you for dinner and the part of the conversation that was coherent."

"You're leaving?" Anthony said.

"Once Stoneville and Kirkwood turn to insulting each other, the evening generally heads downhill. And I have an early morning tomorrow."

So did Anthony.

While Foxmoor settled his part of the bill, Anthony's mind wandered to Mrs. Harris's school. To be there at eight, he'd have to leave London no later than seven, which meant rising before six to dress.

Of course, Miss Prescott had said he could arrive when he wished, but only because she thought him incapable of anything else. And because she would do whatever she must to get her favor, even hide his mishaps from her employer.

He scowled. She probably expected him to stumble in around noon, green to the gills, reeking of liquor and stale perfume and forcing her to lie for him.

If he stayed here longer, that's exactly what would happen. Stoneville would drag him to a private brothel beyond the knowledge of the courts, where the two of them could carouse to their heart's content. He would drink until he fell asleep in some whore's arms, until dawn came and he could face his room alone.

Unless . . .

Unless he showed up bright and cheerful at eight in the morning and proved to the cool Miss Prescott that he could do whatever he set his mind to. Wouldn't it be a pleasure to watch her jaw drop?

Besides, once Tessa lived with him, he'd have to survive the nights alone in the dark somehow. Why not start learning to do it now? Miss Prescott had called wickedness a habit. Well, he'd show *her* he could break the habit whenever he wished. She'd have her rake lessons at eight in the morning, by God, even if he had to toss and turn half the night. The little naturalist would *not* get away with acting as if he was incapable of being responsible.

He rose, annoyed to find himself already unsteady on

his feet. Fortunately, he still had a good part of the night left to sober up.

The duke was heading to the door when Anthony called out, "Foxmoor, wait! Would you drop me at my town house?"

Foxmoor halted in surprise. "You don't have your own carriage?"

"I came with Stoneville." Anthony skirted the table. "He'll want to stay."

"Damned right." Stoneville lurched to his feet. "Come now, you and Foxmoor can't both take off early. Where does that leave me after Kirkwood heads home to the little woman?"

"Alone, old chap." Foxmoor's eyes gleamed. "As Shakespeare says, 'Get thee a wife.'"

Stoneville indicated Kirkwood with a jerk of his head. "And spend my evenings in misery like our friend there? No thank you."

"We'll go carousing another night," Anthony told him. "But I have to be somewhere early tomorrow."

With a snort of disgust, Stoneville dropped back into his chair. "Fine. Run off if you must. Kirkwood and I will drink for the two of you."

As Anthony left with Foxmoor, the viscount was already pouring himself another drink.

The minute they were out of earshot, Foxmoor murmured, "I'm worried about Kirkwood. It's not like him to drink so heavily."

"Has something new happened, other than the usual troubles with his wife?"

Foxmoor glanced back up the stairs. "I don't know. He won't discuss it."

"I'll ask Stoneville if he's heard anything."

"I'll ask my wife, too, since Lady Kirkwood went to that school I recommended to you for your niece, the one run by my wife's friend."

They'd reached the lobby, so Anthony waited until Fox-moor had called for his carriage. "Speaking of that school, I took your advice about enrolling Tessa."

"And Mrs. Harris agreed? Excellent. I wish I could have put in a good word for you, old chap, but—"

"I know, your wife would have been consulted and would have hurried to give her friend a long litany of my sins. I do wish Kirkwood hadn't been quite so forthcoming about our past exploits at your wedding."

"I'll put in a good word for you when your case comes to court."

"So my uncle can tar you with the same brush as he's tarring me?" Anthony stared out at Leicester Square, as busy at 10:00 P.M. as Rotten Row was at five. "No, I won't have my friends soiled by him, too. You're in politics now—you must be careful of your reputation."

"My reputation is secure, I promise you."

Foxmoor meant well, but his enemies would leap on any excuse to hurt him politically, and Anthony wouldn't provide them the means for it. "If I get desperate, I'll take you up on your offer, but I am more optimistic about my chances now."

"Good." Foxmoor mused a moment. "Doesn't your uncle have a daughter with a soft spot for you? Perhaps she will argue on your behalf."

"Jane is on her father's list of witnesses, so I doubt she'd help *me*."

He had only himself to blame for that. He should have

kept in better touch, visited to see how she was doing. But once he'd escaped that wretched house, the very thought of speaking of what they'd endured had frozen his heart. At Eton, he'd ignored her few letters, and they'd stopped once she'd married the new headmaster of the school in Telford.

A pang of guilt gripped him. He should have written then, if only to congratulate her. But marriage to a headmaster implied that she'd succumbed to her mother's rigid ideas, and he couldn't endure hearing her also voice Aunt Eunice's platitudes, claiming that their punishments had been "necessary" for their "discipline." He couldn't bear to hear that she'd become what he'd escaped by going to Eton. There'd been no school for Jane.

Shoving his hand in his pocket, he fingered his snuffbox. Well, there'd be one for Tessa, damn it.

As Foxmoor's rig arrived, it occurred to Anthony that the duke might know more about the person who held Tessa's future in her hand. "Foxmoor, do you ever visit Mrs. Harris's school yourself?"

He could feel Foxmoor's gaze on him. "Occasionally, with Louisa. Why?"

"There's a peculiar teacher there named Miss Prescott. What do you know of her?"

"You mean the blond beauty with the unusual eyes?"

"I hadn't noticed her appearance," he lied, "but now that you mention it . . ."

With a suspicious snort, Foxmoor headed for the door.

"Oh, for God's sake," Anthony grumbled as he followed the duke into the carriage. "I'm merely curious because she claims to be a naturalist, and Tessa is interested in gardening." All right, so that was a lie, but he'd be damned if he'd have Foxmoor speculating wrongly about Anthony's interest in Miss Prescott.

"I can't tell you much." Foxmoor knocked on the ceiling for the driver to go on. "The headmistress of a school in the country—I forget where—recommended her to Mrs. Harris when she and her father moved to Richmond."

"Can't her father support them?"

"I honestly don't know. From what I understand, she is very private. Keeps to herself, doesn't even bring her father around the school."

Interesting. Did she even *have* a father? Or was that some invention to make her appear respectable? "And the mother? What about her?"

"Dead, I think." With a sly lift of an eyebrow, Foxmoor added, "I could ask Louisa to be sure."

Anthony stiffened. "No, it's only idle curiosity." The last thing he needed was the duchess trying to marry him off to a woman of dubious background.

Settling against the squabs, Foxmoor eyed him closely. "Does this have to do with the 'friend' who wants you to instruct his daughter about fortune hunters?"

"No," Anthony clipped out. Good God, had he been *that* transparent? Not even to Foxmoor would he confide what the ladies of the school had convinced him to do. The duke might be a pillar of the community, but he would still laugh his ass off at the thought of Anthony teaching anything to anyone . . . if he didn't rise up in outrage and have Mrs. Harris put a stop to the "rake lessons."

Whatever *those* were.

He stared out the window. Well, Miss Prescott would just have to explain her proposal more thoroughly if she wanted his compliance.

Otherwise, she wouldn't be getting her nitrous oxide party.

A loud scraping noise in her tiny cottage woke Madeline from a dead sleep. She came instantly alert, a talent she'd had to cultivate of late. Hurrying from the bed, she dragged a wrapper over her night rail, then went in search of her father.

She found him in the parlor, stabbing a poker into the fireplace. A glance at the clock made her groan. "Papa, it's three o'clock. Why are you up?"

"Too damned cold in this place," he mumbled. "Can't sleep."

With a weary sigh, she took the poker from him. She was in no mood for dealing with Papa, not after she'd tossed and turned half the night, replaying the viscount's naughty kiss. "Go back to bed. I'll heat you some milk."

He turned a frantic gaze on her, as he sometimes did after his nightmares woke him. "I had a dream."

"Yes, yes, I know." She guided him toward his bedchamber. "You shouldn't take that sleeping draught. It always gives you wild dreams."

"But I can't sleep without it. I keep . . . hearing her whisper at the end, hearing her labored breaths—"

Madeline engulfed him in her arms, wishing she could banish his painful memories. Mrs. Crosby, the vicar's wife, had been Papa's last patient. Why had this one death tormented him for months now?

She clutched him tightly. It was that horrible Sir Randolph's fault. Papa had done nothing wrong while treating Mrs. Crosby. He certainly hadn't committed the disgusting acts Sir Randolph claimed. Sir Randolph hated Papa for trying to bring reason to a town where ignorance held sway, so he'd seized on this nonsense to drum him out of town.

"You did your best, Papa. It was Mrs. Crosby's infection that killed her."

"How many times have I lanced abscesses with no ill effect?" He pulled free and went to stare dolefully at the fire. "I shouldn't have given her anything for the pain, but the poor lady cried so pitifully . . ."

Papa had a bias against laudanum, so he'd decided to try the nitrous oxide after what Sir Humphry had written in his book about its pain-relieving properties.

He glowered at the hearth. "The nitrous oxide killed her—I just know it."

"It did not." Madeline took his arm. "Otherwise, all those reckless lords imbibing it for fun would be dead by now."

"You see, you see?" he cried. "It is good for nothing but frivolity."

"That's not true. We both know it has other untapped properties. Besides, you said yourself that Mrs. Crosby's abscess was worse than it at first appeared."

"Yes, but to have it provoke acute fever and a racing pulse within moments . . ." He shook his head. "That never happened before with a patient." As sudden as the anger came, it fled, replaced by his all-consuming sadness. Dropping into a chair, he buried his head in his hands. "She went so very quickly . . . a breath, two breaths, and she was gone." Tears rolled down his cheeks.

The weeping was what tore at her. Madeline had only seen her father cry at Mama's funeral, until the vicar's wife died. Since then he cried with no provocation, sometimes sobbing like an old man, though he was only fifty.

"I killed her as surely as if I'd shot her," Papa choked out. "Sir Randolph is right—I *am* a murderer for trying that nitrous oxide on her."

"Sir Randolph is a vicious fool, and you know it," she protested.

"Aye, but that doesn't change the fact that she's dead. His other nonsense might be lies, but that part was true. And I deserve to be punished for that part alone." With a woeful shake of his head, he dabbed at his eyes with a handkerchief.

Seeing him like this made her want to run Sir Randolph through with a rapier. It was bad enough that Papa was questioning his medical judgment, but he might have got through that if Sir Randolph hadn't raised such a clamor over it. Then, to accuse Papa of giving Mrs. Crosby nitrous oxide in order to have his wicked way with her—what a ghastly falsehood!

Sir Randolph and Papa had fallen out years ago, but people had believed Sir Randolph's lies because Papa was a widower, and Mrs. Crosby had been the beauty of the town. They'd always been suspicious of his advanced scientific learning, since old wives' tales formed the basis for most remedies in town. He'd spent his life caring for the townspeople, only to have them turn their backs on him at the first hint of scandal.

Her hands curled into fists. The worst part was that he had let them. Once upon a time, he would have fought back. But his misplaced guilt over Mrs. Crosby's death kept him from defending himself, which left only her to defend him.

Why did this plague him so? He'd suffered spells of

melancholy all her life, but they generally passed after a week or two. Even Mama's death from consumption two years ago hadn't resulted in such abject grief.

The thought of her mother made her choke back a sob. Mama would have known how to make him easy; whatever Madeline said merely provoked tears. Or worse, made him lash out in anger—and not just at her, but at their neighbors and tradesmen and even Mrs. Jenkins, the widow she'd hired to keep house.

That was the reason she'd given Papa; the truth was she dared not leave him alone for fear that he would take his own life during one of his melancholy fits. The possibility terrified her.

She'd hoped that moving from Telford and escaping the horrible gossip Sir Randolph kept stirred up would help him, that he might resume his practice in Richmond. But he'd been unable to do so.

Thank heaven the headmistress at the Shrewsbury school, where Madeline used to teach, had been kind enough to recommend her to Mrs. Harris. Otherwise, they'd be facing poverty when Papa's meager savings ran out.

They might end up there yet. Even though the coroner's inquest had deemed Mrs. Crosby's death not a criminal matter, Sir Randolph was bent on convincing Reverend Crosby to have it reexamined by the authorities.

Anger roiled in her belly. If that happened, she would have to hire a lawyer and spend money on Papa's defense. But if she could convince Sir Humphry to come to Telford and speak to the vicar himself, he could assure the man that nitrous oxide was perfectly safe, that other people had used it in such a capacity—and not to "have their wicked way" with anyone, either.

A sigh wracked her. It was a flimsy hope, at best. For one thing, it depended on Lord Norcourt providing a chance for her to meet the famous chemist, and how likely was that?

The snoring from the chair startled, then relieved her. Papa had fallen asleep. Thank the Lord.

Careful to keep her steps quiet, she returned to her own bed. But now *she* couldn't sleep. It was the third night this week that Papa had awakened her at some horrible hour, and she sometimes caught herself nodding off while the girls did an exercise at their desks. She was just so very tired . . .

It seemed like only seconds later that something shook her. She snuggled deeper into her pillow.

"Miss Prescott!" a sharp voice said in her ear.

Her eyes shot open. Why was it so bright? And why was Letty Jenkins here, bending over her—

She'd overslept! "What time is it?" she cried, tossing off the coverlet.

"A little after seven," the woman answered, her face concerned. "Aren't you supposed to be at the school at—"

"Lord, I'm so late!" Madeline wailed as she leaped from the bed. Hurrying to the washbasin, she poured water from the pitcher.

Like the angel that she was, Mrs. Jenkins handed her the washcloth, then headed for the door. "You've missed breakfast at the school. I'll fetch you something to eat."

"No time for that. I'll have something later."

The aging widow clucked her tongue, but took a gown from the closet and laid out Madeline's clothes for the day.

Madeline raced through her ablutions. She never overslept. Her girls would wonder where on earth she was. She must hurry, she must! Mrs. Harris wouldn't notice she was late unless one of the girls alerted her.

Or unless the viscount arrived; today was the day he was to start his lessons! How mortifying it would be if he asked Mrs. Harris about her.

She rolled her eyes as she donned her chemise and corset. Lord Rakehell would *not* arrive on time; she'd be lucky if he even came. All she had to do was reach her class before the students could alert Mrs. Harris, and no one would be the wiser.

"How is Papa?" she asked Mrs. Jenkins, as the woman began lacing her up. "Did you see him when you came in?"

"He's snoring in his chair."

"If he doesn't move to the bed, his muscles will seize up—"

"I'll take care of it." Mrs. Jenkins handed her the gown. "You just leave everything to Letty now. I know how to deal with Dr. Prescott."

Hiring Mrs. Jenkins had been the wisest idea of her life. "Thank you," she said, as the woman helped her finish dressing. "You're a godsend."

"A pity my late husband never thought so. Believe me, caring for your father is hardly a trial after a lifetime of putting up with Mr. Jenkins." The widow pushed her toward the door. "Now go on with you. Everything will be fine."

As Madeline raced out the door, she clung to the widow's words, praying that the woman was right.

Chapter Five

Dear Charlotte,

*Why on earth do you wish to know about Lord
Norcourt? Please say you haven't fallen under his spell.
After what I told you about his outrageous parties, I
should think you'd have more sense than to succumb
to his much-vaunted talent for seducing widows.*

Your concerned cousin,
Michael

Anthony paced the hall, his temper rising. The servant had assured him that Miss Prescott would join him shortly, yet here he stood cooling his heels outside her classroom. A gaggle of giggling girls had trooped past ten minutes ago, come up from breakfast. Occasionally one peered out, then returned to the others to whisper. He felt like a circus attraction.

God rot Miss Prescott—no doubt she was keeping him waiting for some nefarious reason of her own. And he hated being made to look the fool.

Could he have misunderstood her instructions? Surely she hadn't meant for him to begin teaching these silly lessons alone. He still wasn't sure what she wanted him to say.

Just as he'd decided to go to Mrs. Harris's office, he

heard someone racing up the stairs. He whirled in time to see Miss Prescott vault onto the top step, then freeze at the sight of him.

Her glorious hair was a mess, half-falling down about her shoulders, and her cheeks shone the same color as her poppy red gown. A series of ragged breaths stuttered from her lips. "L-Lord . . . N-Norcourt," she stammered, trying vainly to catch her breath. "G-Good . . . morning."

His annoyance faded, replaced by a devilish satisfaction. He hadn't misunderstood. She was simply late.

Oh, this was too rich for words. It made up for his having to rise at an ungodly hour, for the frenzied pace he'd set for his horse, and even for having to forgo carousing with Stoneville.

He could hardly restrain his glee. "Miss Prescott," he drawled. "We've been waiting for you." Removing his pocket watch, he gazed at it with exaggerated interest. "You did say eight, didn't you? In the morning?"

As she restored her hair to its proper condition, she hastened toward him.

"I could have sworn you did." He shook his watch, then looked at it again. "Either my watch is broken, or you aren't terribly—"

"—punctual," she finished for him through gritted teeth. She halted a few steps away. "Very good, Lord Norcourt. You've proved you can tell time."

Without bothering to hide his smile, he restored his watch to his pocket. "And you, Miss Prescott, have proved that you cannot."

If eyes could kill, he would be laid out on the floor. But not even her fiery glance could ruin his enjoyment. He followed her into the classroom in a far better humor.

The students who'd been milling around inside hurried to greet her. "Are you all right, Miss Prescott?" asked one of them.

"You weren't at breakfast," said another, her young face worried.

She turned fond glances on them. "I'm perfectly well, I assure you."

"Your father's not ill again, is he?" one girl asked.

Anthony's enjoyment at her lateness dimmed. Could her interest in nitrous oxide be related to her father's health?

If she'd already begun an article on the subject, surely she knew the gas had no healing properties. Besides, if that had been her aim, why not just say so?

With a furtive glance at him, she said, "Papa is fine. I simply overslept. It was rude of me, and I'm sorry if it alarmed you." A genuine smile crossed her features as she gazed at them. "I appreciate your concern."

He had to admire how she treated her students, a far cry from how he'd been treated at their age. That probably explained why they were so solicitous of her.

She clapped her hands. "Now, girls, it's time to take your seats. We have a special guest, so I'll expect you to be on your best behavior this morning."

Thirty pairs of eyes swung to him in curiosity, but the girls did as they were told without dawdling. He grudgingly admitted that Miss Prescott seemed to be good at her profession. Yet another reason to fight for Tessa's admission, if the other teachers were as competent as she.

"Ladies," she said, as soon as they were seated, "we are honored to have the Viscount Norcourt join us today. Lord Norcourt's niece will be enrolling here soon, so he's been gracious enough to offer . . . that is . . . he will be revealing to you girls . . ."

Taking pity on the flustered Miss Prescott, Anthony stepped forward. "I'll be giving you lessons on men."

That got their attention. They sat up straighter and exchanged meaningful glances that made him wonder again what the devil he would tell them.

Miss Prescott flashed him a grateful smile. "Lord Norcourt shall reveal what he has learned from his vast experience in society. His instruction will focus on how to identify the wrong kind of men."

"So that when you run afoul of them," he added, "you know how to get them to leave you alone."

A hand shot up in the back of the room. He glanced to Miss Prescott, but she gave him the floor. Damn. He'd hoped she'd guide him through it the first time.

Stifling his irritation, he smiled at the girl with the raised hand. "Yes?"

The young lady stood. "I am Miss Lucinda Seton." She tipped her nose high. "My father is a colonel. He says if a soldier or any other man tries to touch me, I'm to slap his face and tell him my father will shoot him at dawn if he tries it again."

Miss Prescott's groan told him this wasn't the first time Miss Seton had offered such advice. No wonder they wanted the girls to have lessons.

"Does that stratagem work for you?" he asked.

Miss Seton blinked. "I-I don't know. I've not had occasion to try it yet."

"With so many soldiers about, you've never had one be impertinent?" He eyed her closely. "Or is it just that no one you *disliked* was ever impertinent?"

With a blush, she sat down.

When the other girls tittered, and Miss Seton's blush deepened, he added, "But your father is right. His tactics will work on a certain sort of man."

Warming to his subject, he began to pace the room. "Listen well, ladies. There are three kinds of men: beasts, gentlemen, and beasts masquerading as gentlemen. Contrary to what your parents may say, neither a man's connections nor his rank nor his money will help you distinguish one from the other. I once saw a blacksmith offer his coat to a beggar girl, and an earl rudely eject a dowager from his carriage because she coughed on his seats. Men are a tricky business, no matter what their rank. Don't let anyone tell you otherwise."

He halted to gaze at the susceptible young females before him, and an unfamiliar panic gripped him at the thought of being responsible for these girls' opinions. Then Tessa's tearful face at the funeral swam into his mind, and he considered what he would tell *her*. Instantly the panic fled.

"That's precisely the problem," he went on. "A beast is easy to spot. He leers at you or paws you when you dance with him. He catches you when you're alone and tries to force a kiss on you even when you protest." He smiled at Miss Seton. "Slapping him and threatening him with Papa's wrath is entirely appropriate. Braining him with a flowerpot wouldn't be amiss, either."

The girls laughed. Even Miss Prescott managed a smile.

"But call them rogues or whatever you wish—beasts masquerading as gentlemen have one thing in common. They're hard to detect. They don't wear signs that say, 'I've come to tempt you into wickedness.' No, they smile and charm their way into your good graces. *Then* they tempt you into wickedness."

The girls' skeptical expressions made him wonder how often they'd heard this from Mrs. Harris and her teachers, probably with a healthy dollop of dull moral instruction. And what girl wanted to believe that all men weren't the dashing fellows they longed to marry? Especially when those dashing fellows deliberately made the girls' hearts melt and their pulses race.

These girls needed something more powerful to convince them.

He waited until their giggles died. "Before I go on, I wish to learn more about you." Gesturing to a plain chit in the front row wearing spectacles, he said, "Why don't we start with you, Miss—"

"Bancroft," she said warily. "Elinor Bancroft."

"That's a lovely name." A familiar one, too. Where had he heard it? "It's fitting for a girl with your elegant manner."

As the other girls giggled, she glared at them. "Thank you, sir."

"And where are you from, Miss Bancroft?"

"Yorkshire, sir."

Now he knew who she was. She was widely deemed the richest heiress in northern England. "Ah yes, I could tell. You have that air of confidence that I find in so many people from Yorkshire. It's the bracing northern air— it strengthens one's stamina." Sidling near her desk, he smiled. "It's probably also responsible for your fine complexion."

Coloring a little, she straightened in her seat. "Thank you, sir."

He picked up the book sitting upon her desk and

glanced at the title. "You're reading Shakespeare's sonnets?"

"They're my favorite," she confessed.

"Mine, too. What is that line, 'a rose by any other name . . .'"

"No, sir," she protested, "that is from the plays. *Romeo and Juliet*."

Pasting a look of chagrin to his face, he said, "You're right." He hung his head. "I'm not good at remembering verse, Miss Bancroft. I'm always embarrassing myself. You must think me a complete dolt."

"No, indeed I do not!" she hastened to assure him.

"Oh, but I'm sure you do, a clever girl like yourself."

"Really, sir, anyone can learn to recite poetry if they work at it."

"I wish that were true. My poor, blind mother is always asking me to recite verse for her, and I can never oblige her unless there's a library near to hand. I so hate how often I'm forced to disappoint her."

"I could show you an easy way to learn if you like."

"Would you?" He seized her hand. "It would mean so much to my mother."

She blushed violently. "I would be honored to help you."

He squeezed her hand. "I'll hold you to your promise, Miss Bancroft."

"Certainly, sir."

She tried to pull her hand free, but he turned it over to look at it. "You have ink on your fingers. I daresay you write poetry, too."

Her hand relaxed in his. "Indeed, I do."

"Might I be permitted to read it sometime?" He played with her fingers as the girls around her strained to see. "I do so enjoy good verse."

"I will give you some of my poems tomorrow, if you like."

"I'd enjoy that very much." He frowned. "Ah, but I forgot—I won't be here. Might you go up to your room later and fetch it? I could meet you in the library."

She blinked at him.

Releasing her hand, he stepped back, then faced the girls who watched him with shocked expressions. "*That*, ladies, is a beast masquerading as a gentleman."

Glancing over at Miss Prescott, he found her fighting a smile. He winked, and she shook her head. But her pretty eyes danced, and the sight of it sent a shaft of need right through him, which he forcibly ignored.

Unfortunately, when he turned back to the students, Miss Bancroft looked devastated. "I should have known you didn't think me elegant," she said softly. "No one really thinks me elegant."

Her wounded tone cut at him. Despite her riches, she reminded him pitifully of Tessa. "I don't know you, Miss Bancroft," he said gently, "so I can hardly think you elegant or otherwise. But our conversation told me one thing. You have a kind heart. And that's more important to a man than any amount of elegance."

When she cast him a grateful glance, he turned to the others. "Unfortunately, girls with kind hearts also make fine prey for scoundrels. Such fellows will say anything to convince you to go off alone with them. They will speak of their poor sainted mothers if that will gain your sympathy. They will tell you with apparent modesty of being wounded in France if that will soften your heart."

Glancing to the back of the room, he called out, "Miss

Seton, if we'd had the same conversation and I'd taken your hand in the same manner, would you have slapped my cheek and threatened to send your father after me?"

Miss Seton chewed her lower lip, obviously debating whether to tell the truth. At last she sighed. "I expect not." Then she thought a moment before gazing at him consideringly. "But you're a better catch than most of the soldiers I meet, so I don't think Papa would mind terribly if I encouraged you."

He laughed. "That depends on how much he knows of my reputation."

A girl sitting near the front muttered, "*I* would never fall for such nonsense."

"Perhaps not," he said, addressing her directly, "but that's because I said only things that suit Miss Bancroft. Any scoundrel trying to tempt *you* would tailor his lies accordingly. The more clever the rogue, the less blatant he is. His compliments will be subtle, of the kind you'll wish very much to believe."

He pinned Miss Bancroft with his gaze. "What was it that first made you soften toward me, Miss Bancroft?"

Coloring, she glanced about at the others. "Your love of verse. I suppose you made that up, too?"

"No, indeed. But the kind of verse I like isn't fit for ladies."

At a strangled sound from Miss Prescott, he looked over to see her fighting a laugh. "Did you have something to add, Miss Prescott?" he teased.

She blinked at him. "No, Lord Norcourt. Pray continue."

He gestured to Miss Bancroft's book. "I said I loved

verse because I deduced from your spectacles and your collection of verse that *you* loved it." He began to pace again. "Remember, ladies, a rogue will seize on any clue to strike up a deeper acquaintance. If you carry a basket of cut flowers and your skin is tanned, he'll profess that he loves gardens more than anything. If your name is McBride and your ribbons are tartan, he'll extol the virtues of Scotland. He'll say whatever he thinks will make you comfortable with him."

A girl's hand shot up, and he nodded to her.

"What if the gentleman really *does* have a blind mother, sir? What if he really does like verse and such. Isn't it rude to assume he's a rogue from the first?"

"Don't assume he's a rogue. Assume he's a stranger. Because until you know him well, that's exactly what he is. A gentleman won't need to press his attentions on you. He'll let a friendship progress naturally. He'll be patient and allow you to learn something of his character by introducing his friends and family before he starts trying to get you off alone with him in a library."

"Mrs. Harris says that if he's a gentleman," Miss Seton put in, "he won't try to get you off alone with him at all."

"Even a true gentleman wants to be alone with the woman he's courting. That doesn't mean you should let him. But he will try."

"Would *you* try?" Miss Seton asked, wide-eyed.

"All men try."

"But—"

"What Lord Norcourt means," Miss Prescott put in, "is that everyone, man or woman, rogue or gentleman, is born with an animal's instinct to mate."

Instinct to *mate*? Casting her a sidelong glance, he smiled. "Leave it to the naturalist to express it so eloquently."

But she wasn't finished. "The difference between people and animals is that people can tame those instincts if they choose."

That depended on how powerful the instinct and how determined the person. He managed to hold his own voracious appetites in check by regularly letting the beast out to play during very controlled encounters. But God save him if he ever took the restraints off fully. He wasn't sure what he'd be capable of.

Of course, she wasn't talking about him. She was talking about the average man. And *that* he could address. "Miss Prescott is correct. A true gentleman will choose to govern his desires. If you refuse to go off alone with him, he'll accept your decision. And if you do happen to find yourself alone with him, you will still be safe, because he lives by the rules that society sets for his behavior."

Hardly aware that he did it, he scowled. "But the *beast* doesn't care about the rules. He'll keep trying to get you alone until he succeeds. Once he succeeds, there will be no controlling him. He will certainly not attempt to control himself. That's why you must learn to distinguish between the beast and the gentleman. Because it's the only sure way to protect yourself from harm."

For some reason, that provoked a flurry of whispers among the girls. At apparent prodding from the others, Miss Seton raised her hand again.

"Yes, Miss Seton?"

She rose, a serious expression on her face. "We were wondering, sir . . . well . . . you seem to be very good at acting sincere, and you have a great deal of knowledge about these matters and . . ." With a glance at her friends, she hesitated.

"Ask your question, Miss Seton. I promise not to bite."

With her friends' titters goading her, she met him with a forthright gaze. "What we'd like to know, sir, is which are *you*? A gentleman? Or a beast masquerading as a gentleman?"

Chapter Six

Dear Cousin,
    In all your alarm I notice you don't reveal whether
you know his lordship personally. Perhaps I shall ask
him about the friends he invites to his parties. It could
be a most enlightening discussion.

Your curious relation,
Charlotte

Madeline had to smother a laugh at Lord Norcourt's
flummoxed expression. Only her girls could render a viscount speechless. Taking pity on him, she said, "Since his
lordship has been kind enough to instruct you girls in
these matters, I don't think we should question—"

"No, no, I want to answer." He stared thoughtfully at the
girls. "Mrs. Harris and your teacher asked me to provide
this instruction because of my reputation as a rakehell.
They've decided I'm a beast masquerading as a gentleman,
and they figure no one knows better how a beast behaves
than another beast. They may be right."

Leaning his hips against the edge of Madeline's desk, he
regarded the girls with an oddly sober expression. "But you
will have to decide for yourselves. Despite what I've told
you so far, a man's character isn't always easy to determine.

Over the days to come, I hope to offer you ways to do so, but in the end your decision on how to regard a man, any man, can only be yours."

What a clever dodge. Still, it wasn't a bad answer under the circumstances. If he came right out and said he was a beast, the girls probably wouldn't believe him anyway. Or worse yet, they'd be fascinated.

They were already fascinated, truth be told. As he described a rogue's sly techniques for touching a woman's hand or arm or even hair without alarming her, he made every female in the room, including her, yearn to receive those touches.

Madeline sighed. Who could blame them? Even dressed in mourning clothes, he managed to look fashionable. Today he wore black buckskin riding breeches with carved ebony buttons. His Hessian boots bore a high sheen, and his merino riding coat and waistcoat of black figured silk were excellently tailored. Even his hair was fashionably tousled, though probably from his ride, not a valet's care.

Unless he was intentionally trying to look unstudied.

Oh, how was a mere schoolteacher to discern such aristocratic whims? Why, the man had just happily illustrated a rogue's ploys. If she had any sense, she wouldn't trust him at all. Yesterday, when he'd admired her interest in natural history and professed to love mathematics, he probably hadn't even meant it. He'd merely been trying to soften her so he could gain her help.

And his kiss . . .

She swallowed. No one could call that hot, unsettling caress the act of a gentleman. It had kept her up half the night wondering how his lips would feel against her throat and shoulder and breasts.

Lord help her, she must be mad. He was driving her mad. She should heed his lessons and be careful around him until she knew him better. Or more importantly, until he arranged the nitrous oxide party.

Guilt stabbed her. She had no business dreaming about the viscount. He was necessary to her aims, nothing more, and she mustn't forget it.

The clock in the hall chimed the hour, and she started. Look how thoroughly he'd unnerved her—now she was forgetting the time.

Stepping forward, she broke into his recitation. "Thank you for your enlightening information, Lord Norcourt, but we'll have to save the rest for tomorrow." At the predictable protest from the girls, she frowned. "We're already forgoing instruction in natural history for these lessons—we shan't forgo your mathematics instruction, too."

"But couldn't his lordship stay during our lessons?" one of the girls chirped.

"I can't imagine why he'd want to listen to me teach mathematics."

"On the contrary," he put in, eyes gleaming, "I'd enjoy that enormously. And how better to improve my own instructional skills than to observe yours?"

"Oh, yes!" Miss Seton said breathlessly. "After that, he can help with our dance class! He can show us the proper way for a gentleman to hold us."

"Your instructor can do that, too, as you know very well," Madeline chided. "Besides, his lordship has only committed to be here for one hour a day, and probably has other matters to take care of."

"Miss Prescott is correct," he said in a faint Etonian clip that tip-tapped along her heightened nerves. "I've arranged to meet my steward this afternoon at my estate near Chertsey."

Relief coursed through her.

"But that leaves me a few hours free." His gaze bore a decidedly reckless glint. "If you ladies can convince Miss Prescott to dance with me during your lessons, I'll stay until they're over. After all, I'll need a partner for this demonstration, and partnering one of you would hardly be appropriate."

An instant clamor rose from her students, making her suppress a groan. The last thing she needed was to spend an hour twirling in the viscount's arms. But he clearly reveled in her discomfort, and that rubbed her raw.

She refused to let him think his sly tactics would make her waver from her demand for her party. Besides, it would be useful for the girls to see how a woman of sense responded to a rakehell. "Very well, sir. I shall dance with you."

As the girls let up a cheer, he winked at them. Devious devil.

"And if you insist upon staying to observe our class," she added, "you may take a seat." While he headed toward a vacant chair near the back, she cast the girls a stern gaze. "But if you ladies cannot concentrate on your studies because of our visitor, he'll have to leave, understood?"

They nodded and made a great show of settling in— laying out their pencils and paper and straightening in their seats. She drew her notes from her desk, then strode to the blackboard to write the problems they were to work.

Until today, she hadn't noticed how her gown hiked up to show a sliver of stocking when she lifted her arm to write. It was all she could do not to pull at her skirts. She swore she could feel Lord Norcourt's gaze on her as a doe felt the predator surveying her strengths . . . and her weaknesses.

She told herself she was imagining it, but when she faced the class, there was no mistaking the half smile playing over his lips. Oh, Lord, *had* he been staring at her bottom and ankles? Or had he merely guessed how his presence unsettled her?

Well, if he thought to change her mind about the party by turning her up sweet, he could think again. He would *not* get what he wanted by using his tricks on *her*, no indeed.

Unfortunately, he didn't seem to care that she ignored him as she began to teach. While she gestured and explained and asked questions of her students, his eyes swept her from head to toe in a slow, interested perusal. And to her horror, whatever part he scanned grew heated beneath his impudent glance.

Yet whenever she paused in her lecture to frown at him, he drew his gaze back to her face with the innocent expression of a lad who couldn't imagine what he was being chastised for.

Outrageous rascal. And she'd agreed to dance with him! How was she supposed to endure it without betraying his alarming effect on her?

Drat him, she'd had enough of his antics. He professed to like mathematics, did he? Very well, let him prove it.

She strode to the board and erased the problems they'd finished, then chalked one very long equation. The girls groaned. Every day for the past week, she'd offered it as a mental challenge. So far, they hadn't figured it out.

"I think we should let Lord Norcourt try his hand at it this time, ladies." She addressed them with a smile. "What do you say? Shall we see if he can solve it?"

As they loudly voiced their assent, he cocked his head. "I thought you didn't want me disrupting your class."

"It's no disruption. My pupils have puzzled over it for days—I thought it only fair we give *you* a chance. Of course, if it's too difficult for you—"

"No, indeed." A smile tipped up his fine mouth, and he raked her again with his gaze, as if to say, *Do as you wish, but you can't stop me from looking.* Then he unfolded his lanky form from the short chair and strolled to the front.

But instead of taking another piece of chalk, he reached for hers, deliberately brushing her fingers when he extricated it.

The light touch sent an electric current sweeping over her skin, and she swallowed. She should never have told him that attempts at seduction left her unaffected. For one thing, she'd begun to think it mightn't be entirely true. For another, it had presented him with a challenge that no rakehell worth his salt could ignore. Nor did she dare report him to Mrs. Harris until she got her party.

Fine. She would give him a taste of his own tactics. Let *him* be uncomfortable for a change.

So when he went to the board, she moved to stand where he could see her out of the corner of his eye. Then she proceeded to gaze blatantly at his bottom the same way he'd gazed blatantly at hers.

It was no hardship. He had a fine bottom, from what she could see of it beneath his riding coat. And his legs were quite attractive, long and muscular, the calves nicely filling out the leather. She could stare at them all day.

And would, if it annoyed him, but he didn't even seem to notice. Apparently the problem on the board absorbed him entirely, for he kept his eyes fixed there and his lips set in a line as he worked. She was still trying to figure out how to make him notice her rude staring when he set down the chalk and faced her.

"There." He wiped the chalk dust from his hands. "Shall I explain the solution as well?"

She gaped at him. Then she gaped at the board. Drat him, that problem had taken *her* thirty minutes to solve when she'd found it in a book of equations. And he'd got it right in no time at all, on the first try, too!

So he hadn't lied about his interest in mathematics. Worse yet, he was better at it than she. That had never happened before. It was awfully disconcerting.

"Please," she said coldly. "Do explain it. If you can."

He laughed. "I'd be honored."

"I'll just step out into the hall to tell Mrs. Harris that you're staying longer—"

"What?" He stepped into her path with a cheeky grin. "But your careful watch over me is what inspired me to complete the problem."

So he *had* noticed her staring and hadn't been the least bothered by it. If anything, it had made him even more of a flirt.

"Come now, Miss Prescott, you're supposed to supervise. You can't supervise if you run away."

"I'm not running away," she retorted. One should never show one's weaknesses to a beast. "What exactly would I be trying to escape?"

His eyes twinkled. "Perhaps the overwhelming effects of my charm?"

As the girls giggled, she forced a laugh. "Oh, but after you've gone to such effort to convince us that your charm is false, sir, I would certainly not be silly enough to succumb to it."

"I revealed that a rogue's charm is false, madam," he said, a slight edge to his voice. "Do you think that *my* charm is as well?"

"You did instruct us to treat every man as a stranger. Since I only met you yesterday . . ."

A grudging laugh escaped him. "You persist in using my own lessons against me. Very well, go off to your employer."

"Oh, no, sir, I can't leave now, or you'll claim I'm running away." She flashed him a smile. "I won't have my girls thinking I'm a coward."

"Only a fool would think you a coward, sweetheart."

The endearment dropped like a stone into the girls' rapt silence, startling ripples of gasps throughout the room. In that moment, Madeline realized he had momentarily forgotten their audience. As had she.

Panic clamoring in her breast, she turned to the girls. "And there, my dears, is another illustration of how a rogue works." With a gesture to Lord Norcourt, she said, "His lordship and I will offer many such demonstrations through the next two weeks of his tenure here. You must be prepared to witness one at any moment."

"Exactly." His husky voice played havoc with her senses. "Now you see how easily it is for a flirtation to progress beyond the bounds of propriety. You may think that sparring with a rogue won't hurt, but it can get away from you before you know it, as Miss Prescott has just shown."

What Madeline had just shown was her horrible susceptibility to his flirtations. Because in the first second after he'd called her "sweetheart," she'd felt a curl of warmth . . . satisfaction . . . pleasure. Oh, Lord.

"And now, sir," she said, not caring that her voice was as breathless as any green girl's, "I will inform Mrs. Harris of our plans."

They'd had a narrow escape, for if one of the girls ever revealed what he'd called her, Mrs. Harris was sure to suspect the attraction between them.

Then there would be hell to pay.

Chapter Seven

Dear Charlotte,

You *do not mention the nature of your connection with the viscount. If my opinion counts for anything, I warn you to take care. You aren't likely to consider a liaison in the same light as he. As for your finding out my identity from the viscount, don't go to the trouble. I only know of his parties from gossip.*

Your concerned cousin,
Michael

$\mathcal{L}$ess than an hour later, they trooped to the ballroom. Anthony watched as Miss Prescott explained to the dance instructor the new plan. Apparently the woman was delighted not to be needed, for she abandoned ship as soon as she heard that Miss Prescott meant to take over that day's lesson.

One of the girls headed for the pianoforte. "Play a waltz," Anthony instructed her. "It's the only dance suitable for demonstrating what's improper."

The girl looked to Miss Prescott, who sighed. "He's right—the waltz provides more opportunities for the wrong sort of touching."

And more opportunities for him to test her mettle.

Yes, their audience would provide some restriction, but he could touch her, unsettle her. Try to determine her real reasons for demanding a nitrous oxide party.

That's all he wanted. Not to put his hands on her. Or dance with her. Or feel her move beneath his hands.

He stifled an oath. All right, so perhaps he did want more than just to unsettle her. But who could blame him? Her veiled glances and challenging remarks were driving him mad, not to mention her prancing about the room and sticking out the tip of her tongue as she wrote and a million other fetching gestures that brought their last kiss painfully to mind.

Even the relatively innocuous glimpse of her ankles had made him want to strip off her stockings and skim his lips up the entire length of her slender calves—

Damnation, he must not lose sight of his purpose. This was about being sure he could trust her, that her scheme wasn't something that could ruin his chances to get Tessa free. It was *not* about seducing her.

"Shall we take the floor?" Miss Prescott asked, dragging him from his thoughts.

He offered her his arm, which she barely touched. Once they reached the middle and faced each other, he smiled down at her. "I'm ready when you are."

"I daresay you're always ready," she muttered.

A wicked retort sprang to his lips that he ruthlessly squelched, unsure if she'd meant the double entendre. No point to provoking her unnecessarily into ending the dance. Although, given her mention of "an animal's instinct to mate," he suspected that the little naturalist had a full understanding of what that entailed.

Taking her in his arms, he began to waltz, trying not to

dwell on the part of him that was "always ready." Around them girls stood observing, but he paid them no heed. All he could think was that Miss Prescott had an even tinier waist than he'd guessed, that she smelled faintly of almonds . . . and that it would take little provocation for him to carry her off to a room and ravish her.

Steady, man, you mustn't let the beast take control, no matter how enticing the woman or how tempting her flirtations.

Unfortunately, her composed expression showed that she was in no mood for flirtation just now. It irritated him. Here he was, chafing at the need to brand her with his mouth, and she acted as if she didn't even notice that he was holding her.

"You're certainly a cool one," Anthony said under his breath.

"Someone has to be. And since you make a practice of saying reckless things and calling me 'sweetheart' at inopportune moments—"

"But you covered my error very well. The girls didn't suspect a thing."

With a scowl, she glanced over at her pupils, who were paying close attention to their whispering. "I can't imagine what possessed you to speak so unwisely. We shared one kiss, probably less than you share with your chambermaids."

His temper flared. "I have never seduced a chambermaid. You, of all people, should know that a beast doesn't soil his own den. It makes a huge mess. And I always avoid messes."

"I can well believe *that*," she said archly. "Are you saying you're a beast?"

"You seem determined to believe I am. I might as well play the part." Sliding his hand to the small of her back, he tugged her close and called out to their snickering audience, "You see, ladies? This is much too intimate an embrace for a man you've only just met."

She raised an eyebrow, then pinched his shoulder. Hard.

"Ow!" He jerked his arm back.

"And that, ladies," she called out, "is how you combat such presumption."

"That's hardly ladylike," he grumbled.

"No, but it's effective."

"For now." He swept his gaze to her mouth, then lowered his voice. "Sweetheart."

"Mind your tongue!"

"Would you rather I called you Madeline? It's a lovely name."

A sly smile curved her lips. "Will you praise my elegant manner, too?"

What did she mean? Oh, yes. He'd forgotten his interchange with Miss Bancroft. "That was in the classroom. With you, I'm entirely honest."

"I can't imagine why you should be different with me than with them."

"I told you—virginal schoolgirls aren't to my taste. I like my women older." Dropping his gaze to her breasts, he murmured, "And more worldly."

She tread on his toe with her surprisingly sharp-heeled shoe. He felt it even through his boot and jerked back, missing a step.

"That, ladies," she called out, "is what you do when a gentleman isn't keeping his eyes on your face, where they belong."

The girls laughed as he found his place again, and they continued dancing.

"Was that necessary?" he ground out under his breath.

"I don't want the girls thinking we're involved in something scandalous."

"Ah, but we *are*." When she blinked at him, he added, "Your party, remember? If that's not scandalous, I don't know what is."

Her eyes brightened. "Have you arranged it?"

"Not yet. I'm still determining who should throw it."

Noticing how her pupils were giggling, she scowled, and called out, "I fear you can't hear what his lordship is saying over the music, but he's whispering nonsense to me as part of your lesson. Remember, it is perfectly acceptable to engage a rogue in conversation, so long as you do not let his lies sway you."

"I am not lying," he bit out under his breath.

"No, you're just dawdling until the two weeks are up," she hissed. " I have half a mind to tell Mrs. Harris you're doing a poor job with these les—"

"Oh, for God's sake, you'll get your party." The clever chit wouldn't *let* him stall her. And he dared not lose Tessa's chance at enrollment. "You'll just have to trust me."

"For whatever good that does," she muttered.

Annoyed, he swung her sharply in a turn. "Do you impugn my honor?"

"You've made it clear you have little honor to impugn, sir."

"Surely you realize I'm merely mimicking men I've observed."

Her eyebrows lifted. "You seem to know very well how to turn the girls up sweet."

"And you seem to know very well how to rouse a man's 'animal instincts.' Yet I haven't impugned *your* honor."

She colored, then glanced away, and just the sight of that hard-won blush made him want to kiss her senseless.

Damnation, he must watch his step. She made him forget where he was, something that never happened with other women. He was supposed to entice her into revealing her secrets, not lust after her with the finesse of a randy bull.

"I'm not as wicked as you assume," he said, partly to convince himself.

Her gaze met his. "I never said you were wicked. Besides, it isn't your wickedness that concerns me." She jerked her head toward their audience. "It's how they perceive the two of us, the suspicions they will form from your unwise behavior toward me, Lord Norcourt."

For no reason he could fathom, her formal use of his title rankled. It had felt unfamiliar ever since he'd ascended to it a month ago, but on her lips it sounded perversely like an insult.

He leaned in close enough to whisper, "I'll behave myself with you when they're near, but only if you'll call me Anthony in private . . . Madeline."

"Step back, sir," she demanded.

"Call me Anthony."

He felt rather than saw her attempt to grind her heel in his foot again. Anticipating the move, he twirled her, an easy task since she weighed next to nothing. Once she faced him again, her face afire with anger, he kept his distance but moved his hand to the small of her back.

She pinched his shoulder.

He winced, but ignored it. "Say you will call me Anthony in private."

She glowered at him. "We will never be in private if I can help it."

By God, they would. It might be the only way to crack her shell of reserve to unveil her secrets. "Then why not use my Christian name? It's a small enough price."

"Not if I slip up and say it before my girls. Not if they go running to Mrs. Harris bearing tales and lose me my position."

Her real worry gave him pause. He glanced over to where the girls watched them avidly, thankfully unable to hear over the thundering piano. "They adore you. They wouldn't tattle to your employer."

A sudden pain darkened the sweet amber of her eyes. "People can surprise you. You think they know your true character, then they—" She broke off with a forced smile. "My girls are no less inclined to spread gossip than anyone else. As you said yesterday, gossip is the legal tender of our society. Even my girls have their price."

The lost look on her face made something twist inside his chest, made him want to shake her and find out who had threatened her with gossip in the past. It made him want to defend her honor.

How ludicrous. For all he knew, she had no honor. Pretty women, even ones without fortunes, usually ended up married by the time they were old enough to help run a school . . . unless for some reason they'd made themselves ineligible for marriage. There was only one way she might have done that.

Still, her anxious gaze haunted him until he grudgingly moved his hand to its proper place. "I'll try to be more careful around them."

A grateful smile touched her lips. "I would appreciate that . . . Anthony."

The sound of his name on her lips stirred up a hot maelstrom of emotion inside him, sweet memories of his parents whispering together. Until Mother had died, and the idyllic life he'd known had ended.

Good God, where had that come from? And why now, with this slip of a schoolteacher? He'd have to keep a much tighter rein on his emotions around her. She wasn't like the featherheaded females he usually seduced—she might get under his skin, and that mustn't happen.

Especially with a woman he couldn't trust. She was as much a schemer as any rakehell—just better at hiding it.

"What shall I play now?" came a girl's voice from the pianoforte.

Damnation, the music had stopped. And neither of them had noticed.

Madeline blanched, then glanced at the clock. "You'll miss your meeting with your steward if you stay any longer, Lord Norcourt."

She was dismissing him, and he knew why. She couldn't take much more of their semiprivate encounter. Nor could he, for that matter.

"Yes, I suppose I should be going," he said.

As a chorus of disappointed protests followed his pronouncement, he turned to smile at the girls. "There's always tomorrow. I have no set appointments then."

"But we'll be elsewhere tomorrow," Miss Seton complained.

Madeline started. "Lord, I completely forgot about our trip to see the menagerie." She turned to him. "The entire school is going. We've planned it for months."

"May I accompany you?"

"That's an excellent idea," she surprised him by saying. "Mrs. Harris likes to have male escorts for such outings if we can get them. So assuming that it's fine with her, we'll meet you here at eight." A taunting smile touched her lips. "If you think you can rise early for two mornings in a row, that is."

"I can if *you* can, Miss Prescott." He added, "Don't worry, I can do just about anything I choose."

Including seduce a certain schoolteacher under the nose of her employer.

The possibility seized hold of him and wouldn't let go. Why not? He watched her walk over to her pupils with her lovely bottom swaying. He'd tried stalling her until he could find out why she wanted that damned party, and that had only made her more determined to force his hand.

So perhaps he should try seduction. That might ensure that she kept her promises, no matter what happened with the nitrous oxide party. If she succumbed, he'd have something to hold over her, to help him hedge his bets.

You said she was the marrying sort, his long-dead conscience clamored. *You were sure she was a virginal innocent.*

At first, yes, but now he doubted it. Her reaction to their talk of gossip, her willingness to risk her position . . . her few blushes proclaimed her to be a woman of some experience. He would swear she was hiding something—an unsavory past, perhaps a feckless lover.

She'd claimed not to be tempted by seduction. And

why not, if morality wasn't important to her, as she'd said? Most women would be eager to have a lord's attentions. They would flirt and try to draw him in, hoping to gain marriage. If she actually believed herself immune to temptation, it had to be because some idiot had put her on her guard around men by bungling his seduction of her.

He wouldn't.

At the thought of the cool Miss Prescott lying naked beneath him, the devil in him danced jigs. How he would relish watching those cat's eyes finally warming to him during the "reckless" pleasures of lovemaking.

You just want her in your bed, said that same niggling voice. *That's the real reason you're determined to believe her a schemer—so you'll have an excuse to seduce her.*

He scowled. He'd never needed an excuse before; he certainly didn't need one now.

Seducing her is dangerous, and you know it. Yet you're willing to risk everything to have her. And why? Because she's the first woman whose company you've enjoyed outside the bedchamber.

The possibility made him break out in a cold sweat.

With a curse, he headed for the door. That was absurd. He might enjoy her quick wit, but he wasn't fool enough to let a sweet-faced schemer turn his life upside down.

Bedding her was just part of his plan to make her keep her promise to get Tessa enrolled here. Nothing more than that.

Chapter Eight

Dear Cousin,

I'll toy with you no longer over Lord Norcourt, though I do enjoy your disgruntlement. I know you will keep this secret—Lord Norcourt wants to enroll his niece here, so Miss Prescott suggested that in return he teach my girls lessons in recognizing the rakehell. He agreed. You will probably disapprove, but after hearing her pupils describe his first lesson, I begin to think her idea inspired.

Your teasing friend,
Charlotte

Madeline slipped inside the school and hurried up the back stairs, grateful no one had noticed her arrival at the rear. Everyone was gathered on the lawn in front, sharing a quick breakfast of cross buns and tea as they awaited the carriages.

But she'd come through the woods, needing a few moments alone to gather her thoughts and prepare for the day.

She had to be in top form when the viscount arrived, and have herself under full control. Anthony would not catch her off guard just because—

A groan escaped her. She mustn't call him Anthony,

even in her head! That was the surest way to slip up and say it around the students. Besides, he'd be gone in two weeks. No sense in thinking there could be any future between them.

Still, his Christian name fit him very well. And he had *asked* her to call him Anthony. Remembering the smoldering glint in his eyes at the time made her feel all swoony . . .

Swoony? That wasn't even a word! She was as bad as her girls, succumbing to his flirtations because he made her light-headed. It wasn't remotely sensible.

If only he didn't excel at flirtation, like his ability to know exactly where to touch a woman. Whenever he'd brushed her hand, her pulse had jumped. And yesterday, when he'd rested his fingers just above the curve of her bottom while dancing, she'd imagined them slipping down, sliding lower . . .

A scowl furrowed her brow. Why was he so blatantly trying to seduce her, anyway? Other gentlemen never attempted it, not after they discovered her peculiar interests. Watching her count the teeth of a dead hedgehog generally dampened their ardor. Especially when she showed the same enthusiasm for her natural history that another woman would show for embroidery.

Men wanted to marry the women who enjoyed embroidery.

Of course, Anthony hadn't witnessed her do anything but teach and dance, so he hadn't yet seen her at her most unmarriageable.

With a snort, she went to her desk to stuff items for their outing into a satchel. As if his flirtations had anything to do with courtship. They were merely a way to keep his rakehell skills fresh while he rusticated at a girl's school. That's why he used his sultry gaze to scour off her clothes and make her feel exposed . . . desired. He was practicing his technique, much as a fencer did lunges to keep his muscles in fine form, nothing more.

Unless . . .

A chill skittered down her spine. Unless he didn't believe her reasons for wanting her party. Unless he suspected she had another motive and was using flirtation to uncover it.

But that was absurd. How could he possibly guess that; he had no reason to do so. She was just being overly cautious.

Something clattered to the floor. Lord, she'd knocked off her notebook in her agitation.

As she bent to pick it up, she noticed that a newspaper clipping had fallen out. Mrs. Jenkins, to whom she'd had to reveal her purpose for being in London, had slipped it to her this morning and she'd thrust it inside her book until she could read it.

Tucking the book under her arm, she straightened to read the clipping:

> According to reliable sources, Sir Humphry Davy, the current President of the Royal Society, and his wife, Lady Davy, are planning a removal to Cornwall next week so that he may recover his failing health at his mother's Penzance home during the Easter season.

Next week! That scarcely gave her any time!

She must impress upon Anthony the importance of arranging this party *soon*.

"You're here early," said a voice from the doorway.

She whirled to find the dratted viscount himself standing there. "I'm always here at this time," she lied.

"Except for yesterday."

She winced. "I overslept. I told you."

He stalked into the room and closed the door behind him, trapping her there like a beast tracking his prey. "Because of your ill father?"

Oh, dear, how to answer that? Did it matter if he knew? Even if it did, he could easily find out the truth from the girls. Making an issue of it would only call attention to it. "Yes. He has . . . trouble at night."

"What sort of trouble? Has he seen a doctor?"

"His isn't the sort of illness anyone can heal." Not with medicine, in any case.

"Is he dying?"

The thread of genuine concern in his voice surprised, then alarmed her. She couldn't have him asking questions about Papa. "Did you want something?"

With an arched eyebrow that acknowledged her refusal to discuss the matter, he pointed to her hand. "What's that?"

Quickly, she shoved the clipping into her pocket. "Nothing. A recipe."

"Ah." Judging from his narrowed gaze, he didn't believe her.

"You shouldn't be in here alone with me. It's dangerous."

A devilish smile curved up his mouth. "I like danger."

"No surprise there," she muttered. "But I don't. And if anyone should realize we're up here by ourselves—"

"They won't. I rode in the back way, then entered unseen from the stables. Everyone else was too busy in front to notice." He lowered his voice to a sensual rasp. "I wanted a few moments in private with you."

Her pulse began to drum most annoyingly. He'd sought her out, which was definitely dangerous. No one knew either of them was up here, so he could do anything to her, and no one could stop him.

Yet since they were alone, what better chance to ask for what she wanted?

"Actually, I'm glad you're here. I need to speak to you about something."

"Oh?" Amusement turned his eyes a vivid, dancing blue as he approached.

"We have little time, so we must make it quick. The others will wonder why I haven't yet arrived. And probably why *you* haven't as well."

"So your employer has agreed to include me in your outing?"

"She suggested it before I could even ask. She must have thought it would be useful to have a man along."

His gaze drifted to her mouth. "And you? Do you find it useful?"

She found it invigorating. "It's useful for the girls."

"I didn't ask about the girls. I asked about you." He stepped close, too close. So of course her pulse launched into its silly drumming, and her belly betrayed her by going all quivery inside. Lord, she was as predictable as a ewe in heat.

And like the ram he was, he let a knowing smile tug at the corners of his lips, then reached forward as if to catch her about the waist. Instead, he tugged her notebook from beneath her arm, where it was still tucked.

Embarrassed, she grabbed for it, but he turned away to read the words inscribed on the cover boards. " 'A Natural History of the Fauna of England, by Madeline Prescott.' " He arched an eyebrow at her. "You're an author?"

Heat rose in her cheeks. "Without a publisher, I'm afraid. Mostly it's for my own use. It chronicles my research into the habits of various animals."

To her mortification, he flipped through it, silently reading until he reached something that made him laugh aloud. " 'Beasts of the Field.' " He lifted his gaze to her, eyes twinkling. "After my lessons are done, you should add a chapter on 'Beasts of the Drawing Room.' That will ensure that you find a publisher."

"Or that I'm drummed out of London by your fellow 'beasts' for exposing their tricks," she said dryly.

He continued flipping through. "I don't see any notations for your article on nitrous oxide," he commented, deceptively nonchalant.

Lord help her, he was prying into things again. "Those are in a separate notebook. One about chemicals." She reached for it once more, but he caught her hand with his free one. As his fingers curled around hers, a tremor coursed through her. "Please return my book, Lord Norcourt."

"I thought you were going to call me Anthony in private," he murmured, turning her hand over so he could rub her palm with the pad of his thumb.

She started to snatch her hand away, but remembered her purpose and didn't. Instead, she let him trace circles in her palm, even though his touch twisted her insides into a knot. "I thought you were going to arrange a party for me to attend."

"I will."

"When?"

He shrugged. "I see my friend this afternoon. But it will take a few days—"

"Saturday. I want it arranged for Saturday."

"*This* Saturday?" He snorted. "Are you mad? Invitations must be sent, a place decided upon . . ."

She tugged her hand from his to take hold of her notebook. "Saturday," she repeated. "It must be then."

Refusing to release the book, he eyed her closely. "Why?"

"Because I don't trust you to keep your promise, that's why."

"I'd be foolish *not* to," he said irritably. "I know what will happen in two weeks if I don't. But nothing was said about arranging the party for so soon."

Realizing he wouldn't budge without a good explanation, she wracked her brain for something convincing. "The following Saturday is our monthly assembly, which I'm required to attend. Nor can I go to a late party on a school night—"

"*I* did."

"You don't have to teach several sessions, then return home to tend an ill father. The only night anyone can sit with him is on Saturday, our usual assembly night," she said, lying for all she was worth. "I can't leave him alone." That much was true at least.

"Ah, yes, the ill father." Rank suspicion glimmered in his eyes as he used her grip on the book to draw her closer. "Very well, I'll see if I can arrange it for Saturday. Providing that you offer me something in return."

"Other than allowing your niece to enroll here, you mean?" she said tartly.

"Something to encourage me to go beyond our original agreement." His calculating gaze drifted down to fix on her mouth. "An additional enticement, if you will."

Perhaps she shouldn't have pressed him to have the party so soon. "What sort of enticement?"

Heat flared in his face. "You know exactly what sort."

There was no mistaking that look. Or what he wanted.

Pretending ignorance, she stared him down. "I prefer to have things spelled out. That way neither of us can complain we were cheated in fulfilling the terms."

"You're always thinking like a teacher of mathematics." His eyes raked her as they had the day before. Only this time they lingered on her breasts, her belly, her hips. "Try thinking like a woman for a change."

"I *am*." She fought to ignore the strange tingling he provoked wherever his gaze touched. "A woman with the good sense to know when a beast is trying to run her to ground."

"If I am a beast, madam, then you are a schemer."

"I am not!"

A thin smile tightened his lips. "You blackmailed me into giving you what you want. What else does that make you?"

Desperate.

But she dared not reveal that. If he knew her situation, he would never help her. It could hurt his cause if his uncle ever found out. The sad truth was she needed him more than he needed her. So she would simply have to find a way to get what she needed from him without losing her virtue.

"Should I assume from your prolonged silence that you

agree with my assessment of your character?" Anthony drawled.

"Certainly not. You told Mrs. Harris you prefer women who know what they want and aren't ashamed to take it. That's all I'm doing."

Eyeing her askance, he yanked her notebook free and strolled over to place it on the desk. "And all *I'm* doing is making sure you don't run roughshod over me with your demands."

"I daresay no woman has run roughshod over you since you were in leading strings," she grumbled.

He froze, then rubbed his left wrist absently, the same motion she'd noticed before when he was agitated. "You'd be surprised." When he faced her, his eyes glittered like glacial gems as they trailed knowingly down her gown of green spotted muslin. "But I don't mean to let it happen again, with you or anyone else. So if I give you your party this Saturday, I'll expect an additional reward."

And he was making it perfectly clear what sort of reward that might be.

Lord help her, this was what she got for behaving like a tart yesterday when he kissed her. That, combined with her frank manner of speaking and her "scheming," had apparently led him to think her rather more naughty than she was.

But if she set him straight, he would lose interest in her since inexperienced women didn't appeal to him. Then she'd have nothing to offer him as an "enticement."

And if the nitrous oxide party didn't gain her entrée to Sir Humphry, she might still need Anthony's connections. As a possible conquest, she had more leverage for the future. After all, she needn't do more than flirt and let him kiss her or perhaps touch her a few times. Nothing *too* risky; only enough to get her what she wanted.

You just want to see what it's like, a voice niggled at the back of her brain. She shushed it. A bit of curiosity never hurt, as long as she didn't let it go too far. Which she wouldn't, given everything she knew about the dangers. What sensible, intelligent woman would? "You still haven't specified what reward."

The smug curve of his lips showed he'd expected her to capitulate. "It's simple. After the party on Saturday, you spend the rest of the night in my bed."

His blunt statement took her so off guard that she let out a burst of nervous laughter. "Don't be absurd."

He quirked up one eyebrow. "You find the idea of sharing my bed absurd?"

She found it alarming, terrifying . . . and horribly tempting. Yet she dared not refuse him outright. The key was to keep him close but not too close until he helped her meet Sir Humphry.

"It's just so predictable." She deliberately imbued her voice with contempt. "I thought you'd use more finesse in your seductions. No rogue worth his salt should need to bargain his way into a woman's bed."

A blatant hunger rose in his face. "Are you challenging me to seduce you?"

"Certainly not!"

"Ah, but I think you *are.* And I love a challenge."

Oh, dear, this wasn't going quite how she'd hoped.

"If finesse is what you require," he went on as he came toward her, "I will accept a less 'predictable' enticement from you."

"We cannot discuss this now. We're expected outside." She swept past him and stuffed her notebook in the satchel, but before she could close it, Anthony came up from behind to trap her against the desk.

Not being able to see him unnerved her exceedingly, yet when she tried to slip from between him and the desk, he caught her by the muslin sash cinched about her waist. "Don't run away." He bent his head so close she could smell his shaving oil. "I only need a moment to explain what I want."

When he slid his finger back and forth beneath the sash along the small of her back, she had to fight the silken shiver that danced along her skin. But she couldn't resist the image that rose in her mind, of his undoing the sash and letting it fall before he unfastened each button of her bodice . . .

"Fine," she said tartly, eager to be rid of him before she went mad. "Tell me what enticement you require, so we can join the others."

"Between now and Saturday you must allow me to give you a private lesson in seduction." His husky voice thrummed along her every nerve. "And it must include more than mere kissing."

He nuzzled her neck, and her pulse leaped into triple time. The man was an artist of sensuality. How in heaven's name could she survive his lesson in seduction?

In keeping with her chosen role, she said, "What makes you think I need lessons?"

"You claim that attempts to seduce you are pointless because 'such things' can't tempt you. At the very least, I mean to prove that they can."

"Has it occurred to you, sir," she snapped, peeved by his

unerring ability to see through her, "that I might not even be attracted to you? That I might find your arrogant confidence and your reckless ways annoying?"

To her surprise, he laughed. "No, that hadn't occurred to me. Especially not after you melted beneath my kiss."

There'd been melting? Melting *he* could notice? Now that she thought of it, yes, she'd experienced a noticeable softening of her limbs. That would explain the swoony feeling. And his determined pursuit.

His mouth moved from her neck to her ear, which he laved with his tongue most effectively. "So we'll have our lesson. Then after the party, if you still consider the idea of sharing my bed 'absurd,' we'll call our private bargain complete. I'll finish out my second week here, you'll speak glowingly of me to Mrs. Harris, and we'll be done with each other."

He nipped her earlobe, sparking little tremors of excitement down to her very toes. "I'll wager, however, that your choice will be anything but that."

That's what she was afraid of. He was even better at this than she'd suspected, evidenced by the artful things his teeth were doing to her ear, things that gave new meaning to the word "finesse."

She'd just about steeled herself to pull away—really, she *had*—when he turned her in his arms and lowered his mouth to hers . . .

Sweet Lord in heaven.

He kissed her with a leisurely enjoyment that sent lightning flashing over her skin. He leaned into her until she was sandwiched between the desk and his unyielding, oh-so-virile body, then took her mouth as if it were his due.

And she melted. No other word sufficed.

As if feeding off her reaction, Anthony ravaged her mouth so thoroughly she forgot where they were. The long, drugging strokes of his tongue made her pulse careen wildly and her skin feel ripe to the point of bursting, eager for his touch, longing for his touch. Perhaps that was why she scarcely noticed when his hand slid up to cover her breast, kneading it through her gown.

Then her nipples began to harden and ache. *That* she couldn't help noticing.

She tried to remember what she'd read about the mating of animals, but her mind was too fogged by his scent of shaving oil and leather . . . by the starkly possessive thrusts of his tongue . . . by his other hand slipping from her chin to her throat and then beneath the fabric of her chemise and her gown—

"Anthony!" She jerked back, staying his hand before it could touch her inside her gown. "You can't . . . we have to—"

"We don't have to do anything." His eyes gleamed down at her. "And you, sweetheart, owe me a lesson."

"But here? Now? It's too dangerous."

"No one even knows we've arrived. They certainly don't realize we're up here alone together."

Logically, she knew she shouldn't listen—there was nothing to stop Mrs. Harris or another teacher from coming in to fetch something. But they *were* on the top floor, nowhere near the office, and the door *was* closed, with no one around, and . . .

And she wanted to see what he would do, how it would feel.

Drat him! He was infecting her with his recklessness.

"We might not get another chance, you know," he continued as he branded her neck with hot, heady kisses. This time she did nothing to stop him when he slid his hand inside her gown to cup her breast, then fondle it in slow, silky motions that soothed the ache in her nipples, only to build it up again seconds later.

She gripped his shoulders, more to keep from collapsing into a boneless heap at his feet than anything else. His fingers were plucking at her nipple now . . . oh, heavens. Lower down, some sort of fluid seeped into the hair of her *mons veneris,* and the flesh beneath it grew tingly and hot.

So *this* was what seduction felt like, this . . . this boiling need to have his hands on her breasts, her nipples . . . on the tight, aching place between her legs . . .

And she'd told him she was immune to such temptations?

No wonder he'd laughed at her.

His mouth sought hers again, kissing her so thoroughly that she didn't notice where his other hand was headed until it slid down her gown to between her legs. But when he rubbed her *mons veneris* through the layers of fabric, and she instinctively arched into his hand, she knew she was in deep, deep trouble.

Because it was the most exquisite thing she'd ever felt. With expert care, he stroked her down where her body had grown tense with the urge to be touched and now began to throb with the thrill of his scandalous caresses. His hands were all over her, thumbing her nipple above, fondling her through her gown below. A whimper escaped her before she could swallow it, and his answer was to cup her fully between the legs, so fully she felt sure he would feel—

She struggled to free herself. "Please, Anthony. If you keep touching me like that, my gown will have a damp spot, and I have no other gown here to change into."

"A damp spot?" After a second, he chuckled. "Ah, yes, a damp spot. Only you would think of such a practicality at a time like this."

"I have no choice."

"There's a way to avoid a 'damp spot.'" He stopped caressing her below, but only to inch her gown up her legs. "Besides, we're not done with our lesson."

"Stop that!" she cried, catching hold of his hand. "I can't risk losing my teaching position. If anyone were to find us together here—"

"They won't," he rasped, though he didn't pull his hand free.

"How can you be sure?"

"The door is closed, we'll hear them coming long before they reach us, and the space under your desk is large enough to hide two people."

The way he'd thought it out gave her pause, yet she didn't resist his fondling of her breast. "I take it you've done this sort of thing before," she breathed.

"Once or twice."

"While trying to avoid jealous husbands?"

He chuckled. "Only if they rose from the grave. I prefer widows, remember?"

"Then why do you want to seduce me?"

He skimmed openmouthed kisses along her cheek. "Why do you want to change the terms of our agreement?"

She jerked back to stare at him, then saw the hint of calculation in his eyes before he swiftly masked it.

Her throat tightened with a sudden raw pain. She'd been right all along. He didn't believe her reasons for wanting the nitrous oxide party. He was only touching and kissing her to make her confess the truth.

And he'd very nearly succeeded in lulling her into forgetfulness.

With a strength borne of anger, she shoved him away from her. "I told you why," she said as he staggered back, taken by surprise. "And this lesson is over." Quickly, she skittered around the desk, eager to put it between them before he could catch her again.

"Oh no, you don't." A dark flush rose over his cheeks as he stalked her, the need in his face purely bestial. "We're not done. Not until I see you reach the pinnacle of your pleasure."

"As if you care about that." She circled the desk to avoid him. "You believe I'm lying about why I want the party and think if you seduce me, I'll tell you the secrets I don't have. That's why you're really doing this."

Though he uttered a rough laugh, his jaw's rigidity revealed his anger. "Is it?"

"What other reason could you possibly have for attempting to bed me?"

"You'd be surprised." His hard gaze skated down her. "Or perhaps you wouldn't. But either way, I mean to learn your secrets, sweetheart. And that's not all. Oh, no."

With eyes burning a hot blue, he took in her parted lips, her rising and falling breasts, and the trembling hands she tried to hide behind her skirts. He bent to plant his hands on the desk between them, so close to her that she stepped back with a gasp.

"I mean to have everything, you see," he growled. "I

mean to watch you reach for your release in my arms, and I mean to be the one to give it to you."

"Why?"

"Because once you taste true passion, you'll crave it every day and night until Saturday, knowing you can only taste it again in my bed. And then I'll have you exactly where I want you."

"I'll *never* share your bed," she said hoarsely, hoping she could hold to that vow when his every word struck an answering chord deep inside her. "It's time for you to leave, Lord Norcourt. I suggest you return to the stables until I make my appearance outside."

"I'm not leaving until we've finished the lesson," he said, half growl, half threat.

"Then *I'm* leaving."

She darted for the entrance. Swift as a hawk, he lunged, catching her at the door, pinning her against it. With fear gripping her, she drove her elbow into his ribs hard enough to make him grunt and fall back.

In that instant, she had the door open. She was halfway out when he cried, "Wait!"

She turned to glare at him, fully prepared to fight.

"We're not done, sweetheart," he vowed. "Run, if you like, but I *will* catch up to you eventually, and we *will* finish our lesson. Or you won't get your party this Saturday."

"Fine, we'll have your lesson," she countered, only too aware of the delicate game she played. "But later, in a safer place, at a time that *I* choose. And that's *if* you can get outside without rousing suspicions."

Hurrying to the stairs, she scurried down until she was out of sight of both the upper and the lower floors. Then she paused in the stairwell to smooth her skirts, straighten her hair, and calm the wild pounding of her heart.

It had been a narrow escape. She'd never seen him like that—ruthlessly intent on getting what he wanted.

Nor had she guessed it would have the unsettling effect of making her want to throw caution aside and let him do as he would with her. Though the throbbing in her breasts and lower down had dimmed, the ache lay just beneath the surface, like an itch needing to be scratched.

Once you taste true passion, you'll crave it every day and night until Saturday, knowing you can only taste it again in my bed. And then I'll have you exactly where I want you.

She only prayed she could prove him wrong.

Chapter Nine

Dear Charlotte,
   I do hope you know what you're doing. Men like
Lord Norcourt aren't as easy to manage as you think.
If you're so curious about the viscount, why not ask
your friend Godwin about him? Godwin's sister is
rumored to have been Norcourt's mistress before
she married the second time. She would know his
character better than anyone.

                          Your concerned cousin,
                          Michael

*I*t took every jot of his will to keep Anthony from running after Madeline. But she was right—this was neither
the time nor place for seduction. She couldn't help him if
he landed her in trouble with her employer.

And yet . . .

When he spoke of her craving him, it was *him* doing
the craving. He'd dreamed of her last night. He never slept
well alone anyway, but last night was worse than usual, full
of fitful, erotic dreams in which she promised to give him
his every desire.

He'd awakened at dawn already pleasuring himself, and
even that hadn't been enough. Eager to see her, he'd come

directly here. He'd told himself it was so he could get answers out of her, so he could make sure her hidden scheme couldn't ruin his chances of gaining Tessa.

He'd lied.

What he'd really wanted was to bed her. And he'd almost done it, too, risking both their aims.

Good God, the woman had a frightening ability to bring out the beast in him. Look at him—standing here like a racing Thoroughbred stopped dead in its tracks, his heart pounding, his blood roaring in his ears, and his bad boy straining the seams of his riding breeches.

He'd spent a lifetime fighting to cage the animal in him, to keep himself from being a slave to his appetites. It had taken years to learn how to rein in his lust until the right moment, how to bring a woman to the point where she couldn't do without him before he took her.

One kiss from Madeline, and all that control vanished. With *her*, there was no finesse, no façade of the gentleman, no ability to shut off his appetite when he was done, the way he could with other women.

The second he'd kissed her, his control had begun to erode, until the very end, when his need had so consumed him that when she'd tried to leave, he'd nearly stopped her by force. She would be wary of him from now on, and who could blame her?

The worst part was, he still hadn't accomplished his original purpose. All he knew was that she wanted the party, and now she wanted it sooner. But *why* was still a mystery. *She* was still a mystery, damn her.

Why do you want to seduce me?

Her pointed question jangled in Anthony's head. This was supposed to have been simple—tempt the chit into unveiling her secrets, so she couldn't refuse to support Tessa's enrollment if something should go wrong with the party. But every time he thought he'd unveiled one, the mystery deepened.

He paced the classroom, fighting for mastery over his body, but he kept remembering the look on her face when he'd cupped her soft breast. He would swear she'd never had a man do that to her before. Yet if that were so, why let him go so far? Was she experienced or no?

She could be just experienced enough to know that a seeming innocence would draw him in. And it was working, too, because with every unanswered question, he grew more entranced by her. It was insanity. He wouldn't stand for it. One way or the other, he would find out what she was about, even if he had to go behind her back and start interrogating her students.

Or Mrs. Harris.

He considered that a moment. The widow was every bit as clever as Madeline. If she thought he was interested in her teacher for whatever reason, she would put a quick end to this bargain. Did he dare risk it?

In the end, the decision was taken out of his hands. By the time he'd regained control of himself enough to join the others outside, no seats were left in the carriages except in the open landau of Mrs. Harris herself. Since she'd made the assignments, she clearly had wanted him there.

Given that Mrs. Harris liked him about as much as he liked her, he could only guess that he was riding in her carriage along with two of her pupils because she wanted to observe his behavior firsthand.

Fine, let her observe whatever she pleased. Perhaps

she'd be so caught up in "observing" that he'd finally get a chance to find out more about Madeline.

Pasting an ingratiating smile on his face, he climbed into the landau and vowed to watch every word. His machinations on Tessa's behalf would come to naught if Mrs. Harris decided he wasn't to be trusted.

Unfortunately, Miss Seton sat beside him, and she seemed determined to flirt. He was sure the headmistress chalked up a mark against him for every one of the girl's coy remarks. At least Mrs. Harris couldn't see how Miss Bancroft, who sat beside her, blushed furiously every time he even glanced at the poor girl.

God save him, he hoped Tessa was more sensible than these two, or he'd be beating the scoundrels off her at every ball.

"It was very good of you to come with us today, Lord Norcourt," Miss Bancroft said, apparently deciding that Miss Seton shouldn't have *all* the fun. "You must have many more important things to do."

He ignored Mrs. Harris's snort. "I had intended to spend today at my estate, but it will keep until tomorrow. This is more important. When my niece Tessa starts here after Easter, I'll want her to learn the same things I'm teaching you. It won't do for her to go into society, only to be plucked up by some rogue." He shot the headmistress a direct glance. "Don't you agree, Mrs. Harris?"

"If I do my job properly, your niece won't be susceptible to rogues at all, sir, with or without your lessons."

Her skepticism inexplicably irritated him. "Forgive me, madam, but your girls don't even know how to recognize a rogue unless he's leering at them or asking pointed questions about their dowries."

"That's not true!" Miss Seton protested.

Forcing a smile, he softened the insult. "Not that it isn't a credit to their good breeding and gentle natures, mind you. Under normal circumstances, I would think ill of any lady who assumed the worst about every man she met. But these are not normal circumstances. An heiress can't be too careful."

Mrs. Harris eyed him narrowly. "On that subject, we certainly agree."

"Let me give our companions a simple test." He nodded to Miss Bancroft. "Who is more likely to be a fortune hunter—an army captain or an enlisted man?"

Miss Bancroft frowned in thought. "Since an enlisted man has less money, it would be him, I should think."

Before he could refute that, Mrs. Harris sighed. "Not necessarily. Enlisted men don't aspire to high society—it isn't a world where they feel comfortable. Army captains, on the other hand, are generally second sons with a taste for champagne and an income for ale. They need to secure an heiress, if only as a means for escaping the army."

"I could have told you *that*," Miss Seton said with a superior smile. "Officers are always looking for a rich wife. The army doesn't pay well at all."

"Very good, Miss Seton," Anthony said. "I'm sure you'll know this answer, too. Who's more likely to overindulge in liquor while in your presence at a family dinner—a fortune hunter or a wealthy squire enamored of you?"

"The fortune hunter, of course. The squire will want to impress me."

"Actually, if the squire is truly in love with you, he'll be so nervous that he'll drink to bolster his courage. But the fortune hunter must keep his wits about him when discussing your future with your father. Unless he's an utter fool, he won't drink at all."

Frowning, Miss Seton sat back against the squabs. "I hadn't thought of that."

Mrs. Harris gave a rueful smile. "I'm not certain whether to be impressed or appalled, Lord Norcourt. You have an uncanny insight into how a fortune hunter's mind works. If I didn't know better, I'd think *you* sought to marry an heiress."

"Me?" He gave an unsteady laugh. "Not on your life. Why marry a green girl, with so many lovely and experienced widows around to . . . er . . . dine with? I can send a widow home afterward and enjoy the rest of my night in peace. Can't do that with a wife, no matter how rich she is."

And with the widows *he* chose, there was never any fear that he'd want them too much, pursue them too much . . . give them too much of himself. Nor any risk that they'd unleash the beast, and he'd frighten them out of their wits.

The way he'd probably frightened Madeline.

He shook off the unsettling thought. If she was the schemer he believed, she wouldn't frighten that easily.

"But what about children?" Miss Seton cried. "Don't you want children?"

"I have a niece. That's enough."

Liar. He did indeed want children, but not at the expense of his sanity. What kind of father could he possibly be? He'd scarcely known his own father, and he certainly couldn't look to the Bickhams for an example since they'd wielded discipline with all the care and subtlety of a sledgehammer. What if he were too lax? Not lax enough?

Better not to attempt it than to rue his mistakes the rest of his days—as Father had, with a simpleton for an heir and a rogue for a spare.

"What about when you're old?" Miss Bancroft asked. "Surely you'll want companionship then. You don't want to be a crotchety old bachelor."

He shoved that unsettling image from his mind. "I needn't worry about that anytime soon. If I get lonely, I can always find a crotchety old widow to marry me." He shot Mrs. Harris a smooth smile. "Do you know any, madam?"

She eyed him askance. "I do hope you're not speaking of me, Lord Norcourt. While I freely admit to being crotchety at times, I am in no respect 'old.'"

"I didn't think you were. You can't be more than thirty-five."

"I just turned thirty-six, as a matter of fact." A perplexed expression crossed her face. "How did you guess? Most people assume I'm older."

"I have a talent for assessing women's ages accurately," he said, unable to keep the smugness from his voice.

"How old do you think *I* am?" Miss Bancroft asked.

"Eighteen. And Miss Seton is nearly nineteen."

"That isn't hard to guess," the colonel's daughter protested. "We're in school and will be coming out soon."

Mischief lit Miss Bancroft's face. "Guess how old Miss Prescott is."

Old enough to make his mouth water whenever he looked at her. "Twenty-nine. Perhaps thirty."

"Actually, she's twenty-five," Mrs. Harris said. "Though I'm not surprised you misjudged *her* age. Miss Prescott always thwarts people's expectations."

Twenty-five! He sat back, feeling as if the wind had been knocked out of him. Good God, she was younger than any of his mistresses. No wonder she looked ripe and fresh enough to eat.

And no wonder his caresses had taken her off guard. Perhaps she really wasn't experienced in the bedchamber, after all.

He scowled. No, he couldn't believe that. The first time he'd mentioned additional enticements, she hadn't blushed or pulled away. She'd started talking about bargains, of all things. What virgin did that?

"Miss Prescott is very attractive," Miss Bancroft said, her young face alight with matchmaking fervor. "Wouldn't you agree, Lord Norcourt?"

Aware of Mrs. Harris's interest in his answer, he chose his words carefully. "Every woman has some attractive features, Miss Prescott included."

"Oh, she's uncommonly pretty," Miss Seton chimed in, "don't you think?"

He smiled. "I *think* you girls are bent upon finding me a wife. But you do your teacher a disservice to assume she can do no better than a scoundrel like me. I'm sure Miss Prescott has far more deserving suitors."

"She has no suitors at all," Miss Seton protested.

"None?" he couldn't resist saying. "But surely she's had some in the past."

"Not since she's been at the school."

"And how long is that?" he asked.

"Six months," Miss Bancroft said. "She'll never have a suitor if she keeps spending all her time at home with her papa. She won't even go to our assemblies."

"That's enough." Mrs. Harris frowned at her charges.

"I doubt Miss Prescott would appreciate our speculating about her marital prospects behind her back."

So Madeline had managed to make herself invaluable to her employer in only six months. Astonishing. She really was a very clever woman. And she'd lied about being required to attend the assemblies too. He'd been right—her reasons for wanting the party soon had *nothing* to do with scheduling her life.

A grim smile touched his lips. He was tired of her evasions. He wanted the truth out of her. And he meant to get it . . . one way or another.

The carriage turned down a familiar lane, and he frowned. They were supposed to be visiting the menagerie of a friend of Mrs. Harris's. But the only person of quality he knew who lived near here *and* owned a menagerie was Charles Godwin.

He groaned. Surely not. It couldn't happen. Not today. Not to him.

But even as they reached Godwin's drive, he knew he was in trouble when he saw Godwin and a woman standing on the steps.

His fingers curled into fists. No wonder Mrs. Harris had suggested he come along. Glancing over, he saw the headmistress watching him with a smug expression. Was this another of her tests? Probably.

Which meant he was in for a day of pure misery. Because the woman on the steps was not only Godwin's sister; she'd also shared Anthony's bed for a few annoying nights.

Damn it all to hell.

Chapter Ten

Dear Cousin,

What a capital idea, suggesting that I speak to Mr. Godwin's sister. How odd that I never knew of her connection to Lord Norcourt, despite my years of friendship with Mr. Godwin. You really do have quite extensive sources of information. I wonder why that is.

Your curious friend,
Charlotte

As they reached Mr. Godwin's estate, Madeline congratulated herself for having kept her emotions successfully in check throughout the ride. The girls' questions about what they were to see had helped distract her.

But not enough. Anthony seemed determined to find out the truth about her party, and he mustn't until it was over. She had to watch her step. Allowing him to play with her was one thing. Allowing that to lower her guard was quite another.

With any luck, Mrs. Harris had used the ride to bedevil him about his past. The man deserved to be taken down a peg, and the sharp-tongued widow was the woman to do it. Madeline almost wished she could have seen it.

But that would have been disastrous, since every glance

he gave Madeline turned her knees to putty. Mrs. Harris would have noticed the wobbly-knee thing; she was quite observant of her teachers and girls. And since Madeline had never had such a ridiculous reaction to any other man, the widow was sure to make something of it.

Thank heaven Mr. Godwin was enamored of the widow. If Madeline was lucky, her employer would have her own romantic entanglement to distract her.

Madeline's carriage hadn't even lurched to a stop before Mr. Godwin was striding down the stairs of his manor to greet Mrs. Harris. And right on his heels was his sister, Lady Tarley.

Madeline had met the woman once, long enough to discover that Lady Tarley's bosoms vastly outweighed her brain. Unlike her brother, the publisher of a radical newspaper, Lady Tarley moved in lofty circles. Her first husband, a barrister, had died of an apoplexy, probably brought on by her twittering nonsense. Her second husband was an earl of some consequence.

But Lord Tarley wasn't around, and as Madeline's group descended from the carriage, she realized why. Apparently the Tarleys had a "fashionable" marriage, judging from her ladyship's manner toward Lord Norcourt as he disembarked.

"Why, Tony," she gushed, "what a wonderful surprise! When Charles asked me to serve as his hostess today, I had no idea you would be here, too."

Tony? She called him *Tony*?

"Good morning, madam," Anthony said in a decidedly cool voice. "How nice to see you again." Then he turned rather pointedly to help the girls down.

Lady Tarley slid her hand in the crook of his elbow.

"Now, Tony, surely you won't be so formal with an old friend."

The vicious stab of jealousy that shot through Madeline caught her off guard. What did she care if Lady Tarley knew Anthony? Even if it *had* been an intimate connection, it was of no matter as long as it didn't interfere with her plans.

In fact, it might work in her favor to have Lady Tarley drawing his attention. Then Madeline wouldn't have to worry about him trying to get her alone, trying to find out the truth about the party.

Yes, it was a good thing—a very good thing—that Lady Tarley had come.

Madeline gritted her teeth as the buxom brunette draped herself over his arm and minced along beside him with a tinkling laugh.

Mr. Godwin, who'd helped Mrs. Harris to disembark, turned to Anthony now, chagrin written across his handsome features. "Norcourt."

"Godwin."

Madeline brightened. If the two men knew each other, too, the connection might be a familial one and not the unsavory connection Lady Tarley seemed to imply. Not that it mattered. It didn't. Not one whit.

Apparently it mattered to Mr. Godwin, for he shot his sister a dark look. "See here, Kitty, we should welcome *all* our guests." He bowed to Mrs. Harris. "I'm so pleased you took me up on my offer to show off my menagerie. I trust that you and your pupils will find it interesting."

"If we don't," Mrs. Harris said, "Miss Prescott will surely chastise us."

"Ah, yes, your resident naturalist." Mr. Godwin smiled

at Madeline. "So glad you could come, Miss Prescott. I'm counting on you to fill in the gaps in my knowledge for your students." Offering one arm to Mrs. Harris and the other to Madeline, he proceeded to lead them toward his gardens.

That left Anthony to follow behind with Lady Tarley, the girls, and the other teachers. Madeline tried not to glance back and see how he fared with "Kitty."

What sort of name was Kitty anyway? It sounded like something you'd call an opera dancer with a penchant for gaudy jewelry and giggling.

Not that she cared.

Mr. Godwin dropped his voice to a murmur. "Charlotte, why on earth is Norcourt here? Or is that why your note last night asked me to include my sister?"

"That's precisely why," Mrs. Harris said. "It's an experiment."

Madeline tensed. "What sort of experiment?"

Mrs. Harris glanced at her, eyes speculative. "To see just how discreet he can be around young ladies."

"I do not want my sister taking up with Norcourt again, damn it," Mr. Godwin grumbled. "He's a bad influence on her."

A sick feeling settled into Madeline's belly. *That* certainly clarified the woman's relationship with Anthony, didn't it?

"I suspect your sister became what she was long before Lord Norcourt came along," Mrs. Harris said dryly. When Mr. Godwin cast her a sharp glance, she shrugged. "She's newly married. Surely she won't take up with a rakehell *now*."

Mr. Godwin's snort said he wasn't so optimistic.

Wonderful. If Anthony couldn't behave himself around

his former paramour, Mrs. Harris would throw him out on his ear, and that would put an end to the nitrous oxide party.

They rounded the house and entered a garden where refreshment tables had been set up. Beyond it, a stout wooden fence surrounded a pasture of cows. The girls were too caught up in attacking the refreshments to notice, but Madeline spotted the other creature in the pasture at once, standing near a copse of trees.

"You have a rhinoceros!" she exclaimed, half in awe, half in delight.

"I do indeed, the only one living in England at present." Mr. Godwin led them to the fence. "Clarabelle is so mild-mannered I needn't even keep her caged. As you can see, she roams free with my cattle."

Lucy Seton had followed them. "Aren't you afraid she'll eat your cows?"

"Rhinoceroses are herbivores," Madeline explained. "They only eat plants."

"That horn looks as if it could tear a cow apart," Lucy said, clearly skeptical.

"It could," Anthony put in. "That's probably why rhinoceros horn is so greatly prized by the Chinese for its medicinal properties."

Madeline glanced at him, which proved a mistake. Bad enough that Lady Tarley clung to him like a barnacle. But when the woman looked at Madeline, then plastered her breast against him while leaning up to whisper in his ear, Madeline wanted to slap her. Especially after Anthony followed her gaze and laughed.

Madeline hated being laughed at. "I thought the Chinese prized it because they consider it an aphrodisiac."

Anthony's eyes danced. "That, too. How good of you to point it out."

Lady Tarley giggled, but Mrs. Harris cast Madeline a warning glance that made her curse her quick tongue.

"I understand that their skin is virtually impenetrable," Mrs. Harris broke in before Lucy could ask for an explanation. "Is that true, Mr. Godwin?"

"Hardly." He launched into a description of the characteristics of rhinoceros skin, which Madeline would generally find fascinating. But she couldn't take her eyes off the cooing Lady Tarley, whose whispered comments to Anthony were met with dry smiles and quiet remarks.

When he caught Madeline glaring, he quirked up an eyebrow, as if he'd guessed what tumultuous emotions roiled through her. Then he skimmed his eyes lower, reminding her of his promise to have her craving pleasure day and night. Just the touch of his gaze down there brought the craving back so intensely she had to squeeze her thighs together to quell it.

Curse him. And Lady Tart, too, for pressing her bosom possessively against him. Grinding her teeth, Madeline turned her back on them, yet she couldn't banish the image of them together. Why did this bother her so? It wasn't as if he'd returned Lady Tarley's fawning attentions. If he'd been any other man, she wouldn't have thought twice of his polite behavior to his overly clinging hostess.

But he wasn't any other man, drat it. He was Anthony, who'd kissed and caressed her and made her feel desire for the first time. Who was also now making her feel jealousy for the first time—over *him*, an unrepentant rakehell who routinely seduced women for entertainment! What was she thinking?

Yes—what *was* she thinking to resent the one woman who might draw his attention away for the remainder of the day?

That steadied her. She must be sensible about this. Only schoolgirls flew into the boughs over a man. She was a naturalist, drat it. Once she got what she needed from the viscount, she would be done with him.

"Shall we move on, ladies?" Mr. Godwin said.

Lucy and Elinor slid up on either side of her to capture her arm. They held her back until Mr. Godwin headed off with Mrs. Harris, and Lady Tarley with Anthony. Only then did they follow, a good distance behind the others.

Lucy bent her head close to whisper, "Lord Norcourt thought you were thirty years old. Can you imagine that?"

Well, now she knew how he saw her—as some pathetic spinster long in the tooth, a challenging female to seduce but no more.

You've known that all along. Why can't you get it through your thick head that this is only an exercise for him? For both of you?

"But we set him straight," Elinor added in a whisper. "We made it clear you're not as old as all that. You're certainly not yet on the shelf."

That brought her up short. Why would the girls—

Oh, dear. She noted their conspiratorial expressions and groaned. The last thing she needed was two little matchmakers. "You needn't have bothered. His lordship doesn't care what my age is, and I don't care what he thinks it is."

"So you don't care he was asking questions about you?" Lucy said slyly.

"Questions?" Madeline's throat tightened. "What sort of questions?"

"About your suitors." Elinor smiled. "Whether you had any or not."

She stared at them. "Why would he ask that?"

The girls exchanged knowing glances.

"Don't be silly, girls." Her heart beat wildly despite her protest. "Lord Norcourt isn't looking for a wife, and even if he were, I wouldn't be his choice."

"I wouldn't be too sure of that. Lord Norcourt—"

"And what are you ladies whispering about so intently?" Anthony asked.

The group ahead had halted before a paddock and now eyed them with curiosity.

Lucy answered. "We were asking Miss Prescott"—she paused, then brightened—"what an aphrodisiac is!"

Oh, Lord, that was almost worse than the truth.

As Mrs. Harris lifted her eyes heavenward, Anthony chuckled. "And what did she say?"

Madeline glared at him. "That it's something believed to enhance a beast's natural instincts."

A simpering laugh escaped Lady Tart. "Not just beasts. Men use it, too, you know." The woman gave Anthony a lascivious glance that made Madeline want to scratch her eyes out. "Although certain men don't need it."

"I'm sure every man could use help occasionally," Madeline snapped.

"Madeline, for heaven's sake, this is not remotely—" Mrs. Harris began.

"Do tell, Miss Prescott," Lady Tart cut in. "Have you a great deal of experience with men and what they require help with?"

The girls might not have understood the exchange, but they could tell she was being attacked, and they flanked her protectively. "Miss Prescott knows a great deal about everything," Elinor shot back. "She's a wonderful teacher."

"Indeed she is." Mr. Godwin shot his sister a disapproving glance. "So I'm sure she'd be happy to identify the lovely creature in the paddock before us."

As the others turned to look, Madeline smiled gratefully at him for saving her from herself. She mustn't let that woman provoke her. Especially with Anthony smirking over the interchange.

She stared at the paddock. "That's a zebra. I've never seen one in the flesh."

"Looks like a painted horse to me." Elinor peered at the stately animal prancing through the grasses. "Can you ride it like a horse?"

"I honestly don't know," Mr. Godwin answered. "He's a new acquisition."

"I'll bet Tony could ride him," Lady Tarley cooed.

"If your brother will saddle him," Anthony drawled, "I'll certainly try."

At the speculative glint in his eye, Madeline tensed. This was the sort of challenge to appeal to him, like that bacchanal at Eton that got Anthony into trouble as a lad. But given what she'd read about futile attempts to break zebras to the saddle, he'd be daft to try it.

Especially if he was merely doing it to impress that ninny, Lady Tarley.

"This isn't like riding a goat, you know," Madeline cautioned. "Zebras are truly wild, Lord Norcourt, and by all accounts cannot—"

"A goat?" Anthony's eyes narrowed. "You knew about me and the goat?"

Her stomach knotted. "Everyone knows. You're famous

for it." Or was that only in Telford? *Oh no, please let it be a tale widely told.*

"Famous for what?" Lady Tarley queried.

"Riding a goat, apparently," Mr. Godwin answered.

"A schoolboy indiscretion." Anthony searched her face. "I nearly got sent down from Eton for that prank. Didn't I, Miss Prescott?"

Something in his tone alarmed her. "I-I wouldn't know."

"Yet you knew about the prank itself."

"I'm sure I read of it in some gossip column," she said hastily.

"My curiosity is thoroughly roused, Lord Norcourt," Mrs. Harris remarked. "Why were you riding a goat?"

She could have kissed her employer for drawing Anthony's attention. After another speculative glance at her, Anthony relented to the girls' demands that he reveal all. "It happened my third year at Eton. My friends and I . . ."

Madeline listened with half an ear, having already heard the tale. Lady Bickham had delighted in telling the populace of Telford how her nephew had degenerated after leaving her care. How Eton had corrupted him, and how he would have been better off if he'd remained with her and her husband.

As a child of eight, Madeline hadn't understood why Lady Bickham made such a fuss over the incident. She'd thought it amusing that he and his friends had ridden a goat. But once she was old enough to understand what a bacchanal was, she'd known exactly why Lady Bickham had reacted so ridiculously. The woman had no sense of humor whatsoever, and she certainly couldn't appreciate a Dionysian revel.

"After some matron saw us dancing about our bonfire

and riding the goat," Anthony was saying, "she ran screaming to the local vicar that Satan himself had appeared in Eton town."

Madeline noticed that he left out the part about the tavern wenches cavorting with him and his friends.

"It seems there was a superstitious belief that the devil rides upon a goat," he went on. "Anyway, we were discovered, much shouting ensued, and my friends and I received a caning for alarming the local folk."

"But what is a bacchanal?" Elinor asked.

"You know, it was in that book about myths," Lucy reminded her. "It's when the Romans used to drink mead and go about naked to worship Bacchus."

"Who is Bacchus?" one of the other girls asked.

"The god of debauchery, I think," Lucy answered.

"The god of wine and intoxication," Madeline corrected her. "Although too much wine often leads to debauchery. Not to mention other idiotic behaviors that a sober person would never engage in."

Anthony scowled at her before turning his gaze on Lucy. "Do you even know what debauchery is, Miss Seton?"

"I doubt it," Mrs. Harris retorted. "And I doubt any explanation would be wise, my lord. Come, girls—"

"I beg to differ," Madeline cut in. This was yet another way women were poorly prepared for their futures. "Knowledge is never unwise. The girls will hear such words bandied about in society. Shouldn't they know their meaning?"

As Mrs. Harris regarded her with a considering gaze, Mr. Godwin said, "Surely such discussions should wait for a husband's gentle guidance."

"What if the husband isn't so gentle?" Mrs. Harris sur

prised Madeline by saying. "Miss Prescott is right. Knowledge is never unwise." She fixed Anthony with an intent gaze. "Tell the girls what debauchery is, Lord Norcourt."

He tugged at his cravat. "I . . . well . . . perhaps Miss Prescott should explain. I'm sure she could do it far better."

Before Madeline could speak, Mrs. Harris squeezed her arm to silence her. "You're the one who brought up the bacchanal. The girls should hear it from *you.*"

"Fine." He glanced at the girls. "First, what do you ladies *think* it is?"

"Something naughty," Lucy said.

"*Very* naughty," Elinor added, as if that explained everything.

When Lady Tarley giggled, Anthony glared at her. "And what did *you* think it was when you were a girl, Kitty?"

Kitty blinked. "I don't remember. I had a vague notion it included beds."

As the girls nodded, Anthony sighed. "Debauchery can mean a number of things—drinking strong spirits to excess, gambling, gluttony—but people generally use it to mean . . . well . . . that is . . ."

When Mrs. Harris laughed, Madeline shook her head. "And you were worried he might not be discreet." She rolled her eyes. "For heaven's sake, the big, bad, immoral rakehell can't even explain debauchery to some girls."

"What do you expect?" he snapped. "They all remind me of Tessa. It would be like . . . telling a child about . . . about my parties."

"Hardly." With a snort, Madeline faced the girls. "You know that book of harem tales you girls were passing around at night in the dormitory, the one I confiscated last week?"

The brilliant blush on Miss Seton's face revealed that she'd probably read the entire thing. "We told you, we don't know *how* that got under the floor."

"What book of harem tales?" Mrs. Harris exclaimed.

"*Stories of a Barbary Harem.*" Madeline surveyed the blushing girls. "I found it when I nearly broke my neck on the board that someone left sticking up after they hid the book under it."

"Why didn't you tell me about this?" Mrs. Harris demanded.

"I didn't want to worry you." And she didn't want Mrs. Harris destroying the book before she could read it herself.

She'd only had time for a cursory glance at it, but she'd seen enough to know it was explicit about certain matters, not to mention full of ridiculously overblown descriptions about the "pleasures of the bed." Although after today, she wasn't so sure they were overblown.

She leveled her stare on the girls. "The things discussed in that book, girls—*those* are debaucheries."

"Ohhhh," Lucy burst out, her eyes wide with understanding. "But those didn't take place anywhere *near* a bed. And there were lots of people about."

"I thought you never read the book, Miss Seton," Mrs. Harris said dryly.

"I-I . . . um . . ."

"Well, *I* never read it," Elinor wailed, "so I don't know what you mean!"

"Good!" Anthony and Mr. Godwin said in unison. They halted to stare at each other.

When Anthony went on, his face was ripe with color. "I can only imagine what nonsense you'd find in it—alarming claims and lurid exaggerations in no way appropriate for a young girl."

"I agree entirely, Lord Norcourt," Mr. Godwin said.

"You think their wild imaginations would serve them better?" Madeline said.

"We'll discuss this further once we return to the school," Mrs. Harris put in with an air of finality. "I'm sure we can find more appropriate ways to educate the girls on such matters." Smiling at the irate Mr. Godwin, she took his arm. "Now, I should like to see the lion you told me about, sir. Come along, ladies."

Anthony looked relieved as he let Lady Tart appropriate him again, and Mr. Godwin looked positively self-righteous. The girls, however, looked confused. They surrounded Lucy in a fury of whispering that probably meant she was passing on her tidbits of information and further muddying the explanation.

In that instant, Madeline swore she would find a way to explain such delicate matters to them. Just see if she didn't.

Chapter Eleven

Dear Charlotte,
 Wonder about my "sources" all you like, my dear.
You know I'll never reveal them. But do write and tell
me about the expedition to Mr. Godwin's menagerie.
Is his collection as wide and varied as rumored?

 Your equally curious cousin,
 Michael

They toured the menagerie for two hours, with Mr. Godwin providing feed buckets and allowing the girls to pet the tame animals. Madeline tried to add to the girls' education throughout, but it was difficult when Anthony kept staring at her with that assessing look. What was he thinking? Was he considering how to get her alone so they could "finish" their lesson in seduction?

An uncomfortable heat pooled in her belly, making her want to squirm, as she'd squirmed earlier when he'd stroked her between the legs. He would surely do it again if she gave him the slightest encouragement.

Any more sessions like this morning's and she would find herself in deep trouble. She couldn't even hold her tongue in public—how would she do it in private once he started . . . turning her to mush?

If only she hadn't blurted out that bit about the goat-riding. She'd covered up her slip, but she couldn't have him finding out she was from Telford. One letter to anyone he might have known when he'd lived there, and he'd have the whole tale about Papa in excruciating detail.

Still, the party must be soon. Which meant she'd *have* to let him give her that dratted lesson. But next time she meant to be better prepared. Tonight, no matter how demanding her father, she was going to read that harem book. It might be lurid, but at least it would explain the wild way Anthony made her feel.

She'd thought she understood the principles of love-making because of her observations of animals, but she hadn't counted on how amazing it felt to have a man kiss her, caress and fondle her private parts, make her feel as if only she—

"Madeline," said a voice at her ear.

Startled, she turned to find Mrs. Harris looking irritated. "Is something wrong?" Madeline asked.

"Lord Norcourt and Lady Tarley have disappeared."

Madeline gave her a blank stare, though she wanted to scream. Going off alone with Lady Tart was *not* going to help Anthony's cause. Or Madeline's.

"We're about to be called in for luncheon," Mrs. Harris went on. "Fortunately, Charles hasn't noticed, and the girls and the other teachers were too engrossed in watching him feed the lion to notice, either—but if the viscount and the countess stay gone much longer, everyone will remark upon it. Someone must find them before that happens. I'd go myself, but then Charles is *sure* to notice."

"Shall we send a servant?"

"No, indeed. Who knows what they might be doing?

Servants gossip, and I cannot risk the school's reputation by having something like this happen at a school function. Bad enough that Charles dislikes him, but if it gets out that I brought them together on purpose—"

"It's not your fault."

"Oh, yes, it is. I let my guard down. I should never have let him inside my school." When Madeline blanched, Mrs. Harris said, "I'm not blaming you, dear; I'm blaming myself. You were merely attempting to help the girls—and his poor niece. But I'm experienced enough to know that rakehells never change."

"I'm sure it's not as bad as you think. Why, they might not even be together at all." When Mrs. Harris snorted, she added hastily, "And even if they are, they're probably just touring the gardens and . . . and talking over old times."

Mrs. Harris's raised brow showed her skepticism. "Nonetheless, you must be the one to find them. I can't risk anyone else catching them misbehaving."

"Of course not. I'll bring them back discreetly, I promise."

Tapping her chin, Mrs. Harris mused a moment. "I'll tell everyone that Lady Tarley headed toward the carriages to look for a shawl she dropped, and I sent you that direction to fetch her in for luncheon."

"Have you any idea where they might actually be?"

"Try the garden pavilion first. It's the only private spot on the grounds. When you find them, instruct Lady Tarley what to say before bringing her back."

"All right." That might be something of a feat, but she'd do her best.

"His lordship can follow later. I'm sure he's adept at

lying his way out of any situation, so he can produce his own explanation for where he wandered. Just make sure you and Lady Tarley approach from a completely different direction."

With a nod, Madeline started to walk away, but Mrs. Harris stayed her. "Later, I shall expect a full report about what you saw."

Madeline's throat went dry. "You want me to *spy* on them?"

The color rose in Mrs. Harris's cheeks. "I want to know how badly my experiment has run awry. Then I can determine how to proceed."

Oh, Lord. This was bad, very bad. "As you wish."

But a flood of anger rose in her throat as she headed toward the carriages until she was out of sight of everyone, then circled back to find the path to the pavilion. All her plans were about to be ruined, and for what? She would *not* let him ruin her plan to save Papa, even if she had to drag him kicking and screaming off that blowsy witch Lady Tart!

By the time she found the garden pavilion half-hidden in some trees, she'd worked herself into quite a temper. The sound of voices as she neared the miniature stone building made things worse, for it proved Mrs. Harris right.

But the voices weren't cozy murmurs. They sounded rather hostile. Creeping up to an open glass window, Madeline peered inside to find Anthony leaning against the central pillar, his arms crossed over his chest and his expression grim as he watched Lady Tarley swish in front of him, halfheartedly tucking her fichu back in the bodice of her gown.

"You could at least help me, Tony," Lady Tart complained in her girlish voice, although her enormous breasts were anything but girlish as they fought to escape her snug bodice.

A pang of envy seized Madeline before she tamped it down. What did she care if Lady Tarley possessed the two attributes that men always seemed to want—a buxom figure and no brain to speak of?

Though Anthony didn't look particularly entranced by either. "It wasn't *my* idea for you to remove your fichu." His voice dripped condescension. "I'm certainly not fool enough to put it back in for you. And stop calling me 'Tony.' You know I hate it."

"I know you used to be more fun." Lady Tarley stuck out her lower lip in a pretty pout that didn't seem to move him. "I can't believe gaining the title turned you into such a dull creature that you can't give a girl a little pleasure."

With a curse, Anthony pushed away from the pillar. "You're not a girl, Kitty. You're a married woman. And I don't dally with married women."

She thrust out her breasts. "Even ones with charms like mine?"

"Yes, damn it! How many times must I tell you I don't commit adultery?"

So he had some scruples after all, did he? That, plus his refusal of Lady Tart's overtures, dissipated Madeline's temper.

"If so," Lady Tarley snapped, "it's the *only* thing you don't do. What a silly rule for a rakehell."

"However it may seem to you, it is *my* rule, and I never break it."

"But the earl hardly notices that I—"

"I don't care," he growled. "I don't care if your husband

bores you in bed or ignores you or prances on your head every night. I am *not* interested in renewing our affair, as I've made clear countless times already today." He grabbed her by the arm and tried to lead her to the door. "It's time for you to return. I'll follow in a few minutes. We don't want anyone to realize we've been off together."

"Why not?" Snatching her arm free, she searched his face. "Don't tell me Widow Harris has caught your eye? That's pointless, you know. My brother Charles wants her for something more than a tumble, so she won't look at you. Besides, she'd never allow a man of your low morals to bed her."

"Then it's a good thing I'm not remotely interested in her."

Lady Tarley blinked. Then her eyes went wide in horror. "Oh, Lord, you want to seduce that scrawny schoolteacher with the outrageous tongue!"

Scrawny! Because Madeline didn't have breasts so big they could float a ship? How dared the witch call her scrawny!

When Anthony uttered a low curse, Lady Tarley tossed back her head. "I'll put a stop to that. I'll tell my brother to have that saucy creature dismissed."

As Madeline's heart dropped into her stomach, Anthony exploded. "You will do nothing of the kind, you nasty little twit," he growled.

With implacable steps, he backed Lady Tarley into a stone bench that caught her behind the knees, forcing her to sit abruptly, her breasts jiggling at the shock.

He paid them no heed as he loomed over her, anger cutting his features into sharp planes. "If you say anything to cause Miss Prescott to lose her position, I'll make you regret it. The woman is necessary to my plans, damn you."

Necessary to my plans. Madeline caught her breath at the sudden stab of pain in her chest. It shouldn't hurt. It was what they'd both agreed to from the beginning. But to hear him state it so baldly tightened a knot in her heart.

"There's naught you can do to stop me," Lady Tarley taunted him.

"You think not?" The menace in Anthony's voice took Madeline by surprise. "No doubt the earl would be interested to hear about your friend in Bond Street who lends you money for your card games without charging you interest. That is, as long as you provide him with certain benefits."

The color drained from Lady Tarley's face. "You wouldn't dare."

"But I would, my dear, with great relish."

Madeline ought to be shocked by his chilling threat. Instead, she was thrilled by his defense of her, even if it *was* only because she was necessary to his plans.

"You can be such a beast sometimes," the countess complained. She stood and shoved him away, then gave a petulant sniff. "Fine, if you want her, take her. You won't be satisfied for long with that bony scarecrow in your bed. And when you come crawling to me, I shall make you beg before I take you back."

Lady Tarley was already flouncing toward the door, so she didn't see Anthony roll his eyes. She was apparently so sure of her power that when Anthony said, "One more thing, Kitty," she gave a secretive little smile before schooling her features into a pout as she faced him.

"Any attempt to ruin *my* reputation will damage yours far more. So when they ask where you've been, tell them you were revisiting your favorite spot on the grounds. Alone. And you haven't seen me. Understood?"

Lady Tarley looked to be on the verge of an apoplectic fit. But though her lips twisted into a bitter line, she nodded before marching out the door.

Madeline shrank back to avoid being seen as Lady Tarley hurried off down the path. She dared not catch up to the countess *now*. Lady Tarley would assume that Madeline had come out here for a tête-à-tête with Anthony, and an enraged Lady Tarley wouldn't exactly go along with Mrs. Harris's scheme. Better to let the woman return and give the excuse Anthony had dictated. Perhaps no one had even noticed her departure.

She sighed. Except Mrs. Harris. She would also notice the countess's return.

Unless . . . Perhaps Madeline could race through the trees and come from the direction of the carriages when Lady Tarley emerged from the pavilion path. With everyone already inside, no one would see. Then Madeline could coax the woman to enter with her so that Mrs. Harris wouldn't be the wiser.

Yes, that might work. She slipped stealthily into the trees.

She might have escaped unnoticed, too, if not for looking back to make sure Anthony wasn't in pursuit. Because that's when she stumbled over a tree stump and landed with a crash in the brush.

As Anthony growled, "What the bloody devil?" she scrambled to her feet in a panic. But she wasn't quick enough. He was out the door to catch her before she'd even steadied herself. Drat it all.

"Skulking about in the woods, Madeline?" he bit out

as he surveyed her hapless state. "I didn't take you for the sort."

She strove for calm while she brushed leaves and twigs from her skirts. "Mrs. Harris sent me to fetch you and Lady Tarley for the luncheon."

He frowned. "Damnation, I made sure no one saw us leave together."

"That didn't keep Mrs. Harris from noticing you were gone." When he reached up to pick leaves from her coiffure, she glared at him. "And given her suspicions about you, you can guess what conclusions she leaped to. Which were obviously well-founded, since she knew exactly where to send me to look first."

"What the devil was I supposed to do?" He threaded his fingers through his hair. "Kitty kept plaguing me to join her on a tour of her brother's new garden pavilion, so it was either get her alone to tell her where we stood or risk having her become increasingly indiscreet in her flirtations before Mrs. Harris and the girls. I did what I thought was best."

With a sniff, Madeline stalked past him. "It's no concern of mine how you act around Lady Tarley as long as it doesn't ruin my plans."

He caught her by the arm. "Where do you think you're going?"

"To make sure 'Kitty' doesn't say anything stupid."

"She won't. She'll not risk having her husband learn of her gambling indiscretions." He eyed her closely. "You should trust me in this—I don't wish to see your plans ruined either. Or your reputation. It wouldn't help *my* plans."

"Yes, I know perfectly well how *necessary* I am to your plans."

The sudden narrowing of his gaze warned her she shouldn't have revealed what she'd overheard, no matter how much his words had rankled.

"Well, well, a schemer *and* an eavesdropper," he said.

"It's hard not to overhear people when they're practically shouting. Besides, I didn't dare interrupt while Lady Tarley was dressing herself."

The brittleness in his gaze softened a fraction. "If you overheard us, you know she never removed more than her fichu. So the only reason I can think of for this burst of pique is that you're jealous."

"Of you and that hen-witted tart with her rhinoceros-sized breasts?" Her ire only increased when he smiled. "I don't care one whit what you do together."

Twisting free of his hold, she tried once more to leave, but he caught her about the waist from behind to drag her up against him. "She means nothing to me, you know," he murmured in her ear. "We shared a bed years ago when she was between husbands, but I could only bear a few nights of her inane chatter before I had to end it. I'm not interested in Lady Tarley."

"I told you, I don't care!" She tried to pry his arm from about her waist, but he was surprisingly strong.

"If you don't care, then why are you annoyed?" he drawled. "And why are you angry that I said you were necessary to my plans when you know you are?"

"If I'm so necessary," she snapped, "let me go clean up your mess!"

"My mess is already taken care of." Heedless of her struggling, he pulled her inside the pavilion. "Besides, sweetheart, it's time you and I have a little talk."

Only after he had shut the door and leaned back against

it did he release her. She backed away, her hands fisting at her sides. "Talk? About what?"

His gaze pierced her. "How you heard the story of the bacchanal at Eton."

She froze. "I already told you. I read it in a newspaper."

"Impossible. No one writes about schoolboys, especially ones who are merely second sons."

"But you weren't the only one involved. Your society friends were there, too: the heir to the Marquess of Stoneville and the heir to—"

She broke off as she realized, too late, that she'd only dug the hole deeper.

"How do you know all that, damn you?" He shoved away from the door to stalk toward her. "Our fathers spent a great deal of money to keep the tale from leaking out beyond Eton."

"Apparently not enough," she quipped, frantic to assuage his suspicions as she backed away. But the distrust darkening his face knifed a chill of foreboding through her belly.

"I want to know how you heard the tale," he demanded, "and I want to know *now*."

She scrambled for some plausible lie. A brother at Eton? No, Anthony would just ask for a name, and she'd be sunk. But she could hardly tell him that she'd heard it in Telford, because then he would seek out the truth of who she was.

"Damn it," he growled as he backed her into the pillar, "where the devil did you hear about that bacchanal? How do you know so much about me? What—"

"I grew up in a town near where you lived!" she burst

out, praying she could convince him it was Shrewsbury or some other place.

He blinked. "Near Chertsey?"

Chertsey, of course! His childhood home, where his estate was, lay far away from Telford. She'd even visited the town once as a child, when her father had gone there on some business, so perhaps she could pretend to know it.

"That's where you lived, isn't it?" she answered. "The townspeople gossiped about your family often, and that was one tale that made the rounds."

He searched her face, as if trying to determine her truthfulness.

With a toss of her head, she stared him down. "There, are you happy? Can I please return to the others now?"

"Not yet." His eyes darkened to an unfathomable blue as he gripped her waist to keep her from sliding away from between him and the pillar. "Your answer merely makes me wonder why this is the first I'm hearing of it. Why the bloody devil didn't you tell me from the beginning that you knew my family?"

The bottom dropped out of her bravado. Lord help her, now what?

Chapter Twelve

Dear Cousin,

I carried your suggestion one step further and invited Lord Godwin's sister to join us. That should make for an interesting day at the menagerie, if nothing else, and it will let me observe Lord Norcourt's behavior for myself.

Your friend,
Charlotte

"I want an answer," Anthony clipped out.

Every time he began to rethink his assumptions about her, something else spilled out of her mouth to give him pause. Who was she, damn it?

"Most people who meet a person they've heard of say, 'I know you—we come from the same town.' But you pretended to know nothing about me. So what is it you don't want me to know? Is it what's prompting you to push for this bloody party that any fool can see—"

"I was embarrassed!" she cried.

He stared at her. "Embarrassed over what?"

"We may come from the same town, but not remotely the same station." A pretty blush pinkened her cheeks.

"My family isn't . . . well, they would be far beneath your contempt. I wasn't sure you knew them, but if you did . . ." She set her shoulders defiantly. "I didn't want you to tell Mrs. Harris about them. She thinks I come from a family of more consequence than I do."

The ring of truth to her words gave him pause. Pride was something he understood. He'd spent half his childhood shoring up the ruins of his own after his trials at the Bickhams'.

"You don't know what it's like to have everyone whispering behind your back, looking at you as if you're nothing." Her voice shook. "Mrs. Harris thinks I'm clever. She trusts me."

"And you didn't want me to ruin that."

She nodded.

Even if he hadn't remembered her words about the pain caused by idle gossip, he would have believed her explanation. He'd witnessed firsthand how she thrived upon the mutual respect between her and her employer.

Mrs. Harris *did* trust her, and with good reason—Madeline admirably shouldered her responsibilities. She seemed genuinely to care about her pupils, too. Could a woman of such character really be as devious as he'd assumed?

"It wouldn't have mattered to me who your family is," he said.

"You already thought I was a schemer who wanted your money." Dropping her gaze to his cravat, she went on haltingly. "I didn't see any point in telling you about my miserable connections."

"Well, you can tell me now."

Her gaze shot to his. "Why? So you'll have something

to hold over me, something to allow you to wriggle out of your promise—"

He kissed her. He couldn't help himself. Every time she showed what she really thought of *his* character, it inflamed him. So he kissed her to shut her up.

But within seconds, the kiss exploded into intimacy. Her lips parted beneath his, allowing him to plunder and thrust, to sink his tongue into the hot silk of her mouth over and over, the way he wanted to sink into other parts of her. She had the softest mouth he'd ever tasted, scented with something citrus so that her every breath reminded him of spring.

Kissing her made him crave more. Much more. He slid his hand over her breast, molding it, thumbing the nipple through the fabric. She responded by leaning into the caress . . . until she came to her senses and pushed his hand away.

Tearing her mouth free, she shoved at his chest. "Anthony, I must go back."

"Not on your life." His blood pounded in his ears as he branded her neck with kisses, then tongued the hollow of her throat. "We never finished our lesson in seduction." And he still didn't have the answers he sought. Although, judging from how his cock was stirring, he might have trouble asking questions. All he wanted was to swive her silly.

"Th-there's no time for this." But her halting words told him that she wished there were. So did her quickening breath and her fingers curling into his lapels.

He would make the time. He had to touch her . . . fondle her . . . discover her secrets. "They won't be looking for us yet, and Kitty's explanations will work in our favor, trust me."

She laughed shakily. "Trust you? What kind of fool do you take me for?"

"A very desirable one," he rasped against her throat.

"Desirable because I'm necessary to your plans," she said with a trace of bitterness.

He could kick himself for having said that, no matter how true it was. It might sound to her as if he held her in contempt. Which wasn't the case. "Necessary to my sanity, more like," he muttered to himself.

When she stilled, he groaned. Damnation, he hadn't meant to reveal how thoroughly she fascinated him. But then she drew back to stare at him with wide, innocent eyes that showed she found *him* fascinating, too, and he decided that he'd say anything if it kept her looking at him like that.

"What if someone sees us here?" she whispered.

"They're going in to luncheon, remember? You said Mrs. Harris wasn't even sure where Kitty and I had gone. And if she does send someone else after us, we'd hear them coming in plenty of time. But just in case . . ."

He went to close the window and draw the curtains. As he walked back, her eyes grew sultry, and the sight of her lips shining a luscious red in the dim light made him crave that mouth on his chest, his belly . . . his cock.

He groaned. Not today. The lesson he intended was supposed to entice her to share his bed, not send her running from him in shock.

"I never agreed to your terms, you know," she pointed out, as he reached her.

If she meant to tease him, she was doing a good job of it. "Very well," he said with a shrug. "Then we'll have the party next week as I'd initially planned."

He turned for the door, but she caught his arm. "No. Now that you've gone to so much trouble, you might as well finish the lesson in seduction. But do be quick about it."

A choked laugh escaped him as his bad boy leaped fully to attention. "The first thing you need to learn, sweetheart, is that 'quick' and 'seduction' don't belong in the same sentence." He led her to one of the stone benches. "And seduction is never any trouble."

"It could be trouble for me," she pointed out, as he seated her on the bench.

"I won't let it." After removing her tucker, he lowered her gown, stays, and chemise, so he could gaze his fill of her twin beauties, so pert and high, with small pink nipples that he ached to suck.

"You have perfect breasts," he rasped as he dropped to his knees before her.

"Really?" She stared at him, her gaze oddly guileless, showing no trace of embarrassment. But when she spoke again, her voice held a tremor. "They're . . . they're not very big."

True, yet they suited her somehow. And they were by no means paltry. "Big enough to please me," he murmured. Then he covered one with his mouth, relishing the tiny gasp she gave in response.

That was all the encouragement he needed. He took his time, teasing one nipple with teeth and tongue while he fondled her other breast. As he drank in her sighs and moans, he fought to ignore his rapidly growing arousal. She smelled of citrus and sun, tart and hot together, and he wished he could taste her for hours.

Taste *all* of her. His fevered brain could think of nothing else. He told himself it was because nothing softened a woman and turned her confessional better than a thorough tongue-lashing in just the right place.

But that was a lie. He ached with the need to have some part of him inside her. Ruthlessly, he ignored his own need. He meant to show her he could hold his beastly self in check.

Perhaps then she would see that their joining was inevitable. And once she let him seduce her, *he* would be in control. Then he would have what he wanted from her—the agreement to Tessa's enrollment, the truth about who she was . . . her presence in his bed every single lonely night . . .

The dangerous thought stiffened him to painful heights. Shoving her skirts up to her knees, he pushed her legs apart, eager to survey her domain.

"Anthony . . ." she said, a throaty warning that drove him mad.

"Let me finish the lesson." He inched her skirts up enough to bare her drawers. "I swear I won't do anything to ruin—"

He gulped. He had a full view of everything now, and with her legs parted, her sweet little honeypot peeped between the slits of her modest drawers, turning them into the most erotic piece of clothing he could have imagined.

The widows and whores he'd bedded had been lusty women showing off for a lusty rakehell. They hadn't worn drawers, and tossing their skirts up had generally given him instant access to their allurements.

He'd never dreamed that sublety could turn him hornier than a rhinoceros in the wild. His bad boy was fairly
dancing in his trousers.

"What's wrong?" she whispered.

He glanced up to find her face awash with color. "Not a
bloody thing," he rasped. Then he buried his face between
her legs.

At the first taste of her, he groaned. Who would have
dreamed a woman could hide such a delicious treat beneath practical linen drawers and bluestocking talk? God
save him, she was dewy and warm, and her drawn-out sigh
told him she was every bit as eager for this as he. Which
was a good thing, because this time he meant to make her
scream.

And scream was exactly what Madeline wanted to do as
she stared down at Anthony's head between her legs. How
could she let him do these . . . amazing . . . incredible . . .
things to her . . . with his mouth? She'd never guessed a
man could use it like this! Or that she'd want him to continue.

But ever since this morning, she'd been unable to stop
thinking about how he'd touched her . . . how he'd roused
an undeniable craving between her legs, more powerful
than any she'd roused with her own caresses in the dark of
the night.

Hardly realizing what she did, she gripped his head
to hold him fast, and he paused long enough to cast her
a smug glance. Curse him for that. She would make him
regret it later. But right now, she'd go mad with curiosity if
she didn't learn what she craved.

The more he drove his tongue inside her and the more

his teeth strafed that little nodule of flesh nestled between her legs, the more she yearned and burned.

Caressing herself there had never achieved quite this astonishing sensation. It had merely frustrated her, made her impatient. It had never sent a flood of heat from her toes up her legs to just where his tongue and teeth worked that pebble of flesh with a delicacy that had her gasping. He churned the hot need in her belly into a frenzy that made her thrust her pelvis hard against his mouth.

And scream. The keening cry shocked her, but she couldn't seem to stop it. It poured out of her as she reached the pinnacle of pleasure he'd referred to this morning, reached it and soared over it into bliss.

"That's it, come for me, sweetheart," he demanded, as his fingers took over the work of his mouth. He straightened, an unholy light shining in his eyes. "Now do it again. I want to watch you come apart."

"Enough," she whispered, because his fingers tickled.

But then the tickling became an echo of before, and an ache built in the back of her throat that mirrored the quivering ache between her loins. Now it was tightening, throbbing, the ache worsening, the cry rising in her throat . . . and she screamed again.

This time she actually felt herself spasm around his fingers, as if to drag them deep inside her. The spasming seemed to please him, too, for a dark satisfaction leaped in his face.

His eyes were hot on her, drinking up every mew of pleasure, every gasp. He breathed as hard as she and seemed to be fighting for control.

While she still shook and quivered, he drew back his hand to wipe his fingers on his handkerchief.

"What . . . was that?" she asked when she could finally speak.

His eyes narrowed. "Don't you know? It's the little death."

"I-It didn't feel like death at all. Or what I would imagine death feels like." She struggled to regain her reeling senses. "It felt . . . oh, how to describe it . . . like heaven. Except reckless."

He uttered a rough laugh as he drew her skirts down. "You've never done that before, have you?"

Uh-oh. She was supposed to be experienced, remember? But she could hardly lie about this. "No," she whispered.

"That lover of yours must have been more inept than I thought," he said.

She blinked. "Lover?"

"The man who seduced and abandoned you." His gaze searched her face. "The man who drove you into exile at a girl's school in Richmond rather than marrying you as he should have."

She choked back a hysterical laugh. My, my, he'd invented quite a tawdry little past for her. She couldn't have come up with a better tale herself.

"Who was he?" he demanded. "Who was the selfish oaf who took your innocence without bothering to give you pleasure?"

Making use of his outrageous story was one thing. Expanding it was quite another. "I don't want to talk about it," she said as she drew up her corset.

He rose. "Madeline, I understand." He caressed her hair. "It's all right. You can tell me what the bastard did—or didn't do, more likely. I can well imagine your encounters—a lot of fumbling in the dark and him stuffing himself inside you with little preparation. Clearly, *something* he did made you wary of seduction."

"I'm wary of seduction for the same reasons I told you before."

"Fear of disease and illegitimate children? There are ways to prevent both."

"Really?" she said, then wanted to kick herself for encouraging him.

"Really." He tipped up her chin until she stared into his flushed face. "Alas, today I didn't bring anything with me, but next time I'll show you."

She dropped her gaze again. There wouldn't be a next time. Not that she could tell *him* that. "One of us must return before Mrs. Harris grows suspicious." And she must get him off this dangerous subject.

"It can't be me, or they'll see what I've been doing. I can hardly hide it." He stepped nearer, making it impossible for her not to stare at his trousers, since they were at eye level and quite close. Not to mention bulging.

Her mouth went dry. She did know about *this*, how a male animal's penis grew erect when aroused. It only stopped being erect once the male emitted his semen inside the female. Which she hadn't let him do. *Mustn't* let him do.

But hadn't she read some tidbit from the harem tales . . . Ah, yes, a man could pleasure himself the same way a woman could. She'd seen a crude picture of it—the man emitting his semen while being aroused by his own hand. And surely if a man could do it to himself, a woman could do it to him, too.

Not that it mattered—she would never do such a thing. Certainly not. "Then I'll go first, and you can follow when you're . . . presentable. That would rouse less suspicion anyway."

She started to rise, but he pressed her down with one hand. "You're not going anywhere until you answer my questions."

Him and his questions, drat it. She stared ahead, right at his bulging trousers. How better to distract him? Besides, the thought of touching Anthony's erect penis sent excitement swirling through her senses.

She squelched it at once. This had nothing to do with her eagerness to see what he looked like *there*. Or how he would feel in her hand. And how he would react to having her touch him.

She just had to keep him from figuring out what she was up to with her party.

"You could either ask your questions," she said, gazing at him from beneath lowered lashes. "Or I could relieve your condition. It's your choice."

He hesitated. She could almost see him weighing the choice in his mind.

"Relieve my condition how?" he asked warily.

"With my hand," she clarified, hoping she'd guessed right about what a woman could do to pleasure a man. Judging from how the bulge in his trousers swelled before her very eyes, she had indeed.

"Oh, God," he groaned, "you're a witch."

"Because I'm offering to pleasure you?"

"Because you're only doing it to keep from answering my questions."

"So you *don't* want me to pleasure you?"

"I didn't say that." Desire flared in his face. "You know damned well I want your hands on me."

"Then let me put them there." She unbuttoned his trousers. How difficult could it be to stroke a man to release?

His face flushed. "I still want answers . . ." he said hoarsely, though she noticed he didn't stop her as she unbuttoned his drawers.

"You'll have your answers," she assured him. "After the party, all right?" She had to give him some concession, and by then it wouldn't matter anyway, because if Sir Humphry didn't attend, she would have no choice but to beg Anthony to introduce her.

Pausing with her fingers on the last buttons, she lifted her face to his. "All right?" she repeated, making it clear this was the only choice she offered.

He stared at her a long moment. "All right," he said, the words almost guttural. Then he brushed her hands away and finished unbuttoning his drawers, unveiling the instrument that she'd seen only on animals or in drawings before.

Her mouth went dry. It was hard not to gawk. The thing was huge—not as large as a horse's, of course, but larger than she'd expected. Long and thick, it jutted out like a compass needle pointing north. To her.

"Stroke it," he commanded. "Oh, God, please stroke it."

Though she nodded, a moment of panic seized her. What if she did it wrong? What if she displeased him? A pity she hadn't read more of the girls' cursed book. One picture was hardly enough to inform a woman about proper technique.

Feeling at a disadvantage in her seated position, she rose and took his flesh in her hand. "I don't know . . . exactly how this works," she felt honor-bound to admit, since she didn't want to damage his lovely organ in any way.

"I'll show you." Closing his hand around hers, he moved it up and down his erect shaft.

"Ohhhh," she exclaimed, "it's like milking a cow."

A ragged laugh escaped him. "I suppose. Haven't ever . . . milked a cow." He guided her hand easily, as if it was a motion he did often. And the thought of him caressing himself the same way she touched herself in bed at night made her feel hot and quivery all over again.

Amazing. Only think how it would be if his flesh were inside her—

No, don't think about it. It's unwise, and you know it.

Releasing her hand so she could continue her caresses without his help, he eyed her closely. "Your lover must have been a very . . . dull fellow. Didn't he even have you do *this* to him?"

She avoided his gaze. "Just tell me what *you* like. Am I pleasing you?"

"You're driving me insane." When she tightened her grip, he moaned low in his throat. "Yes, like that. Ah, sweetheart, that feels like heaven."

"Except reckless," she said.

"Definitely reckless." He caught her chin with one hand. "Thank God."

Then he kissed her, his tongue mimicking the thrusts of his shaft into her fist as his other hand fondled her breast. The quivering between her legs started all over again, startling her with how easily he could rouse it.

She did seem to be rousing *him* fairly easily, since he was soon panting against her mouth. He dropped his hand to grip hers again, urging her to stroke faster. "Ah, sweet

Madeline, so practical . . . so naughty . . . you make me want—"

He broke off, fumbling for the soiled handkerchief he'd shoved in his pocket, then wrapping it around their joined hands. "God, I'm there . . . yes . . . yes!"

With a hoarse cry, he spent himself into the handkerchief, his hand squeezing hers to halt her motions. Wondering what he'd meant by "you make me want" and what exactly she made him want, she stared down at their hands. It fascinated her to feel every jerk of his penis, every spurt of his seed.

She'd never done anything so intimate. Who'd have guessed it could be so beautiful, even without completing the seduction? When he bent his head to hers and brushed a kiss to her forehead, she felt a sudden urge to cry, for what could never be, what they could never share.

Because now she knew the truth—if she ever allowed him to take her innocence, she would give her heart to him, too. And a rakehell was a terrible guardian for a woman's heart.

Even a heart as practical as hers.

Chapter Thirteen

Dear Charlotte,
You are quite mad. Do you really think Norcourt and Lady Tarley can behave around impressionable young girls? What does Miss Prescott think of your plan?

Your cousin,
Michael

Anthony came slowly to his senses, drifting down from his heady release to find Madeline drawing back her hand. Once again, she'd brought out the beast in him, keeping him from doing what he should.

He wanted to be angry, but he couldn't regret a moment of it. Besides, she looked so awkward and uncomfortable that he only wanted to reassure her.

"Are you all right?" He wiped her fingers with the dry part of the handkerchief.

"Fine." But she refused to look at him as she straightened her clothing.

"Do you regret tarrying with me?" he probed.

"No, of course not," she murmured. Before he could even smile at that response, she added, "Since I've met your terms, we can go on with our bargain."

A sudden flood of anger took him by surprise. "Is that all this meant to you? A way to get your party?"

"What did it mean to *you*?" she countered with a little lift of her chin.

The question arrested him. His anger made no sense—he'd had his pleasure, so why did it matter how she felt about what they'd done?

He didn't know why—it just did. He stared at her vulnerable expression, and he wanted . . . more. For the first time, he wanted more. But he wasn't about to tell her. She'd already taken enough advantage of his strange obsession with her.

Besides, how could he explain he'd never met a woman like her? Never even dallied with one? She'd think him a fool if he revealed he'd fought all his life to avoid any affair that could lead to more, any affair that could end badly, leaving both parties scarred.

He certainly couldn't tell her that the more time he spent with her, the deeper he sank into the very thing he'd always avoided. And that he couldn't for the life of him figure out why. Or how to stop it.

"This was unlike anything I've ever experienced," he finally admitted.

She blinked, then frowned. "I have trouble believing that no woman has ever pleasured you in such a manner."

"That's not what I meant." He lifted his clean hand to stroke her cheek, noticing the sheen of unshed tears in her eyes. So this *had* affected her, even if she wouldn't admit it. "I only meant that you . . . have a way of taking a man out of himself, making him forget things he shouldn't."

Like the flaws in his character. Or the fact that he

shouldn't dally with the one woman who'd agreed to help him with Tessa's situation.

A small sigh whiffed from her lips. "Then we're alike in that. You take me out of myself, too." She stared at him wide-eyed. "And I didn't even know I wanted to escape myself."

He suddenly got the sense he was on the verge of discovering something important about her. If he dared to probe further. If he dared to let this become . . .

No, that was unwise. Instead, he reverted to the comfortable role of practiced seducer.

"That's understandable." Dropping his hand from her cheek, he began to button up his clothes. "If done right, 'swiving' does have a tendency to take one out of oneself." The words sounded hollow even to his own ears.

"If you say so." Though her tone matched his for nonchalance, the trembling in her hands as she finished setting her clothes to rights showed he'd wounded her by becoming the consummate rakehell once more.

Yet he pressed on. "Trust me, it will be even better on Saturday."

She stiffened. "I haven't said I will share your bed."

"No, but you will."

Her eyes were round and solemn as she stared at him. "We'll see."

He let her tell herself she would avoid any further entanglement. They both knew it was a lie. A woman could return to celibacy if her first experience with a man was bad, which was undoubtedly what had happened to her before. But let that woman once experience the full glory of her sensuality, and she would never deny it to herself again.

For proof of that, he had only to look at every widow he'd ever seduced—no matter how much they missed their husbands, they missed being bedded more. If they didn't, it was only because their husbands had bedded them badly.

Or so he'd been telling himself for the past ten years. Better to believe that than to think that women only came to him because they were lonely. And because his need to assuage his own loneliness was as plain to them as letters on a page.

He swore under his breath. That was ridiculous. He bedded women because he required release for his unruly urges, because he wanted to get through the dark nights. Not because he was lonely.

And he wanted Madeline for the same reason. He did, damn it!

Madeline headed for the door, but he caught her arm. "Do you swear to give me my answers Saturday night?"

"Yes. After the party. Now I must go."

Reluctantly he released her, watching as she slipped out of the garden pavilion. He waited a few moments, then walked out to perform a quick survey of the area. Satisfied that no one was nearby, he headed for the house.

When he entered the manor, Madeline was seated at the luncheon relating a story of how she'd gone to look for Lady Tarley near the carriages, not realizing that the countess was somewhere else. Judging from Mrs. Harris's reaction, the headmistress and Madeline had agreed beforehand on what tale to tell.

So it was his turn. He feigned surprise at learning they'd been looking for him. He explained he'd gone for a stroll around Godwin's small lagoon. Though Mrs. Harris eyed him closely, and the girls whispered together, they seemed to accept his tale. There *was* a brief moment when Kitty looked as if she might contradict him out of pique, but his cold stare stifled whatever trouble she thought to cause.

Thankfully, they boarded the carriages a short while later and headed back to the school. This time, the two girls didn't seem to mind that he was inordinately quiet as they chattered about what they'd seen. Only Mrs. Harris noticed, casting him a few searching glances though she said nothing.

Once at their destination, he took his leave and headed back to London. It was later than he'd expected to be, and he had some unsavory business to discuss with his solicitor before he could meet with Stoneville as planned.

As Anthony strode into his solicitor's, pausing to hand his hat to the clerk in the outer office, Mr. Joseph Baines rose from behind his desk in the inner office. "My lord. To what do we owe this unexpected pleasure?"

The family solicitor had never been fond of Anthony, a feeling that was entirely mutual. But Anthony could live with that as long as he was sure the man deserved the trust that Wallace and Father had placed in him.

Anthony waited until Mr. Baines closed the door and resumed his seat before he spoke. "I thought you should know I've dismissed the steward at Norcourt Hall."

Disapproval was plainly etched in the solicitor's overly powdered face. "Dismissed him?"

"Yes." Anthony sat down and propped his ankle on his knee. He drew out two folded sheets of paper and unfolded them on the desk. "This is only a sample of his shenanigans with the books. It took me but a few hours to discover how much money he'd been secreting away by underpaying the staff." He watched Baines's face carefully.

"It's no wonder we've had trouble keeping footmen in our employ. And the butler was near to giving notice when he learned that his salary was actually supposed to be higher."

The shock that spread over Baines's features didn't appear feigned, nor was there a trace of guilt in his face. Perhaps the man hadn't been part of the steward's deception. Anthony had hoped not.

Baines skimmed the paper, then said in a hushed voice, "My lord, I had no idea. He came highly recommended, and I drew up the contracts with the assumption—"

"I'm sure that's true. But I thought you should be made aware of his character."

"Certainly, sir." He stiffened, then folded his hands on his desk. "I shall, of course, resign my position at once. I am the one who hired him, and consequently, I am the one responsible for this travesty."

For half a second, Anthony was tempted to accept the man's resignation. But the fact that he'd proffered it absolved him of any misconduct. And the truth was, the solicitor had a keen legal mind and the ambition necessary to benefit from it. His personal dislike of Anthony might be annoying, but it would never keep him from performing his duties to the greatest of his ability. Anthony admired him for that alone.

"I'm afraid I shall have to refuse your resignation, Mr. Baines. I don't hold you at fault in this matter. I merely thought you should be apprised of it."

"Thank you, sir. I shall try to be worthy of your faith in me."

His palpable relief took Anthony by surprise. Perhaps Mr. Baines wasn't entirely opposed to being the Norcourt solicitor after all. "Now then," Anthony went on, "I'll need you to find a replacement for the steward as soon as possible." A thought suddenly occurred to him. "Also, have you heard of any talented cooks who might be looking for a new position?"

Mr. Baines jerked his head up. "Surely the cook at Norcourt Hall has not left, as well."

"No. I'm asking on behalf of an acquaintance of mine. A Mrs. Harris."

The man's chilly manner returned. "A widow, I take it?"

"Yes, but not the merry kind." To his surprise, he rather enjoyed defying his solicitor's bad expectations of him. "She runs the girls' school that has agreed to enroll Miss Dalton." Or would agree, if he had anything to say about it. "Perhaps you've heard of it? Mrs. Harris's School for Young Ladies?"

Baines nodded as if in a daze. So much evidence of responsibility on Anthony's part was obviously more than he could take. "You said no school would consider enrolling her until you gain guardianship."

"It turns out I was wrong."

For the first time since Anthony had met him, there was a glint of respect in Baines's eye. "The Harris school is excellent, very prestigious," Baines said. "If you have secured your niece a place there, it will help your cause enormously. Especially with the change in your situation."

"What change?" Foreboding settled in his belly.

"I wasn't going to discuss it with you until I confirmed the rumor, but my sources say the court is already leaning toward giving guardianship to your uncle."

"What! But the barrister hasn't even had a chance to plead my case."

"As I told you before, they'll be considering more than

the mere facts of your fortune or rank. According to statements submitted by Lord Tarley—"

"What has the Earl of Tarley got to do with this?" Anthony said hoarsely.

"He has the ear of one of the judges and seems not to like you."

No surprise there. Damn! If he'd ever guessed that his dalliance with Kitty would cling to him for eternity like the smell of dead fish, he would never have spent one minute in her bed. It had certainly not been worth it.

"Is there anything to be done about the court's bias?" Anthony asked.

"Merely the same things I've urged. Avoid gaming clubs, eschew ladies of the evening, try not to be seen in the company of known profligates—"

"And attend church and apply for sainthood and God knows what else," Anthony snapped. "All to satisfy some dubious idea about what makes a man respectable."

"Dubious it may be, my lord," Baines said, reverting to his more usual manner, "but it is how most people live."

"Then most people be damned!" When Baines frowned, Anthony bit back another curse. "Forgive me, sir, I haven't been myself lately. This matter of Tessa's future is very distressing."

"Perhaps you should abandon her to her relations."

"The bloody devil I will. I won't let the Bickhams sink her in misery." He rubbed the scar on his wrist, then leaned forward. "Can we win? Despite Tarley?"

Baines glanced to the papers showing the steward's perfidy, then squared his shoulders. "I believe we can, yes. Your securing of her enrollment in that school will weigh well in your favor. And I have procured a barrister unparalleled in arguing cases of this kind. *If you can show the court—*"

"That I'm capable of being a decent guardian. I know. I'm working on it."

But when he left Baines's office half an hour later after more discussion of strategy, his unease wouldn't abate. It bothered him he had to provide Madeline with this party at a time when he was supposed to be lying low. It bothered him she was so obviously deceiving him about why it was important to her. Most of all, it bothered him that Lord Tarley was now involved.

Fortunately, Kitty wasn't likely to fuel her husband's dislike by speaking of her recent encounter with her former lover. If she was dim-witted enough to do so, he had only himself to blame, for giving her this power over him in the first place.

His years of thumbing his nose at society had brought him to this, a prison of his own making. Perhaps he *should* have lived his life more wisely.

Gritting his teeth, he climbed onto his horse. No, he had no regrets. Why should he have catered to the madness around him? Why should he have given his aunt and uncle the satisfaction of believing that their despicable methods had been right and just? Wasn't it better to have proved them wrong by his very life?

Yes, and they're certainly suffering for it, aren't they? They'll have Tessa to torment now, all because you couldn't be more circumspect.

He scowled at his conscience, which had chosen a damned fine time to show up. Where had it been while he was cutting a wide swath through society's widows?

Banished by you. Remember?

Bloody insolent conscience. All right, so he'd made mistakes he was paying for now. But Tessa wouldn't pay for them—not if he could help it.

He glanced at his pocket watch. Damnation, that discussion with Baines had taken longer than expected. He'd be late to meet Stoneville at Brompton Vale to discuss the nitrous oxide party. And it was never wise to keep Stoneville waiting.

Just as he'd feared, by the time he reached Stoneville the man was well on his way to being foxed, thanks to a whisky flask he brandished as Anthony approached.

"Oh, for God's sake," Anthony bit out, "when did you start carrying whisky with you everywhere?"

"About the same time you turned into a prig." Stoneville took a last swig, then tucked the flask inside his immaculate riding coat. "Just because you're trying to prove something to the world doesn't mean the rest of us have to be dull."

"I hate to disappoint you, old chap, but you're far duller when you're drunk than when you're sober."

It was true. Why had he never noticed that before? And was he the same—a blithering idiot when he was foxed?

Too much wine often leads to debauchery. Not to mention other idiotic behaviors that a sober person would never engage in.

Wonderful, now Madeline and his damned conscience were working together to plague him. Ruthlessly, he ignored them both. "I need a favor."

"So I gathered from your note," Stoneville said, as they set their horses off at a walk along the perimeter of the vale. "But what was so bloody important about coming to this deserted spot? I much prefer Rotten Row."

"For once, you can do without your daily ogling of the opera dancers in their carriages. I'm not supposed to be 'seen in the company of known profligates' like you. Your servants talk, my servants talk, and I couldn't think of anywhere else to meet that wasn't a brothel, club, or gaming hell. No one will notice us here."

"Very well. What's the favor?"

"I need you to throw a nitrous oxide party."

Stoneville's eyes lit up. "I *knew* you couldn't keep up this monastic life for long. By all means, we should have a party."

"Not *we*. You. I'll be there, but I have to stay out of sight during the affair. My solicitor was very clear on that subject. That's why I need *you* to be the one throwing it— because I can't be connected with it."

"Then why have it?"

He wasn't about to tell Stoneville how he'd been blackmailed into it by a slip of a schoolteacher. "Why do you care? Just throw the party, for God's sake."

Stoneville held up his hands. "Fine. There's a bevy of beauties over at Mrs. Beard's place that I've been eager to try out—"

"Not that kind of nitrous oxide party, damn it. The other kind. One with people of a certain . . . stature."

"The boring kind?" Stoneville complained. "I never went to those affairs when *you* held them. Well, except the ones attended by those chaps from the Royal Society. At least they know how to enjoy themselves."

"So invite them." He thought a moment. "She'd like that."

"She who?"

Anthony blinked. But Stoneville would have to be told

about Madeline eventually. He just didn't need to know the truth. "My . . . er . . . cousin. I've been promising for years that if she ever came to town, she could attend one, and now she's holding me to my promise. That's why I need you to host it."

"Ah. Is she pretty?"

Gritting his teeth, Anthony glared at his friend. "Do you ever ask any other question about a woman?"

"Don't care about the answer to any other question. So, is she pretty?"

"Pretty enough, I suppose." If he even hinted to Stoneville that he had feelings for Madeline, the man would flirt with her just to torture him. "But very dull—the bluestocking type. She has a scientific interest in nitrous oxide. Wants to see its effects on people."

Stoneville guided his horse past a barking dog. "She could see its effects on whores just as well as on the Royal Society sort."

"She's my cousin, damn it. I don't want her exposed to such a thing." Alarmed by the glint of calculation in Stoneville's eye, he added hastily, "And she's married, too. To a . . . er . . . parson."

Stoneville's eyebrows arched high. "You have a cousin married to a parson? Why have I never heard of her?"

"I've never heard of your cousins, so why would you have heard of mine? She's a distant country cousin."

"Is her husband coming to the party?"

Damnation, he shouldn't have invented a husband. But no unmarried woman would risk her reputation to attend such a party. Even a married woman would think twice. "Her husband isn't in town. She's staying with her friend and wants to live a little while out from under his thumb." He brightened. That was quite good. Perfect explanation.

"Wants to live a little. I see. Definitely your cousin."

Uh-oh, that look was back in Stoneville's eyes. "Stay away from her," Anthony growled. "She's a respectable woman."

"Whatever you say." A half smile played over Stoneville's lips. "And I can't stay away from her. Someone's got to introduce her round, and since you're in hiding, that leaves only me."

He hadn't thought of that. Damnation, this got worse by the moment. He couldn't have too many people speculating about his country cousin, or they'd soon find out she was a fabrication. "Don't introduce her as my cousin, or they'll say I corrupted her. Just . . . don't introduce her at all. Bring her out after the party is in full swing, and everyone will be too drunk on nitrous oxide to care who she is."

"Someone is bound to ask, and—"

"Damn it, handle it however you must. Just be careful what you say. Now, will you throw the party or not? I need it for this Saturday."

"This Saturday! But I've got plans."

"Have I ever asked you for a favor before?"

Stoneville sighed. "No, can't say as you have."

"And have you ever asked *me* for one that I haven't given you?"

Stoneville knew better than to answer that. He still owed Anthony money for the last favor. "Oh, very well, I'll host the damned party."

"And you'll invite the right sort of people?"

"Yes, though I can't promise they'll all come. Faraday is

off somewhere, Barlow went to visit friends in Yorkshire, and Lady Davy has been keeping a close eye on our friend Sir Humphry." Sarcasm laced his voice. "She doesn't let him step out of the house for fear he'll seduce some hapless female admirer."

Lady Davy was a good example of the sort of wife Anthony intended to avoid—paranoid and tyrannical. "Do you really think he beds them?"

"Hard to say. With all the bluestockings who used to follow his every lecture, swooning at his pearls of wisdom, I wouldn't be surprised. He may have retired from lecturing, but he's not dead, you know."

"True." The man had a certain charm that women responded to, facile though it might be. And considering how browbeaten Davy was by his wife, Anthony could hardly blame him if he *did* occasionally stray. "Invite him anyway. You know how much he likes his nitrous oxide. He may exert himself to come."

And Madeline would be delighted, no doubt, to meet the very chemist who'd experimented with nitrous oxide so famously. Assuming she wasn't lying about that article of hers, which might be a large assumption.

"Any other demands for this party?" Stoneville asked. "Preferences for food, type of wine, cushions—"

"Very funny," Anthony said. "Let me know the time as soon as you've arranged it." He reined in his horse. "Now I have to go. I'm dining with friends."

It was a lie, but he wasn't in the mood for Stoneville right now. Something in the man's careless manner rubbed him wrong, which had never happened before. Anthony felt as if he were watching himself the way he was just a year ago, and what he saw unnerved him.

Then a thought occurred to him. "Stoneville, do you remember that bacchanal we had at Eton, the one that got us in trouble?"

"Remember it? I've been living it ever since, whatever chance I get."

Anthony rolled his eyes. "Was it ever gossiped about outside your family? Did anyone mention it to you, or—"

"Don't be daft. My father would have had their heads. He spent a vast deal of money and pulled a great many strings to keep it hushed up. Don't you remember how obsessive he was about keeping up appearances?"

"Yes." Anthony stared off across the field. "As was mine." It still made no sense that Madeline had known of the bacchanal. He'd never heard a whiff of scandal about it in Chertsey.

It was possible the servants had talked, and God knows villagers loved to chatter. Still, with Madeline being so reticent to reveal things, who was to say she hadn't lied about that?

His eyes narrowed. There was one way to find out. Nitrous oxide had the interesting effect of making one more honest, if not terribly coherent. Though everyone reacted differently, he might learn more if she were under the influence.

All he'd have to do is convince her to indulge, perhaps after the party was over and the guests were gone. How hard could that be?

Chapter Fourteen

Dear Cousin,

*It seems my "impressionable young girls" have
been secretly reading a book that explains physical
relations between the sexes. Miss Prescott confiscated
it, but I daresay any minor flirtation they witnessed
between the viscount and his former paramour
pales by comparison. I swear, sometimes girls can be
frightening.*

Your alarmed relation,
Charlotte

No indulging in the nitrous oxide at the party tonight.

Madeline decided that much after three days of Anthony's odd behavior at school and a day at home dealing with her father.

Anthony clearly had some plan up his sleeve, something beyond seduction. Another woman might have been lulled into complacency by his gentlemanly behavior since the outing, but not Madeline. She didn't trust him one whit.

Well, not much, anyway. All right, so he could be rather ... wonderful at times. During their spirited discussions about science, he never dismissed her opinions as those of a "mere woman." He showed her the utmost respect around her pupils. And his behavior to the girls was downright admirable—gentle but not weak, firm but not harsh. Miss Dalton would be very lucky to have him for a guardian. He'd even found a cook for the school.

A pity that he excelled at being a rakehell. And that even his rakish qualities appealed to her. She would have to be very careful not to land in his bed, especially since she'd spent the last three days reliving that cursed lesson in seduction.

She wasn't fool enough to let the man seduce her again. No, indeed. No more kissing, no more caressing . . . no pleasuring him with her hand.

Or her mouth.

With a blush, she reached for the slim volume of harem tales in her apron pocket, the one she'd now read cover to cover. With her blood running hot, she reread the part about a woman bringing a man to "raptures of joy" with her mouth. It sounded absurd—Madeline had never witnessed animals doing such a thing.

Yet the very idea sent a delicious tremor along her spine. Having Anthony reduce *her* to a quivering mass of "rapture" with just his mouth proved it could be done. Also, it would preserve her innocence if she should happen to—

She closed the book with a snap. What was she thinking? She must never attempt such a thing. It could only lead to more recklessness. Besides, she didn't understand how it worked. The dratted book didn't explain the mechanics.

How did a woman fit such a large appendage in her mouth without choking? Why was having his penis in the woman's mouth pleasurable for a man? Yes, a mouth was soft and wet like . . . like a woman's inner passage, but the presence of teeth so very near a man's tender parts couldn't possibly be pleasant. Although Anthony had used *his* teeth to good effect on her own tender parts.

She groaned. Bad enough she spent half of every night replaying what they'd done; she mustn't do it during the day as well.

"This way, sir," came Mrs. Jenkins's voice through the kitchen door, "we've got some nice soup for you."

Madeline shoved the book into her pocket just as Mrs. Jenkins and Papa came through the door.

"I don't want to eat, I tell you," he complained, as Mrs. Jenkins led him to the table. He pulled his arm from her grip. "Leave me be! I'm not hungry."

That was why his clothes hung on him. "Come now, Papa, it's barley soup, your favorite." Madeline ladled it into two chipped china bowls and carried them to the scarred oak table. "And you know how I hate to eat alone."

Scowling, he sat down, gazing into the bowl as if it held the answers to combating his misery.

She glanced over to where Mrs. Jenkins waited in the doorway. As soon as he lifted his spoon, Madeline gave a tiny nod, and the woman slipped out.

"Where's *she* going?" he snapped, taking Madeline by surprise.

"To tidy up," Madeline lied. If he realized that the woman was pressing Madeline's satin evening gown in the adjoining room, her plans would be ruined. He might demand answers, and she'd be forced to reveal the truth.

He glowered down at his soup, then stirred it. "I don't know why you hired that female. She's trying to kill me with all her walking me up and down the road. She always needs something from the costermonger and orders me to go with her."

Madeline was about to say that exercise was good for him, when he lifted his spoon, then froze with it midair as he gazed out the kitchen window. A chill swept over her. His vacant stares were more disturbing than any tantrum.

"Though perhaps she's got the way of it," he said in a faraway voice. "It might be best if I died."

Madeline's stomach roiled. "That's not true, Papa."

His spoon dropped into the bowl. "Your life would be better without me. You could live and work at the school, have some beau to squire you about—"

"Don't be absurd." She grabbed his hand, which lay cold and clammy beneath her fingers. "I'd rather have you alive than any beau."

"It would be so easy to manage," he murmured, still in that eerie voice. "I'd only need some laudanum to mix into my sleeping draught, and I'd slide into—"

"Don't say that, Papa," she hissed, jumping to her feet. The very fact that he would mention laudanum, which he'd always disapproved of, sent her into a panic. "Don't you dare even think it!"

He blinked. Then his gaze met hers, vaguely surprised. "But I am such a trial to you. It would end your suffering. And mine."

"It might end yours, but it would increase mine threefold." Her voice shook as she laid her hand on his shoulder. "Promise me you won't consider laudanum or any other . . ." She couldn't even say it. "Promise me you won't leave me."

He looked as shaken as she felt. "Very well."

"Swear it! Swear you'll never consider such an awful thing."

"I swear," he said, then covered her hand. "I swear, my little Maddie-girl."

Her breath caught at the endearment. He hadn't used it in months. "Good." When he squeezed her hand, then turned to eating his soup, she was able to breathe again. Pray God he kept his word. Anything else was unthinkable.

As she sat beside him again, she said, "This will pass with time, you know."

He grunted in answer.

It *would* pass. With any luck, tonight would signal the beginning of that.

Unfortunately, much as she hated to leave just now, she had no choice. "Papa, I need to go to the school tonight to balance the account books."

She abhorred lying to her father, but he would never let her attend a nitrous oxide party, no matter what famous chemist she meant to meet there. He would certainly not approve of her going alone with a rakehell like Anthony.

Focusing on her soup, she strove to sound casual. "Mrs. Jenkins will keep you company. I thought it might make a nice change. You can play cards."

He frowned but made no protest. She almost wished he would. But he was too absorbed in his own misery to notice anything odd in her life. Why, he hadn't even asked how she would get home after dark.

The kitchen door cracked open, and Mrs. Jenkins nodded to indicate that the gown awaited her in her bedchamber. Madeline rose and took the bowls to the washbasin.

"You didn't eat your soup," Papa said. "Are you well?"

The question was so much like his old self that tears stung her eyes. She flashed him a watery smile. "I'm just not very hungry." She walked to the door. "Why don't you come sit by the fire in the parlor? I have to pack my satchel."

With a mute nod, he followed her. Once he was settled in his comfy chair, she knew she could safely leave him. He would sit staring for some time.

As soon as she entered her room, she and Mrs. Jenkins sprang into action. They peeled off her day gown, then got her into the golden satin gown she'd brought from Telford.

As Mrs. Jenkins began to fasten it up, Madeline said, "I appreciate your coming this afternoon to help me prepare for tonight and look after Papa. I know you probably went to some trouble to arrange it."

"Nonsense, what else would I be doing of a Saturday? It's not as if I have suitors beating down my door, dearie." Mrs. Jenkins fastened the last hook. "I'm pleased you're finally attending a social affair, even if it *is* only a fellow teacher's party. But if your friend can introduce you to Sir Humphry, it will be worth it."

"Indeed it will." If Mrs. Jenkins knew that the "fellow teacher" was a notorious rakehell, she would worry, but Madeline dared not take the widow too much into her confidence.

Mrs. Jenkins puffed out the cap sleeves. "Now, that's lovely, isn't it?"

As the widow dressed her hair in the simple chignon they'd agreed upon, with sprigs of white lilac blooms interspersed, Madeline stared at her best dinner gown in the mirror. Her heart sank. It was almost *too* lovely. Of course she must dress appropriately for Anthony's circle of friends, but she did wish she owned a gown a bit less . . . provocative.

Odd how she'd never thought of this gown that way before. Though it was cut low enough to show her bosom quite effectively, that differed little from most evening gowns. Indeed, her only ball gown was cut exactly the same. She'd worn both of them without a thought in Telford.

But now she knew how dangerously thrilling it was to have a man admire her breasts, first with his gaze and then with his touch. Now she knew Anthony.

"What time is your friend's carriage calling for you?" Mrs. Jenkins carefully laid Madeline's French cloak about her head and shoulders, completely encasing her in black glazed cotton.

"In half an hour. But it's not coming here. I'm meeting it on the outskirts of town. I didn't want Papa to be suspicious of why I'm not walking to the school."

Aside from not wanting anyone in town, including Mrs. Jenkins, to know that she was going out alone with a man, she didn't want to risk Anthony's meeting Papa. Ever. There was a chance that Anthony might recognize him, and Papa would certainly recognize Anthony's name if she had to introduce them.

"That's probably wise. You don't want to get your father's hopes up about Sir Humphry. Still, what about when you return?"

"He'll be asleep by then, and I'll have my friend leave me here." Actually, she intended to slip out of the party without Anthony's knowledge and take a hackney home.

It would cost her dear, but at least she'd keep her secret.

"Well, if you're walking to the edge of town," Mrs. Jenkins pointed out, "then you'll need pattens with your cloak. Can't have you dirtying up your pretty shoes before you get there. I'll go lay them outside, so your father won't see."

Before Mrs. Jenkins could leave, Madeline squeezed her hand warmly. "You don't know how much I appreciate the trouble you go to for me and Papa."

"Nonsense, it hasn't been a bit of trouble, dearie." With a kind smile, Mrs. Jenkins squeezed her hand back. "Besides, I never had children of my own to fuss over. This is the next best thing."

Tears clouded Madeline's vision as she remembered Mama's fussing over her.

"None of that now," Mrs. Jenkins clucked. "You just go off to your party and don't be worrying about us. Your father and I will play cards until he dozes off, and I'll make sure he doesn't notice if you come in late. We'll be fine, I swear it."

Madeline hoped so. Because tonight might be her one chance to change everything. And no matter what, she meant to make good use of it.

Chapter Fifteen

Dear Charlotte,

    *Yes, girls can be a trial. So I hope you know what
you're doing by having Lord Norcourt at your school.
What little I've heard of the man makes me wonder if
he is capable of behaving himself around any woman.
How did he acquit himself during your outing?*

         Your concerned cousin,
         Michael

As the hackney sped toward Richmond, anticipation
built in Anthony's chest. Three days of hell were near an
end. He'd acted the consummate gentleman with Madeline, he'd danced to Mrs. Harris's tune, he'd given their
girls lesson after lesson, and he'd arranged Madeline's
damned party. Now he deserved a reward.

Madeline. At last she would be his.

She'd as much as said so at Godwin's. And even if she
came to the party determined to resist him, that would
last only until he got her alone and kissed her. Her natural
sensuality would lead her right to his bed.

Then perhaps he could return to being himself, to
seeing her as merely a lover. Perhaps he could return to
when he didn't crave the sight of her, didn't wonder how

she would respond to someone's idiotic comment at a party . . . didn't consider whether she'd approve of the renovations at his ancestral manor.

Good God, he sounded like a besotted fool. But it would end tonight. It must.

Jerking the curtain open, he scanned the roadside for the curve near the school where Madeline was supposed to meet him, with two oaks marking the spot. And there she was, emerging from beneath the sheltering trees.

Swathed in a voluminous black cloak, she awaited him nervously. But beneath the cloak's hem peeped a pair of pattens attached to evening slippers, and just that glimpse of her formal attire had him wondering what gown she wore, how well it might skim her curves . . . how easy it might be to remove.

A pity they had no time for private enjoyments between here and Stoneville's estate. But tonight . . .

He grinned.

Signaling the coachman to stop, he didn't even wait until it completely halted before leaping out. "May I offer you a ride, good lady?" he said, gesturing to the coach with a courtly flourish.

"Very amusing." Casting a furtive glance up the road, she hurried over. "Let's go quickly, before someone sees me."

"Ah, an intrigue. Are you playing the spy now, sweetheart?"

"You know perfectly well that I must be careful about my reputation. Why do you think I didn't want you fetching me from my house?"

"Because you like to be mysterious?" He helped her into the coach, jumped in behind her, and ordered the coachman off.

"I like to be careful." She settled into the middle of the seat facing forward.

Paying that no mind, he pushed in beside her. When her gaze shot to him, blazing high, he simply bent his head and kissed her.

After only a moment's stiffness, she softened, melting beneath his lips, opening her mouth to the plunges of his tongue. But when he undid the ties of her cloak, she tore her lips free. "We can't do anything like that now."

"I only want to see what you're wearing. To make sure it's acceptable."

Though she looked skeptical, she let him push the cloak from her shoulders and her coiffure. The setting sun filtered through the curtains to reveal a gown of shimmering golden satin cut low enough to reveal the dainty swells of her breasts.

His pulse thundering, he bent to kiss her again, but she pulled back. "Your note to me yesterday said you would tell me in the coach what to expect tonight."

Damnation. She was right—he did have much to say to prepare her. With a frustrated sigh, he sat back against the seat. "We're going to a friend of mine's estate—the Marquess of Stoneville."

"Lord Stoneville is our host?" she queried, a note of panic in her voice.

"You know him?"

"I know *of* him. Everyone does. He's even more notorious than you are." Her lips tightened into a thin line. "You said this wouldn't be one of *those* parties."

"It's not. But he was the only person I could browbeat into giving it on such short notice." When alarm deepened on her face, he added, "For God's sake, you've nothing to worry about. There won't be any cavorting females."

She searched his face. "If there are, I'll walk out. I swear I will."

"Don't you trust me?" he said lightly, though the answer meant more to him than he'd like.

"Should I?"

Her eyes shone so luminously he could easily lose himself in their depths. That would be unwise. He must resist the sweetness offered by those beautiful eyes.

"Of course. I'm unlikely to do anything to anger the only person who can get Tessa into Mrs. Harris's school."

A pained smile touched her lips. "I forgot about that."

"I didn't." It was the only thing keeping him from letting his randy bad boy loose right now to ravish her. Their bargain had to be finished first, so she could never accuse him of reneging. "You needn't worry about the guests. Stoneville invited several respectable men of science, along with our usual friends who enjoy indulging. You'll have a healthy sample of subjects to observe."

She smoothed her cloak. "And . . . er . . . what do they know about *my* attendance? Surely you didn't allow your friend to mention my name."

His eyes narrowed. "Why? Are you afraid a guest might recognize it?"

"No!" Her gaze shot to his. "I'm sure I can safely say I've never met any of your friends. But I don't want word getting back to Mrs. Harris—"

"Of course." He relaxed. "You needn't worry. I told Stoneville you're my bluestocking cousin, who wanted to see a more exciting part of London life while in town. He thinks you're married to a parson and visiting friends."

She stared at him quizzically. "Why have me married to a parson?"

"Have you something against parsons?"

"Well, no, but . . . it's just odd." She mused a moment. "Do I have a name?"

"I didn't give him one. But I was thinking Brayham, my maternal grandmother's maiden name. My mother's side of the family is less well-known, so any cousin from there would be harder to trace."

Curiosity leaped in her face. "You never mention your mother."

"You never mention yours, either."

"That's because she died two years ago of consumption."

So Foxmoor had been right. "Mine died when I was eight."

"That must have been difficult," she said, her voice soft with sympathy.

A lump lodged in his throat. How odd. It had been a long time since that age-old grief had arisen. It disturbed him that Madeline was the only one to rouse it.

He attempted to sound nonchalant. "I imagine it's harder to lose your mother after you've had her for so many years. You have more to regret, more to miss."

"Perhaps. But a boy of eight needs his mother far more than a full-grown woman needs hers." When that made the lump in his throat thicken so much he couldn't speak, she added, "Do you remember much about her?"

"A few things. Her scent." He smiled. "She used to chew on cinnamon sticks for her breath, and the spicy smell would waft over me whenever she—" He broke off before he could reveal how much he still missed her.

"Whenever she what?" Madeline prodded.

She wasn't going to let this go, was she? "Whenever she hugged me. Father disapproved of how she coddled me, said she hugged me too much." Idly, he rubbed his wrist. "My aunt and uncle agreed."

"You can never hug a child too much."

Her fierce tone startled him, then made something uncurl deep inside him that had lain tightly coiled for years. Damnation, he couldn't have her crawling so far under his skin.

"You might need a Christian name tonight, too," he said, the words terse from his haste to change the subject.

She cast him one last tender look before turning her face to the window. "Fine, then I'm . . . Cherry."

He followed her gaze to a stand of cherry trees they were passing. "Thank God we weren't driving by shrubbery. I couldn't have called you Viburnum and kept my countenance." When she eyed him askance, he added, "You do mean it to be short for Charity, right? I've never heard of anyone named Cherry."

"It's no worse than Kitty," she said archly.

"No, I suppose not." He dearly loved her being jealous. It showed she wasn't as immune to his charms as she pretended. "But we'll call you Mrs. John Brayham if Stoneville is forced to introduce you."

"Why would Lord Stoneville be introducing me?"

"I have to stay out of sight, remember? That's why we're arriving at the party early. I'm not taking the chance that my uncle will hear of this and use it against me to prove I'm still set in my old ways."

"I forgot about that. So Lord Stoneville will be my

escort for the party." She looked decidedly uneasy about that.

He didn't blame her. "I don't like it either, but I warned Stoneville that he must treat you with the respect due my cousin. Besides, you're not his sort. He prefers women with less brains than br—" He broke off, cursing his quick tongue.

"Than breasts?" she finished for him. "Many men do. Are you sure you don't share his preference?" Her smile was teasing. Her eyes were not.

"I might have, once." He let his gaze rake her with a thoroughness that left no doubt of his desire for her body. "But people do change," he murmured as he took her gloved hand in his, then pressed a kiss to the back of it.

He was rewarded by the trembling of her hand, which prompted him to turn it over and kiss her palm, then her wrist, frustrated by the kid shielding her bare flesh from fingertip to elbow. God, he couldn't wait until the party was over and he could get her out of her clothes.

Though her breath quickened at his kisses, she slipped her hand from his. "You said something about *if* your friend is 'forced' to introduce me. Why wouldn't he introduce me?"

"I told him to avoid it as much as possible. The fewer people you meet, the less chance of Mrs. Harris hearing about your presence at the party."

She stared at him. "But I have to know who my subjects are. I can't report on my observations without that."

Wariness stiffened his spine. "What do you mean?"

"If I write an article and expect it to be published, men of science will want details. They'll have to confirm what

I observed. They'll need witnesses. And since *you* can't be my witness—"

"You may not mention a single guest's name in your damned article, do you understand?" His blood chilled at the very thought.

Her lips thinned. "Why not, if they're all men of science?"

"You know perfectly well that such parties are considered scandalous, even laughable these days. My friends have already had enough fun poked at them over their use of the gas. I don't want them enduring more because you use their names in some article." As an odd panic spread over her face, he forced a smile. "Can't you just call them Subjects A and B?"

"I'll still need to record somewhere who Subjects A and B are, so that someone can confirm my methods if anyone doubts my conclusions."

"That isn't acceptable," he bit out. "Observe whatever you wish, write down whatever you wish, as long as you're discreet about it. But no going around at the party seeking introductions to the guests. If anyone starts digging too deeply into who 'Mrs. Brayham' is, we could both be sunk. Understood?"

An icy smile froze her lips. "Certainly, Lord Norcourt."

Lord Norcourt indeed. *Certainly* was probably her code for *I'll do whatever I damned well please, and you just try to stop me.* Which he couldn't manage since he had to cool his heels somewhere else during the party. He'd have to warn Stoneville to keep an eye on her.

Though he sure as the devil didn't like that idea either.

He liked it even less once they arrived and her cloak was taken. The shimmering satin clung as she walked, teasing him with hints of the lovely form beneath, and the delicate curls at the nape of her eloquent neck roused the urge to run his tongue down the sweet ridge of her spine. For a woman of such small stature and such little opportunity to buy fashionable attire, she had an uncanny ability to look ravishing.

And ravish her was just what Stoneville would want to do the minute he saw her. Indeed, as soon as they were shown into the man's study, Stoneville rose with a wolfish grin. It was all Anthony could do not to glare while making the introductions.

When Stoneville stepped forward to take her hand, the rogue not only used the opportunity to kiss it but to scan her attributes as he straightened. It was a technique Anthony had used many a time in the past, but watching Stoneville use it on *her* made him want to throttle the man.

Good God, what was wrong with him? He couldn't be jealous, could he?

He might not have encountered the emotion before, but he recognized it now. And he didn't like it. Not one whit.

"In your description of your cousin, Norcourt, you said she was 'pretty enough,'" Stoneville drawled. "Pretty enough for whom? A king? An emperor? A god?"

Before Anthony could tell him exactly what to do with his lavish flatteries, Madeline let out a laugh. "Do women usually respond favorably to such exaggerations, sir?"

"Depends on how much wine they've drunk." Stoneville flashed her one of his patented bedroom glances, and Anthony had to forcibly restrain himself from rushing over to pummel the man.

"Well," she said sweetly, "I don't know if it's my lack of

intoxication or just simple good sense, but I find that men who exaggerate in their compliments tend to exaggerate in nearly everything else. As a woman of science, I prefer men who speak the unvarnished truth."

Stoneville blinked, clearly taken aback by the reasoned response emerging from so pretty a woman. "She really is a bluestocking, isn't she?" he told Anthony.

"And my cousin," Anthony stressed. "Which means I expect you to behave."

"I always do," Stoneville said with a small smile that was none too reassuring. "Depending on one's definition of 'behave,' of course."

"Stoneville—" Anthony began in a warning tone.

"Don't fret yourself. It will be fine." A clamor outside the house made Stoneville glance at the clock. "I should greet my guests. Since you can't attend the party, Norcourt, I've arranged for you to sit in here. No one will enter my private study, and besides, I'll give you a key, so you can lock the door. You know where to find the brandy, and there's books if you wish to read. Will that suit you?"

"It'll do."

"Excellent. Then I'll come back to fetch Mrs. Brayham—" Stoneville began.

"I'd rather go with you now." Madeline hurried to Stoneville's side.

"You can't," Anthony put in, irritated by her transparent desire to be with Stoneville as he greeted the guests, so she could take note of their names. And after he'd forbidden it, too. "The only way to preserve your anonymity is if you wait to join the party until everyone begins to be inebriated. If you stand at Stoneville's side when the guests enter, he'll have to introduce you." As she well knew.

Stoneville offered her his arm. "Then I'll tuck her away in the kitchens so she can speak to the chemist to learn how nitrate of ammonia is turned into the desired gas. Once most of the guests are here, I'll fetch her."

The disappointment on her face was so palpable, Anthony knew he'd guessed right.

"You could fetch her from here," Anthony pointed out.

"Oh, but I'd like to meet the chemist," she said hastily. "I'd like to find out how the nitrous oxide is made."

More likely she wanted to sneak out to learn their friends' names, and he couldn't stop her—especially with Stoneville ignoring his admonitions. He'd just have to make sure she showed her article to him before she got it published.

Stoneville offered Madeline his arm, and Anthony forced himself to resist the urge to whisk her off to the hackney before anything could happen to her. She wanted this, after all. He was being foolish to worry.

Nonetheless, as he watched them leave, he realized he couldn't just sit here reading and drinking brandy while she was at the party with Stoneville.

He'd wait until everyone was fully involved in their entertainment, then he'd move about on the outskirts and keep an eye on her. What with the servants making the rounds to provide fresh bags of nitrous and the poor light and the general confusion that nitrous caused in imbibers, no one would notice one man in the shadows.

Better not let Stoneville see you, or he'll torment you end-lessly. He'll say you're acting more like a jealous husband than a cousin.

Husband? Nonsense.

Yet as he waited, the idea of Madeline as his wife rose

up to tempt him. Yes, he was supposed to marry some virginal chit of appropriate rank from a respectable family, but when had he ever done what he was supposed to? Madeline was the only woman who even came close to thinking as he did. They would never lack for interesting conversation, to be sure.

But marry her? Why her? Why did *she* make him want to abandon his firm resolution about not marrying yet? She was no prettier than other women, possessed of no more charms and graces. Yet something in her peculiar blend of innocence and knowledge stimulated his mind and body like no other. Just when he began to think her incredibly young and naive, she would say something that showed her wise beyond her years. The incongruity of it utterly fascinated him.

That was the trouble—her mysteriousness bewitched him. But that wouldn't last past tonight. Once he'd bedded her, once he'd learned her secrets, he could go back to being detached.

Or so he tried to convince himself as he waited for the party to be in full swing. An hour later, when his obsessive thoughts began to annoy him, he decided to carry on with his plan.

He slipped into the hall, then nearly tripped over a man sitting in the middle. It was his friend Dr. Roget, whose project of grouping words by their types absorbed his every hour these days. Anthony tried to sneak past, but no such luck.

"Norcourt!" Roget said, the words slurred from inhaling the contents of the silk bag he held. "Didn't know you were here."

"I'm not. You're dreaming this."

"Ahh," Roget answered, as if that explained everything. "Quite right."

As Anthony hurried off, he heard Roget mutter, "Don't know why I had to dream about Norcourt. Much rather dream about some pretty filly."

Though Anthony doubted that Roget would remember the incident later, it served as a warning to him to be careful. And it left a bad taste in his mouth for other reasons that became apparent the moment he got a good view of the first room filled with guests.

Usually by this time Anthony was well intoxicated himself. Unlike some, his experience of the gas tended to be mild and benign—a pleasant sense of well-being, some laughing, and thoughts that seemed brilliant until he came to his senses later. Still, it did distort his perceptions, so that he viewed the party through the same rosy lens as everyone else.

The rosy lens was gone now, and for reasons he couldn't quite fathom, it left him staring at a scene he found utterly unnerving. The laughter bore an unnatural quality, and the sight of so many intelligent gentlemen—and ladies—comporting themselves like fools made him wonder how *he* appeared when he indulged. Did he giggle idiotically like that man over there, whom he knew to be a well-respected barrister? Or twitch his legs, like the prominent headmaster in the corner?

After a week teaching schoolgirls, Anthony found the headmaster's behavior particularly disturbing. What if the man's students were to see him acting like a fool? How much harder would it be for them to listen when their headmaster cautioned them against the ills of society?

To his horror, he caught himself wanting to stride over

and lecture the man on responsibility, something he'd never wanted to do in his entire life. Perhaps Stoneville was right. Perhaps he had turned into a prig.

That was absurd. He was plotting Madeline's seduction, wasn't he? That wasn't the behavior of a prig.

Yet he couldn't shake his uneasiness as he skirted the party looking for her and Stoneville. When he found them, he was relieved to see his friend soberly escorting her about the room. She was safe.

Unexpectedly, he felt a desperate wish to join her. They would laugh at the others together, then leave before the nitrous oxide could taint them.

He resisted the fanciful impulse, and not only because she'd be angry at him for cutting short her period of observation. He resisted it because it demonstrated just how thoroughly he craved her.

And that would not do.

Chapter Sixteen

Dear Cousin,

Lord Norcourt behaved more admirably than expected at Mr. Godwin's. Although Lady Tarley took him off with her, he rebuffed her entirely, judging from her annoyance when she rejoined the group alone. I questioned Miss Prescott, who said she'd never seen them together. He returned a while later, which supported her assertion. And why would she lie, anyway? She's as suspicious of the man as I am.

Your anxious relation,
Charlotte

The party had been going on for two hours, and Madeline began to despair of ever finding Sir Humphry. He must be here somewhere—the few names she *had* managed to learn belonged either to his friends or members of the Royal Society.

Clearly this wasn't the first time most had attended such an event. As if it were their everyday practice, they took their silk bags off the trays and sucked the wooden mouthpieces with cool aplomb. Most sat in chairs or reclined on the many cushions strewn about. Early on, Lord Stoneville had explained that the gas could make one insensible of one's body, so the safest way to inhale it was while seated.

She'd read Sir Humphry's book and the different accounts his friends had given of their experiences with nitrous oxide, but that still hadn't prepared her for the wide variety of reactions. Some guests lapsed into a near swoon, their faces spread in beatific smiles. Others seemed unable to stop laughing. A few even danced, capering into walls. It was like observing a madhouse peopled with well-dressed gentry.

The few females present appeared to be wives of other guests, but their experiences seemed no different from the men's. One lapsed into a fit of giggles. Another exclaimed about the "music, the glorious music."

Normally, Madeline would be rapidly scribbling notes, asking questions, recording what she witnessed. But scientific observation wasn't her aim tonight.

Unfortunately, Lord Stoneville was making it very difficult for her to *achieve* her aim. He hadn't left her side after fetching her from the kitchen. Worse yet, he'd taken very seriously Anthony's admonition not to introduce her to anyone, and the rules of society meant that people couldn't introduce themselves.

Under normal circumstances, anyone curious about her would simply beg an introduction from the marquess, but the guests were too single-minded in their desire to imbibe the gas to pay her much mind. And if anyone did venture near, Lord Stoneville's frigid manner put them off.

By now they probably assumed she was his paramour. She didn't really care, since the likelihood of her seeing these people again was remote. But she did care that she hadn't reached her goal.

So she took a different tack. If she couldn't meet the guests, she could at least find out who they were. Then, once she discovered Sir Humphry, she would introduce herself, society's rules be damned.

She began questioning the marquess about the guests, careful not to sound too nosy. Since she had to intersperse her queries with polite conversation, it was a painfully slow process. It took another half an hour to identify only six men.

"That fellow looks interesting," Madeline said casually to her too-attentive escort. "Is he a good friend of yours?" She nodded toward a gray-haired fellow who could be Sir Humphry's age. Soberly dressed, the man with the pointed chin and full lips was sprawled on a settee, where he kept up a conversation with a thin, red-faced gentleman between shallow puffs from their silk nitrous oxide bags.

"I know him well enough."

Drat it, why wouldn't he give her a name? "Is he famous?" she said in a breathy voice meant to sound like that of a typical provincial visitor to London. "Would I have heard of him?"

Lord Stoneville cast her a searching glance. "Perhaps. That is Mr. Coleridge and his friend Sir Josiah Wedgwood. As a woman of learning, you might have heard of Mr. Coleridge—he writes poetry. And Sir Josiah—"

"Is a potter. Yes, I know." Although they'd participated in Sir Humphry's initial experiments, they could hardly help her with Papa's problem. The opinions of a poet and a potter wouldn't sway Sir Randolph and the vicar.

"Shall I introduce you?" Lord Stoneville asked.

Her gaze shot to him, the unexpected question making her wary. Why offer to introduce these particular men and why now?

The marquess was clearly up to something. She'd best

proceed with caution. "Lord Norcourt thinks meeting people would be dangerous for my reputation."

"Ah, there *is* that. Norcourt doesn't want the parson to hear any gossip. Wouldn't want your husband finding out how exciting your trip really was."

"Exactly. My cousin knows Mr. Brayham wouldn't approve."

They wandered into a smaller room, where the light was so dim that some guests had nodded off. Out of the corner of her eye, she saw someone pass a nearby doorway, but when she glanced over, he—or she—was gone.

It was probably a footman. They were everywhere, waiting to replace the guests' empty bags.

"Your poor husband," Lord Stoneville said as they strolled the room. "He must hate being left alone in— Where did you say you were from?"

"I didn't say."

"Oh yes, I forgot—it was Norcourt who said you hail from Kent," Stoneville remarked in a deceptively casual tone.

She tensed. She didn't know what Anthony had told his friend, but she doubted he'd have invented something so specific. "I can't imagine why he would say that. He knows perfectly well where I live."

Lord Stoneville searched her face. "I must have misunderstood."

She forced a smile. "You must have."

"Or perhaps I simply forgot what he told me. He brings so many beautiful women into our circle, you know. It's hard to keep them straight."

Though her heart raced madly, she fixed him with a cold glance. "I'm sure that's true. But I'm his cousin, not one of those women. That should make it easy."

"Oh, don't worry, Mrs. Brayham. I shan't forget *you* for quite some time."

What did *that* mean? Did Lord Stoneville even believe Anthony's story? She began to think he might not.

Shifting her gaze to the reclining guests, she said casually, "I notice you aren't partaking of the gas yourself. I should hate to think that squiring me around is preventing you from enjoying your party."

"Hardly. Your presence is intoxicating enough to satisfy me."

She rolled her eyes. "Spare me your flatteries, sir. I'm no green girl."

"Odd, then, that Norcourt thinks he must protect you from everyone."

"He's only behaving like a cousin."

"A kissing cousin, perhaps."

Her blood slowed to sludge in her veins. She leveled him with a chastening glance. "Why on earth would you say such a thing about a parson's wife?"

The marquess looked decidedly unrepentant. "Because I've never seen Norcourt want to throttle me just for flirting with a woman. It smacks of jealousy, and one isn't generally jealous of one's cousin, is one?"

She fought to keep her voice even. "He's protective, that's all."

"Yet he brought you to a nitrous oxide party and left you to me."

"Because I begged him to."

"And he complied, even though he has sworn off such things. Even though he refuses to attend himself. Very strange behavior, wouldn't you say?"

"Not at all. He's merely trying to please me."

"I'm sure he is. But no one tries that hard to please a relation, and certainly not Norcourt. He's behaving like a man being forced to a woman's will."

The comment hit too close to comfort. "Pray tell me, how on earth would I force a man of Lord Norcourt's position to my will?"

"I haven't yet figured that out. But I would guess it has something to do with his determination to have you in his bed."

She released his arm, the sudden clamor in her chest making it hard for her to breathe. "For shame, sir," she said, trying to sound outraged instead of defensive. "I know such shocking talk is de rigueur in your circles, but I shan't tolerate it."

His expression was as stony as his name. "Nicely done, madam." He leaned close. "You almost sound like a parson's wife. Just not enough to convince me."

"I was unaware that I had to convince you of anything. Now, if you don't mind, I'd prefer the company of complete strangers to that of a man who apparently thinks me a deceiver." With that, she walked away, hoping that her affronted mien would keep him from following.

It was a foolish hope. As she picked her way through the murmuring, half-slumbering guests lying or sitting on the floor, the marquess followed her at a leisurely pace. "Does Norcourt know that you're looking for someone here?"

Her heart skipped a beat.

"I've been watching you all night. You scan every face, take note of every name spoken. And your questions aren't those of a disinterested observer."

"I know no one in this area," she said, fighting for calm. "Who could I possibly be looking for?"

"It's just a theory."

"A ridiculous theory." And if she didn't squelch it, she would get no more information out of him. "Why don't you talk to your chemist? He'll tell you how many questions I asked *him* about the properties of nitrous oxide."

"Yet you've shown no interest in trying it yourself."

She blinked. "What?"

"The nitrous. You have yet to ask for a bag."

"Neither have you."

His black devil's eyes glittered. "I'm the host. I must keep my wits about me. But you've no need to do so. And I would think your keen interest in scientific matters would make you eager to inhale some."

The truth was, she'd inhaled nitrous oxide years ago under the careful supervision of her father, who'd always been willing to further her store of knowledge. The effects had been minimal. But she could hardly tell Lord Stoneville that, because it would unleash a whole slew of questions about who she was. Nitrous oxide wasn't that easy to come by, after all.

"I can witness its effects in your guests," she hedged. "I don't need to experience them for myself."

"But it does seem a shame for you to go to so much trouble to attend a nitrous oxide party and then not have the main experience. Wouldn't you say?"

He had a point, and the more she denied him, the more suspicious he would become. She had to allay his suspicions before he voiced them to Anthony.

Perhaps she *should* inhale some. Given her experience last time, it shouldn't cause any harm. And since the effects were notoriously short in duration, a few puffs should satisfy him. Indeed, if she pretended to be under the influence longer than she was, she might question him about the guests with impunity.

And this time she'd ask about Sir Humphry. "You're right." She smiled sweetly at her tormentor. "I really should try it if I'm to form any reasonable opinion. But only if you try it with me." Yes, that would be even better. Then he might not remember her questions at all.

The smile playing about his lips was decidedly unnerving. "Very well." He offered her his arm. "Let's go to the library. Nitrous tends to amplify sounds—it can be uncomfortable in too noisy a room."

True, but his reason for wanting to go to the library probably had more to do with privacy than noise. And given her own aims, privacy might be wise for her as well. She didn't need anyone overhearing her questions about his friends.

She tucked her hand in the crook of his elbow. "Lead on, sir."

Lord Stoneville snagged two bags as they passed a footman. Moments later, they left the crowded drawing room to head down a long gallery. When they reached the end, he ushered her into a dimly lit room lined with bookcases.

He started to close the door, but she said firmly, "No, leave it open. I'm a married woman, remember?"

Though annoyance flicked in his eyes, he shrugged and led her to a couch. After they were seated, he handed her a bag, then took the stopper off, holding his finger over the opening. "Start with a few shallow puffs to get yourself used to it."

She did, making sure he put *his* bag to his lips as well. Like last time, she felt nothing, no strange visions, none of the "thrill" to the "extremities" that Sir Humphry had described in his book. She might have been disappointed . . . if not for the fact that she needed to keep her mind clear.

"Well?" he asked after her fourth small puff.

"It's interesting," she said evasively.

"Interesting? Try it again."

She put the mouthpiece to her lips. Without warning, he squeezed the bag, forcing her to inhale a larger amount.

"*Now* tell me what you think."

"I . . . I think it's fine." The word ended on a giggle. That was most strange.

She glanced over to see how he reacted to the gas, but he wasn't taking in any nitrous. Or she didn't think he was. It was hard to think when a strange warmth was spreading through her limbs, down her belly, into her *mons*, which felt hot, very hot. Her chest seemed to expand, grow heavy, as if filling up with the gas.

Wait, was she still breathing it in? She hadn't meant to. Had she?

White spots appeared before her eyes, beautiful, glorious white spots. They danced like little fairies, making her giggle.

Then the white spots formed a face, which loomed closer. "Tell me, Mrs. Brayham," Lord Stoneville asked, "are you really married to a parson?"

A parson! She laughed. Why would she marry a parson? They were dull fellows, who often disapproved of science. "I . . . I don't recall. But I don't think so." Was she supposed to say that aloud? It seemed wrong somehow.

The looming face smiled broadly. "His cousin, eh? You're Norcourt's new mistress. I knew he couldn't keep up his façade. He's a rakehell to the bone."

"Oh, yes," she agreed, thinking of how Anthony had

made her feel in the garden pavilion. It was rather like she felt now—warm and tingly. Very, very warm and tingly. Although she didn't like that her head tingled. That was odd.

She splayed her free hand through her curls in an attempt to stop the tingling, but that only dislodged her pins, making her hair tumble down. "Oops!" She giggled, and then, fascinated by the sound of it, giggled again.

"All that rot he spun me about preserving your reputation," Lord Stoneville said. "You probably wheedled this party out of him by promising to do something naughty."

"No. No-o-o-o." The long, low sound of the drawn-out word fascinated her, so she kept repeating it. "No no no no. No thing naughty. No thing. Nothing." Why, *no thing* and *nothing* were the same words. What an important realization!

Apparently its huge significance didn't occur to her new friend. "Nothing naughty, eh?" he murmured. "Methinks the lady doth protest too much."

When had he moved up next to her?

"And why did you persuade Norcourt to give you this party in the first place?" Lord Stoneville continued. "Who are you looking for? Who are you using him to get to?"

She *was* looking for someone, wasn't she? "The chemist!" she said cheerily. No, the chemist had a name. Hummy? Sir Humph? Didn't seem quite right.

"It's not the damned chemist," he growled, pushing the nitrous bag from her lips. "You already talked to the chemist, for God's sake."

He forced her chin up so she stared into his face. Lord Stoneville had a very cold face. How had she not noticed before?

"I want to know who you're looking for here." He shook her by the shoulders, further dislodging her coiffure. "Tell me, damn you!"

A figure appeared in the library doorway, with menacing shadows shrouding his face. It roused fear in her chest until the candlelight caught his features, and she recognized him. "Anthony!" She was *so* very glad to see him.

"No, not Anthony—" Lord Stoneville began.

"Let go of her!" Anthony demanded.

The marquess stilled, then twisted around to watch Anthony stride into the room. "You were supposed to stay in my study."

"Why, so you could seduce my cousin?" Anthony snapped as he hauled Stoneville up from the couch.

Stoneville shoved him away. "I'm not seducing her, you smitten fool. And she's not your cousin either, as you well know. Whoever she is, she's using you. I'm only trying to find out why."

"By forcing nitrous on her?" Anthony shouted, making Madeline wince.

"I didn't force it. She wanted to try it. She said so. Ask her yourself."

Who did they mean? Madeline could hear what they said, but it didn't make sense. The words jumbled up into nonsense once they reached her brain. She shook her head to clear it of nitrous, but that only made her dizzy, and she swayed forward.

Anthony hurried to catch her, then urged her back onto the couch. "Be still, Madeline." His eyes mirrored his concern. "Wait until the intoxication passes."

"Anthony." The name was like a talisman, bringing a smile to her lips. "I feel . . . I feel . . ." Warm, now that he

was here. Content. Oh, how to describe the perfect pleasure that surged through her at his touch? "It's so . . ."

"I know, sweetheart." Anthony brushed her hair from
her face. "Shh, now."

She nodded, perfectly happy to do what he said. She
liked Anthony. Unlike Lord Stoneville, who stank of
brandy, Anthony smelled like sweet Russian oil. When he
looked at her with his kind eyes . . . she heard bells tinkling . . . tingling . . .

She giggled at the rhyme she'd made.

"Can't you see she's in no condition to answer your
questions, Stoneville?" Anthony cupped her face tenderly.
"Or mine."

"On the contrary, she's in exactly the right condition,"
the marquess said. "Let me give her a bit more nitrous, and
she'll tell you whatever you need to learn. Then you'll see
that she's here under false pretenses."

"I know that already, damn it." Anthony shifted her
to sit more comfortably on the couch. "At the moment, I
don't care. And yes, I know she's using me."

"To do what?"

"I . . . it doesn't matter. Anyway, it's none of your concern!"

"You don't know why, do you? Well, it *is* my concern
when she's in my house asking about *my* friends." Leaning over Anthony's shoulder, Lord Stoneville put the bag
of nitrous to her lips and squeezed, forcing her to inhale
more gas.

"Stop that!" Anthony ripped the bag away and tossed it
aside. "Come, sweetheart, we're leaving."

No, leaving seemed . . . wrong, very wrong. Even
through the haze of her thoughts, she knew there was a
reason she was here. What was the reason again?

Ah yes. "Can't leave," she mumbled. "Can't. Not yet. Not till I meet Sir Humph. Free. Sir Humphry."

"Davy?" she heard Lord Stoneville say through the encroaching fog in her brain. "The chemist, of course! That's what she was trying to tell me, who she's been looking for all night. I knew she was here for someone. She probably brought you here so she could find him since she couldn't get to him otherwise."

"What would she want with Sir Humphry?" Anthony asked.

"I don't know. Perhaps his wife isn't paranoid after all, and he *has* been seducing his female admirers. He could be her lover—wouldn't surprise me."

"No!" she cried as she tried to rise. She didn't have a lover.

"Stay there, Madeline." Anthony pressed her back onto the couch, then turned to glare at Stoneville. "Go back to your guests. It's my problem."

"Can't you see she's making a fool of you?"

"Get out!" Anthony roared. "Leave us, damn you!"

"Fine," the marquess retorted. "But you're a bloody besotted idiot if you let her twist you about her finger."

"Better than being an arse," Anthony muttered under his breath, as Lord Stoneville headed for the door.

She watched the marquess disappear through the doorway. He couldn't go yet—he hadn't introduced her to Sir Humphry. "Wait! Come back!"

Frantic to catch him, she stumbled to her feet. Then crumpled to the floor.

"Madeline!" cried an anxious voice floating above her somewhere.

That was the last thing she remembered.

Chapter Seventeen

Dear Charlotte,
   *Do not misunderstand—you and Miss Prescott
may fancy yourselves good judges of character, but
men of this sort can be very deceptive. And Miss
Prescott is young, exactly the kind of woman a
rakehell feeds on. She could easily be misled if you do
not keep a tight rein on her.*

                    Your suspicious cousin,
                    Michael

*A*nthony gazed about him in a panic as he cradled
Madeline in his arms. Her reaction wasn't unusual, especially the first time. Some people had a ringing in the ears
or spots in the vision, while others occasionally swooned.
And once in a while, someone reacted very badly—

No, he wouldn't even think it. That wasn't going to happen to her!

He started to lay her on the couch, then hesitated when
sounds from the party filtered in from the gallery. He
didn't have the key to lock the door. No one was at this end
just now, but the last thing he needed was to be discovered
lurking in Stoneville's library with an insensible woman.
Madeline would certainly not want to risk that herself.

As he stood there undecided, she turned into his chest and mumbled something, sending relief coursing through his veins. She was regaining consciousness. But she needed a safe place to recover. Somewhere private, where he could get to the bottom of her tale.

The back stairs to the guest bedchambers lay mere feet away. No one would be up there for hours. Not even Stoneville would think to look for her there.

Swiftly, he carried her up, his heart lurching to see her lying so pale and still in his arms. And he'd thought to use nitrous to get the truth out of her? He must have been mad. He still wanted to pummel Stoneville to a bloody pulp for doing it, mostly because another notorious effect of nitrous was to act as an aphrodisiac.

Not that Stoneville had intended to seduce her. Apparently the marquess really had been trying to determine Madeline's true aims. But that didn't assuage Anthony's anger, not when he remembered Stoneville shaking her until her—

"Anthony?" she croaked out as her eyelids fluttered open. "My head hurts."

Not surprising. Some people did suffer from headaches a short while after inhaling nitrous. "It'll pass, sweetheart," he said soothingly. "I promise."

Having reached the next floor, he charged through the first open doorway. He laid her on the bed, then went out to the hall to fetch a candle. When he returned, he closed the door, shooting the bolt to so they wouldn't be disturbed.

"What . . . what happened?" Her lovely amber eyes followed him as he circulated the room lighting the other candles from his.

"You fainted." He paused by the bed to look at her, then caught his breath at the sight of her displayed so deliciously on the coverlet. Her gown had fallen off one shoulder, revealing a more-than-generous swell of bosom, and her legs were parted, the satin outlining each thigh in loving detail. He'd had no idea her hair was so long and thick. It spread out beneath her like a pool of golden silk lapping at her body. The body he wanted desperately to ravage.

The body still recovering from nitrous oxide.

With a curse, he forced himself to abandon the fetching image and head for the fireplace. The fire was already set, so he had only to light a piece of tinder to ignite it. Once it was well and truly started, he returned to her side.

As he tucked a pillow under her head, she gazed up at him. "I fainted?"

"Occasionally that occurs with nitrous."

"Not to me." She looked bewildered. "I mean, when I had it once before . . . it had no such effect."

His blood stilled. She'd certainly never mentioned *that*. "When did you inhale nitrous? Who gave it to you?"

"My father." Sitting up on the bed, she touched her hand to her head.

"Your *father*!" He gaped at her. "How old were you?"

"Nineteen."

"What kind of father lets his daughter experiment with nitrous oxide?"

"The kind who's a physician." She shook her head as if that might untangle her muddled thoughts. "We read . . . Sir Humphry's book, you see."

"No, I don't see." Perhaps Stoneville's speculations about her looking for Sir Humphry hadn't been far from the mark.

He shrugged off that disturbing thought. She'd probably mentioned the chemist in the first place because she knew of him from his book. Then again, how many girls had read that 550-page tome? None, he would wager.

With a frown, she rubbed her temples. "After reading about it, I begged Papa to let me try it. Since he always encouraged my interest in science, he agreed." She lifted a still disoriented gaze. "But . . . but it had no effect on me. Not like tonight."

"That doesn't surprise me. Unless your father was a complete idiot, I doubt he actually gave you nitrous oxide. It can have unpredictable effects—surely no physician would risk it. He probably gave you oxygen. Or a diluted dose that wouldn't affect you much."

"That does make sense." She screwed up her brow in thought. "He did seem to give in to my begging awfully easily."

The fire now blazed high, revealing a bedchamber done up in Grecian style, in golden yellow wallpaper and dark woods with gilt dappling the furniture and fittings. The Kidderminster carpet, the chintz bed hangings and curtains all mingled black with gold, lending the room an exotic air.

For the first time since they'd left Stoneville's library with its heavier masculine furnishings, Madeline gazed about her and seemed to realize that they had changed their surroundings. She glanced to him in a panic. "Where are we?"

"Still at Stoneville's, but in a guest room. I figured it would afford us privacy while you recovered." An edge entered his voice. "While we talk."

She seemed to shrink into herself, her eyes dropping to

her gown. With the nitrous wearing off, she was returning to her usual cautious self.

It didn't matter. She would give him his answers this time.

"Talk about what?" Her fingers plucked idly at the satin, a residual effect of the nitrous.

"You know what. Sir Humphry Davy."

"Why would we talk about him?" Her gaze flicked to the door, suddenly hopeful. "Is he here, too?"

Damnation. She *had* come to the party to find Sir Humphry.

Stoneville's insidious words assailed him. *She probably convinced you to bring her so she could find her lover, since she couldn't get to him otherwise.*

Surely not. He couldn't believe it. Still, the man *was* known for his bluestocking lady admirers, and she *had* read his book. "Sir Humphry Davy is not here, no."

"Downstairs, I mean." She slid to the edge of the bed, looking as if she meant to rise. "At the party."

He hurried over to stay her. "It's not safe for you to stand yet."

"I feel fine," she protested, trying to push him aside.

"That doesn't mean you are. Sometimes certain effects linger."

"But I have to return to the party—"

"He isn't here, I tell you!" Jealousy gnawed at his gut. The thought of the fresh young Madeline yearning for his aging ruin of a friend sickened him. "So you won't be meeting up with your quarry after all."

The blood drained from her face. "I don't know what you're talking about."

"Ah, but you do." He could see it in her expression.

"Don't play the fool with me, Madeline. It's much too late for that. You came here for Sir Humphry. You said so while under the influence of the gas."

"I-I don't remember that. I don't remember what I said." Sinking back onto the bed, she stared past him at the closed door. "Are you . . . sure he's not here?"

The plaintive request tugged at his sympathies, which only further enraged him. Had she used him to meet another man, the man she really wanted? Could her flirtations and kisses have been intended only to bring about this?

Then a more painful thought occurred to him. What if Sir Humphry had been the incompetent lover who'd seduced her the first time, thus ruining her? By God, he'd have the arse's head on a platter.

"Yes, I'm sure he's not here," he said tersely. "I overheard the other guests discussing it. He was supposed to ride with Wedgwood, but his wife told Wedgwood he was unwell. She probably put her foot down, as she often does. I'll wager you know exactly what I mean."

Her face now bore the dull gray pallor of despair. "Indeed I do. She guards him most jealously." She sighed. "Otherwise, I wouldn't have had to resort to this subterfuge in order to meet with him."

Every word stabbed like a dagger to his heart. When had he let her creep so far beneath his defenses? How could he have given her such power to hurt him?

Yet, like a child picking at a sore, he had to know all of it, the why and the how. "What had you hoped to gain by accosting him here? A renewal of his affections? Did you hope to make him feel guilty for what he'd done?"

Her gaze shot to his. "His affections! Make him feel guilty? What in heaven's name are you talking about?"

The clear surprise on her face gave him pause. "Sir Humphry and you. I'm assuming he's the lout who seduced you. The incompetent lover."

She gaped at him, then burst into laughter. "Lover! You must be daft."

This wasn't quite the reaction he'd expected. "I don't . . . understand."

"No, you certainly don't, if you think Sir Humphry was ever my lover." Her amusement faded. "I wish he had been. Then I wouldn't be in this predicament."

Relief swamped him. God save him, he was thinking like a jealous idiot. That's what he got for listening to an arse like Stoneville.

"So what *is* your predicament?"

The question seemed to put her on her guard. She rose from the bed, stood a bit unsteadily, then wrapped her arms about her waist. "It's complicated."

Complicated was never good. "You promised to answer my questions if I gave you your party, and I did. It's not my fault it didn't provide what you wanted."

"I know."

"I fulfilled my end of the bargain. Now you must fulfill yours."

"Yes, you're right," she said, the words so low he had to strain to hear them.

When she remained silent, he approached her warily. "Come, sweetheart, you can tell me about it." He saw the confusion on her pretty face. "No one will disturb us—Stoneville doesn't even know we're still here. And the door is locked."

"You locked the door?" Alarm laced her words.

"So you could recover in private." He started to caress

her cheek, then dropped his hand before it could make a fool out of him. "Tell me why you need Sir Humphry's help." *Instead of mine. Yes, why not ask* me *for help?*

Because he was a rakehell. Because she trusted him as much as a gamekeeper trusted a poacher. With his reputation, she wasn't likely to turn to him for help with anything but a wicked nitrous oxide party. "Madeline—"

"My father had a medical practice in the town where we used to live."

He nodded. "Chertsey."

She flushed. "Or thereabouts."

"*Where* exactly?"

"I can't tell you."

"Why not, damn it?"

"I just can't."

He released a frustrated sigh but allowed her that. For the moment. "Go on."

"Papa's work as a physician was enough to keep us relatively comfortable." Her voice shook. "Until he treated a woman for an abscess. Because she was in pain and he dislikes using laudanum, he used nitrous oxide. Having read Sir Humphry's book, he was aware it could be useful to dull pain."

"But something went wrong," Anthony guessed.

She nodded. "The woman died within an hour of when Papa excised the diseased flesh. There was an enquiry, as you might imagine, and they determined that Papa wasn't at fault." A sudden anger tightened her lips, flavoring her words with bitterness. "But my father's enemies didn't agree. And in their ignorance, they convinced others that he'd killed the woman. They destroyed his practice."

A chill went through him. He knew how easily people

could believe nonsense in a small, provincial town. "So you moved to Richmond to start anew."

"Exactly. I got the position at Mrs. Harris's school, hoping Papa might begin his practice here." A profound sadness swept her features, making something catch in his throat. "But he was too devastated by what had happened and the ensuing gossip. For the last several months, he's done nothing but go over and over what he perceives as his mistake, drowning in guilt."

"While you," he said tightly, "try to save him."

Her startled gaze lifted to him. "And myself. I can't support us for long on a teacher's salary, and I have few prospects for marriage." Her tone turned defensive. "What am I supposed to do? Stand back and watch him wither and die?"

He couldn't wait to meet this selfish fellow who let the burden of his sins lie on his daughter's back. He would give the man a piece of his mind.

She sank onto the bed. "Mama always knew how to bring him out of his fits of melancholy, but I confess that this time I . . . begin to despair. He's never had one run so deep or last so long. That woman's death shook him terribly."

Anthony had friends who suffered such bouts. Samuel Coleridge was one—it was why the man took laudanum and inhaled nitrous. From what Anthony could gather, breaking from the prison of melancholy was damned difficult.

Still, the man shouldn't neglect his duty to his daughter. Here she was, doing reckless things—associating with a rakehell, attending a scandalous party . . .

Yes, what of that? "This doesn't explain why you're desperate to meet Sir Humphry."

She swallowed. "Papa's enemies are clamoring for the incident to be reexamined and Papa charged with a crime. They want the woman's husband to press for a trial."

"Good God." Anthony knew how justice could operate in such provincial towns. Once the populace decided you were guilty, you could find yourself hanging from the end of a rope very easily.

"*That's* why I need to meet Sir Humphry. He's my last hope. If he would travel to my town and speak on Papa's behalf, they'd have to listen." As she warmed to her subject, her face grew more animated. "They keep saying that Papa's use of the nitrous is what killed her. You and I know that's not true."

"It's unlikely, yes."

"And Sir Humphry knows that more than anyone. He has reams of documented evidence that prove it, as well as the fame to overpower their ignorant objections. If he would only speak to them, convince them—"

"Did you ask him to do so? Approach him?"

"I tried. But unlike you, my lord, I cannot gain entrée merely by leaving my card. I wrote letters asking for an audience, and they were ignored," she said in a hollow voice. "So I wrote letters explaining how dire the situation was. The last one was refused unopened. That's how I know that he—or someone close to him—must have read the previous ones."

Anthony paced before her. "Why didn't you tell me this from the first? Ask me to introduce you?"

"And what would you have done? Take a stranger to

your friend's home?" She shook her head. "You would have asked why I wanted to meet him. Once I revealed the truth about Papa, you would have balked at involving your friend or yourself in my troubles when you already had difficulties of your own."

Her perfectly valid point annoyed him. "You could have held my niece's enrollment over my head the way you did to get your party."

"And that would have convinced you to help a woman whose father might be taken to trial for murder? What if your uncle heard of it? What then?"

Oh, God, his uncle. He'd forgotten all about him. Damn, damn, damn! If the man learned of Anthony's involvement with anything unsavory, he would use that knowledge to destroy Anthony's chances at guardianship.

"At least with the party," she went on, "you were kept out of it. I hoped to meet Sir Humphry on my own and make my case without involving you."

"But you did involve me," he snapped. "You just didn't have the courtesy to tell me why."

"If I'd told you why I needed to meet Sir Humphry, you might have warned him off. Then I'd have lost my chance. Trying to meet him in society seemed more prudent, and your parties are—"

"—the only events he attends these days." He gritted his teeth. "That's true."

Everything she said was true, damn it. If she'd asked him to introduce her, he would have insisted on knowing why. He would at least have mentioned her name to the man. Given the letters she'd sent—letters that had been refused—the matter would have ended there, without her even gaining her audience.

"I did what I had to do," she whispered. "Surely you can understand that, given your situation with your niece."

With a nod, he began to pace again, unable to keep still. "I see why you were worried about telling me of Sir Humphry. He's not even home to his friends half the time." He shoved his fingers distractedly through his hair. "But I still say you could have asked for *my* help. Perhaps not at the beginning, but later, after I kissed you. Caressed you. Couldn't you have trusted me then?"

"It's not a matter of trust. Other than by introducing me to Sir Humphry, how could you help me without damaging your situation with your niece?"

"It's not as if my uncle is omnipotent," he clipped out, frustrated by her view of him as some ineffectual idiot. "He wouldn't know if I went to a provincial town to use my influence in helping a physician. How would he find out?"

Her gaze grew shuttered. "He might. You never know."

"Not if I greased the right palms. Money and rank often accomplish things that logic and reason cannot. You should at least have given me the chance to help."

"I couldn't risk your making matters worse."

"I wouldn't have." He marched up to her. "I won't. Let me try." He wasn't sure when he'd gone from suppositions to a determination to help her, but he couldn't stop himself. Her anguish tore at him. "Let me go to your town and—"

"No."

"Come now, Madeline, you're being stubborn." He laid his hand on her shoulder. "At least let me make enquiries."

"No!" She shoved his hand away, then rose to go stand by the fire. "You can't be involved to that extent."

Her demeanor set off alarms in his head. "There's something you're not telling me. This isn't the whole story."

She wrapped her arms about herself. "Leave it alone."

"I'm not going to leave it alone." He didn't like being used. He was tired of her keeping secrets. And the fact that she continued to do so gave him pause.

What if she'd invented the tale about her father? What if Stoneville's initial suspicions were correct? She could have any reason for wanting to meet Sir Humphry, and surely the man wouldn't have refused her letters without good cause.

What did Anthony really know of her, anyway? She wouldn't even tell him exactly where she was from, yet she seemed to know a damned lot about *him*.

"Madeline," he said sternly. "I want the truth. All of it."

She whirled on him, desperation in her features. "Then find some way for me to meet Sir Humphry. Do that, and I'll tell you everything."

"Not this time. Tell me the whole story tonight, or I bring you home and wash my hands of you." It was a bluff, but she couldn't know that. She couldn't know she'd sunk so deeply inside him he couldn't seem to root her out.

"You wouldn't," she said uncertainly. "You still need me to get your niece enrolled in the school."

His temper flared. He strode up to loom over her with hands clenched. "Ending Tessa's chances won't help your situation. Because if you tell Mrs. Harris I'm unfit to be Tessa's guardian, I'll ruin you at the school, I swear. All it would take is one word to your employer about your father and his background, not to mention your attendance at this party, and you'd be without a position."

"I would never hurt your niece!" Tears pooled in her

eyes, and she turned away to hide them. Her voice dropped to a whisper. "If you want me to trust you, you'll have to stop saying such horrible things."

The sight of her distress clutched at his heart, bringing him back from his dark suspicions. He'd never seen her cry. She always controlled her emotions around him, and the fact that he'd brought her to tears—which even now she tried to hide—made him realize she was just a frightened young woman with the weight of the world on her shoulders.

"Don't cry, sweetheart, please don't cry," he said hoarsely.

"I'm n-not," she stammered, turning his stomach into knots.

He tugged her into his arms. "Shh, now, shh, it will be all right."

"You mustn't a-ask me to tell you. I can't. I-I won't."

"How can I not ask when it's breaking your heart?" And his. He stroked her back, holding her close in his embrace. "We both have much to lose in this matter. We should be working together, not fighting each other."

Cupping her head in his hand, he lifted it so her tear-filled gaze met his. "Just tell me everything. Tell me what this is really about. Then I'll do whatever is in my power to help you. I swear."

Chapter Eighteen

Dear Michael,

Keep a tight rein on Madeline? She is not a horse, sir—she is perfectly capable of looking after herself. I know her character well enough. She may be mad for science and too curious about certain matters, but she is no fool.

Your friend,
Charlotte

Madeline was sorely tempted to do as Anthony bade her. How lovely it would be to lean on someone else, to reveal the entire sordid tale and let him fix everything. She could see that he wanted to. He'd even defended her to Stoneville!

That part of the night was still hazy, but she had flashes of memory—Anthony's fierce expression as he'd come to her aid, his tender treatment of her, the concern shining in his beautiful eyes. He'd been so sweet, so gentle.

And later, so jealous. Of her with Sir Humphry—imagine! A sob caught in her throat. No man had ever cared enough about her to be jealous. And to have Anthony feel that way . . . oh, how she wanted to unburden herself to him.

But she couldn't.

Even if she did tell him everything, hearing that Papa had been accused of trying to seduce a woman using nitrous oxide was sure to give him pause. Anthony would know how easily a man could do such a thing. And just because his despised uncle had made the accusations didn't mean Anthony would assume Papa was blameless. A whole town believed the gossip. Why should Anthony believe *her?*

And even if he did side with her and Papa, he might fear that Sir Randolph would find out if he helped Papa.

She couldn't predict how he'd react if he knew the full story. It would be difficult enough for him to get her in to see Sir Humphry—she couldn't risk his refusing to do it entirely. Or worse yet, warning Sir Humphry off.

"Come now, sweetheart." He brushed a kiss to her forehead as if sensing her uncertainty. "You know you want to confide in me. After everything we've shared, surely you can trust me not to hurt you."

After everything they'd shared . . .

She froze. Therein lay her answer. He wanted her in his bed. Since he didn't deflower innocents and erroneously believed she was unchaste, she'd have some hold over him if she gave herself to him. Once he discovered he'd taken her innocence, he'd feel so guilty he would surely do whatever she asked, even introduce her to Sir Humphry. Especially once she said she didn't expect him to marry her.

But what a low trick, to use his desire for her in such a scurrilous manner!

She sighed. What choice did she have? Besides, if she was willing to give him something he wanted in return, how was that wrong?

Her innocence wasn't likely to be of use to her any-way—she had little chance of marrying. She'd never had viable suitors before—it was even less likely now that scandal tainted her family.

"Sweetheart . . ." Anthony whispered against her ear, and her heart fluttered.

Right now Anthony cared about her, but how long would that last if she told him the whole sordid tale about Papa?

That was the real reason she balked at telling him everything, wasn't it? Because he mattered to her. Because, fool that she was, she liked having him care about her. She liked having him jealous and defending her. If what she told him ruined that, she couldn't bear it.

She deserved to have some part of him, if even for one night. Tomorrow, she would deal with the rest of it, but tonight . . .

Lifting her gaze to his, she ignored the clear hope in his eyes that she would trust him with the truth. She couldn't do that yet, but she could trust him with something else. And perhaps that would be enough for him for now.

"I don't want to talk about Papa," she whispered. "Or Sir Humphry or what we can do." She let her desire for him show in her gaze as she began to unbutton his waistcoat. "I don't want to talk about anything at all. Kiss me, Anthony."

He groaned. "Madeline, for God's sake, don't . . ."

"Kiss me," she begged. "A few days ago, you told me that 'swiving' has a way of taking one out of oneself." She unknotted his cravat and drew it off, then nuzzled the whiskers along his jaw. "I need to be taken out of myself tonight. And you're the only one who can do that."

"Damnation, sweetheart," he choked out, though his fingers dug into her waist. "This won't change anything."

Yes, it would. But he didn't know that, thank heaven. "I don't care."

"Then let's return to my town house, where we'll have privacy."

So he could keep her trapped while he plagued her for the truth? Not on her life. If she went home with him, she would need his help to return to the cottage in Richmond. At least here she could follow her original plan and take a waiting hackney. "You said you locked the door. You said Lord Stoneville doesn't know we're here." She unfastened his shirt buttons. "Why wait?"

"You know why, damn it." His gaze bore into her, the smoky blue of storms and night. "You always try to make me forget everything by offering me what you think I can't resist."

"You've got it all wrong—I'm the one who wants to forget." Her voice caught on a sob. "Please, Anthony. For tonight, just help me forget."

He raised his hands to her shoulders, and she feared he meant to push her away. But then he caught her head between his hands and brought his mouth to within a hairbreadth of hers. "You're a witch, do you know that?" he said hoarsely. "A witch masquerading as a bluestocking."

"Then I'm a fitting consort for a beast masquerading as a gentleman."

Fire leaped in his eyes, and a choked laugh escaped him. "God save me, but I'm going to regret this in the morning."

"Morning is a long while off," she whispered. Then she kissed him.

He froze, and she thought he might refuse her. Then an inarticulate sound erupted from his throat, half growl, half moan, and his lips took hers.

His kiss was savage and needy, everything she could have wanted and more. He ravaged her mouth with heady thrusts of his tongue, and when that no longer satisfied him, he swept his hands down her neck to shove her gown free of her shoulders so he could strafe her bared flesh with urgent, openmouthed caresses.

She was almost as fierce, yanking on his coat until he shrugged it off, then removing his waistcoat as he dragged down her corset. His mouth seized her breast and sucked it through her chemise so ardently that the warmth she'd felt while inhaling nitrous returned, leaping to flame inside her, licking along every nerve.

Then everything began to move swiftly. Too swiftly. He tore at tapes and buttons, divesting her of her gown and corset with amazing speed, then kicking off his shoes and jerking off his trousers.

When he reached for the ties of her chemise, she caught his hand. "Wait, wait, wait!" she cried.

A sudden anger suffused his features. "Now you want to stop?"

"No! That's not what I mean."

He thought her experienced, and she couldn't tell him otherwise or he wouldn't make love to her. But neither could she run headlong into it as if she knew everything. She had to slow him down without revealing her inexperience.

Then it hit her. "I want a good look at you." She nodded to his shirt and drawers. "I want to watch you undress." That was certainly true.

Judging from his rakish smile, she'd hit on a reason that he liked. "Whatever you say," he rasped. "As long as I get to do the same when you're done."

"Of course."

As she backed up to get the full view, he shucked his shirt, then paused to let her look her fill, his rapid breaths making his magnificent chest rise and fall like a buck's at the end of a hard run. A line of hair bisected the slabs of muscle down to his navel and beyond, disappearing beneath his drawers.

He reached for the buttons. "Shall I go on?" he asked impatiently. When she nodded, he removed his drawers in one swift motion, taking the stockings with them.

As he straightened, she swallowed hard. "*That* is certainly interesting."

"Interesting?" A dark amusement resonated in his voice. "If I didn't know better, sweetheart, I'd think you hadn't seen my privates before. But you did get an excellent view in the garden pavilion."

But not so eloquently displayed. He ambled toward her, and she watched in fascination as his ballocks swung with his gait, an integral part of the wealth of muscle and bone that was his body.

That's when maidenly alarm struck her. Not because his thrusting flesh looked any more daunting than before, and not because she feared it wouldn't fit. Nature made a man's penis to fit inside a woman—she knew that logically.

But logic didn't tell her *how* it fit or how to make it feel comfortable, not to mention pleasurable. Even that cursed harem book hadn't told her that.

He reached for her chemise again, and she blurted out, "It's not the same."

A smile touched his lips as he untied her chemise. "What isn't?"

"Seeing a man's privates and seeing him completely unclothed. Except for artist's renditions and statues, I've never seen a real man entirely naked."

His fingers froze on the ties. "Never?"

Drat it, she was supposed to be experienced. But she couldn't invent details about some imaginary lover, not now, not with Anthony.

"It's hard to undress fully in a carriage," she said obliquely. That was a bald statement of fact. If he took it as something else, at least she hadn't lied to him.

His face cleared. "I should have figured that your incompetent lover would take you in a carriage. It's just what a blackguard would do."

He sounded so . . . so *moral* she had to laugh. "Why do you assume he was a blackguard?"

"He seduced and abandoned you, didn't he? That's what a blackguard does."

Guilt choked her. "And you've . . . never done anything like that."

"Absolutely not." His voice grew husky. "But I don't want to talk about him." He dragged off her chemise, then removed her drawers. "Tonight is for us."

Silently she agreed. Tomorrow she'd do whatever she must, but tonight was theirs. And the ardent way he scoured her nakedness made her feel, for once, as if she truly was his.

"You're a witch, I tell you." He lifted his fingers to caress the curve of her waist, then the swell of one breast, before wrapping his hand in a long lock of her hair. Bringing it up to his lips, he pressed a worshipful kiss to the silky strands. "The most exotically beautiful witch I have ever encountered."

The extravagant compliment embarrassed her. "You sound like Stoneville."

"Don't say that," he retorted, his eyes suddenly solemn. "I've never been more sincere in my life." He tugged her into his arms. "You're a wonder, Madeline Prescott. Anyone who told you different is a liar and a fool."

Then he kissed her, a soul-searing sharing of mouths that made her badly want to believe him. But how could she? She wasn't a "wonder"—he only said that because he thought her pretty . . . and experienced and easy to seduce. Once he realized that his tastes were more sophisticated than hers, he would lose interest. For now, he found her amusing, but it could never go beyond that.

And yet . . .

Other men who'd found her pretty in Telford had balked when they discovered that her pretty face hid a peculiar and clever female with a fascination for very unfemale things. Anthony had not. Didn't that mean something?

She clung to that as he backed her toward the bed. And when he tumbled her down upon it and covered her body with his, then kissed her again, slowly, sensually, she allowed herself to believe that he truly did find her a wonder.

Because she wanted desperately to lose herself in him tonight, and that would be easier if she could believe he cared for her. That he felt even a tiny part of what she'd begun to feel for him. So she wrapped her arms about his neck and gave herself up to the delicious sensations of his tongue teasing her nipple, the exquisite delights of his hand stroking her below. Within moments, he had her gasping, straining against him, wanting more.

"I begin to believe that the rumors about nitrous being an aphrodisiac are right," he groaned against her breast. "I want you, sweetheart. Now."

"Yes," she whispered. "Now."

He pushed her thighs apart with one knee, then halted, lifting his head from her with a pained expression.

"What is it?" she asked.

"Damnation, I forgot something." Pushing himself off of her, he left the bed.

Feeling self-conscious splayed naked atop the coverlet, she crawled between the sheets, then propped herself up on one elbow to watch perplexed as he searched his coat pockets.

"I promised to protect you from disease and such," he explained, "and I mean to keep that promise." He rummaged another moment, then shot her a quick grin. "Ah. French letters. I knew I'd brought them."

Before she could ask why on earth he would want to read foreign letters at a time like this, he unfolded a silklike tube that had tiny ribbands hanging from it.

"What in heaven's name is that?" she asked.

"A cundum." He cast her a rueful smile. "It's the only way to be sure you don't conceive. It's not foolproof, mind you, but fairly reliable."

She stared in rapt fascination as he pulled it on over his aroused shaft. But when he actually tied the ribbands close to the base, as if dressing his penis, she couldn't prevent the laugh that escaped her.

He scowled, his erection flagging a little. "You're not helping, sweetheart."

That only made her laugh harder. "I'm sorry, it's just so . . . odd."

"So says the woman who refers to lovemaking as mating," he said dryly. As she struggled to restrain her amusement, he stalked to the bed, looking annoyed. "Do you want to prevent conception or no? Because I'd just as soon dispense with the whole thing, trust me."

She fought back the giggle rising in her throat. "No, no . . . preventing conception is good. I certainly want that." This was probably not the time to ask him how his cundums were made and such. Forcing a serious expression to her face, she said, "Forgive me, it's just the lingering effects of the nitrous."

"Nitrous, my arse," he muttered as he pulled down the sheets, then stretched out on his back beside her. "That stopped affecting you half an hour ago, admit it."

His arousal was swiftly waning, thanks to her, and that was the last thing she wanted. Especially now, with him displayed so gloriously naked beside her. "That's not entirely true . . ." She pressed her hand to his chest, marveling at how his muscles bunched beneath her fingers. "I still have that tingly feeling it roused."

With a quirk of his eyebrow, he glanced at her. "Tingly feeling?"

"You know," she said coyly. "Here." She laid his hand upon her *mons*, where she'd dreamed of his touching her again ever since that day at Mr. Godwin's.

That was all it took to return the heat to his gaze and rouse his penis anew. "Ah," he rasped as he began to fondle her with deft strokes, "*that* tingly feeling."

"Yes," she breathed, "oh, Anthony . . ."

His mouth sought hers, hungry, eager, while he delved

inside her below with first one finger, then two, each caress maddening her further. Within moments they were back to where they were before, him kneeling between her legs, parting her thighs . . . replacing his fingers with something larger and thicker.

Lord help her, they'd come to the deflowering already.

As he eased inside her, she fought the urge to resist, knowing instinctively that would only make it more difficult. At least he took care with her. And it wasn't too awful, just an intrusive pressure in an unexpected place.

Still, having his penis inside her was more intense, more intimate than when he'd stroked her with his fingers. And when he thrust, burying himself deeply, she was grateful his eyes were closed, so he didn't see her sudden grimace at the sharp pain that apparently signaled the loss of her maidenhood.

He didn't seem to notice, thank heaven. Indeed, it hadn't been nearly as bad as she'd feared. It didn't compare to the awkward fullness created by her being joined to him down there.

"Good God, you're so tight," he whispered, the words hot against her brow. "You feel incredible, sweetheart."

"So do you . . ." she managed to choke out.

Incredibly thick and uncomfortable. What a disappointment. She should have known that his talk of pleasures would come to nothing.

Then he began to move, in and out, in long, slow strokes. At first that seemed uncomfortable, too . . . until his repeated pressing against her *mons* roused a strange urge to squirm against him. When she did, a faintly pleasurable sensation shot through her that was so delicious she tried it again. And again.

With every motion, the sensation intensified a little. How intriguing.

"Here, sweetheart," he gasped against her ear as he pulled her knee up to shift her position. "You're so much smaller than I'm . . . used to. Put your legs around my waist. Yes, like that."

Sweet Lord in heaven. *That* was more like it.

Now he was pounding right against that aching spot he'd been fondling before, and excitement uncurled throughout her senses, opening her to him. Something broke free inside her, rising toward the surface like the first bubble floating up from the bottom of a water tank heated to boiling.

"That's it, my sweet wanton," he said hoarsely as he thrust harder, deeper. "You're . . . so tight, so warm . . . God save me . . . you really are . . . a witch."

"No such thing . . . as witches," she pointed out.

A strangled laugh escaped him as he gazed down at her, his black curls plastered to his brow from his exertions. "You never . . . cease to amaze me."

"Good." She wanted nothing more than to keep amazing him, to hold him beyond tonight. She wanted this. With him. Forever.

Then tears stung her eyes. A rakehell viscount marry a scandal-tainted schoolteacher? Never. So she would take what she could of him now, store up every bit against the famine when he was no longer hers.

His eyes slid shut, and he drove into her with quickening strokes that sent more bubbles rising inside her, taking her with them, edging toward light and air and the sun, until he gave one mighty thrust that sent her boiling free of the surface to burst into the air.

With his choked cry of pleasure echoing in her ears, joining with hers, she strained up against him, feeling weightless and for once, free.

Wrapping her arms about him, she clung to the feeling, not allowing herself anything but this joy.

But as the minutes marched by, and she floated down from her lofty heaven, dragged down as much by the warm weight of him atop her as by the waning of her pleasure, reality began to intrude.

Now was the time to point out that she was an innocent. That he'd taken her virginity. That he owed her something in return.

And she couldn't. She just couldn't.

"Ah, sweetheart," he murmured against her ear, "I'll be happy to take you out of yourself at any time. I am at your command."

The words were so sweet that she clutched him to her, cursing herself for her weakness. "I'll remember that," she choked out, letting the moment of confrontation pass.

Now she had another secret to keep. She could never let him know he'd deflowered her, or she'd have to explain why she'd allowed it, and the thought of tainting this wonderful night by revealing her sordid plan was too appalling to bear.

But neither could she stay here and risk his plaguing her for answers again. He refused to help her unless she told him everything, but doing that meant risking his warning Sir Humphry off, so she couldn't.

Neither could she have him find out where she lived and plague Papa for answers, too. Time to return to her original plan and sneak away in a hackney. She wasn't sure how to manage that, but the late hour might work in her favor. Yes, she would let nature take its course and wait until he dozed.

Then what would she do about meeting Sir Humphry?

She would take a chance on Anthony's good heart. Now that she knew he had one, she knew she could trust him. Monday, she would urge Mrs. Harris to enroll Anthony's niece. Once he learned of it, he might be willing to introduce her to Sir Humphry, no questions asked.

But if he wouldn't help her, she'd find another way. Because telling him the truth meant possibly alienating Sir Humphry entirely, and she dared not risk that.

Chapter Nineteen

Dear Charlotte,

I bow to your greater knowledge of the young Miss Prescott. Forgive me for being so presumptuous as to question your judgment in the matter, but it was only my concern about Lord Norcourt being at the school with you that made me even broach the subject.

Your ever-anxious relation,
Michael

Sometime later, Anthony lay on his side with Madeline tucked neatly against his sated body, her back to his chest. He ought to renew his questioning of her. He ought to use the intimacy of the moment to find out what she was hiding. But after what they'd shared, he couldn't bear to, not yet.

Perhaps he was indeed the smitten fool Stoneville took him for. At the moment, he didn't care. Gazing down at her tumbled golden hair, he felt a tenderness for her as sweet as it was alarming. Did she realize how profoundly she affected him? Or how amazing their joining had been? It had been everything he'd imagined and more . . . a progression of wonders so glorious, his head still reeled. He'd never felt like this with any other woman—as if he'd met his match.

Certainly, no other woman had dared laugh at him when he'd donned a French letter. He chuckled. Leave it to Madeline to see cundums for what they were—necessary perhaps, but very odd indeed.

"What do you find so amusing, sir?" she turned her head to ask. "Not what we just did together, I hope."

Her teasing tone held a thread of uncertainty that he was eager to banish. "No, indeed." He nuzzled her shoulder, drinking in her unique scent of almonds and citrus. "You bewitched me entirely, as I'm sure you know."

With a hesitant smile, she shifted to lie on her back. While her hand stroked up and down his arm, she stared at him from beneath shyly lowered lashes. "Then what struck you as funny?"

"Your reaction to my cundums."

"Oh, I forgot about those!" Her eyes sparkled with curiosity. "I meant to ask—what are they made of?"

He shook his head helplessly. "Only *you* would want to know such a thing."

Her smile faded and her gaze dropped to where her hand still caressed his arm. "And does that bother you?"

"No." He brushed a curl from her brow. "It's what I like best about you. And to answer your question, they're made of lamb intestines turned inside out, macerated, scraped, washed, cured, blown up, and dried, then cut to a nice, convenient length on one end."

"And fitted with ribbands," she teased. "But what chemical do they use to macerate it? How do they cure it? How long does it take to dry?"

A laugh erupted from him. "I should have known you'd want the entire process described in excruciating detail. You're as bad as I am, with your insatiable curiosity about how things work." He feathered a kiss over her nose. "Let me just go remove the thing, and you can examine it to your heart's content."

"No, that's all right." A strange alarm filled her face. Pulling his arm about her waist, she returned to her former position, curled up against him. "Don't go anywhere yet. Stay here with me a while longer."

"If you wish." Tucking her head beneath his chin, he held her close, relishing the moment.

She took his hand in hers, then stared at his wrist. "You have a nasty scar here. How did you get it?"

His enjoyment of their cozy moment instantly fled. Should he tell her the whole mortifying tale? No, he couldn't. He cringed even to think of how she might react to such evidence of his wicked character. But he could tell her the bald facts of the incident, just not why and how it had occurred.

"When I was a boy, I . . . got caught in something and tried to cut myself free with my penknife. Instead I cut myself."

"It looks like a very serious cut," she said softly. "You were lucky you didn't die."

Thank God she didn't ask what he'd been trying to cut himself free of. "So said the doctor who sewed me up. Right before he abandoned me."

A strange stillness came over her. "Abandoned you? What do you mean?"

He shouldn't have revealed even that. "Nothing. It was a long time ago."

But she wouldn't let it go. "Was this in Chertsey?"

Ah, so that's why she wanted to know. "No, in Telford, while I lived with my aunt and uncle." He smoothed his cheek over her shoulder. "So it wasn't your father who sewed me up, if that's what you're afraid of."

"Of course it wasn't," she said hastily. "So . . . er . . . how did this doctor abandon you?"

"It's nothing, not worth mentioning. Forget I said it." The very thought of her knowing about that mortified him. She would surely see it as evidence of his inherently bad character, and he didn't want to add to that impression.

Why he cared so much what she thought, he chose not to examine too closely.

"All right." She surprised him by pressing a kiss to his wrist before holding it against her breast. "I'm just very glad you didn't die."

"So am I," he said with a flippancy he didn't feel. Her tender remark resonated through him to the depths of his hollow heart.

He held her close although he knew they ought to be thinking about returning her to Richmond. She hadn't said what she'd told her father about where she was going and why.

A sigh escaped him. Instead of revealing his darkest secrets, he ought to be questioning her about hers. But he was none too eager to do so. Lying entwined with her was the most sublime experience of his life. He couldn't bear for it to end.

So he savored it as long as he dared, while the fire crackled behind them, and the ormolu clock atop a nearby writing table ticked away the moments. After a while, when he caught himself starting to doze off, he glanced at the time. "Sweetheart," he murmured, "it's past midnight. Won't your father worry?"

No answer. And her deep, even breathing told him she'd fallen asleep. Not surprising. Between the nitrous, their exertions, and the late hour, he was amazed she'd stayed awake as long as she had.

He should rouse her, but he hated to. Why not let her rest a while longer before he took her home? Once they were in the carriage, there'd be plenty of time to get answers to the rest of his questions about her father's situation.

You're making excuses to put off an uncomfortable discussion.

Perhaps so. But who could blame him for being loath to leave her bed? It had taken him long enough to get here, after all.

Still, it surprised him how fiercely he wished to lie all night with her. That had never happened with any other woman. He buried his face in her hair. Mmm. Such soft hair. So pleasantly scented. He breathed deeply.

He wondered what she did to . . . make her hair . . . smell so good . . .

It seemed only moments later that he opened his eyes again, but it had clearly been longer. The fire had burned out, as had the candles. Black as pitch. All around him darkness.

For a second, the familiar panic swelled in him. Alone. In the dark. Trapped.

No, he was *not* alone, was he? He felt for Madeline next to him but found nothing. God save him, he *was* alone.

But not trapped—not that, at least. He could move his arms and legs with perfect ease, and did so, just to be sure. His fingers brushed something wet and cold, which made him start violently . . . until he realized it was just his French letter, which had slipped off while he'd slept.

While *they'd* slept. "Sweetheart," he said, fighting the ancient feeling of helplessness that stole over him. "Where are you?"

She'd left the bed, that's all. She was probably searching for a flint box at this very moment so she could light a candle. He waited a second, then said more sharply, "Madeline, damn it, answer me!"

The echo of silence chilled him.

Light. He needed light to see. At home, this was rarely a problem. He went to bed so late that the fire never had a chance to burn out. But it had been early when he'd dozed off, early enough that the fire hadn't outlasted the night. So he would have to manage this in the dark.

Trying not to think about the darkness, Anthony left the bed to inch carefully toward the fireplace, nearly tripping over the chair in front of it. That gave him his bearings enough to find the mantel so he could feel for a flint box. When he found it, his anxiety receded a little, but his hands still shook so badly that it took him a few moments to get a spark. Once he got that, he was able to have a fire blazing high fairly quickly.

Dropping into the chair, he fought to regain his equilibrium. Good God, he hated this. After twenty years, he ought to be able to handle being alone in the dark without feeling such waves of helpless anger and confusion. He wasn't a child anymore, damn it. And where the bloody devil was Madeline?

Taking in a great gulp of breath, he steadied his nerves, then rose and lit all the candles. A glance at the clock revealed that it was after 5:00 A.M. He'd slept all this time? No wonder the fire had burned out. Why hadn't she awakened him?

Quickly, he searched the room. Her clothes and shoes were gone. Either she'd headed downstairs, which he found unlikely, given her reaction to Stoneville, or she'd left the place entirely.

Rage coursed through him. She'd sneaked away like some thief? After they'd shared the most glorious night of his life? How could she, damn it!

Calm yourself, he chided. *She might still be here. You won't know until you talk to the servants.*

And if she *had* left, there might still be time to catch up to her. She might not have been gone that long. He might even discover where she lived if she'd had the footman give a direction to the coachman.

After drawing on his drawers, he went to sit on the bed to pull on his stockings. He couldn't find his garters, and as he tossed the bedclothes aside looking for them, he froze.

Something dark and unmistakably red stained the center of the sheet. Blood. There was blood on the sheets.

For a moment, he could only stare at it in confusion. Had he hurt her? Was that why she had fled, because he'd been too rough with her somehow? No, that made no sense given how she'd reacted after they'd—

Oh, God. The truth hit him with brutal force. Madeline was a virgin.

She *had* been a virgin, anyway. Until he'd deflowered her with all the care of a rampaging bull.

"Damnation!" She'd been an innocent?

He moved the sheets about until he found his cundum, then examined it by the light of the candle. Blood stained it, too. She'd most assuredly been an innocent.

He should have realized it at once. She'd been incredibly

tight. He'd chalked it up to her limited encounters, but he ought to have known what it meant.

Now other things came to him, too—her reaction to his nakedness, her surprise at their sensual explorations. He cursed foully. Why hadn't she told him? He would have been more careful with her, more gentle. And how dared she lie to him all this time, claiming to have lost her innocence to some inept lover?

The thought arrested him, made him sift back through every conversation between them. He groaned. She'd never claimed that at all. She hadn't needed to. He'd concocted an inept lover for her.

Granted, she'd known precisely what he'd thought and had never set him straight, but she'd never actually said she'd had a lover. She'd even laughed at the idea of Sir Humphry in that role. And when he'd expressed surprise at her assertion that she'd never seen a man naked, her answer had been an evasion.

By God, he'd deflowered a respectable virgin.

The door to the room abruptly swung open, and a feminine squeal startled him. A maid stood there, blinking at him. "Oh, Lud, sir, I didn't know anybody was up here. His lordship didn't tell us anybody was staying the night."

"I'm not." As she started to leave, he called out, "Wait!"

"Sir?" she asked, keeping her gaze averted from his half-naked body.

Hastily he donned his trousers, then his shirt. "Have all the guests gone?"

She nodded. "The last one left over an hour ago. We heard something fall up here while we were cleaning downstairs, and they sent me up to see what it was."

That must have been when he'd tripped over the chair.

"Did you happen to notice if a Mrs. Brayham left? She's blond, very pretty, wearing a yellow satin gown." When the woman looked blank, he added, "Or a black cloak."

"Yes, she's gone," said a new voice.

Anthony let out a low oath as Stoneville entered the room, still dressed in his evening clothes. He was the last person Anthony wanted to see at the moment. But apparently Stoneville didn't give a bloody damn, for after dismissing the maid, he closed the door.

"Why are you still up?" Anthony growled as he fastened his shirt. "You should be passed out in the bed by now."

With a shrug, Stoneville leaned back against the door. "I wasn't tired. Then the servants told me they heard something up here, so I came to investigate."

Damnation. It looked like Anthony had no choice but to involve Stoneville now. "Did you actually see her leave?"

"Who? Your little cousin?"

Anthony scowled at him.

"Ah, right, not a cousin. A beautiful female named Madeline." When Anthony started, Stoneville eyed him askance. "I heard you call her that last night in the library. What's the rest of her real name?"

"I'm not going to tell you that. And I'd prefer that you kept to yourself anything having to do with her."

"Even after she abandoned you?" At Anthony's coarse curse, Stoneville added, "Yes, I did see her leave. I thought you'd left with her. I caught her heading out the front door, but she said you'd gone ahead to fetch the hackney because you didn't want to bother the servants. I should have known that was a lie."

Gazing about him distractedly, Anthony threaded his fingers through his hair. "What time was that?"

"One o'clock. Or thereabouts."

She'd been gone four hours already. By now, she was tucked up in her bed somewhere in Richmond.

Stoneville glanced about the room, taking note of the tumbled bedclothes. "I can't imagine why she'd want to leave so tidy a love nest."

No point in denying it. The state of his clothing and the condition of the room made it painfully clear what he and Madeline had been doing.

Plucking up his cravat, Anthony went to the mirror to tie it. Too late, he saw Stoneville head for the bed. Damnation!

Anthony turned to find Stoneville staring at the bed with unmitigated shock, a rare occurrence indeed.

"She was a virgin," Anthony said flatly.

"I see that." Then Stoneville's expression grew calculating. "Or else she brought some pig's blood to make you think she was."

The man's cynicism infuriated Anthony. "Then she somehow managed to smear it on my cock without waking me, because it's on the cundum as well."

With a world-weary sigh, Stoneville dropped into a chair. "How can you be sure she didn't? Christ, you know how that age-old game works. She claims you deflowered her, hoping to get you to marry her so she can become a viscountess."

The idea of Madeline aspiring to be a viscountess was so ludicrous that Anthony snorted. "Some women might try a trick like that, but not her." He picked up his waistcoat. "For one thing, she knew my reputation from the first. She had no reason to believe I would marry her just because I deflowered her. If that was her game, she took a very big chance." Especially given the situation with her father. "And this isn't a woman who behaves recklessly. Ever." He shook his head. "No, she had a logical reason for doing this."

"You mean, other than the obvious one? Your irresistible charms?"

"She's been resisting them fairly well until now. You should have heard her lecture me on the reckless behavior of rakehells. I doubt marrying one would appeal to her. Besides, why didn't she reveal I'd stolen her innocence when it happened? Why isn't she here now demanding reparation?"

"Perhaps she went home to bring her father back, so *he* could witness what had been done and make you marry her."

"Don't be an idiot." Anthony buttoned his waistcoat. "She couldn't have been sure I would sleep the whole time. Besides, she doesn't live far from here—she could have been home and back three times by now. Not to mention that her father doesn't sound as if he's in any state to force anybody into anything."

Anthony bent to pick up his coat. Could her father's problems have caused her uncharacteristically reckless behavior? Now that he considered it, it was only after he'd turned into the Grand Inquisitor, swearing to have the truth at any cost, that Madeline had turned into Lady Seducer.

But surely she wouldn't lose her innocence just to distract him from the truth. She must have known that eventually he would plague her for answers again. She wouldn't get to meet Sir Humphry otherwise, and that seemed to be her goal.

Anthony froze in the act of pulling on his coat. Oh, God, had that been her plan? To let him deflower her, then hold that sin over his head until he introduced her to Sir Humphry? But then, why wasn't she here seeing her plan to fruition?

"None of this makes sense," he told Stoneville. "If she'd wanted to use my reckless behavior, she should have stayed around. Running off serves no purpose."

"If you say so." Stoneville gazed at him intently. "So what will you do?"

"Talk to her." Though that would have to wait until Monday at school. He had no idea where she lived, and Richmond was too sizable to search in one day. Besides, perhaps it was time to seek elsewhere for information about her since she wouldn't confide in him. "For today, I mean to go to Chertsey."

"Chertsey! I don't see what good going to your estate will do."

"I know you don't. And I'd rather keep it that way." He donned his shoes. "The less you know, the better." At least until he could get to the truth.

"What am I to do if she *does* return with her father to make demands?"

"She won't." He didn't know why, but he felt sure of that.

"All the same . . ." Stoneville rose, removed the sheet with the cundum rolled up in it and strode to the fireplace, where he tossed the bundle onto the fire.

"What the devil—"

"No point in leaving behind any evidence, old chap."

Anthony didn't know what to make of that. "Why do you care?"

Stoneville shrugged. "You may not believe this, but I really am your friend. And I don't want to see you end up like Kirkwood."

"I could end up like Foxmoor instead, you know."

"You? Happily married? That will happen when pigs fly and the sky falls."

"Thank you for your opinion," he said testily as he headed for the door. "You must really think me a matrimonial lost cause if you need *two* clichés to express it."

"Norcourt!" Stoneville called after him. "All the hackneys are gone."

He halted. "Damn." Gritting his teeth, he faced Stoneville once more.

But before he could speak, his friend said, "Yes, you may borrow my phaeton."

"Thank you." Anthony gazed at the man who'd accompanied him on many an orgy of excess. They'd been friends for years, yet he'd never felt as if he really knew the man, so to have his help in this delicate matter felt odd. Was there more to his friend than Stoneville let on?

"Thank you for everything," he added. "Not just the phaeton, but the party and your meddling last night. Even if I didn't like your methods for gaining information, they proved more useful than you can possibly know."

"Happy to be of service. Feel free to bring your 'cousin' to visit anytime. Just warn me so I can have the room prepared and the nitrous bag ready."

"That's not the least bit amusing," Anthony shot back, "and you know it. Besides, I have no intention of letting this sort of thing happen ever again."

"The deflowering? Or the nitrous oxide party?"

"Both," he said, and meant it.

Much later, as he set off in Stoneville's phaeton toward Chertsey, the man's cynical comment about Anthony and marriage rose up to haunt him.

Was Stoneville right? For years, Anthony had been convinced that marriage was impossible for him. That the intensity of his sexual urges would alarm any respectable woman, and he'd end up in a miserable marriage like Kirkwood's. The respectable women he'd met had been fragile sorts, wanting husbands who were half poet, half saint. He was incapable of either.

But Madeline was the least fragile female he'd ever met. She'd even let him deflower her without complaint. Even if she'd done it out of some desperate attempt to save her father, he truly believed it had meant more than that to her.

Not that it mattered. He'd ruined her; there was only one way to make that right, even if she *had* lured him into it by hiding her past experience. He drew the line at debauching innocents and then abandoning them to the fate society usually designated for the "fallen." He wouldn't be that sort of man. He couldn't.

In truth, he didn't want to give her up for any reason. For the first time, he could actually imagine bedding the same woman every night, spending evenings by the fire with her . . . having the sort of enviable marriage his parents had shared.

Perhaps he'd finally found a woman who could tolerate him and his fierce urges, who might even be happy to share them. After all, she was the only person who'd never called him wicked. Reckless, yes, but not wicked. She was the only person who'd seen past his reputation to the man beneath.

But he was getting ahead of himself by thinking of

marriage. First, he had to figure out what her situation was, so he would know how he could really help her. A day in Chertsey ought to take care of that. Then come hell or high water, he and she *would* discuss marriage.

Madeline paced the cottage as her father slept, wondering if she could just wake him and be done with it. She hadn't slept a wink since her furtive return at 2:00 A.M. Mrs. Jenkins had roused to help her undress, and if she'd noticed anything different about Madeline, she certainly hadn't mentioned it.

But Madeline felt it within herself. She was a woman now. She felt gloriously, triumphantly a woman. She was as bad as Anthony with her recklessness, yet she couldn't dredge up any guilt over her ruination.

Except in the matter of how things had been left between them.

She sighed. She'd truly hated leaving him asleep. It was a nasty thing to do, especially since he'd wrapped himself so tightly in the covers that she'd been unable to check the sheets to see if there was evidence of her deflowering.

But she doubted he would notice if there was; that's why she'd extinguished the candles. When he awoke to find her gone, the dwindling fire wouldn't provide him with enough light to examine the sheets. Besides, men didn't notice things like that, did they? Not when they weren't looking for them.

And if he did?

Then he would consider himself lucky to have escaped a marriage trap.

You don't really think that. He isn't as reckless as you pretend.

Perhaps. Perhaps not. It didn't matter—he couldn't marry her even if he wanted to. Any association with her scandalous family would make it impossible for him to gain guardianship of Tessa.

A tiny part of her wished he would choose her over his niece, given the chance. But that was selfish. Besides, he didn't even completely trust her. And she was so far beneath him . . .

No, marriage was impossible. He would decide that for himself the minute he learned of her background.

Which she wasn't going to tell him. Now, more than ever, she had to be cautious. His mention of a doctor treating him worried her. It *had* to be Papa.

But what had he meant when he'd said the doctor had abandoned him? That didn't sound like Papa. Still, when she calculated the last possible year Anthony could have stayed with the Bickhams before going to Eton, it was the year she'd turned six. And given what she remembered, that alarmed her indeed. She had to know the whole story before she could even think about involving Anthony further.

"You're up early," said her father's voice from the end of the parlor.

Finally, he was awake. "I couldn't sleep."

When she faced him he stared at her oddly, and a fleeting fear seized her that he could tell she was unchaste, that it was somehow branded on her forehead. Then he shuffled over to his usual seat before the fire and lapsed into his brooding.

Thank heaven. Although now came the difficult part. "Papa, I need to ask you something important."

He didn't respond.

She hated to press him, but only he could tell her what she needed to know. "Do you recall when you took me to Chertsey years ago?"

"Chertsey! You remember that?"

"A little, yes. We went to a very grand house, and the housekeeper let me play with her pug while I waited for you to finish your business."

A shadow passed over his features. "I would have left you with your mother, but she was recovering from scarlet fever, and the servant had her hands full caring for her."

It must have been a very important matter indeed if he'd left Mama still ill to travel to Chertsey. Which only reinforced the suspicion that had been growing in her ever since last night. "What sort of business was it?"

He cast her a perplexed look. "Why on earth are you thinking about Chertsey?"

"I just need to know what sent you there. I can't explain why."

It was a tribute to how much her father had changed of late that he didn't demand an explanation. "I don't know if I should say. The old viscount swore me to secrecy— didn't want the scandal and all."

"But he's dead now, Papa, so what does it matter?"

"Aye. I suppose that dunce Wallace is the new viscount."

"Wallace is dead, too," she said impatiently. When he gazed at her oddly, she added, "Or so I hear. His brother Anthony is now the viscount."

"Ah, yes, poor Master Anthony." Papa grew pensive. "That's what started the troubles between Sir Randolph and me. I couldn't stomach being his physician after what happened. The lad's father promised he wouldn't tell anyone that I'd brought the tale to him, but Sir Randolph was no fool. He knew someone had spoken to the viscount. He's been suspicious of me ever since."

"What tale?"

Her father blinked. "Why, about what they were doing to poor Master Anthony, of course."

Her heart leaped into her throat. "And what was that?"

"Don't know as if I should say."

Madeline held her breath.

"But I don't suppose it matters anymore." He stared into the fire. "Lady Bickham made the boy kneel for hours at prayer and gave him cold baths to curb his 'licentious' behavior. But that wasn't the worst of it. No, the worst was them tying him to the bed at night, hand and foot, without even a fire to give him light."

Horror filled her at the thought of poor Anthony being kept tied up in the dark like some dangerous creature.

His voice grew distant. "The night they called me in, he'd been desperate enough to hide a penknife behind the bedpost before they tied him down. Later, in the dark, he nearly killed himself trying to cut the rope while still bound. By the time I reached him, he was faint from loss of blood. He told me he wanted to go home, that they hated him. He told me everything they'd been doing."

A chill swept her. "How long had it been going on?"

"From what I gathered, for nigh on to four years. He didn't say why, but Sir Randolph said it was to keep him from running off. He missed his dead mother so much that he kept trying to run back home."

Who wouldn't? she thought, furious on his behalf. How dared they treat him like that? What sort of monster did such a thing?

And if they were so horrible, why hadn't Anthony

simply told the courts about it in order to gain his niece? Or *her*, for that matter, to emphasize why she should help Tessa? He must have thought it would hurt his chances—but why?

"So you went to Chertsey to tell his father what was going on," she said.

"Aye, as soon as your mother was on the mend. Couldn't leave her until then. I wrote a letter at first, but when no answer came, I decided to go myself. Turned out his lordship hadn't been at home for a month, and no one had sent it on to wherever he was. It was still sitting there when I showed up to speak to him."

That's why Anthony had thought Papa abandoned him. Because it had taken a month for Papa to talk to his father.

Madeline turned her face to hide her tears. Her poor darling Anthony. The thought of him suffering like that broke her heart. No wonder he hated the Bickhams. No wonder he wanted to save his niece.

Though surely they wouldn't be so cruel to a girl, would they? She thought of Jane, and reconsidered that. Who knew what might have been going on in that house all those years? What might still be going on?

I must get Tessa out of that unspeakable place. Neither of those two are fit to raise a child, especially my aunt.

This changed everything—and not necessarily for the better. She couldn't in good conscience risk that poor young girl's future. She would have to find another way to save Papa.

But what?

Chapter Twenty

Dear Cousin,

I find your persistent dislike of Lord Norcourt strange, given that you claim not to know him personally. I have observed him with my girls this week, often without his knowledge, and he always behaved like a gentleman. His lessons have truly helped the girls. Which makes me wonder if your dislike of him might stem from something other than a mere concern for the school's reputation.

Your perplexed relation,
Charlotte

𝒜nthony pushed the team of his traveling chariot to its limits, determined to arrive at the school in time to catch Madeline alone. Because he'd learned one thing in Chertsey yesterday. There was no physician named Prescott. There'd never been a physician named Prescott anywhere in the vicinity. Nor had anyone heard of any scandal involving nitrous oxide in the county.

Before Saturday night, he might have assumed that Madeline's tale about her father was a lie, just another scheme.

But after what had happened between them, he couldn't believe it. For one thing, he'd reexamined her comments about Chertsey enough to realize she'd never claimed to be from there. As with her lack of experience in the bedchamber, she'd let him believe what he wanted but had taken great pains not to lie to him.

There was her virginity, too. She'd given up her innocence to protect her secrets, and then she'd fled. Those weren't the acts of a scheming woman. Those were the acts of the desperate.

The very thought of her being that desperate sent fear spiraling through him. She'd been trying to protect him by keeping the truth to herself—he was almost sure of it. That meant that she and her father must be in very dire trouble indeed, trouble so dire that she'd relinquished all hope of his helping her.

Were her father's enemies friends of his? That would explain how she knew of his boyhood antics and why she didn't want to confide in him. He had to know—he had to make her see he could help her without making either of their situations worse.

He stopped just short of the school so he could sneak in unnoticed. Slipping inside the back entrance, he took the servant's stairs to the next floor. Now he could only pray she showed up early again.

Unsure of her response, he strode into the classroom swiftly so she couldn't avoid him. To his relief, she was there. But so was Mrs. Harris.

His heart dropped into his stomach. Good God, what was *she* doing here?

"Good morning, Lord Norcourt," the headmistress said with a stern expression. "You're here rather early, aren't you?"

"So are you." He glanced to Madeline, but her face wore

a panic that mirrored his. Apparently, she'd been caught by surprise, too. What the bloody devil was going on?

Mrs. Harris regarded the two of them with interest, her expression unreadable. "I suppose you were hoping to speak with Miss Prescott alone."

"Of course," he said, going on the offensive. "She and I need to review my lessons for this week. We can hardly do that with the girls underfoot." Mimicking his father's supercilious viscount manner, he cast Mrs. Harris a withering glance. "I assume that's allowed."

Mrs. Harris ignored his remark. "I have a serious private matter I need to discuss with both of you. If you will follow me, we'll adjourn to my office."

God save them both, she knew something. That became more evident when she ushered them out with Madeline ahead of her, so that he had to follow behind, separated from Madeline.

By the time they reached her office, his frustration knew no bounds. He needed to speak to Madeline, not be corralled like an errant schoolboy.

"Please." Mrs. Harris gestured to two chairs before her desk. "Take a seat."

As they did so, Madeline cast him a speaking look, but he couldn't read her mind, damn it. What was she trying to warn him of?

"What's this about?" he demanded, tired of the headmistress's mysterious manner.

"Forthright as always." As Mrs. Harris sat down behind her desk, she surveyed him with cool aplomb. "Except in certain matters. You might as well admit the truth, Lord Norcourt. Your early arrival has nothing to do with lessons and everything to do with the nitrous oxide party your friend threw on Saturday night. The one Madeline attended."

As his blood rose to a roar in his ears, Madeline leaned forward. "Mrs. Harris, I told you I did not—"

"Be quiet, Madeline," Mrs. Harris ordered. "I want to hear his side without your interference. If necessary, I'll banish you from this discussion entirely."

Fortunately, Madeline had said enough to warn him that she hadn't been the one to reveal the secret.

He schooled his features into the expression of someone hearing shocking news for the first time. Years of wicked living had taught him how to cover for himself very well, and no mere headmistress would trick him into confessing all.

But how had she learned about the party? What had she heard?

It couldn't be much, because if she actually knew anything, she would already have dismissed Madeline, and a footman would be escorting him from the property.

"I have absolutely no idea what you're talking about," he said, in a voice of astonishing calm.

"Don't you?"

"No. Which friend of mine threw a nitrous oxide party? Why on earth would Miss Prescott have attended? It's hardly appropriate for a lady of her situation."

"Exactly." She searched his face. "So you know nothing of it."

"Nothing." He hated lying to a woman he'd come to respect, but what choice did he have? He couldn't risk Tessa's enrollment. Or Madeline's reputation.

She tapped a sheet of paper on the desk. "So I should

discount this letter that came by special messenger last night from my best source of gossip?"

Bloody hell, her mysterious "source." After a week at the school, he knew exactly who she meant—Cousin Michael, her anonymous benefactor, whose identity the girls speculated about endlessly. "I don't know if you should discount it or not. What does it say?"

"That the Marquess of Stoneville, your intimate friend, hosted a nitrous oxide party this weekend at his estate." She glanced at Madeline. "That he escorted a young lady who went by the name Mrs. Brayham, but who, from her description, sounds remarkably like Miss Prescott. What have you to say to that?"

He ignored the twisting in his gut. "I'd say you should ask your source for more details since he was obviously a guest himself."

She flushed. "He wasn't a guest—he made that quite clear. But he did hear other guests talking about it."

"Ah." He fixed her with his coldest gaze. "That is what I believe my attorney friends call 'hearsay.' It isn't even admissible in a court of law."

"This is not a court of law, sir," she said with a considerable amount of starch in her spine. "I make the laws in this school, and I want to know the truth."

Out of the corner of his eye, he could see Madeline's hands trembling in her lap. It turned his frustration to rage. "Then I'm afraid I can't help you. If my friend threw such a party, I was unaware of it. And I find it highly unlikely Miss Prescott would risk her position and reputation to attend that sort of affair. As I'm sure she would tell you if you asked *her*."

"I did ask her," Mrs. Harris said. "She denies it as well."

"Then there you have it."

"Not exactly." She rose to stand behind the desk. "Before we continue this conversation, I wish to make one thing very plain. Your behavior at the school until now has been better than I anticipated. I would even go so far as to say that you've helped my girls quite a lot. So I am inclined to hold you blameless in this matter."

Her face darkened. "Except for one detail. I understand that Brayham is the family name of your maternal grandmother, which indicates that the woman at the party might have had some connection to *you*." She looked at Madeline, then back to him. "So either she was a relation of yours, or Miss Prescott decided that taking a name from your family would deflect suspicion from her and onto you."

His blood chilled. How the bloody devil did her source know Grandmother's maiden name? Mother's side of the family didn't even appear in Debrett's. Of course, someone with access to public records could learn such things. A newspaperman, perhaps. Like Godwin. But not in the space of a day, surely.

Whoever he was, this Michael person deserved to be thrashed for trying to ruin Madeline over a damned nitrous oxide party.

"So here is the situation, sir," Mrs. Harris went on with an impassive expression. "Either you tell me exactly what you know—including the identity of Mrs. Brayham, her connection to you, and how she came to be at your friend's party—in which case I will reevaluate whether I choose to help you in the matter of the guardianship of your niece."

He swallowed hard. "Or?"

"Or you continue to deny any knowledge of the party,

leading me to assume you had nothing to do with Miss Prescott's appearance there, except perhaps for letting slip the family name of your grandmother, something I can hardly fault you for. If such is the case, I will enroll your niece."

"And what will you do to Miss Prescott?"

"End her employment, of course."

Madeline's pitiful little gasp made his blood run cold. He jumped to his feet. "End her employment! Based on evidence so slight as to be laughable?"

"I have other evidence. My friend tells me that a guest overheard the marquess call Mrs. Brayham 'Madeline' as she left. And Madeline is a rather unusual name, wouldn't you say?"

Damn, damn, damn. It was quite likely that Stoneville had done so, too, given what he'd said during their discussion after she'd left.

What the bloody devil was he to do? Anthony shoved his hand in his coat to close his fingers around Tessa's little snuffbox. He couldn't invent any tale about "Mrs. Brayham" without admitting he knew about the party. And though Mrs. Harris hadn't said for certain she would refuse to enroll Tessa under such a circumstance, she had implied it.

But neither could he sit here and watch Madeline lose her position while he got everything he wanted. After all, he still didn't know her situation. She seemed to think he couldn't help her and her father. What if that were true? What if Sir Humphry were indeed the only person who could save Dr. Prescott? Without knowing the facts, he didn't even know if marrying her would help her.

If he were to believe what she'd told him last night,

then her father's very life was at stake. It had to be something at least that serious, or why had she been willing to sacrifice her virginity to keep him out of it? Even now, she sat trembling in fear of what he might decide.

He knew how these dismissals worked—it took very little for information to appear in the paper, especially if a scandal was involved. If she lost her position, it might get back to her father's enemies. He couldn't be responsible for helping a group of ignorant fools see a man to his grave. Especially when the man was *her* father.

Compared to that, even Tessa's situation paled. Which left him only one alternative.

He squeezed the box. *Forgive me, my dear girl. If Mrs. Harris doesn't enroll you, I will find another way to free you, I swear.*

"Well?" Mrs. Harris snapped.

"As it happens," he said, "Miss Prescott had absolutely nothing to do with any of this. Mrs. Brayham is my distant cousin on my mother's side. It's merely coincidence that her Christian name is also Madeline."

"Ah," Mrs. Harris said, a strange expression crossing her face. "And your cousin—how did she come to be at your friend's party?"

He gritted his teeth. "She wanted to experience the more exotic delights of town, so I arranged with Lord Stoneville for her to attend."

"I see."

"No, you don't see. She's married to a parson. I wanted to preserve her reputation. That's why I lied about the party."

Madeline rose from her chair. "Mrs. Harris, you must let me speak!"

"You may leave now, Madeline," the headmistress said curtly. "I'm sure your students are waiting for you."

"But he's ly—"

"Go!" he said sharply before she could ruin everything. He put as much of what he felt into his gaze as he could manage. "It's all right, Miss Prescott. Don't invent some complicity in this to spare me embarrassment. I'm willing to take responsibility for my actions, foolish though they were. I'm sure I can make Mrs. Harris understand the situation."

Madeline shook her head. "Please, my lord—"

"If you don't go now, Madeline," Mrs. Harris said, "I shall assume you are both guilty of something and throw you both out."

That was the only thing that got her to leave.

As soon as she was gone, Mrs. Harris closed the door. "So you think you can make me understand the situation, do you?" She strolled before him, a calculating gleam in her eye. "You aided your married cousin, a respectable lady, in going to a scandalous party thrown by your friends. You did this without regard for the risk she took to her reputation or her marriage. Have I grasped the particulars?"

"Yes," he said, his stomach sinking at the harshness of her tone.

"And you didn't even accompany her to make sure none of the inebriated guests—or your friend, I might add—took advantage of her."

He debated, but decided on the truth. "I did accompany her. But because of concern over my gaining guardianship of my niece, I didn't actively participate." When she frowned, he added, "I know it was reckless of me to indulge her request, but when Madeline wants something, she is hard to dissuade."

She cocked one brow. "Yet you think you can be a firm guardian to a young girl."

Though he knew she was probably headed toward the complete destruction of his hopes, he couldn't resist making one last plea for his niece. "I have no idea if I can be a firm or even a good guardian. I've never had children, never been responsible for anyone's future except my own."

His voice grew thick. "But I can promise always to put Tessa's interests first, to do all in my power to ensure she has a safe and happy home. Having seen how well this school is run and how appropriate the curriculum, I would consider it a great honor if you would overlook my flawed character and enroll my niece anyway. After all, her only sin has been to lose her parents at too young an age."

Mrs. Harris regarded him intently, then held out her hand. "Very well. She may begin as soon as the courts settle the matter of guardianship. I will write a letter supporting your petition and have it sent round to your home."

He stared dumbly at her hand, not sure if he'd heard her correctly. He'd won? And without ruining Madeline?

"That *is* what you want, isn't it?" she said, a faint amusement in her tone.

"It is, it is!" Grabbing her hand, he pumped it up and down. "Thank you for giving me a chance. For giving Tessa a chance. You won't be disappointed."

"I hope not." Turning her back to him, she returned to the desk. "There is, however, one favor I wish you to do in exchange."

More favors? "Anything you ask."

She quirked up a brow at that. "Since I have agreed to

your request, there is no need for you to continue the rake lessons. So I want you to leave the school."

"Of course," he said.

"This morning. Now. Without speaking to Miss Prescott. Indeed, I want you to promise that you won't approach her ever again, here or elsewhere."

It wasn't a promise he could make. "Why?" he said hoarsely.

She faced him with a steady gaze. "Because, sir, we both know that it was Miss Prescott at that party."

Had he won one fight only to lose the other? "I swear to you—"

"You needn't keep lying about it, for heaven's sake." Folding her hands, she leaned back on the desk. "I have connections of my own in society, and once my cousin informed me of her presence at the party, I spoke to someone who actually attended. His account satisfied me that it was indeed her."

At his look of alarm, she added, "I'm not planning to do anything about it, I assure you, especially after you made your noble sacrifice on her behalf." Her tone grew faintly annoyed. "I can easily imagine what sort of scientific curiosity led her to request such a thing of you—she is always trying to learn. And your willingness to protect her from the consequences of such curiosity does you credit."

"Then why did you just threaten—"

"Because I knew you helped her." She sighed. "Because I believed—wrongly, apparently—you were just using her to get what you wanted. That's why I brought you both in here. I wanted her to realize it, too. I wanted her to watch you throw her to the wolves, so she would know not to trust you."

She gave a self-deprecating laugh. "But you surprised me, sir. You lied for her, at the risk of your own aims." Her expression turned serious. "So I must concede that you probably care for her, at least a little. And if you do, then you have to leave her be."

He drew a ragged breath. "I can't. I won't."

Temper flared in her features. "She isn't like your other women—she doesn't understand how easy it is to slip from respectability into a pit of horror with little more than a kiss or two."

"Actually, she understands more than you give her credit for," he said heatedly. "In any case, my intentions toward her are honorable."

"Honorable!" She looked at him as if he'd grown another head. "But you're a viscount, and she's merely a teacher, with an ill father and no connections."

"That doesn't matter to me."

Her eyes narrowed. "Are you thinking to fob off on her your responsibility for your niece?"

"Certainly not!" He drew himself up to his full height. "You insult me by saying so, and you insult her even more by implying she isn't worthy of a titled gentleman's attentions."

For the first time all morning, Mrs. Harris looked entirely discomfited. "I wasn't implying any such thing. Indeed, she has been a jewel ever since she started here. She came highly recommended by the school in Shrewsbury where she worked before, and she has lived up to that promise in every—"

"Shrewsbury?" He pounced on that bit of information. "She comes from Shrewsbury?" No, that couldn't be, for Telford was only fifteen miles—

Damnation. *That* was the town she was from. Telford. Not Chertsey, not Shrewsbury. Telford. *That* was why she'd refused to reveal her secrets.

"You didn't know she was from Shropshire?" Mrs. Harris asked, suspicion in her voice. "She hasn't revealed *that* to you?"

He shook his head wordlessly, still trying to figure out the ramifications of her being from Telford.

"Is she even aware of your honorable intentions? Have you approached her father for permission to court her?"

"No," he said in a faraway voice. Her father, the physician. Oh, God, surely it wasn't . . . it couldn't be his uncle's—

But it had to be. Why else would she be so secretive, so mysterious in her machinations? Her father must have been the one to treat him all those years ago.

Oh, of course, he thought cynically. First, her father had abandoned him to the "tender" ministrations of his aunt and uncle. Then Madeline had run off in the middle of the night. It must be a family trait.

Something even worse occurred to him. Surely it was no coincidence that the daughter of Uncle Randolph's physician had proposed that he take her to a nitrous oxide party. Or that she'd tempted him into bedding her. Deflowering her.

God save him, what if Madeline had planned—

"Then perhaps you should consider doing that first."

He forced himself to attend to the headmistress's words. "Doing what first?"

"Asking Madeline's father for permission. Because you will not be allowed to see her here anymore. I cannot have you paying her court on the grounds of the school. It would rouse all sorts of gossip and speculation."

"I understand."

Oh yes, he began to understand a great deal. And what he understood changed everything he thought about the deceitful Miss Prescott. He felt as if she'd reached in and ripped out his heart by the roots. What fanciful ideas he'd had about them marrying after he gallantly took care of her father's situation.

He would bite off his hands before he'd pay court to her now.

Indeed, it took every ounce of his control not to ask where she lived so he could go right there and corner her *and* her wretched father. But if Mrs. Harris was suspicious because he didn't know where Madeline was from, she'd be doubly suspicious if he asked where she lived now.

It didn't matter. He would simply accost Madeline the moment she left the school today. There was only one road into town, and she had to take it.

Somehow he got through the end of the discussion with Mrs. Harris. They parted on as good terms as could be expected, given that she was still wary of him, and he was reeling from the blow he'd taken to his perception of Madeline.

Because the only explanation for her behavior Saturday night that made any sense was too unsavory to be borne. If his suspicions were correct, she'd kept her secrets not out of a desire to protect him, but because of a truly despicable plan.

How had he let her slip so far under his guard as to accomplish such a scheme?

He knew how. All this talk of changing the way he lived for Tessa had fooled him into believing he could live like other men, that he could have a wife who actually cared for him, who could see him not as the wicked devil he pretended to be but as a man still afraid of being alone after all these years.

Well, he wouldn't be a fool anymore. His uncaring façade had served his purpose admirably all these years. He should never have let it go. But he would don it now with a vengeance.

And pray he hadn't waited too late to prevent the worst of her plans . . . and his uncle's.

Chapter Twenty-one

Dear Charlotte,

. . . So you can see from Lord Norcourt's scurrilous attempts to lead poor Miss Prescott down the garden path that my concern over his involvement with the school has naught to do with any personal feelings toward the man. It is always concern for you and your teachers, not to mention your pupils, that prompts my interference.

Your disinterested cousin,
Michael

Madeline hurried from the school at noon, cinching her pelisse tightly about her as a sudden gust of March wind threatened to tug it off. Thank heaven Mrs. Harris had allowed her to leave early. Even after the headmistress's explanation for her cold words and harsh behavior this morning, Madeline was sorely shaken.

Anthony had lied for her. Knowing what he risked for his niece, he'd still lied to save her. And that was without her having confided everything in him, without her trusting him. Well, she trusted him now. But she didn't know how to find him to tell him, especially since Mrs. Harris had banished him from the school.

At least he'd gained Mrs. Harris's agreement to help Tessa. Madeline would have been horrified if his lying to protect her had damaged his niece's chances. Ever since Papa had related what Anthony had endured at the hands of the Bickhams, she'd been unable to think of anything else. It was evil for a child to suffer so. No wonder he loathed any mention of morality. Given the Bickhams' twisted perception of it, how could he not?

The sound of horses' hooves coming slowly along the road behind her made her veer over to stay out of their way. Absorbed in her thoughts, she only noticed that the team had halted when a harsh male voice said, "Get in."

She turned to find Anthony holding open the door to a traveling coach as he threw down the step. He offered a gloved hand to her, but his face was so rigid, and his eyes held such a deep chill that she didn't at first take it.

"Get in!" he demanded. "Before someone sees us."

That jarred her from her surprise. Taking his hand, she let him pull her into the coach. She took a seat opposite him, but hardly recognized the Anthony she knew. His remote and cynical expression fleetingly reminded her of Lord Stoneville, sending a frisson of fear skittering along her nerves.

"So you're from Telford," this new strange Anthony said.

The bald statement took her so off guard that she could only gape at him.

When she didn't answer, he went on in that awful, frigid tone that struck dread in her heart. "Mrs. Harris let it slip that you'd been recommended by a school in Shrewsbury. Apparently she had no idea you were lying about where you were from."

"I never lied, not to her and not to you," she protested, his manner alarming her more by the moment.

He leaned forward, his eyes marble-cold. "You knew damned well what I thought. And you let me think it."

"Yes."

"Was that my uncle's idea?"

She gaped at him. "Why on earth would that be your *uncle's* idea?"

"Because your father is his physician."

"Not anymore!"

"No, of course not. After the scandalous death of that woman you told me of, I'm sure Sir Randolph ended the connection." His eyes narrowed. "Unless your story about your father's fall from grace was a lie, too."

"Certainly not!" His battery of accusations confused her. "I mean, none of the part about Papa and the scandal was a lie . . . but Sir Randolph—"

"My uncle is the reason you seized on me to help you, isn't he?"

"Only because—"

"I showed up at the school, and you saw a chance to regain your father's position with my uncle."

"No!"

"You knew about the situation with my niece, and you probably guessed that my uncle would give you anything in exchange for evidence of how irredeemable a scoundrel I am. All you need do was drag me back into precisely the sort of behavior that would ruin my chances of gaining Tessa forever."

Madeline gasped. *That's* what he thought? That she'd been trying to help his *uncle*? "Now see here," she said, horrified by his assumptions, "I didn't drag you into anything. We had a bargain."

"A bargain concocted by *you*. I was against it from the beginning, but you told me you would support Tessa's enrollment—"

"And I did! I have. I went to Mrs. Harris this morning to urge her to enroll your niece, but before I could broach the subject, she surprised me with that letter."

The icy quality of his gaze showed he didn't believe her. "Ah yes, Mrs. Harris. You should have included *her* in your machinations if you'd wanted them to turn out right."

"They *did* turn out right." Given what Papa had told her, she understood why he'd leaped to these conclusions, but why couldn't he give her a chance? "You've got this all wrong."

"Have I?" His eyes trailed down her with an insolence he'd never shown before. "I suppose you're going to tell me now that our swiving meant something to you, that you made love to me because you cared about me."

"Yes!"

"Which is why you ran off as soon as I fell asleep."

She groaned. "No . . . I mean . . . You can't possibly think after what we shared at Lord Stoneville's that I was only gulling you—"

"You gave me your innocence!" he hissed.

Her mouth dropped open. Obviously men were more observant than she'd given them credit for. And *that* must be why he was behaving so awful. He'd attributed the wrong motives to her.

"Did you think I wouldn't notice until it was too late?" he ground out. "Until you'd gone to my uncle with your pitiful tale of how I'd ruined you, offering to drag me through a scandal if he would restore your father's position?"

"Stop this! You've taken a mad idea into your head that is utterly false!"

She grabbed for his hands, but he snatched them away with a look of sheer horror before he caught himself and regained his remote expression.

Forcing herself not to panic, she said, "You're not making sense. Didn't you notice this morning how terrified I was that I would lose my position over some stupid party? You can't actually believe I'd reveal to *anyone* that I had given myself to a man, just on some chance that Sir Randolph would help my father."

"Why not?" His harsh words dripped acid upon her heart. "Everything else you've done has been on behalf of your father. You misled me into thinking you were a woman of the world, you coaxed me into having that party so you could meet Sir Humphry, you shared my bed . . ."

"I didn't do that for Papa," she whispered. "I mean . . . it started out that way, but not for the reasons you think."

When he just stared at her, his gaze still chillingly distant, she realized she had to tell him the truth, even the ugly truth about herself. "I knew if you took my innocence, you'd feel guilty and—"

"I'd offer marriage. *Then* you could use my influence to save your father however you pleased. Never mind that it would materially damage my chances of getting Tessa. Never mind that—"

"Would you please just listen?" she snapped, tired of his determination to believe ill of her. "I never thought you would offer marriage. I'm too far beneath you for that. But

I thought you'd feel guilty enough over taking my innocence to introduce me to Sir Humphry. Without my having to reveal I was from Telford."

"You mean, without your having to reveal who your father really was, in case I guessed his connection to my uncle, and thus guessed *your* connection—"

"I have no connection to that horrible devil, unless you count my absolute hatred of him. He's the one who put Papa in his present position, drat you!"

He blinked.

"Yes, your uncle. Surely you know him well enough to realize what he thinks of science. He's the one trying to coax Vicar Crosby to press for a trial. He's the one determined to ruin my father at all costs. I would no more side with him against you than I'd side with Lady Tarley against Mrs. Harris."

That, at last, seemed to punch through his assumptions, for the ice in his eyes melted enough for her to see the Anthony she knew and loved.

Loved? Yes, sometime in the past week she'd fallen in love with him. How, she wasn't sure, except that the seed had been planted from the moment he'd argued on his niece's behalf . . . and it had bloomed yesterday after she'd heard how a small boy missing his mother had been handed over to a half-mad aunt. How he had, for a brief period, lived a life consisting of one long succession of punishments.

He stared at her now, the cold and logical Anthony clearly warring with the one who'd made love to her. "Why would my uncle try to ruin your father?"

"Why does he do anything he does? Why does he want Tessa?"

"For the money, no doubt. My brother arranged for a handsome allowance for her guardian. That's why they wanted me when I was a boy—because I brought more money into the household."

And because Lady Bickham had needed someone new to bully. Or so it seemed to her after what Papa had said.

"Well, in Papa's case, it's more complicated. Sir Randolph and Papa have been at odds for years. That's what I tried to tell you—Papa hasn't worked for Sir Randolph since I was a girl." *Since you were a boy.*

How she wanted to tell him about that, too, but given his hasty retreat from the subject two nights ago and his present feelings for her, the surest way to bring this conversation to a halt was to rip that bandage off. First, she had to make him see she wasn't the enemy.

Which might be difficult given how he was scowling at her. "Why should I believe anything you tell me?" he snapped. "You could have come to me from the beginning to ask my help in fighting my uncle, yet you didn't."

"And if I had? Without knowing me, you would have avoided me like any other leech in society. I only wanted to meet Sir Humphry. I was afraid that if you knew the accusations Sir Randolph had made against Papa, you would refuse to help me because involving yourself might damage your niece's case. After all, you had no reason to believe me, no reason to take Papa's side."

His hard stare unnerved her. "What reason do I have now?"

"None. Except that you know my character. You know I won't hurt you. Until now, I've done my best to keep you and your niece out of my situation."

Some emotion flickered deep in his eyes before he

masked it. "Ah yes, your 'situation.'" He settled stiffly against the squabs. "It's time you revealed exactly what that situation is. The truth. All of it."

She nodded. Leaving nothing out, she told him about the death of Mrs. Crosby. She even included Sir Randolph's nasty assertions. At this point, the situation couldn't get any worse than it already was.

By the time she'd finished, he was watching her as a magistrate watches a thief at the bar. "I'll admit my uncle is heartless, but he doesn't act without reason. You expect me to believe that because of a falling-out with your father years ago, he would suddenly fabricate a tissue of lies to ruin a respectable physician? To possibly even bring about his death?"

"I don't expect you to believe anything. Why do you think I didn't tell you? Despite knowing how Sir Randolph prides himself on his moral standards, I still find it rather fantastical myself. But it's true."

The reference to Sir Randolph's morality seemed to shake him. Then his gaze froze over once more. "And of course I have only your word for the truth of it. Because in the time I could travel to Telford to determine how much of it is true, you could easily speak before the court here on my uncle's behalf."

"Oh, for heaven's sake, Anthony, why would I do that?"

"I don't know—to get him to stop persecuting your father?"

"You know better," she said softly. "You've seen me with my girls—you know I would never hurt your niece. How could you ever think it?"

Muttering a low oath, he stabbed his fingers through his hair, but at least he wasn't remote anymore. "I don't know what version of your tale to believe," he said hoarsely. "I don't know how to understand a woman who gives her innocence to a man out of calculation—"

"I told you—it started that way, but it didn't end that way. You know it didn't. That's why I left. Because what we shared was too beautiful to ruin." When he buried his face in his hands, clearly wavering over how much to trust her, she added softly, "That's why I tried to stop you from lying for me this morning. I didn't want you to give up your niece's future on my behalf. Not when you didn't know everything."

She laid her hand on his shoulder, and he started, then cast her a tortured glance. "What do you want from me? Isn't it enough that you nearly put an end to my chance to gain Tessa?"

"I just want you to believe me," she whispered. "Not to think these awful things about me and your uncle. I don't want anything from you other than that."

"No?" With a snort, he threw himself back against the seat. "So you've given up on trying to meet Sir Humphry? Or was that all a ruse, too?"

His continued suspicion tore at her, even knowing the cause of it. "If it was a ruse, then I planned it awfully well, since I wrote letters to him long before you came along. How clever of me to guess that you would show up at the school to bring my dastardly plan to fruition."

He regarded her closely. "You wrote him letters."

"I *told* you I did." What did that have to do with his distrusting her?

Taking her by surprise, he knocked on the ceiling. When the coachman opened the panel, he bit out an address.

"Where are we going?" she asked.

He shot the panel to, his expression grim. "You wanted to meet Sir Humphry, so that's where we're going."

Something in his manner made her wary. "Why now?"

"Because if you're telling the truth, then he has a record of everything you've just been saying to me. But if you're lying . . ."

A shiver wracked her. This could go wrong in so many ways. "You're assuming that he saw the letters. That his wife didn't tear them up before he even got them. That he kept them. Or that he will remember them if he happened not to keep them."

"You'd better hope he remembers them." Suspicion limned his features.

"Or what?" she asked. "What will you do to me if it all comes to naught?"

The question seemed to unnerve him, for he shifted his gaze to the window. "Think of it this way—you wanted to meet him, and now you'll get to."

That was true. And since she had few other choices available to her, she'd better seize this one. "Very well." She sat up straighter in the seat. "Let's go meet Sir Humphry."

Chapter Twenty-two

Dear Cousin,

Methinks you protest too much, sir. I suspect that you dislike the viscount not out of any noble concern, but because you don't like his drawing my attention from you, especially given his reputation for seducing widows. But you need not worry on that score—Lord Norcourt has made it perfectly plain that he has eyes for only one lady. Thus you remain my most important advisor among your sex. For now.

Your fair relation,
Charlotte

*B*y the time they reached Sir Humphry's, Anthony realized he was already losing this duel of wills. He'd begun losing it from the moment Madeline had parried his first accusation with her sword of reason and logic.

She was right—his assumptions about her made no sense. If she *had* chosen to betray him in some devil's bargain with his uncle, then why involve Sir Humphry? And why the whole business with the nitrous oxide party? If she'd meant to use it to expose Anthony as an unreformed profligate, then she'd chosen her tactics badly—

he'd made it clear from the beginning that he wouldn't participate in the party itself.

For that matter, why wait so long to share his bed when she could have seduced him in a way more certain to expose him? She could have arranged for them to be caught by Mrs. Harris—she wouldn't have had to lose her innocence for that. In one fell swoop, she would have destroyed his chance to gain Tessa.

He grimaced. Their joining Saturday night was the real reason he'd clung to his position as long as he had. He was still smarting over her abandonment of him afterward. No woman had ever left *his* bed. He'd always been the one to leave.

And he didn't know how to handle it. God save him, she was introducing him to all manner of things he didn't know how to handle.

Anthony studied her unobtrusively while they waited in the foyer for the butler to take in Anthony's card. Like a magpie, she flitted from one glittering object to another—an intriguing display of crystals, a print of the Strand framed with its engraved copper plate, a vase carved from agate. To anyone else she would seem a casual observer, but he knew her too well for that. Strange how a week of dealing with her in a classroom had taught him how to tell when she was nervous.

Like now, when her trembling hands betrayed her. She wasn't as confident of what might happen as she pretended. And yet . . .

On some gut-deep level, he knew she'd told the truth in the carriage. Every nuance of her voice had trumpeted her loathing for his uncle. Clearly, the idea of selling her soul to regain her father's position in Telford disgusted her.

"Lord Norcourt, how kind of you to call on my husband."

The lilting voice of Lady Davy made Anthony groan. He looked up to see her gliding down the stairs, disapproval stamped upon her sharp features.

"Good day to you, madam." He offered her his most charming smile. "I hope my friend is available to visitors."

Her gaze flicked to Madeline, and Anthony knew what the jealous wife of the chemist saw—a very pretty, very young rival for her husband's affections.

"This is Miss Prescott," he said as Madeline hurried to stand beside him. When the name seemed to register with Lady Davy, he took Madeline's hand, tucked it into the crook of his arm, and added, "She's my fiancée."

Madeline dug her fingers into his arm, but Lady Davy softened. "Fiancée?"

"I wanted to introduce her to Sir Humphry. Is he here?"

The woman offered a faint nod. "He's in his laboratory in back. But I don't think he'd want me to fetch him—"

"We wouldn't want you to interrupt his work. I know the way. If you don't mind, we'll just go on back ourselves."

Lady Davy frowned. "He's been quite ill of late. I'm not sure a visit—"

"I promise not to keep him long. We have other calls to pay." He gazed down at Madeline with as tender a glance as he could muster under the tense circumstances. "I've been showing off my dear Madeline all over town."

Madeline's startled expression swiftly gentled into a yearning one that made his feigned tenderness suddenly feel very real.

Apparently it was enough to convince Lady Davy to

take pity on a courting couple, for she said, "I suppose it would be all right then. If you don't stay long."

Casting the woman another ingratiating smile, he led Madeline into the hall, relieved that Lady Davy had chosen not to accompany them. This conversation would be better conducted in private.

Still, he held his breath until they'd passed far enough down the hall to be out of hearing. Only then could he relax.

"Why did you tell her we are engaged?" Madeline whispered.

"It was the only way to get past her. She seemed to remember your name. Besides, the arrival of a rakehell with an unmarried lady in tow was bound to rouse her suspicions. She doesn't even allow female servants in the house."

"Why?"

"Because she fears he'll dally with them."

Madeline snorted. "Then she shouldn't have married him. What point is there in marrying a man you can't trust?"

A sharp pain struck his chest. "I agree." Could Madeline ever trust *him* to take care of her? She certainly didn't trust him at the moment, or she would have revealed more of her real situation sooner.

They found Sir Humphry sitting bent over a table covered with a sheet of copper and several flasks. Although nearly forty-five, he still possessed the slender figure, peerless brow, and full head of brown curls that had earned him the scornful name of dandy in his youth. But now he looked worn with care, and his pallor was none too good.

Not that it kept the man from working. Oblivious to their entrance, Sir Humphry poured a chemical onto the copper, then shook his head when a plume of smoke arose. When he began making notations on a sheet of paper, Anthony cleared his throat, having learned long ago never to startle a chemist at work.

Sir Humphry looked up. "Norcourt!" he cried, setting down the flask. He started to rise, then fell back into his chair when an attack of coughing hit him.

Ever the physician's daughter, Madeline hurried to his side. "Are you all right, sir? Can I fetch you some water?" She started to push the smoking sheet of copper aside, but he stayed her hand.

"No, no, my dear," he choked out, "it's . . . not the chemical." He hacked another moment. "Devilish cough. Plagues me at the worst times." He regarded Madeline with interest. "And who might you be? Norcourt's latest lady friend?"

"This is Miss Madeline Prescott," Anthony said, watching to see how the man reacted. It wasn't so much to gauge her truthfulness as to gauge Sir Humphry's knowledge of her situation. There was still a chance his wife had kept him unaware of the letters.

Sir Humphry's brow wrinkled. "Why does that name sound familiar?"

"Because I wrote to you, sir," Madeline said hastily. "About my father, a physician in Telford."

It took Sir Humphry no more than a second to shoot Anthony an accusing glance. "And what have you to do with this?"

"I take it you know what she means?" Anthony countered.

"Answer my question, Norcourt."

He stiffened. "I'm here because I'm her friend."

A cynical expression hardened Sir Humphry's features as his gaze swept insolently down her body. "A recent friendship, I'll wager."

When Madeline went rigid, something in Anthony snapped. He was tired of his friends making assumptions about her character. Never mind that he'd made the same ones only an hour ago—that had been a temporary madness.

His friends only made them because she was with *him*. She'd certainly chosen her champion badly, hadn't she? A man she couldn't trust, a man who until now had been nothing but a fribble and a disgrace to his family name, who couldn't even get her an audience with his own friend without risking the niece he held dear. And that very niece wouldn't even be with his damned aunt and uncle if he hadn't spent his entire life thumbing his nose at the world.

No more. "Actually," he said with a viscount's dignity, "we lived in the same town for some years, so I'd say the friendship is long-standing." When Sir Humphry's expression grew more thoughtful, Anthony pressed his point. "I would greatly appreciate whatever you could do to help her and her father."

The chemist frowned at Madeline. "Why didn't you say Lord Norcourt was your friend in the first place, madam?"

"I didn't think I should presume." She thrust out her chin. "To be honest, sir, I thought you would want to defend your findings about nitrous oxide to the world."

"Defend them!" Sir Humphry cried. "Are you mad? Now that nitrous has become the favorite entertainment for parties of a certain sort, any discussion of its medicinal properties is laughed at."

"The people of Telford wouldn't know that. They aren't familiar with society's ways. They're still clinging to the superstitions of their neighboring Welshmen. So if the great Sir Humphry Davy were to come and explain how my father was acting upon sound medical assumptions regarding the effects of the gas, they would probably listen."

He hunched down in the chair. "Or they would claim that it was my foolish statement about its pain-relieving effects that had caused this woman's death—the one you wrote to me about. Then *I* would be vilified in the press."

"I don't think that would happen, sir—"

But he was already shaking his head. "I'm not taking that chance. I've got a reputation to uphold. I can't be haring off to some provincial town on the word of some friend's friend." He nodded to Norcourt. "No offense, sir."

"I would pay for your expenses," Anthony persisted, "and arrange for you to stay in a comfortable inn. It would take a few days at most."

"That's not the point!" Sir Humphry shouted, then lapsed into a fit of coughing that shook his spindly frame. When he could speak again, he glared at them both. "Don't you understand? I can barely drag myself from the bed each morning, and rarely go more than an hour without a fit of coughing. Such a journey, into the wilds of Shropshire, is likely to kill me."

Madeline stepped forward. "But, sir, the newspaper said you're planning a trip to Penzance this week."

"The paper lied. My wife planted that tale to keep people from importuning me. My mother is ailing, but I have yet to see her. These attacks keep me from it."

"Humphry, this is a dire situation," Anthony said.

"And so is mine," the chemist shot back. "Forgive me, but I cannot do it."

"Then perhaps if you were to write a letter—" Anthony began.

"Without first speaking to the individuals involved?" Sir Humphry regarded the two of them with a skeptical eye. "How do I know you haven't been gulled by this woman into participating in a matter better left to the authorities of her town?"

Anthony bit back an oath. "Does a man offer marriage to a woman who gulls him?"

Sir Humphry blinked.

"She is to be my wife," Anthony went on. "Surely you would help the wife of a friend."

"If you're marrying her, then you can bloody well use your own influence to save her father," the chemist ground out. "For myself, I want none of it."

"Damn it, Humphry—"

"Anthony," Madeline coaxed in a low voice, placing her hand on his arm. "We've tried our best. It is time we leave Sir Humphry to his conscience."

That made the chemist's face darken into a scowl. "My conscience is clear, madam. So I suggest you take my friend away before I lose my temper entirely."

Anthony's own temper was perilously close to exploding, but he still had enough presence of mind to allow Madeline to draw him from the room. They passed through the house and out to the carriage in silence, but once they reached it, he turned to her, her expression of defeat rocking him back on his heels.

"Where to now, sweetheart?" he asked hoarsely. "Have

you some other alternative you'd planned to pursue if Sir Humphry could not help you?"

She shook her head, her eyes sadly distant. "I don't know . . . I hadn't thought beyond . . ."

"I'll take care of it." He barked a direction to the coachman, then helped her into the carriage, alarmed by her dazed expression. The only time he'd seen her like this was when Stoneville had been forcing nitrous oxide on her.

They traveled a short way in silence. Then she seemed to muster herself, for she cast him a glance so pitiful it clawed at his insides. "Where are we going?"

"My old bachelor quarters are nearby. The entrance is discreet, so no one will see you enter, and no one will disturb us while we talk."

His coach stopped outside an alley, blocking entrance to it except from the carriage, and he leaped out, then handed her down. Momentarily grateful to the women who'd demanded discretion of him in their liaisons, he hurried her the few feet to the private door, unlocked it, then hustled her inside before waving the carriage on. His coachman knew where to wait for a summons.

While he closed the door, leaving them in a dim stairwell lit only by a transom above their heads, Madeline watched him in clear confusion. "You kept your bachelor quarters? But surely your family has a town house."

Debating whether to tell her the truth, he led her up the spindly stairs to his modest rooms on the next floor. As he let her into the suite and locked the door behind them, her gaze fell on the licentious prints hanging on his walls.

When she shot him a questioning glance, he sighed. No point in hiding any of it from her now. "I initially kept my rooms with the intention of using them once I gained guardianship of Tessa. But I haven't been here since I began that process, for fear that my uncle might be having them watched."

Alarm flickered in her eyes. "What if he is? Now that he's seen *me*—"

"It no longer matters."

"Of course it matters! I don't want to cause trouble for your niece. You've already done too much for me as it is, by introducing me to your friend."

"Which did you no good," he pointed out, still angry at Sir Humphry.

"That's not true. You believed in me even before he revealed he'd received my letters, and that touches me more than you can imagine. I'm so sorry you've been forced to lie for me twice today, inventing an engagement and—"

"That wasn't a lie." The words left his mouth before he could consider them, but he wouldn't take them back. "Sir Humphry is right, you know. The best way to combat my uncle is for you to marry me."

She paled. "I couldn't allow you to make such a sacrifice, Anthony."

"It's not a sacrifice, damn it!" Striding up to her, he seized her hands. "If anyone would be making a sacrifice, it would be you, having to put up with me."

A self-deprecating smile touched her lips. "That's very sweet of you to say, but we both know you could do much better."

"I don't know that at all. You're an amazing woman, Madeline. I knew it the moment I met you. So please don't punish me for briefly losing sight of it in my madness this afternoon."

"Punish you! By keeping you from yoking yourself to a woman whose family is steeped in scandal?"

"I don't care."

"Your niece will care," she said softly. "If you marry me, you'll lose custody of her for certain. Sir Humphry's comments about my gulling you are only half of what your uncle will say to the world. He'll claim you're helping an evil man, that I sold myself to you to gain your influence on my father's behalf . . . He'll make you out to be a wicked reprobate allying himself with another wicked reprobate."

That she was right didn't alter his purpose. "We'll fight my uncle together, then. We'll keep fighting until we get her back, even if it takes years."

Her voice dropped to a whisper. "So she can suffer the same things you suffered all those years ago? Would you see *her* tied to the bed at night as well?"

His heart dropped into his stomach. "You know about that?"

"I asked Papa about it yesterday after what you said about his abandoning you. He didn't, you know."

She related a sequence of events that made perfect sense and absolved her father of blame, but he heard them with only half an ear.

No wonder she hesitated to marry him. His secret was out.

Chapter Twenty-three

Dear Charlotte,

   If you mean Miss Prescott, then I should warn you that even if his lordship professes an interest in marriage, you should advise her against it. Rakehells are rarely faithful to one woman. As for my being upset about his drawing your attention from me, that wasn't the case, but think what you will if it soothes your pride.

                    Always your concerned cousin,
                    Michael

*A*nthony?" Madeline cried, alarmed when he dropped onto a divan that had clearly been designed for seduction, sudden despair sweeping his face.

She hurried to sit beside him. "Anthony, what's wrong?"

He stared at the empty fireplace. Ample light from the windows fronting the street turned the walnut furnishings and rich yellow walls into a cozy blend of amber and bronze. It contrasted sharply with the desolation in his eyes. "How did you find out about my being tied up?"

Why was he so upset? He'd just asked her to marry him, for heaven's sake—*that* was more astonishing than anything she'd learned about his childhood. Marriage between them was impossible, of course, but the fact that he'd asked warmed her to her very soul.

"My father told me what the Bickhams did," she said. "I just explained that."

"So he knew *why* they tied me up?"

"Because you kept trying to run away. Sir Randolph said you missed your mother."

A strange relief suffused his features. "Ah. I did miss my mother, that's true." He dropped his eyes to where his hands gripped his knees. "So . . . er . . . that has naught to do with why you won't marry me."

"It has *everything* to do with it. The thought of them tying your niece to a bed is appalling! You have to save her."

"I intend to save her." His gaze shot to hers. "And I intend to save you, too. I took your innocence. I won't let you suffer the consequences of that. We'll be married, and that's an end to it."

So *that's* why he wished to marry her. Tears welled in her throat that she ruthlessly squelched. What had she been thinking? Of *course* that was his reason. He was an honorable man—that did him credit. She mustn't be hurt by it.

She would simply ignore the part of her hoping that he could feel more.

"The thought of living my life without a husband doesn't frighten me." Not much, anyway. "So don't let my loss of innocence prod you into offering for me."

"I'm not," he said fiercely.

His answer perplexed her. "If you're worried about my bearing a child, you shouldn't be. We used that contraption of yours, so we're safe."

"That's not why I'm offering, either." He settled his arm about her shoulders. "Can't you see, dearest? I want *you*. You're the only woman I can imagine marrying." His voice roughened. "Surely the advantages to you are enough to outweigh your scruples about marrying a man as wicked as I."

She placed a finger against his lips, her heart breaking for him. "Don't say such things." He *did* care. Perhaps he hadn't yet said he loved her—perhaps he never would— but at least he wasn't proposing merely out of a desire to behave honorably. "You aren't wicked. I don't care what you did before—in the past week, you've proved yourself to be a good, and, yes, moral person. And if not for your niece—"

He cut her off with a long, needy kiss that seared her to the soles of her feet. Several moments passed in which he possessed her mouth so thoroughly she actually forgot to breathe. She even forgot her objections.

Until he drew back and released her from his spell. "Marry me," he urged.

"Oh, Anthony, if you only knew how badly I want to be your wife. But we have time for that later. Your Tessa doesn't."

"Time? How long will it be before my uncle wins his attempt to have your father charged with a crime? Once that happens, saving him will become harder." He stroked her cheek tenderly. "Uncle Randolph's desire to ruin your father is likely born of revenge for the help your father gave me years ago. I won't repay his kindness by doing nothing to save him."

"Then pay for Papa's lawyer if I have to hire one. But marrying me—"

"Might make a lawyer unnecessary. Your vicar may bring charges against a defenseless physician with a spinster daughter, but I doubt he'll bring them against a viscount's father-in-law."

That was true, and Anthony's willingness to throw his rank behind Papa touched her to the heart. Made her want to give in. Except for one thing. "If you involve yourself in this, it will almost certainly mean the end of your chances to gain Tessa. Your uncle will gleefully point to your scandalous association as proof that you're unfit to be guardian to a child."

"Yes, he will. And I'll argue that being a respectably married man counts for something. After all, *you* aren't the one accused of scandalous behavior, only your father. And I have Mrs. Harris on my side, too." He seized her arms. "I can help your father and Tessa both. It's better than taking a chance on his life, isn't it?"

"If it comes to that, you may handle it however you please. But until it does, work to gain guardianship of your niece first. I can't bear to think what she might be suffering even now. The thought of them tying *her* to the bed every night—"

"They will not tie her."

"How can you be sure?"

"I just can." He rose to pace the spare wood floors. "They'll preach and read lectures and make her kneel on cold marble and other such creative punishments, but they won't tie her. They didn't tie Jane, and they won't tie Tessa."

"Their daughter suffered such punishments, too? No wonder she married the first man to offer for her, even though he was only a headmaster. Her parents were very angry over it, you know."

He didn't know. To his shame, he hadn't kept up with Jane at all since he'd left the Bickhams. "So is she friendly with her parents now?"

"They hardly speak." She wouldn't let him change the subject. "But when she lived with them, they had no cause to tie her up—she had nowhere to go if she ran away. Your niece, on the other hand, has you to run to, so—"

"That's not why they tied me, Madeline," he said in a voice so wrought with emotion she could hardly make out the words.

"What?"

"They didn't tie me to prevent my running away." He let out a frustrated oath. "They tied me because of . . . how I am. What I am."

The shame on his face filled her with unnamed dread. "What do you mean?"

Refusing to look at her, he leaned against the mantel to stretch out his arm atop it. "Do you know what the sin of onanism is?"

She blinked. "Masturbation, you mean?"

His startled gaze shot to her. "Yes, that would be the naturalist's term. And what do *you* know of it, anyway?"

A blush touched her cheeks. "One of Papa's patients gave him a copy of *Onania; or the Heinous Sin of Self-Pollution.* I overheard Mama and Papa discussing it, so I . . . read it in secret."

A bitter laugh escaped him. He focused his gaze on his hand as it curled into a fist. "Well, then you know what I'm speaking of, since my uncle had the same book. I committed the sin of onanism several times a day, beginning when I was nine and only lessening when I could sate my desires in other ways."

The Bickhams had tied him to the bed to keep him from pleasuring himself? Oh, her poor sweet dear!

How could they have humiliated him so cruelly? She'd also read the other book Papa had mentioned, one by a doctor who'd debated what the first writer said. There seemed no agreement on the matter.

Besides, he'd been only a boy! As she stood up, she chose her words carefully. "You must have been a precocious child."

"Precocious?" His gaze shot to her, dark with anger and shame. "That's what you call a child who can read Latin and recite Shakespeare at three, not one so consumed by his desires that he can't keep his hands off his own penis."

"Anthony," she said in a soothing voice, approaching him with the caution she might show a wounded fox caught in a trap, "other children do—"

"At nine? So persistently that no amount of lectures and cold baths and nights spent in futile prayer can keep them from touching themselves? How many children are so hungry for it that they must be tied to a bed to keep from . . ."

He trailed off with a curse, but when he started to push past her, she gripped his hand to pull him to her side. "Now see here—everyone explores their bodies, don't they? I can't see what's wrong with it, no matter what the Bickhams said."

"What's wrong is the frequency and intensity of my urges." His eyes met hers, shadowed by uncertainty. "I still have very strong desires, Madeline. Sometimes I fear I won't be able to control them if I ever loose them completely."

Squeezing her hand compulsively, he gazed past her out the window. "I almost wish the writer of that damned book had been right about how pleasuring oneself weakened your 'healthy' urges once you grew to a man."

"Don't say that! There's nothing wrong with your urges. Papa called that book sheer quackery, and he's right. Only your ignorant relations would read it to a child." She laced her fingers with his. "Besides, if pleasuring oneself is evil, then why do animals do it? Horses, for example. I heard about it from the stableboys."

"Are horses so desperate for it they nearly kill themselves trying to get free?"

"You were desperate for it *because* they tied you down. It made you focus on it even more. That's not why you tried to get free; anyone would." She kissed his hand, her heart twisting inside her for what he'd suffered. "You were just a boy, my darling. What boy wants to spend his nights tied to a bed?"

Silent tears slid down his cheeks that he rubbed away with a furious gesture. "I hated it so much," he whispered. "Some nights . . . I just wanted to die."

"Of course you did." Her own tears fell freely.

"I lay there alone in the dark, wondering what creatures might crawl up my leg." He spoke as if from far away, every word rousing an answering ache inside her. "To distract myself, I'd think of the last pretty maid I'd seen and my cock would stiffen and I couldn't stop it, and I would wish to God I weren't so very wicked—"

"You weren't wicked!" She pulled him into her embrace.

"You were a young boy in a strange house, who didn't understand why his body betrayed him, who only wanted someone to care about him. That house *was* unspeakable. You should never have been sent there."

He buried his face in her neck, his body shaking so violently she had to stroke him to soothe his emotions. "My father never knew what they did."

"But he did find out you were being tied down at night after Papa told him."

He shuddered. "That would explain why Father brought me home." Lifting his face to her, he choked out, "But he behaved so oddly upon my return, as if he couldn't bear the sight of me."

"He was probably too plagued by guilt to face you." She smoothed a lock of hair from his flushed brow. "He had sent you where he thought you'd be safe, and then he learned that you were anything but. He probably blamed himself. Did he talk to you about it?"

"Only once. Right after I came home, he asked if I wanted to tell him anything about living at my uncle's. I said nothing . . . I was afraid to tell him." He dropped his gaze. "I was afraid he'd find out how debased his son was."

"You are *not* debased! You had a natural desire that ignorant people tried to stifle—that's all." Something dawned on her. "Is that why you haven't told the courts what happened to you at their hands? Because you're ashamed?"

"Because I knew the courts would merely consider it further evidence of my bad character." His voice dripped sarcasm. "My aunt and uncle would claim that they'd been trying to save my soul, and that their lack of success only proves how wicked I am. I daresay the courts would believe them."

"They shouldn't!"

His usual dry self began to return. "You were the one who pointed out that I've wasted my life in the reckless pursuit of pleasure, remember? You were right, too."

She blushed to hear her own words thrown back at her. "I merely didn't understand why you chose that path. I still don't. You say you have strong urges, but surely now that you're grown you can control them—"

"That's *how* I control them." He swept his hand to encompass his bachelor's domain, moving away from the mantel to stand before a closed door that probably led to the bedchamber. "With short encounters, different women, brief but frequent liaisons." He added, almost to himself, "Anything to give me release and hold the dark nights at bay."

"Why not do that with a wife?"

He shook his head. "Gently bred females aren't prepared for the likes of me, sweetheart. I've always been afraid to overly tax one woman. I'm still afraid that during the long years of a marriage I might not be able to maintain my control."

Clearly, he meant that to be a warning. She caught her breath, fighting to make her words casual. "You mean you might be tempted to take a mistress, like other married men of your rank?"

"No, not that," he said with all the fervor she could have asked for. "My parents were faithful to each other; they had a wonderful marriage. I want no less for myself. But that means inflicting my unruly urges on a wife, and no woman should have to suffer that simply because I can't face the dark nights alone. If I hadn't taken your innocence, I would never . . ."

When he trailed off, she suddenly understood. He'd buried his boyhood fears in the soft flesh of women, but only under strict circumstances, terrified that if he didn't watch himself, he would loose the monster his aunt had convinced him he was. And he'd known marriage wasn't conducive to watching oneself all the time.

He went on in a subdued tone. "That's why you needn't worry I'm making a sacrifice by marrying you. You'll be the one enduring my insatiable appetites."

"Drat it, you're *not* the half-crazed fiend you make yourself out to be. Look how easily you controlled your 'appetites' that day at Mr. Godwin's. If you were incapable of restraining yourself, you would have attacked Lady Tarley the minute she brandished those breasts of hers."

His eyes darkened. "I damned near lost control with *you* in your classroom."

"But you didn't." She gave him a tender smile as she walked up to him. "And I've never felt truly afraid with you. Never."

Sudden yearning leaped in his features. "Then marry me." He cupped her face in his hands. "I need you. I've never needed anyone so much. Marry me."

Her throat felt tight and raw. "I will, I swear. Once you've got Tessa away from your horrible relations."

He let out a low oath. "That could take months, and anything could happen to your father in that time. I can handle both."

"I won't take the chance." Not after hearing what *he'd* endured. He might think the Bickhams had only been cruel to him because of his "debased" character, but she wasn't so sure. And how could she be happy in a marriage built upon his niece's suffering?

Releasing her, he leaned back against the door to cross his arms over his chest. "You mean, you won't trust me with anything so weighty as my niece's future and your father's life." His eyes held an unreadable emotion. "That's why you kept me in the dark from the time we met, why I had to drag the truth out of you . . . or stumble over it by accident. Because you knew you couldn't trust me."

"That's not true! I trusted you with my innocence, didn't I?"

He uttered a harsh laugh. "No, you didn't—you sacrificed it to me, trying to keep me in the dark. Not that I blame you—God knows I haven't done much in my life to inspire trust. But let's at least have the truth between us now. Tessa is merely an excuse for not yoking yourself for life to a man like me, whom you're probably not even sure you can trust to keep his prick in his trousers."

The bleak accusation tore at her. He seemed to really believe what he was saying—that she considered him unworthy to be her husband. And he probably thought he was. He'd spent an entire life railing at the Bickhams, while secretly believing they were right about him, that he was a monster inside.

That's why he donned his devil-may-care façade—to hide the "debasement" within him. As long as she refused to marry him, he would continue to believe it.

Not if she could help it. Since she refused to let him risk his niece's future, she'd have to prove him wrong by other means. Even if it meant taking a chance with her heart.

"You're wrong about me," she said softly. "I want us to delay our marriage until your niece's situation is settled, but until then, I mean to be yours in body and soul, no matter how reckless that may be."

As he stared at her with such powerful longing it made her chest hurt, she added, "I trust you implicitly, Anthony. How could I not trust the man I love?"

He blinked rapidly, then glanced away. "You mustn't say that. About . . . loving me."

Her heart caught in her throat. "Why not?"

"Because it's already hard enough for me to control myself around you. If I thought that you really loved me—"

"Oh, but I do." Ignoring his protective stance, she moved close enough to catch his head in her hands and force his gaze back to her. "And I'm not afraid of you. You aren't this beast you seem to think yourself."

Taking her by surprise, he grabbed her by the arms and then pivoted to shove her back against the door so hard it knocked the wind out of her. "You don't know what I am," he growled as he loomed close. "You've never seen me out of control, never seen me as myself. Even when taking your innocence, I showed a restraint that required every ounce of my will. But if you keep saying—"

"That I love you? I can't help myself, you know." She felt small and helpless with the bulk of his body against hers, yet any fear it gave her was fleeting. "I do love you. Caution me if you will, but it won't change anything."

"You don't understand." As his heated gaze raked her, his fingers dug into her shoulders, sending a thrill chasing over her flesh. "With other women, it's easy to be careful—they only rouse my body. But with you . . ."

His voice grew ragged. "You rouse my mind, my senses, my soul. I spend my nights dreaming of you, and my days aching to be with you. When we're together, it's too much to bear, and when we're not, it's the only thing I want."

"That's love, my darling—not the beast," she whispered, recognizing some of the same things she felt. "Because I, too, lose control whenever we're together. I think I proved that Saturday night."

"You didn't lose control. You did exactly what you set out to do."

"I didn't set out to lose myself in you. Or forget my purpose." Looping her arms about his neck, she brought her face up close to his. "I didn't set out to fall in love, I promise you. But if you think a paltry thing like the supposed violence of your desires will frighten me off now that I love you, then *you* don't know *me*."

She kissed him, desperate to make him see that he had her, no matter what. Within seconds, he took over the kiss, grasping her head to hold her still as his mouth plundered and ravaged and yes, devoured hers.

His teeth nipped at her lip, his rough whiskers raked her skin, and his hands tore at her buttons and tapes as they had that night at Stoneville's, but this time she didn't try to slow him or do anything to halt the urgency of his desires.

He was the one to do that. He stopped abruptly, halting her hands on his cravat as she tried to unknot it. His hot breath came hard and fast, and the tumult of need in his eyes made her shiver beneath her gown.

"I won't . . . I mustn't make love to you *here*," he said with an outraged dignity utterly at odds with his supposed debased character . . . and the rising bulge of his erection against her *mons*. "Not in this place where . . . You aren't like the others. I refuse to see you sullied."

In a flash, she understood, and his reluctance angered her. "Well, I refuse to let *you* put me on a tidy shelf labeled 'wife,' where you have to restrain yourself with me. I'm not one of your fragile society females."

"You have no idea how—"

"—fierce you can be when you 'loose yourself'? Actually, I do. And if you'll recall, I didn't crumple beneath your rough advances that day at the school." She snorted. "You and your half-baked notions about what a woman can bear—you're the one who has 'no idea' about *me*. I can be just as ungoverned as you."

Fire leaped in his face. "You don't know the meaning of the word." The hint of challenge in his tone was unmistakable.

"We'll see about that."

She dropped to her knees on the floor. "Prepare yourself, my love. I'm about to demonstrate my lusty side. Because this is one woman you'll never have to worry about overtaxing in the bedchamber."

Chapter Twenty-four

Dear Cousin,
I share your skepticism about rakehells reforming,
but Lord Norcourt isn't like other men of his kind. If
anyone can keep him settled, it is Madeline. She has a
way with him unlike any I've seen. I believe they suit
each other.

Your friend in all things,
Charlotte

Anthony watched in shock as his practical little blue-stocking unbuttoned his trousers with clear intent. She couldn't mean . . . she wouldn't know how . . .

"What the bloody devil do you think you're doing?" he ground out.

Her smile was downright witchy as she unfastened his drawers. "Proving we're meant for each other. You claim to have an insatiable appetite. Well, *I* have an insatiable curiosity. Ever since I read in that harem book about pleasuring a man with one's mouth, I've wondered how it worked. And I intend to find out."

His already half-roused cock stiffened unbearably. "It isn't something . . . that is, only whor— . . . women of a certain kind—"

"Do this? Are you sure?" Her eyes shone a hot, inquisitive gold that sent his blood rushing to his head. "You don't know what a man and his wife do in the privacy of their bedchamber. Can't a wife pleasure her husband in this manner?"

"Well, yes, but . . . *I* don't usually . . . That is, I have found . . ."

With her cheery muslin gown pooling on the floor about her, she shot him a bemused smile. "Don't tell me the jaded rakehell hasn't tried this particular act."

Perversely, color rose in his cheeks. "I have. But I . . . prefer not to."

"Oh?" She drew his trousers and drawers down, and his bad boy sprang out, practically doing a dance for her. Her eyes glittered up at him mischievously. "Your body says otherwise."

"My body's a damned fool. It happily ignores my attempts at restraint."

A sudden awareness touched her features. "*That's* why you don't like this sort of pleasuring. Because it means giving up control of the act entirely."

Oh, she read him too well for his comfort. But it was more than that. The first few times a woman had sucked his cock had been like lying in that damn bed at the Bickhams', helpless to stop his bad boy from pushing up his nightclothes. He'd hated being unable to govern his impulses, and he'd avoided it from there on.

That was why the idea of *her* taking him that way, in her respectable teacher's day dress, tantalized him beyond reason. She was the only woman who'd ever tempted him to lose himself in her. The only one who'd ever loved him.

Love *him*? She must be insane. Or at least unaware of

what she was getting herself into. But if she took him in her mouth, she would learn just how uncontrolled he could be. Then she'd never marry him.

"It has nothing to do with control," he lied. "I just don't want you to . . . it's not right for you to . . ."

She cast him an earnest glance. "It's no more wrong for me than for any other woman, especially if you intend me to be your wife."

As she leaned back to stare at him, her hair fell in a delicious tumble about her shoulders, making his breath catch in his throat. He tried to ignore the alluring image she made, but that was damned hard to do.

"You have odd notions about marriage," she went on. "It needn't be limited to only one kind, where you are forced to withhold your strongest impulses and I faint at the sight of your manly excesses. We're different from other people, so why not have a different marriage? We can make it whatever we want."

He uttered a choked laugh. "You only just lost your innocence two days ago, sweetheart—you have no idea what you're talking about."

"That is precisely why I want to try this. How else can I learn?" She leaned forward to lick him, sending his blood into a frenzy. "Besides, I think it's time you discover I can handle your lack of restraint perfectly well."

"Madeline . . ." he said, half demand, half plea.

But her mouth already encased his cock. A groan erupted from low in his chest. He fought the urge to grab her head and force it roughly up and down on his eager flesh. Her caresses were too soft, too gentle, yet even so, he let out an audible moan when she drew back.

"You must tell me what to do," she said, as her finger

circled the damp crown of his cock, driving him insane. "The book wasn't specific enough." A rare blush touched her cheeks. "And I don't think I can take all of you in my mouth."

"You don't need to," he choked out, giving up the fight. "Just close your hand around the root and suck what's left." As she gripped him as instructed, he added, "Only do not be too gentle, I pray you. Hard is better."

She grinned. "I would imagine hard is always better."

He let out a garbled laugh that turned to a sigh of pure pleasure when her mouth seized him, drawing on him so strongly that he gasped.

God save him. He'd as good as given her permission to reduce him to a pile of rubble—not that the impudent chit needed permission. She would do as she pleased with him anyway.

His sane half wanted to keep protesting her behaving like his fancy woman. The insane half, guided by his willful cock, prayed to God she would suck him dry.

The insane half got precisely what it wanted, for she began a motion that sent him reeling back against the wall. Within moments, he'd grasped her head and was thrusting into her mouth, unable to control the impulse. She weathered it admirably, and seconds later, he could feel his release building.

It was too soon, too fast, and he tried desperately to halt it, but watching her pleasure him made that impossible, and when he then tried to pull free, she grasped his naked hips to hold him prisoner. Before he knew it, he'd exploded in her mouth like the unconscionable scoundrel he was.

Cursing his lack of control, he fumbled in his coat for his handkerchief so she could spit into it, but she was already swallowing his seed. He gaped at her, having only seen whores do that before. "You didn't have to . . ."

"What?" She took the handkerchief and wiped her mouth with a look of pure innocence. "That's how they described it in the harem book." An uncertain frown touched her brow. "Did I do it wrong?"

"God, no," he gasped as he collapsed weak-kneed against the wall. He hadn't kissed her, fondled her breasts . . . anything. For God's sake, he hadn't even removed her clothes! And she worried about doing it wrong.

Drawing her up into his embrace, he struggled for breath. Had she no idea what she'd done to him? How appalled he was that he hadn't pleasured her once?

"I told you I could handle you," she murmured, her teasing smile stirring his cock to life again.

Anger surged through him. She thought she'd made her point with her little show of wickedness, as if one encounter proved everything. "You have no bloody idea how to handle me," he warned.

When she drew back, clearly shocked by his tone, he forced her hand to his rising erection. "I wasn't lying about being insatiable. Already I want you again."

"Good." Her eyebrows lifted in challenge. "I am more than happy to oblige."

He pinned her against the wall, grabbing her hands on either side of her to hold her captive. "Don't play with me, Madeline. You'll regret it."

Thrusting her breasts deliberately against his chest, she said, "I doubt that." She brought her mouth up to his, then whispered, "Show me the beast, my love. I want to see the beast unleashed."

His bad boy went into a frenzy at the idea of doing as

it pleased. Yet he hesitated. What if he did show her? And what if she fled screaming from him?

Better now than after they married. If she wanted him as he was, then by God, she would have what she wanted.

Abandoning his usual care, he stripped her clothes from her, heedless of what tore in the process. He ripped her chemise right off, partly out of eagerness to see her naked, partly out of need to shock her into sense. She could handle him, could she? Did she know what that could mean?

Apparently, she did, for her eyes burned with excitement throughout his performance. Then she actually returned the favor by tearing his clothes, too, popping off buttons, shredding the ends of tapes. She even took the initiative by kissing him, and when it rapidly exploded into something hot and wild and raw, with both of them fighting for mastery, he wanted to throw back his head and crow.

He never allowed himself to be like this with a woman. And the fact that it was with a woman who claimed to love him—*love* him, what madness!—was every bit as intoxicating as he'd feared. The feel of her naked flesh against him further inflamed him, and even though he knew he should fondle her and utter soothing compliments, all those things he did to keep a firm rein on his wild appetites, he couldn't think beyond wanting to be inside her.

Then she hissed, "Take me, Anthony. Take me now."

That was all he needed to lift her legs, still encased in their stockings, and enter her without preamble, hard and fast, shoving her against the door like an animal. Yet she was dripping wet as he drove into her, and she met him thrust for thrust, eagerly enfolding him in the warm velvet of her honeypot.

"God, you really are a witch," he ground out as he pounded into her with blind need. "You drag me . . . out of my mind . . . every . . . single . . . time."

"I do my best," she said, kissing his jaw, his neck, everything she could reach, then locking her legs about his waist like the temptress that she was, until they writhed like two sea serpents against the door.

Then he was coming again, too soon, and yet as he spilled himself inside her with a guttural cry, she cried out her own pleasure almost at the same moment.

He collapsed against her, his heart full. She had let him come inside her twice now without any hint of regret. What if she were right about the two of them? What if he'd found the woman who could match him in desire *and* wit? The woman he could share his whole life with? Who understood him?

The sweet possibility swelled through him like a lyric that lingered long after the song was finished. "Dearest," he murmured, as she fell back gasping. "Are you all right?"

With a softly contented sigh, she stretched up to nip his ear. "I was about to ask you the same thing."

Just the feel of her hot breath in his ear roused his cock yet again. "I still want you," he said, curious to see her reaction.

Her laugh soared through him. "I should hope so, or I'd have to chide you for your definition of insatiable." She drew back to give him a dazzling smile. "If the beast wants more, then by all means . . ."

With a growl, he scooped her up and shoved open the door, then carried her into the adjoining bedchamber, where he laid her out on the bed, determined to feast on her as long as she would allow.

But with his first sharp pangs of hunger abating, his frenzy began to ebb. Now he wanted to enjoy her at a more leisurely pace. Exulting in her mews of encouragement, he indulged every desire he'd had from the moment he'd first met her. He stripped her stockings from her, then tasted every part of her, fondled every inch—licking at her perfect bottom, teasing her breasts to taut pebbles, rubbing his scent all over her like the possessive beast he'd become.

She explored him, too, with a curiosity so endearing it made him laugh more than once. She seemed to find his ballocks fascinating, asking him questions that only a naturalist would think to ask. It was what he loved most about her—her thirst for knowledge.

Then he turned to pleasuring her with his mouth. He took his time, not out of need to maintain control but for the sheer joy of watching her reach ecstasy beneath his caresses. Reveling in her easy response, he stroked and sucked and teased until she'd screamed herself hoarse with her climaxes. Only then did he enter her again, this time with less urgency and more feeling.

And as he buried himself inside her warm flesh, a contentment like he'd never known washed over him. This was home—*she* was home. For the first time, he wanted to stay inside a woman forever, be with her forever. That was the real reason he'd never married—because there'd been no Madeline to love.

Love?

He pulled back from the thought. That way lay madness. She'd rapidly become all that was good in his life, all that was pure, and while her endurance of one afternoon's frenzy of lovemaking heartened him, he wasn't ready to give his heart over fully. Because if he took that step only to find that he'd frightened her off, he didn't know how he'd bear it.

Still, as he began to take her again, sliding into her with long, slow strokes, he knew he was falling fast. This was where he wanted to be, for the rest of his life.

He held on to his release until she launched into hers. Then he let himself go as he never had. And as he spilled himself inside her, he prayed he'd given her a child. Their child. Then she'd have no choice but to marry him. Either way, she was his now, in body *and* spirit. If she thought he would let her go blithely on without him after this, she was mad.

It took some time for them to come to earth, but he was perfectly happy to lie there with her curled into his arms. He would lie there all night if not for the waning hour.

"Are you satisfied at last?" she whispered, after they'd caught their breaths.

With a faint laugh, he jerked his head down to his flaccid cock. "Do you really need to ask?"

"Not about *that*, you dolt," she said, though she softened the insult with a tender smile. "Are you satisfied I can handle you and your 'insatiable desires'?"

"Sweetheart," he said with complete sincerity, "I begin to worry that I won't be able to handle *your* insatiable desires. Not to mention your insatiable curiosity."

She gave a mock sigh. "Oh dear, I feared as much." Her eyes sparkled as she ran her hand up his arm. "It's why I've never married, you know—I didn't want to inflict my unruly curiosity on a husband."

"Watch it, minx," he warned, though he couldn't restrain his smile at her parody of his earlier assertion.

"When we're married, I'll expect a good deal less impudence and a good deal more respect from you."

"Oh, you shall, shall you?" she taunted him. "Well, my lord, you may expect whatever you like—you'll get whatever I choose to give you."

He gave an exultant laugh. She hadn't gainsaid his mention of marriage, which meant she intended to accept him. She might run him a merry dance, but he didn't care. Indeed, he could hardly wait to begin.

With a glance at the window, he drew back from her. "Your father will be expecting you soon, if he isn't already."

Her expression grew shuttered. "Yes, I should go home."

"I'll take you."

"No, you mustn't."

When she slipped from the bed and went into the other room to dress, his heart dropped into his stomach. He followed her, watching uneasily as she donned her drawers and her torn chemise. "Why not?"

"Because you'll want to ask Papa for my hand. I can't let you do that yet."

Damn her and her stubbornness. "You have no choice," he said as he, too, began to dress. "I'm not waiting another day to make you my wife."

"For a man who rails against morality, you can be strangely rigid in your morals," she grumbled. "But I won't let you ruin everything for Tessa by marrying me too hastily." She slid into her loosened corset, then presented her back to him in an unspoken request for help.

He caught the laces, but instead of tightening them, he used them to draw her up against him. "You have to trust me, dearest," he murmured against her hair. "I can take care of you both somehow. You must leave the matter to me."

"And if you fail? If you marry me, and she is lost to you as a result?"

He hesitated only a second, but apparently that was enough for her.

"You know it's wiser to be cautious," she continued. "We should stay apart until you've gained guardianship. Papa and I will be fine. And in the meantime, you and I have this place . . . I can come here and—"

"—whore for me?" he said harshly.

When she stiffened and pulled away, attempting to tighten the laces herself, he uttered a curse and brushed her hands away so he could take care of it. "Forgive me," he said as he tightened them, "but the thought of your living in such a limbo is unbearable. You might as well resign yourself to my interference."

She faced him with a scowl. "And what do you mean to do?"

"Speak to your father, for a start. I know he's desperate, but he shouldn't have relied so heavily on you to save him, letting you go to that party and—"

"He didn't know about that. That was all my doing."

"What?" he said, incredulous.

"I was the one who hoped that Sir Humphry might help us." Her voice turned bitter. "Papa wouldn't act, no matter how much I begged, and anytime I mentioned a way of bettering our circumstances, he lapsed further into his melancholy." She thrust out her chin in defiance. "So I had to rely on myself."

His gut knotted at the thought of all she'd risked in trying to protect the man. But that was Madeline, determined to protect the innocent. "Well, that's going to stop. At the very least, your father must be made to see he can no longer wallow in his pain while you take such chances. I mean to tell him so myself."

"You can't!" she cried. "I don't know what he might do! You have to let me break it to him gently. I have to have time . . ."

"Good God," he said in a hollow voice, "*that's* why you won't let me offer for you—because of your father. It has nothing to do with Tessa. You're still trying to protect him."

"That's not true." Wriggling into her gown, she fastened it with only a little help from him. "We shouldn't marry until Tessa's situation is settled, and you know it." When he merely lifted an eyebrow, she added, "You don't understand. Only two days ago Papa was talking about ending his life to make things easier for me. He won't want to see your niece harmed, either. And if he thinks that his situation might help the Bickhams win her, he might—"

"—kill himself over it?" he said skeptically. "So you're going to take upon yourself the responsibility of keeping him from that, too?" He scowled at her. "He had no right to speak of suicide to you, damn it, not after what you've done for him. It was just his way of getting you to keep catering to his sickness."

"No! That's not how Papa is. You don't know him!"

"You won't *let* me know him! You won't even let me speak to him. You're worse than I am about relinquishing control. Everything must be according to your plan, and you only confide what you think we can handle. I daresay even Mrs. Harris doesn't know your situation."

"That's only because I didn't want her to—"

"Dismiss you? Your employer fell over backwards this

morning to keep me from 'taking advantage' of you. She cares about you. *I* care about you. Sometimes you have to give up control and allow the people who care about you to help you."

For a moment, she looked defiant, and he thought she might argue more. Then she smoothed her features. "Fine. Take me home if you must, and talk to Papa. You won't be satisfied until you do."

"Damned right," he muttered, relieved that she'd finally seen sense.

He finished dressing as she put the final touches to her attire. But as she went to put on her shoes, she paused. "Drat it, where are my stockings?"

"In the bed, probably. That's where I took them off you."

"Would you get them? I still have to find my gloves."

"Certainly," he murmured and headed back into the other room.

When the door closed behind him, it took a second for that to register, but by the time he rushed back, she'd already found a way to brace it closed.

"Madeline!" he roared, pounding his fists against the door. "What the bloody hell do you think you're doing?"

"I'm sorry, Anthony!" she cried back. "I can't let you ruin everything because of your misplaced sense of honor. Let me talk to Papa, see what he can handle right now. I swear I'll return here tomorrow evening, no matter what he says. By then we'll both have a better idea of what's the right thing to do."

"My idea of what to do is fine, damn it!" He kicked at the door, then let out a howl as he realized he hadn't put his boots on yet.

"Anthony, my love?" she said, just on the other side. "Are you all right?"

Her concern and calling him *my love* didn't mollify him a bit. "What do you care?" he growled as he nursed his foot. "You're running off—again, I might add—because you think me an impulsive idiot who will bungle this for you and your father and Tessa."

"I don't think you're an idiot," she said through the door. "I think you're impassioned. And right now, impassioned is the last thing that's needed."

"Says you!" He drove his fist into the door, then realized he was reinforcing her argument. "Good God, do you mean to leave me here until tomorrow?"

"I'll send someone to release you as soon as I've got my hackney."

A hackney. He relaxed against the door. Thank God for small favors. The little fool didn't realize he knew every hackney driver working this section of town, another remnant from his days of wild living. Once the coach returned from taking her home, he would simply find out where she lived, then go after her.

He hurried to the window to watch futilely as she climbed into a hackney, called a boy over, gave him a coin, then pointed up to the window. Ignoring Anthony's black scowl, she set off, but not before Anthony took note of the driver.

Ten minutes later, her paid urchin rescued him, but as he paced and waited for the hackney's return, his mind replayed their conversation.

Impassioned. Misplaced sense of honor. She talked about him as if he were a reckless fool, which was clearly how she thought of him, too.

Now that his temper was passing, he could examine that idea with less ire. Could he really blame her for being uncertain of his ability to take care of her and Tessa both? What had he done in his life to prove himself worthy of her respect?

He'd thumbed his nose at the world, angered by the injustices he'd suffered as a boy. What good had that done him? Yes, he'd amassed funds for himself, but instead of using it for a good purpose, he'd wasted it on profligate living. Madeline might be reluctant to trust people with her secrets, but he was worse. He didn't trust them with his true self. Instead, he'd spent his life hiding behind witty retorts.

Then Madeline had slipped beneath his armor. She hadn't balked at what she saw there or chided him for how he was; she'd simply given him her heart even when he'd been too much a coward to give her his.

Now his niece's future lay in the balance and it was *Madeline,* not he, who kept Tessa's well-being constantly in her thoughts, even though Madeline had unimaginable responsibilities of her own to handle.

He dropped into a chair. Instead of agreeing to be cautious, as she'd wanted, he'd selfishly tried to keep her for himself. Yes, he'd had her best interests at heart—as well as those of her father—but she was right. He didn't know her father. It wasn't his place to barge in on the man, making demands, until he did.

And despite what he'd told her, he knew Madeline's reluctance *was* largely due to concern for Tessa. He'd witnessed her compassion toward her girls. It would plague her to marry him if it came at Tessa's expense.

He'd loftily proclaimed that it didn't, but she'd seen

through his blustering. Because the truth was, she might very well be right about that, too. Marriage might not improve their tangle. If he saved her father, the Bickhams would almost certainly retaliate by convincing the courts to let them keep Tessa.

A frustrated curse escaped him. What he needed was the facts of her father's situation, which she couldn't give him since she only knew her father's side. But questioning her father would almost certainly distress the man. And then Anthony would have betrayed his interest in the matter, which would necessitate declaring his intentions, and that would distress *her*.

That left only one way to find out everything. He must question the vicar and whoever else could give him information. He should probably even talk to the local magistrate. But to do all that, he'd have to go to Telford.

A shiver passed through him. Telford, a place he'd avoided for over twenty years. Telford, where the Bickhams lived, where he'd suffered countless humiliations . . . where he'd learned to close his heart off. Telford held the answers. And the thought of going there sent a shudder along his spine.

He stared bleakly ahead. No wonder she couldn't trust him to take care of anyone, when the very name of a town could reduce him to a shivering boy again.

Well, no more, he thought, a grim determination settling into his bones. He was tired of hiding from what had happened, tired of letting it govern his life. Madeline loved him, and Tessa was counting on him to save her, too. The least he could do was brave his past to get some answers.

Then perhaps he could finally earn Madeline's respect. And his own.

Chapter Twenty-five

Dear Charlotte,

  After all these years, you can sometimes be naive. Do as you please in the matter of Lord Norcourt and Miss Prescott. From now on, I will keep my concern to myself, though I pray, for your sake, that nothing terrible comes of your teacher's involvement with a rakehell.

                                    Your disinterested cousin,
                                    Michael

$\mathscr{M}$adeline fumed all the way back to Richmond. How dared Anthony blame *her* for this mess! Apparently he thought she should have gone about willy-nilly begging people for help with Papa. And to accuse her of delaying their marriage only for Papa's sake! He didn't understand, drat it!

You won't let me.

She winced. That was true. Had she done the wrong thing by once again delaying him from meeting Papa? By not letting him handle the situation as he wished? By trying to consider his niece's needs as well as their own?

His account of his childhood at the Bickhams' rose in her mind again. She'd taught other places than at Mrs.

Harris's school, so she knew how easily girls could be mis-used by their guardians. He blamed his "wicked" nature for the severe treatment, but she put the blame squarely where it belonged—on the Bickhams.

Yes, she'd done the right thing. Once he considered it, he would realize that.

You're worse than I am about relinquishing control. Everything must be according to your plan.

No matter how hard she tried to ignore the accusation, the words rankled. Because they, too, had a ring of truth. But what did he expect? Her world had been crumbling even before Papa's fall from grace. She'd been trying to hold things together ever since Mama's death, and that required some control, drat it!

Now she had another problem. They were fast approach-ing the cottage in Richmond. Without money to pay the hackney driver, her only choice was to get his fee from in-side. Which meant alerting Papa to what was going on.

She sighed. Or perhaps not. These days he was so oblivi-ous to her activities he might not even notice.

That hope was dashed, however, upon her arrival at the cottage a few minutes later. Before she could even descend, Papa rushed out to greet her. And Mrs. Jenkins was right behind him.

"Where the devil have you been?" he growled as he jerked open the hackney door. "We've been sick with worry! I sent Mrs. Jenkins to the school for you this after-noon, and Mrs. Harris said that you left there at noon. It's nearly seven now!"

Oh, dear, she hadn't counted on anyone going in search of her. "Let me pay the man, Papa, and then I'll explain."

The words barely left her mouth before her father took

out the purse he hadn't carried in months and thrust some shillings at the driver. When the hackney driver raised an eyebrow, she added more to match what they'd agreed upon.

"Good God!" her father cried as he saw the amount. "How far did you go?"

"I had to pay a call in town." It was partly true, after all.

But when his skin turned to ash, she realized she shouldn't even have said that. With a grim frown, he hurried her inside. Mrs. Jenkins came, too, concern written in her aging features.

As soon as he'd shut the door, her father faced her. "You went to Sir Humphry's, didn't you?"

Shocked that he knew even that much, she glanced at Mrs. Jenkins.

"I'm sorry, miss," the woman murmured, "but he plagued me until I told him all—"

"Damned right I plagued her," her father interrupted. "What else was I supposed to do when I found her cleaning your evening gown? I knew you hadn't gone to an assembly this weekend. And then she tells me you've been up to all manner of shenanigans on my behalf. You had no right!"

Fury boiled up inside her. "You had no right to give up!"

Despite his flinch, she couldn't prevent words from pouring out of her, the sum of her long-repressed anxieties. "For months I've begged you to *do* something to change our situation, yet you could only bemoan what happened to Mrs. Crosby. What about what happened to *me,* Papa? I lost my home and my life in *one* instant when she died on your table. I'm sorry for your pain, but I have pain, too!"

Tears streamed down her cheeks, but she scarcely heeded

them. How dared he play the father now, after months of not caring?

His stricken expression melted into remorse. "Maddie-girl, please . . ." he murmured as he reached for her.

"Don't call me that ever again!" She batted his hand away, her anger nowhere close to being spent. "You hadn't said it in months until two days ago, directly after threatening to take your own life. And you can speak to me of rights?" She swiped tears furiously away. "*You* are the one who had no right, Papa. *You!*"

She merely echoed Anthony's words to her earlier, but only because she'd recognized their veracity the moment he'd said them. She just hadn't wanted to acknowledge it. And now that she did, she couldn't seem to stop crying.

Her father laid his arm about her shoulder and led her to a chair. "There, there now," he said soothingly, "come sit down."

As she complied, still sobbing and unable even to resist his attempts at comfort, he glanced at Mrs. Jenkins. "Fetch my girl some wine, will you?"

With a nod, Mrs. Jenkins slipped into the kitchen, leaving them alone. Papa pulled a chair up next to her and grasped her hands. "I'm sorry, Madeline."

"You always . . . s-say that," she stammered, "and th-then . . . the next day . . ."

"I know, I go back to my brooding. Don't you think I realize I've been a trial to you? But things will be different. I mean it this time."

She shook her head. He'd claimed *that*, too, before.

"You don't believe me, do you?" he said softly. "I don't blame you. But I swear to you, if I'd realized how much you'd taken upon yourself . . ."

When she said nothing, he sighed. "No, that's not true either. I did realize. Somewhere in my sunken spirits, I knew you were the one keeping us afloat. I just couldn't muster myself to care." He squeezed her hands. "Well, I'm mustering myself now."

"Oh?" Her tears were spent, but anger still roiled in her belly. "Why now?"

A guilty look stole over his face. "Your headmistress told Mrs. Jenkins about you and Lord Norcourt."

Her breath caught in her throat. What had Mrs. Harris said? How much did Papa know? Did he know about the party? Sweet Lord, did he know she'd gone there with Anthony?

He went on grimly. "That's when I learned you've been friendly with the man. Yet I hadn't a clue about it. I'd had no idea what was going on with you. I found that more chilling than anything." He hung his head. "You spoke the truth about one thing—I had no right to give up. On you. On your future."

"On yourself," she prodded, the last of her tears drying on her cheeks.

"Perhaps that, too." His voice grew anguished. "But once I heard about him, I remembered that you asked about his childhood and wouldn't tell me why you wanted to know. So when you went missing, I started to worry . . ."

She had to tell him about Anthony. And she honestly didn't know how.

"I haven't been much of a father to you of late, I know that," he whispered, his grip on her hands almost painful, "but I mean to change. I don't care what has happened between you and—" He swallowed. "If you took up with Lord Norcourt, there won't be a word of reproach from me. God knows, you've had good reason to seek comfort outside this house. But I can't—"

His breath caught. "I can't stay out of that, dear girl. I need to know if the man has taken advantage of you. You must tell me. I don't care what happens with Sir Randolph; I just want to make sure that Lord Norcourt does right by you."

"He wants to marry me, Papa," she said softly. "He wants to marry me and protect you from Sir Randolph."

Her father looked stunned, which pretty much mirrored how *she'd* felt when Anthony first offered for her.

"But there's a problem involving his niece," she went on, "so I told him we should wait. He doesn't want to wait. After our interview with Sir Humphry this afternoon, he wanted to come directly here and ask you for my hand in marriage. I wouldn't let him. I wanted to speak to you first."

With a still-dazed expression, her father sat back against his chair. "I see." He rubbed his chin, then glanced at her. "Apparently a great deal has happened without my knowing it."

She nodded, a little ashamed. She still thought she'd been right not to tax him with her plans, but she couldn't get Anthony's words out of her head. *You only confide what you think we can handle.*

"Well then," Papa said, "it's time you tell me what I've missed. I have a right—" He caught himself. "I have a *need* to know. So start at the beginning, will you, dear girl? And take it slow. My brain's been in a fog for a while, but I won't let that stop me from trying to understand this time. Tell me it all."

So she did. While Mrs. Jenkins prepared supper for them

and silently went about the place doing her usual house-keeping duties, Madeline and her father talked. It took two hours—and a few false starts—to tell him everything. It had been a long time since she'd felt free to share problems with her father. She tried not to find too much hope in his rational response to her tale, especially when he lapsed into long silences, but at least he was listening. At least he was no longer shutting her out. That was something, wasn't it?

Of course, she didn't tell him about sharing Anthony's bed. He was her father, after all. But he now knew the rest of it. When she was done, they were no closer to a solution than before, yet she felt as if the vise tightening around her chest for months had suddenly loosened. She could finally breathe.

"I'm right about his niece, aren't I, Papa?" she said at the end. "Isn't it better for us to wait?"

"I don't know." A weary frown beetled his brow. " 'Tis a vexing situation indeed. I can't see the Bickhams inflicting the same punishments on her, but you're right that she shouldn't be there. And Sir Randolph will certainly use any association between his lordship and me to gain what he wants."

"Neither of you will solve this dilemma tonight," Mrs. Jenkins said, the first time she'd interrupted them since they'd begun their long talk. "You're both exhausted." She glanced kindly at Madeline. "Nothing can be done until the morrow anyway, can it, miss? Isn't that when you're to meet his lordship?"

Madeline nodded, not terribly surprised that Mrs. Jenkins had listened to every word. She'd become so much of the fabric of their family that it seemed right she should know their darkest secrets, too.

"Fine," Mrs. Jenkins went on in her motherly fashion. "Then you might as well sleep on the matter. Everything looks brighter in the morning, I always say."

Papa arched one eyebrow at Mrs. Jenkins. "Are you this cheery with everyone, woman? Or do you only inflict your homilies on us?"

"Papa . . ." Madeline began.

"Oh, I save them all up for you, Dr. Prescott," Mrs. Jenkins said with an airy smile. "Men like you who dwell too much on their trials can use a cheery homily now and again."

"Rubbish," he muttered, but he then took Mrs. Jenkins's suggestion and urged Madeline to retire. She was only too eager to comply.

She wasn't sure when *he* retired, but for once she didn't lie awake listening for it. And for the first time in a long while, she wasn't awakened in the middle of the night by his moving about.

Instead, she was awakened the next morning by the sound of urgent voices outside. Swiftly she left the bed, pulled on her wrapper, and went to see what was going on.

Papa was arguing with a footman in livery. "I insist that you leave the letter with me, young man. I'll give it to her as soon as she rises."

"But his lordship said it was to be put into her hand alone," the anxious fellow fretted. "I can wait if you don't wish to wake her."

"I'm awake, Papa," Madeline said, recognizing the livery. She pushed forward. "Have you brought me something?"

"Are you Miss Prescott?" the man asked.

She nodded.

He handed her an ornate envelope with a wax seal. "My master said I was to give this directly to you."

She eyed him curiously. "How did you know where to find me?"

"I believe Lord Norcourt got your direction from the hackney coachman."

Yet he hadn't come here himself. After all his insistence that he be allowed to meet her father, the appearance of a letter instead distressed her. Her hand trembled as she opened the missive.

> *Dearest Madeline,*
>
> *I've gone to Telford. I wanted you to know so you wouldn't await me at my lodgings this evening. Our tangle can only be resolved if I assess your father's situation thoroughly, which requires finding out how bad the case is against him and seeing what I can do to improve matters. I intend to speak to the vicar as well as the local magistrate. It may be a few days before I return, but do not fret. You can trust me to be perfectly discreet.*
>
> > *With all my love,*
> > *Anthony*

The precious words "with all my love" were overshadowed by her alarm. "Discreet!" she cried as she held the letter to her heart. "How can it be discreet to ask such questions there? His uncle will know of it within an hour of his arrival, and then there will be hell to pay."

"What is it? What's wrong?" Papa asked.

She handed him the letter to read. "I have to go after

him, Papa. I have to stop him before he hurts his niece's chance of escape from those dreadful people."

Her father looked up from the letter, one eyebrow raised. "He calls you 'Madeline' and signs it 'with all my love,' but I see no mention of marriage."

"We have bigger concerns, Papa!" She turned to the footman. "How long has he been gone?"

"A few hours now, miss. He left before dawn."

"There's no time to waste," she told her father. "I have to go to Telford."

Papa frowned. "You won't catch up to him."

"I have to try!"

"We don't have the money," he pointed out. "Do you know how much a trip to Shropshire will cost? To catch up to him, we'll have to travel post, and there will be meals and inns . . . It's a two-day journey at least. Unless you've been sticking your pay from the school under a mattress, we can't manage it."

She groaned. He was right about that.

"I don't even think Mrs. Jenkins could cover it, though I'm sure she'd be willing to loan you—"

"A loan, yes! I'll borrow the money!"

"From Mrs. Jenkins?"

Anthony's words yesterday came to her. *Your employer fell over backwards this morning to keep me from "taking advantage" of you. She cares about you.* "No. From Mrs. Harris."

"You'll have to tell her everything then: about the scandal and your reasons for going to that party, the whole thing."

"I know." She squeezed his hand. "It'll be fine. She'll understand."

He nodded thoughtfully, then turned for the door. "Well, if we're to be off soon, we'd better dress ourselves and go talk to her."

"We?" she whispered.

"If you think I'm letting you trot off to Shropshire alone, girl, you're mad."

She caught her breath. "But you haven't been back since—"

"I know." He brushed a lock of her hair back from her cheek. "I have to face it sometime. This is as good a time as any, don't you think?"

What she thought was that her world had taken such a strange turn in these past few days that she was still reeling. She was terrified that Papa's seeming recovery would be overset by a trip to Telford, or that Anthony's interference there would ruin his niece's life and make him resent her for it.

Only one thing kept her from falling apart: Anthony's words to her yesterday. *Sometimes you have to give up control and allow the people who care about you to help you.*

She was about to take that advice with a vengeance. Lord help her.

Chapter Twenty-six

Dear Cousin,

You'll disapprove when you hear that I just loaned money to Miss Prescott and her father. You would have done the same if you'd heard their tale. As it turns out, nothing is as it seems with either her or Lord Norcourt, so I was happy to help them. Think what you will, but I believe you and I were wrong about them. A reputation isn't always the measure of a man.

Your daft relation,
Charlotte

Two days later, as Anthony stood before the white-painted door of the elegant brick cottage, his palms began to sweat inside his gloves.

He hadn't meant to come to this particular door. But after his arrival in Telford midmorning, he'd been told the vicar was in a nearby village performing a funeral service and wouldn't return until evening, so he'd been left with time on his hands. After conversing with the magistrate, then discussing the Prescotts' situation with their neighbors, he'd headed toward the inn where he was staying.

That's when the sight of a school had arrested him. Although classes for that term had ended, he'd managed to learn from a clerk where the headmaster lived, and now he stood here with his hat in hand, unsure whether to knock.

Would Jane want to see him? Or hate him? Would she resent him for intruding on her now-settled life? She must feel some resentment, or she wouldn't have agreed to be a witness for her father in the guardianship case.

He sighed. Perhaps this was a mistake.

He started to turn away, but was nearly mowed down by two strapping lads carrying a large carp. They stopped short, the eldest giving him the same survey Anthony had been subjected to all afternoon. "Good day, sir. May we help you?"

Jane's children? Could it be? He glanced at the fish. "Seems to me that you two are the ones in need of help." The fish looked easily twenty pounds, quite a handful for boys who could be no more than eight and eleven.

The younger boy puffed out his chest. "We caught it ourselves, we did. It's a great big thing, don't you think? Mother will be so proud."

A lump caught in his throat. "I'm sure she will. Let me help you." He took the smaller boy's end, and the three of them entered the house, with the youngest racing ahead to announce their arrival.

"Mother! We caught the big carp!" he cried, as his brother and Anthony tramped through a parlor toward a kitchen.

"If you boys forgot to wipe your muddy boots again, I swear I will—" The woman stopped short as she entered and saw Anthony.

He would never have recognized her. Gone was the frail wraith with pinched cheeks and sad eyes. This woman was plump and hearty, if a bit harried, with a smile that reminded him of his mother and a halo of curls so unruly they encased her head in a brunette cloud.

"Jane?" he asked, wondering if perhaps he'd got the wrong house.

With a wary frown, she wiped her hands on her apron. "Do I know you?"

"I hope so, cousin."

Her eyes went wide. "Oh my word. Anthony?"

"Unless you have another cousin I don't remember."

To his surprise, she rushed over and grabbed him in a hug, no small feat since he was still holding one end of a carp. She drew back, her features alight, and said, "Anthony! I can't believe it! Oh heavens . . . Jack! Come help Christopher with this fish, will you?"

The youngest hurried over to take Anthony's end. This time when Jane hugged him, he hugged her back, tears stinging his eyes. She squeezed him exactly as Mother used to squeeze, with the pure affection of a dear relation.

Then she jerked back to hold him at arm's length, laughing and crying all at once. "Lord, let me look at you! I can't believe you're grown." She dashed away a tear. "Of course you're grown. What a silly goose I am! You look wonderful, too."

"So do you," he said past the thickness in his throat. He nodded to the lads. "Are they yours?"

"Yes, my youngest two." She dragged out a handkerchief to wipe her eyes. "This is Jack and Christopher. My oldest, Nicholas, is in Shrewsbury with his father, and Rachel and Alexandra are upstairs." She turned to her boys, who were watching in awe. "Come now, lads, and shake your cousin Anthony's hand."

"We can't," said young Jack. "We've got the fish!"

"Is this your cousin Anthony who rode the goat?" asked Christopher.

Anthony laughed, feeling a weight lift from his chest. "Yes, I'm *that* Anthony."

"Heavens, Christopher, what a thing to say! Go put that fish in the kitchen, will you? And wash up. And put those boots out by the pump." They headed out as she added, "Oh, and go call the maid in to prepare us some tea!"

"Yes, Mother!" the boys called as they tramped off.

She turned to him with a rueful smile. "I'm sorry, you've caught us all at sixes and sevens. Which isn't unusual around here, I'm afraid."

"No, no, it's fine. I should have given you fair warning."

"Indeed, you should have," she chided. "I could have had a feast prepared."

"I wouldn't want you to go to such trouble. Especially under the circumstances."

That dashed the smile from her lips. Taking a seat on a settee, she patted the place beside her. "Come tell me what brings you to Telford after all these years."

He sat next to her, still hardly able to believe how cozy her cottage was and how well she looked. "First, I need to apologize. I should have come a long time ago."

"It's all right," she said softly. "I knew why you didn't."

Her voice held such a wealth of compassion that he knew instantly he was forgiven. And that struck his conscience sorely, for he didn't deserve it. "Oh, God, Jane, I'm so sorry I never answered your letters or tried to see you—"

"Shh," she murmured, "you wanted to put this place behind you. I can't blame you for that." She bumped her shoulder against his. "I'm just glad you're here now. I'm glad Mama and her madness didn't drive you off forever."

"As always, you're the soul of generosity." Idly, he rubbed the scar on his wrist, hardly aware of doing so until she caught his hand.

"Let me see," she murmured, then examined his wrist.

"It's not bad, really. After so many years, you can scarcely see the mark."

She bit her lower lip. "I'm sorry you had to suffer it at all."

"You've nothing to be sorry about. You were pure kindness to me. Don't think I didn't notice how often you put yourself in harm's way to focus my aunt's ire away from me. I was always grateful even if I couldn't tell you. I thought of you as a kindred spirit."

"In more ways than one." She lifted her gaze to him. "I suppose I should thank you for that episode with the penknife."

"Oh? Why?"

"That was what made Mama stop tying me to the bed at night, too."

He froze. "You? What do you mean?"

"Did you really think you were the only one?" she said, half-incredulous. Then she shook her head. "Of course you did. I always regretted that we couldn't talk about it, with Mama never allowing us to be alone together. Not that I'm sure we would have, given how mortified she made us feel about her reason for binding us . . ." She broke off with a blush.

All he could do was stare at her. Aunt Eunice had tied Jane. Sweet, innocent Jane, who'd probably never had a lascivious thought in her head.

He amended that. Her five children hadn't been brought by fairies, after all. "I thought she tied me up because I was so wicked," he admitted.

"You *were* wicked." A smile curved her lips. "But no more wicked than my boys, I'll wager. Fortunately, their father and I believe that wickedness is better countered with hard work and intense study than with cold baths and lectures." She patted his hand. "And a little fishing never hurts, either."

Tears started anew in his eyes as the knot of self-loathing that Madeline had loosened with her sympathy and love unraveled even more. All this time, he'd let himself believe it was his fault. All this time, he'd let it rule his life and his future . . . What a waste.

He gazed about her comfortable parlor, where a doll sat on the writing table and a child's crooked sampler hung over the fireplace, all of it radiating family and warmth and home. He could have had this, if only he hadn't held on to his anger and self-doubts so long. "I take it that you're happy with . . . forgive me, I've forgotten your husband's name."

"Lawrence. Yes, I'm quite happy with him. He's a good man." Then she added, in the dry tone he remembered her having even as a girl, "I stay happy by keeping Mama out of my life. Or I did until Tessa came."

"Tessa!" he said, appalled he'd forgotten his niece for even one moment. "Good God, does Aunt Eunice tie *her*—"

"No. Mama learned her lesson with you. Besides, she and Father know they must treat Tessa well to gain guardianship, though I look in on the dear girl when I can."

He tensed. "Is that why you agreed to be a witness in

your father's case? Because you figured you could make sure they didn't harm her?"

"What are you talking about?"

"You're on the list of witnesses for your father."

"The devil I am!" She sat back against the settee with a black scowl. "How dare he! That is so like Father, to do something like that without consulting me." She glanced at him. "I would never have agreed to it, and he knows that. No doubt he intended to drum up some excuse for my bowing out at the last moment, without ever telling me."

Relief washed over him. "I suppose he knew they would find it suspicious if his own daughter didn't appear to support him."

She nodded. "And I certainly wouldn't have. Age has softened Mama very little. She still spouts her nonsense at every turn. Poor Tessa is pretty thoroughly miserable, I'm sorry to say." She eyed him closely. "Is that why you've come? To try and convince them to give her up? Because I don't think that will work."

"I know. And there's the rub. And the real reason I'm here." Leaning forward to plant his elbows on his knees, he stared blindly across the room. "I'm getting married, Jane."

"Why, that's wonderful!" she exclaimed, then caught herself. "Oh, please don't tell me that your fiancée is balking at your taking in Tessa."

"That's not the problem, I assure you." Wanting to gauge her reaction, he turned to look at her. "My fiancée is Miss Madeline Prescott."

Jane appeared startled. "*Our* Madeline Prescott? The doctor's daughter?"

"Yes. We met in Richmond. She teaches at the girl's

school where I mean to enroll Tessa." He then told her as much as he dared about how they'd met and what he'd discovered about her father.

When he got to the part about how Dr. Prescott had sunk into a debilitating melancholy as a result of what had happened to Mrs. Crosby, Jane paled and stared down at her hands.

"That's why Madeline won't marry me just yet," he went on. "She's concerned that her father's situation will hurt mine and Tessa's. And *I'm* concerned that her father's situation is too dire to ignore. I came here hoping to find a way out of this tangle."

"And have you?" she asked, oddly reluctant to meet his gaze.

"I've discovered he's not as disliked here as his daughter thinks. People seem to respect him." He gave a faint smile. "They respect him more now that they have no reliable physician to care for their ills, which is usually the way of things."

"He was a good doctor," she conceded. "I liked him quite a lot."

"Unfortunately, that does him no good. Everyone seems to think it's only a matter of time before Dr. Prescott is charged with murder." He cast her a grim glance. "I want to help the man and I want to help Tessa. I honestly don't know how to do both."

Swallowing hard, Jane netted her fingers together nervously. "I do."

For a second, he wasn't sure he'd heard her right. "What?"

"I think I can help you. But it means betraying a confidence and . . ." Her troubled gaze met his. "Why do you want to marry Miss Prescott? It's not because of her father's kindness to you as a boy, is it? Or just to strike back at Father?"

"I love her." He spoke without thought, but the moment he said the words, he knew they were true. Why had he not acknowledged it from the first? Because he'd been a coward and a fool.

But he wasn't now. "I love her very much. I'd do anything for her. She's the only person who ever saw me for what I am." He smiled. "Other than you."

"Oh, Anthony," she said with a heartfelt groan. "I'm happy for you, but . . . it has placed me in a most difficult situation."

"How so?"

"I have to tell you something. I should have told this to someone when this whole mess with her father began, but . . . well . . . they're still my parents, you know, and I was sworn to secrecy . . ."

When she trailed off with a frown, he prodded, "What is it?"

"I hoped Father would stop badgering the vicar once the Prescotts left town. I swear I didn't know how badly the scandal had affected Dr. Prescott. I assumed he'd opened a practice elsewhere, and the entire thing would come to naught."

"Damn it, Jane, what do you know?"

"Something about Father that no one else knows. He doesn't even realize I'm aware of it. Mrs. Crosby was the one to tell me, and she made me swear I'd never tell a soul."

"But she's dead," he pointed out. "And I can't believe she would want Dr. Prescott to suffer for trying to help her."

"You're right." She nodded to herself, as if making a decision. "Someone has to end this madness. I suppose it will have to be us."

"Stop watching me like that, will you?" Madeline's father snapped as he settled back against the squabs and stared out at the houses of Telford. "I'm fine."

"Sorry, Papa." They'd entered the outskirts of town a few minutes ago, and she'd been trying to gauge his reaction ever since.

"It's not as if I'm going to leap from the carriage to my death," he groused. "You should realize that by now."

She did. Sort of. They'd spent much of the long trip talking, and she'd come to realize that his deep despair hadn't resulted just from Mrs. Crosby's death. He'd already been suffering from the melancholy that Mama's death had triggered. Back then, he'd shoved his grief down deep, partly so he could be strong to comfort Madeline and partly because he'd been unable to face his guilt at not being able to save his wife from death.

As a doctor, he'd known it was impossible with consumption, but that hadn't stopped him from feeling helpless. So when Mrs. Crosby had died, all those lingering feelings of helplessness had mingled with his honest guilt over Mrs. Crosby's death, paralyzing him in grief. Madeline prayed that the paralysis was finally ending, but after months of living with it, she was still afraid to hope.

"Where do you think Lord Norcourt will go first?" Papa asked her now.

The practical question heartened her, for it illustrated the clarity of his mind. "The vicar's house, I suppose. He spoke of talking to the magistrate, too."

As their post chaise trundled down the main street of Telford, a coach and four suddenly rushed by them. Her glimpse of it made her cry, "Stop the carriage!"

"What?" her father exclaimed. "Why?"

"Anthony's traveling coach just went past us, headed back out of town. I recognized the Norcourt crest on the door."

Papa ordered the post chaise to halt, then instructed the driver to follow the other coach. As he sat back down, he said, "I'd like to know why you recognize the fellow's crest. When were *you* in his traveling coach, and how exactly—"

"Not now." She thrust her head out the window. "Where is he going? He's not leaving town. He just made the turn at— Oh, no. He's headed for the Bickhams."

"Why ever for?"

"I don't know! But I imagine we're soon going to find out."

They pulled up in the drive right behind Anthony's coach to see him starting up the stairs. He swung around when Madeline leaped down without waiting for the post boy's help. "What the bloody devil are you doing here?" he asked.

"Watch your language, young man." Papa climbed out behind her. "I'll have you know that my daughter is a gentlewoman, no matter what *you* may think."

"Dr. Prescott!" Anthony flushed. "I meant no disrespect, sir. I was simply startled by—" He grabbed Madeline's hands, his expression turning to one of concern. "Truly, sweetheart, is something wrong? Why have you come?"

"To prevent you from making a terrible mistake. Papa and I agree that you shouldn't take any chances with your niece's future, not on our behalf. I only hope I'm not too late to stop you."

"It's all right," he said, his face clearing. "I have the situation well in hand."

"But Anthony—"

"Will you just trust me? I love you, Madeline—too much to ruin our future."

His words sent her heart into the heavens. "You . . . you love me?"

"More than life." He lifted her hands to his lips and tenderly kissed them. "And I'm not fool enough to risk losing you for any reason."

"What about Tessa?"

"She'll be fine. I mean to make sure of that. So it's time to give up control, sweetheart, and let the ones who care about you—"

"—help me." She smiled through anxious tears. "Very well. I shall try."

Before they could say more, the door at the top of the imposing marble steps opened, and a figure emerged. Madeline's blood chilled. Sir Randolph himself had come to greet them.

With a squeeze of her hands, Anthony turned to face his enemy. "Good afternoon, Uncle. I've come to fetch Tessa."

Sir Randolph's eyes narrowed. "If you think I'll just give her over—"

"I think," Anthony said coldly, "that you'll do precisely that once you hear what I have to say." He glanced about at the coachman and other servants drinking in every word. "But this conversation should take place in more private surroundings. May we come in?"

Sir Randolph hesitated, his gaze flicking over the three

of them. Then he shrugged. "*You* may enter, nephew." He glared at Papa. "But your miscreant companion must stay right where he is, him and his accomplice."

"Now see here, sir—" Papa began, but halted when Anthony laid his hand on his arm.

"This is my fiancée and my future father-in-law," Anthony replied, "so I expect you to refer to them with more respect. And since this discussion largely concerns them, I demand that they be part of it."

As Madeline groaned, Sir Randolph's lips curved up in a sly smile. "Your fiancée, is it? My solicitor will be pleased to hear of your new . . . domestic arrangements." He stepped back and indicated the open door with a flourish. "Do come in, all of you. We can settle this matter for good."

"Indeed we can," Anthony muttered under his breath as he offered Madeline his arm.

She took it, still anxious about what he intended to do, but when he laid his hand over hers and cast her a fleeting smile, she found comfort in it. At least they were together in this.

After they entered the baronet's spacious manor, Sir Randolph ushered them into his study but didn't offer any refreshment or ask them to sit. Clearly, he thought to have this interview over with swiftly.

He faced Anthony with a look of cool contempt. "Well then, get on with it. Say your piece. It will not change anything."

"Before I address the matter of Tessa," Anthony said, "I mean to address the matter of Dr. Prescott. We both know why you've held a grudge against the man all these years— because he had the courage to speak to my father about how you and my aunt were treating me."

"Did he? I was unaware of it."

"I doubt that. Just as I doubt your reasons for tormenting him in this matter of Mrs. Crosby's death."

"My reasons are the pursuit of justice. He killed the wife of my vicar."

"Given the results of the enquiry afterward, there's some difference of opinion on that matter. And I do find it interesting that the woman's own husband hasn't demanded that charges be brought against the good doctor."

"Ah, but he will." Sir Randolph cast Papa a vile glance. "Watching a profligate like you take his side will convince the vicar of what I knew all along—that Dr. Prescott is a sly seducer of women who doesn't deserve to live."

When Madeline tensed at the thinly disguised threat, Anthony tightened his grip on her hand to keep her silent. "You have no proof of your assertions, nothing but ranting."

"Leave it to you to fall back on the rule of law." His uncle sneered at him. "You never understood the rule of morality, did you? For you, the world is simply a playground—"

"It has been, yes. After experiencing *your* version of morality, I was more than eager to find some other rule by which to live my life. And I admit I made a less-than-stellar choice." He slid his arm about Madeline's waist. "Fortunately, this good woman here has shown me that morality has many faces. It's only the one worn by hypocrites like you that I have trouble with."

"I am not the one who committed a crime," Sir Randolph said loftily. "I am not the one who gave a woman a dangerous gas—"

"A woman?" Anthony cut in. "Mrs. Crosby was no mere

woman to you, was she? Otherwise, her death wouldn't have incensed you so."

Sir Randolph went quite pale. "I don't know what you mean."

Anthony's hard gaze was unrelenting. "How odd, considering that you've been paying for the maintenance of her mother in Shrewsbury all these years."

As the ramifications of that began to sink in, Madeline exchanged a look with her father, who appeared stunned.

"But I guess I shouldn't be surprised," Anthony went on. "Only a hypocrite would deny the existence of his natural daughter."

Chapter Twenty-seven

Dear Charlotte,
   Have you never heard the saying, "Neither a borrower or lender be"? Those are sound words in this day. But I suppose there are times when a man must venture out beyond his principles. That may be true for a woman, too.

                           Your philosophical friend,
                           Michael

$\mathcal{P}$erhaps it was a measure of Anthony's wickedness that he found an intense satisfaction in the alarm spreading over his uncle's cheeks, but if so, he didn't care. Sometimes revenge truly was sweet. And the fact that Jane had been responsible for helping him strike the blow made it even sweeter.

"I can't imagine . . . I don't know where you could have heard such a tale," his uncle began to bluster.

"From a reliable source." Anthony had promised Jane not to reveal that she'd told him. She had only found out because Mrs. Crosby, eager to know her half sister better, had confided in her. To Jane's knowledge, even the vicar didn't know he'd been a pawn in Uncle Randolph's scheme to gain respectability for his bastard daughter by passing her off as the legitimate daughter of a widow.

"Your source is mistaken," his uncle said.

"I doubt that. And I'm sure if I were to pursue the matter, I could find someone to attest to Mrs. Crosby's illegitimacy. Then the vicar might not be so eager to press charges. Indeed, I rather think he'd prefer to have nothing to do with you. By all accounts, he loved his wife. It would be a shame to sully that love by embroiling him in a scandal."

"You wouldn't dare!" his uncle said, horror turning his skin a mottled red. "To ruin the good name of a sweet and innocent young creature—"

"I wouldn't want to, no," Anthony countered. And he'd promised Jane he wouldn't. But that didn't mean he couldn't use the threat of it to force his uncle's hand. "The vicar seems innocent of your machinations on your daughter's behalf."

He glanced over at Dr. Prescott, whose face wore a mixture of anger and remorse and confusion, then looked back to his uncle, hardening his voice. "But Madeline's father is innocent as well. We both know doctors lose patients every day. It's time that you acknowledge you acted blindly out of anger at the loss of the only daughter still fool enough to love you."

"Anger and ignorance," Madeline said hotly. "You always hated that Papa shined the light of reason on your nonsense, Sir Randolph. You used Mrs. Crosby's death to be rid of the only check to your power in Telford."

"My daughter was the fairest thing ever to grace this village, and your father—"

"Tried to save her," Anthony finished. "And you'll admit as much to the vicar when we leave. You'll also spread the news about town. If necessary, you'll get down on your bloody knees and beg the man's forgiveness before half the populace, so that he can return to his home!"

When his uncle bristled, Dr. Prescott stepped forward with quiet dignity. "No need for that, sir. I mean to set up a practice elsewhere. I find I can no longer stomach living in Telford."

"As you wish," Anthony replied. "We can always use a good physician in Chertsey." He returned his gaze to Sir Randolph. "But I have a more important demand, Uncle. As of now, you will withdraw your petition for guardianship of Tessa. You will explain to the court that you and my aunt are growing too old to raise a young woman."

The veins stood out on his balding forehead. "And what if I refuse?"

"You'll force me to reveal the existence of your mistress. I somehow doubt that the blunt you gain from my niece's estate will afford you much pleasure once your reputation is destroyed."

His uncle's hands curled into fists. "You've been far more wicked than I."

"Perhaps. But I never lied about it. Funny thing about country folk—they forgive the peccadilloes of men like me if we confess our faults and strive to do better. They never forgive being lied to." He lowered his voice to a menacing thrum. "Now, I wish to see my niece. Where is Tessa?"

Sir Randolph released an inarticulate growl of outrage, but he knew he'd lost the fight. Anthony had left him no alternative but to comply. "I will have her fetched," gritted out.

That was enough to rouse Anthony's suspicions. "No. Tell me where she is." When his uncle merely glared at him, Anthony headed for the door. "Very well, I'll find her myself."

"Now see here, boy—" his uncle snapped from behind him.

Anthony stopped short to fix him with a dark look. "I am no longer a boy at your mercy, Uncle. You will address me as Lord Norcourt or not at all. *Where* is my niece, damn you?"

His uncle's eyes burned with resentment. "She is in the garden with your aunt, meditating upon the beauties of nature."

Knowing only too well what *that* meant, Anthony rushed out the door. Madeline lifted her skirts and broke into a run to keep up with him. To Anthony's relief, he still remembered his way about the house, so he was able to reach the garden within moments.

And there, kneeling on the bricks in a shift of rough fustian, was his golden-haired young niece, chin held high and eyes glittering her defiance as his aunt strode in front of her, railing about some infraction. For a moment, he flashed on Jane at that age and was catapulted back to the age of ten, when feelings of helplessness were his daily companions.

Then Madeline came up beside him to slide her hand in the crook of his elbow, and his world was set to rights once more.

"Tessa," he said, interrupting his aunt in midlecture. "Come, dearest." He held out his free hand. "We're going home."

"Uncle Anthony!" Tessa's face lit up as she leaped to her

feet and rushed to throw her arms about his waist. "I knew you would come. I knew you would!"

As Madeline slipped off her muslin pelisse and laid it over Tessa's slender shoulders, Aunt Eunice turned on Anthony, her eyes sparking with hatred. "How dare you! The girl is ours, and there's naught you can do about it!"

"Let her go," said his uncle's tight voice behind them. "I've agreed to relinquish guardianship to An— . . . to Lord Norcourt."

The look of mad outrage on Aunt Eunice's face as she faced her husband was truly frightening to behold. "You spineless worm! You let him browbeat you, did you? Well, I'm not about to let the girl go off with a blackguard who consorts with whores and—"

"Shut up!" his uncle said. "You will do as you are told, woman."

She blinked. Aunt Eunice had been the only person Uncle Randolph never attempted to cow. "How dare you use that tone with me!"

Her husband stepped toward her with clenched fists. "You will have the servants pack Teresa's things and send them down to Lord Norcourt's coach, do you hear?"

"And why should I do that?" she snapped.

"Because if you do not, I will have the footmen carry you bodily up the stairs and lock you in our bedchamber until our nephew and the others are gone."

Anthony took a bittersweet pleasure in how the blood drained from her face.

"Why are you giving her up?" she hissed. "I deserve to know that, at least."

"Because I have decided it," Uncle Randolph said. "That is all."

The inadequate answer took Anthony as much by surprise as it did his aunt. Suddenly the truth dawned on him, making him turn to his uncle with an incredulous look. "She doesn't know, does she?"

His uncle glared daggers at him, confirming that Aunt Eunice had no idea her husband had kept a mistress and sired an illegitimate daughter.

Anthony burst into laughter. "My God, she doesn't know! That's too rich!"

"Know what?" his aunt demanded.

"Nephew . . ." his uncle choked out.

Ignoring the man's mute plea, Anthony turned to her, the truth hovering on his tongue. How he'd love to tell her that her husband was as much a cursed profligate as the nephew she despised. How he'd love to bring her world of strict principles crashing down about her ears, to leave her in a shambles the way she'd sought to leave him and Tessa and Jane.

Jane. That halted him. He'd promised to use her information carefully. If he revealed it to his aunt, God only knew what could result. At the very least, his uncle's mistress would suffer.

And for what? His fleeting moment of vengeance? It would hardly make up for the years he'd lost.

He stared at his aunt then, at the lines of bitterness on her brow, the ugly twist of her lips, all the signs of a truly unhappy woman. He could do nothing more to hurt her than her own life and philosophy had already done.

Glancing over at Madeline, he saw the love shining in her eyes, and his heart caught in his throat. He already had what he wanted. Tessa was going with them, and the doctor stood tall beside the slumped form of Uncle Randolph. No point in letting the ugliness of the Bickhams alter his life anymore.

"What is it I don't know?" his aunt demanded again. "What secret do you think to tell me?"

"Only this, Aunt. Life needn't be misery. Not when those you love surround you." He cast her a pitying glance. "If you had shown me one ounce of kindness after Mother died, you'd have had my heart for a lifetime. You'd have had a nephew in your corner as well as a daughter, and probably scores of grandchildren to brighten your old age. But you threw my heart away with both hands, along with Jane's. From what I understand, she's already taken her family away from you. I'll take my family off, too, and leave you to the cold comfort of your principles."

"Your family!" She sneered at Madeline and Dr. Prescott. "These two?"

"Aye," Dr. Prescott put in. "Your nephew is marrying my daughter, you old witch."

"That doesn't surprise me." Contempt laced her voice as she stared Anthony down. "I always knew you were worthless. Who else would you marry but a chit of no rank or birth, who spends her days examining dead creatures and probably spends her nights wallowing in the same immorality as you?"

Years ago, her self-righteous words would have sent a knife through his heart, but now he saw them for what they were—the poisonous rantings of a woman who had no other use for her tongue.

"Immorality? That 'chit' has more morality in her little finger than you do in the whole of your soul, madam.

You'd be lucky to have such a woman in your corner. But since you're too foolish to realize it, we're only too happy to leave."

Sliding one hand around Madeline's waist and the other about Tessa's, he gazed into their sweet faces and smiled. "Come, my darling family. Let's go home."

Epilogue

Dear Cousin,

    *A few months ago, you pontificated in your letter
about loans, and in the wake of excitement over
Miss Prescott's wedding to Lord Norcourt, I forgot to
respond. Today a bank draft arrived to remind me—
payment of the loan I made to her and her father
months ago. So now I'll point out that if you'd taken
your own advice eleven years ago about not giving
loans, I would have been in dire straits indeed. Thank
you for going against your own principles.*

                    Your grateful relation,
                    Charlotte

"That's enough giggling, girls," Madeline chided. "Or I'll tell my husband what you're giggling about."

As Anthony arched an eyebrow at her, Tessa, Lucy, and Elinor subsided into blushes from their seats at the dining room table. Although Madeline adored having them at Norcourt Hall for her birthday celebration, she'd forgotten what girls their age could be like. The subject occupying them on *this* visit was the recent Harvest Ball that Lucy and Elinor had attended, since they'd had their come-outs shortly after Madeline had left the school to marry Anthony.

Tessa had taken well to life at the school, and for her second term she'd begged to live there, too, so she could be closer to her new friend Elinor, who'd lived with a relation nearby during her debut. Madeline had to hand it to Elinor and Lucy, who'd left the school but still attended the teas for graduates—they'd both taken Tessa under their wings so eagerly that she'd become like a younger sister to them.

"I remember when *you* used to giggle at the table, Maddie-girl." Madeline's father winked at the others from his seat beside Mrs. Jenkins, soon to be Mrs. Prescott.

"I never giggled in my life!" Madeline protested.

"I seem to recall some giggling when you imbibed a certain gas . . ." Anthony teased.

When that roused the girls' questions, Madeline shot him a look that said she'd repay him for that little comment later. Outrageous devil that he was, he merely laughed. And despite having been married to the man for nearly five months, she still responded to that laugh with an increased pulse and a silly fluttering in the pit of her belly.

"Uncle Anthony," Tessa chirped, "Lucy has a question for you."

Poor unsuspecting Anthony said, "Ask away, Miss Seton. You know I'm always happy to help you girls."

Lucy seemed to debate something, then thrust out her chin. "If a gentleman asks a lady to meet him, say, in the garden, say, at night, so he can show her the constellations, is he . . . well . . ."

"Who asked you to meet him in a garden at night?" Anthony growled, tossing down his fork.

"No one in particu—"

"It was Lord Westfield!" Elinor offered. "He said he'd show her the stars."

Tessa and Elinor giggled together.

"I'll show *him* stars," Anthony muttered. "Westfield isn't good enough for either of you, considering that he spends half his evenings at Mrs. Bea—"

"Anthony, darling," Madeline cut in before he actually named the popular brothel, "I'm sure Lord Westfield meant nothing by it."

Anthony snorted, then gave the girls a warning look. "Stay away from Lord Westfield, understand? He's most definitely a beast in gentleman's clothing."

"What about his younger brother?" Tessa asked in wide-eyed innocence. "He told his sister—she goes to the school with me—that he couldn't wait until I was old enough to dance at our assemblies, because he wanted to dance with me."

Anthony's mouth dropped open; then he cast Madeline a glance of sheer fatherly panic. "God save us, she's already lining up dance partners for the assemblies!"

"Don't worry, that's a few years off yet," Madeline said, biting back a smile. "The girls don't get to dance with boys until the age of sixteen."

"I don't suppose Mrs. Harris would add ten years to that," he said hopefully.

"Don't be silly, Uncle Anthony." Tessa gave him an airy smile. "Then I'd be twenty-six, and that's far too *old*."

When she said it in the faintly disgusted tone of the very young, Madeline burst into laughter, since this was her own twenty-sixth birthday. "Yes, darling," she told Anthony, "and we *old* people never dance. We're too busy polishing our canes."

"And lying in our invalid beds," Mrs. Jenkins said with a twinkle.

"And snoring in church," Papa put in as he squeezed Mrs. Jenkins's hand.

The four of them laughed together while the girls exchanged perplexed glances.

But much later, after everyone else had retired and Madeline had finished dressing for bed, she entered the master bedchamber to find her husband frowning at himself in the mirror.

"Do you think I'm old, sweetheart?" he asked as he peered closely at his hair.

Coming up behind him, she wrapped her arms around his waist. "Not particularly. Why?"

"I found a gray hair this morning."

She laughed. "I take it back. You're doddering on the edge of the grave."

"That's not funny," he grumbled as he faced her. "I *feel* old whenever Tessa and her friends start talking about young gentlemen." He scowled. "Gentlemen, hah! They're a lot of scurrilous scoundrels who ought to be horsewhipped before being allowed anywhere near young ladies."

Another laugh escaped her. "Whatever happened to the rakehell I married?"

"He now remembers every minute of his misbegotten youth and fears for the safety of females around men like him." He sighed. "Good God, listen to me. I *am* old. I've become quite the stodgy fellow."

"Hardly," she said, brushing a kiss to his lips.

Yes, he'd grown into a responsible gentleman determined to build a good life for them in Chertsey, but he was a long way from stodgy. A stodgy man didn't stop what he was doing to go on a picnic when his niece requested it. Or build a laboratory on his estate so his wife could pursue naturalist studies to her heart's content. Or chase said wife around the table with reckless abandon.

"The girls continue to ask you questions about rogues without the least concern about your stodginess," Madeline went on. "Clearly, they still regard you as quite the authority on the subject."

He gave a rueful laugh. "I knew those rake lessons would prove the bane of my life."

"Probably for years to come. Or at least until Tessa marries." She backed toward the bed with a grin. "Now *I* have a question for you, Lord Norcourt."

His look changed at once to that of the rakehell she knew and loved. "And what might that be, minx?"

She slipped her wrapper from her shoulders, letting it slide to the floor. "If a gentleman asks a lady to meet him, say, in his bedchamber, say, at night, so he can show her the stars, is he . . . well . . ."

"Grateful to her for indulging his beastly nature?" he rasped as he caught her about the waist and drew her to him. "Delighted to be married to such a wise and clever woman?" He bent his head. "Wildly, deliriously, ecstatically in love?"

"I was going to say, 'angling to seduce her,' but I like yours better."

"Then the answer is yes."

"To which question?" she teased.

"All of them." He nuzzled her cheek before whispering in her ear, "Now come on, sweetheart. Let me show you the stars."

And he did.

Author's Note

The anesthetic properties of nitrous oxide (otherwise known as laughing gas) were discovered by Sir Humphry Davy in 1799. The famous chemist really did write a 579-page tome about his experiments on it, in which he included accounts of use by such celebrities of the day as poets Robert Southey and Samuel Taylor Coleridge, Peter Roget (yes, *that* Roget), and Josiah and Thomas Wedgwood. But not until 1846 was the gas actually used to numb pain, and by then ether and chloroform had also been discovered. In the intervening years, the gas was primarily used for entertainment at parties, a practice which continues to this day. Sir Humphry's wife was indeed a jealous woman, and he did have health problems stemming, some say, from his addiction to nitrous oxide.

I based the incident with Dr. Prescott's patient on a real-life occurrence that happened to a friend of mine. He had an abscess, and when the doctor began to probe it, he went into sepsis. They had to rush him to the hospital to prevent his dying on the table. It made me wonder what happened in times when knowledge of sepsis and a means for combating it weren't available.

Condoms have been around for centuries, with the oldest extant specimen (dating from 1640) having been discovered in Sweden, along with its Latin user's manual. And yes, it has ribbons. Pictures of it appear on the Internet.

As for my other elements about sexuality, until the seventeenth century, masturbation wasn't considered that awful. Some medical works even touted it as a remedy for unwise liaisons. That changed in 1710 with the release of *Onania; or the Heinous Sin of Self-Pollution and All its Frightful Consequences in both Sexes considered,* written by a clergyman, and the subsequent release in 1760 of a book by a Swiss physician, Samuel Tissot.

Despite the occasional pamphlet refuting those anti-masturbation critics, the furor continued, with the practice being decried throughout the Victorian Age, when it reached its height with ingenious devices invented to prevent it. Voices like those of Madeline and her father who criticized the hysteria were widely ignored. And yes, animals do masturbate.

Animals have been a source of fascination to humans for years, which is why menageries like the one on Charles Godwin's estate sprang up everywhere in England in the nineteenth century. Clarabelle is based on a real-life rhino named Clara who was exhibited throughout Europe in the mid-1700s, entertaining thousands. She was reported to be tame and friendly. So how could I resist putting her look-alike in a book?

Want even more sizzling romance from *New York Times* bestselling author Sabrina Jeffries? Don't miss

The Secret of Flirting

the next installment in her sizzling and sexy Sinful Suitors series.

Coming in Spring 2018 from Pocket Books!

$\mathcal{M}$onique fought panic as Lord Fulkham expertly maneuvered them through the crowded rooms of St. James's Palace toward the garden. Curse the count for throwing her to the wolves. And after he'd said he and Lady Ursula would always be at her side, too!

She should have known not to trust him. Ever since they'd left Calais she'd had the sense that he was hiding something. Still, she hadn't expected him to sabotage her masquerade after he'd gone to such trouble to set it up. Could he not see that Lord Fulkham was baiting him? Baiting *her*?

Probably not. To be fair, he didn't know of her former association with Lord Fulkham. He must never find out, either. Because she had to secure help for Grand-maman in her final days, and this pretense seemed the only way to do so.

But why oh why did Lord Fulkham have to be the man at the center of these proceedings? And why must he seem to have recognized her? All his veiled remarks and his intense scrutiny—he remembered her. She was sure of it.

And why hadn't the count warned her that there was a portrait of Aurore in the *Lady's Monthly Museum*? She must finagle a chance to see it. She dearly hoped it was indeed of poor quality and not a likeness that highlighted the few ways in which she and Aurore did *not* resemble each other.

When they reached the garden, her heart sank to see it so deserted. Apparently she hadn't been the only one to think dinner might soon be served. Even the band they'd heard playing out here earlier had packed up and moved inside, closer to the banqueting room.

You can handle this, she told herself. *You're an acclaimed actress, for God's sake. This is what you do—play roles. Why, you've even played a princess before. So get to it, and show this pompous gentleman what you're made of.*

With that in mind, she went on the offensive. "Please forgive me if this is rude, Lord Fulkham, but I'm confused by what my uncle said concerning your part in these negotiations. I was unaware that undersecretaries were of such profound importance in English political matters. I thought they were little better than clerks."

If she'd thought to insult him, his laugh showed that she'd failed. "Some of them are. It just so happens that England has two kinds. I'm the political kind. Especially these days, with the foreign secretary laid up in bed." He cast her a searching glance. "You have a better knowledge of English affairs than I would have expected."

She had her half-English grandfather to thank for that. He'd always kept up with politics in his mother's country. "And you, monsieur, have a better facility for 'diplomacy' than I would have expected. I think my uncle is right. You *do* have a silver tongue."

"I hope not. It would make it awfully hard to eat," he quipped.

A laugh sputtered out of her. Curse him. She didn't remember him having a humorous side. "You are very droll, monsieur."

"And you are very . . . different," he said.

She tensed. "From what?"

"From what I expected. I'd heard that the Princess of Chanay was a rather haughty young lady."

She had no idea if Aurore was haughty. Though it would stand to reason. Weren't all princesses haughty?

Not the way Monique played them. And it didn't matter how Aurore really was. According to the count, no one outside Chanay had ever met the princess, so Lord Fulkham couldn't be sure what she was like. He was merely trying to catch the woman he *had* met in an error.

Which meant she must be as different from Monique Servais as possible, to throw him off guard, make him doubt his eyes. Monique Servais had given him the sharper side of her tongue, so Princess Aurore must be engaging, flirtatious.

"A man like you should know better than to listen to rumor," she told him.

"Actually, rumor is my lifeblood. There's generally a bit of truth in every piece of gossip. It's my job to find out which bits are true and which bits are trumped-up lies." He led her down a path. "For example, I heard that you were partial to theatrical entertainments. Is that the case?"

Curse the fellow, he'd heard no such thing. He was just baiting her again.

She fought the urge to stiffen, keeping her grip on his arm deliberately loose. "I enjoy the occasional play, yes. Doesn't everyone?"

"It depends. I like plays, but only tragedies." He shot her a veiled look. "Comedies set my teeth on edge."

She remembered only too well his ridiculous opinion of comedies. "I prefer operas," she said lightly. "Doesn't matter to me what the story is about as long as there's singing. Do you enjoy the opera, monsieur?"

That seemed to catch him off guard, for he frowned. "Not at all, I'm afraid. In real life people don't speak to each other in arias."

"In real life people do not wear elaborate costumes to go to the market, either, but one can still enjoy seeing such attire in that setting on the stage."

"Yes, those powdered wigs are quite entertaining," he drawled. "Especially when the actors and actresses are running in and out of the boudoir."

She could feel his eyes on her. Clearly he was referencing *Le Mariage de Figaro* directly. Silly man. As if *that* would make her lose her control and spill her secrets. "Oh, I do like that kind of opera myself. *Otello* is *so* dramatic. And that scene in Desdemona's boudoir makes me weep every time."

He halted to eye her closely. "You've seen Rossini's *Otello*?"

"Of course. In Paris. It was quite moving."

A triumphant look crossed his face. "I thought you rarely left Chanay."

Too late she remembered what the count had told her about Aurore's secluded life. She scrambled to cover her error. "That's true—I rarely do. But Maman took me to

Paris to see *Otello* once when I was a girl. It's her favorite opera."

"You said that it 'makes me weep every time.' That implies you've seen it more than once."

Her heart thundered in her chest. "I meant 'every time I think of the scene.' I misspoke. English is not my native tongue, you know." She tipped up her chin. "And why do you dissect my words so, monsieur? Is it necessary for the prospective Queen of Belgium to speak your language perfectly?"

"That's not why I 'dissect' your words, as you are well aware."

Merde, obviously he'd figured her out. She would have to tread carefully, or else he would swallow her up, and with her, all her hopes for her and Grand-maman's future. "I have no idea what you are talking about."

"Come now, mademoiselle." He leaned close enough to show the hardening planes of his face. "It's time that you relinquish this pretense. Because you and I both know that you are Monique Servais and *not* the Princess of Chanay at all."

Gregory had expected guilt. Shock that he'd found her out. Horror that he'd actually confronted her over it.

He had *not* expected the damned woman to laugh at him, long and loud, before saying, "Who on earth is Mona Servet?"

"*Monique* Ser— Damn it, you know whom I mean. You. *You're* Monique Servais."

Eyes twinkling, she cocked her head at him. "Oh? Tell me more. Why do you think I am not myself and instead am . . . am . . ." She waved her hand airily. "Some Frenchwoman."

"What makes you think she's French?" he countered.

That made her falter, but so briefly he could almost think he'd imagined it. Except that he hadn't.

"Servais is a French name," she said stoutly.

"Actually, there are Servaises in Belgium, Sweden, Luxembourg, and Canada, as well as Dieppe, France."

She didn't even blink at the mention of Dieppe. "Are there? I had no idea. Nor do I care. This Monique Servais is nothing to me." She arched an eyebrow. "And you still have not told me why you think I am she."

He crossed his arms over his chest, annoyed now. This wasn't going as expected. "So you intend to brazen it out, do you?"

"Brazen *what* out? That I am some other woman pretending to be Princess Aurore? The idea is absurd."

"I agree. But true, nonetheless."

She shook her head. "You, monsieur, are quite mad."

When she turned on her heel as if to head back inside, he caught her by the arm. "No more mad than you and the count if you think you can perpetrate a deception of such proportions without consequence."

A cool smile crossed her lips as she faced him once more. Oh so delicately she removed his hand from her arm. "Why would my country attempt such a thing at this critical moment in the negotiations? You must realize that the very idea is ludicrous."

"It is. Which is why I must know the reason for it."

"You tell me. I have no idea." As if to erase the feel of him, she rubbed her arm where he'd been gripping it. "But you must have *some* theory."

Sadly, he didn't. He could think of no reason for such a subterfuge. Yet.

"Well?" she prodded, obviously sensing the weak point in his argument.

He threw out the first thing that came to him. "Perhaps the princess is dead. And Chanay doesn't want to lose their chance at having Belgium in their pocket."

"The princess isn't dead." Just as he was about to pounce on that slip, she added, "She's standing right here before you." Then she fluttered her fan again in what he'd come to realize was a telltale indication of her nervousness. "And if she *were* dead, then how could anyone reasonably expect her to be made Queen of Belgium? Unless you believe that the royal family of Rochefort means to put an impostor on the throne. Not only would they be risking the royal line, but such a conspiracy would require my subjects—excuse me, the *princess's* subjects, according to you—to accept another woman in her place."

Another woman. Gregory kept waiting for her to forget herself and say, "an actress," which he had deliberately not mentioned as the impostor's profession, but so far Mademoiselle Servais had been better at maintaining her role than he would have expected.

So Gregory fell back on his usual tactics—fix her with a stare, keep his silence, and wait for her to crumble. Unfortunately, she seemed to be familiar with the strategy, because she did the same thing to him. And as the silence between them lengthened, it gave him time to look her over, to remind himself of her sensuous curves, to be drawn in by her beauty.

Damn her.

Meanwhile, she'd shown no sign of being the least affected by him in that way. Though she *was* an actress, which meant that showing no sign of her true feelings was her forte.

Apparently growing emboldened by his silence, she snapped, "Have you no answer to that?"

It was his move now. He'd best make it a good one. "For all I know, the royal family of Chanay *does* intend to put an impostor on the throne—someone they can manipulate, someone they can control. The real princess is not such a person. And there *is* a resemblance between the two of you, after all, which might even be good enough to fool the citizens of Chanay."

As he'd hoped, that seemed to startle her. The only reason this subterfuge was working was that no one outside Chanay had ever met the real princess. Including him. But Mademoiselle Servais needn't know that.

"Are you saying that you and I have met before?" Her voice was strained. "Because I do not remember that. And I think I would remember a man of your sort visiting Chanay."

He gritted his teeth to hear her persist in the deception *still.* "Of course we've met before, as you well know. Not in Chanay but in Dieppe, where you lived as Mademoiselle Servais."

That didn't seem to faze her. "So, you have *not* met me then. And all your talk about the 'real' princess not being able to be manipulated is just . . . what? Speculation? Because you have some notion that I am this woman from Dieppe?"

"It's not a notion, damn it!"

He caught himself. The chit was annoyingly adept at making him lose control of his temper. And if he'd learned anything it was that controlling one's emotions was essential in his position.

Forcing a measure of calm into his voice, he asked, "Why would I invent such a thing?"

"Because you once encountered a woman who looks like me, and have mixed us up." A brittle smile crossed her lips. "You saw that poor likeness of me in the *Lady's Monthly Museum* and think that I look different. But men do not realize how easy it is for a woman to change her appearance merely with a touch of rouge to brighten the cheeks, a bit of kohl to darken the eyebrows. We can make them doubt their very eyes just with our crème pots. And we often do."

True. Most men were unaware of such female secrets. But he was not just any man. Secrets were his game.

"How interesting that you should mention cosmetics," he said, "when I would imagine a princess of your standing is forbidden to wear them. But Mademoiselle Servais wore them all the time. She was an opera singer."

Would she correct him? He watched her expression, but she gave nothing away.

Instead, she broke into a smile. "An opera singer? How droll! Comic or dramatic opera?"

"That is hardly relevant."

She made a face. "No, I suppose not. But it is no wonder you are confused. An opera singer wears wigs and face paint and patches. How could you even tell what she looked like?"

He tried another untruth. "I saw her without all of that."

Only the sudden sharpening of her smile betrayed her reaction. "Did you, indeed?"

"Yes. Though even if I had not, I never forget a face, cosmetic changes or no. And I noticed Mademoiselle Servais's prominent chin in particular. The real princess has a very small chin, nothing like the opera singer's."

She laughed. "*That* is the source of your evidence? My *chin*? You do realize, sir, that no woman wishes to have, as you call it, 'a prominent chin.' So, of course I asked the artist to reshape my chin for the painting. Even a princess wants to appear beautiful in her portraits."

"You know damned well that you're beautiful, prominent chin and all," he snapped. "You're certainly more beautiful than Princess Aurore."

"I'm not sure how that's possible, given that I *am* the princess." Her eyes shone merrily in the lamps of the garden. "But I shall take the compliment regardless."

God, she was as sly as a courtesan, and twice as tempting. "If you didn't, I'd be shocked, since you didn't seem to mind such compliments when I made them before." He tried to provoke her with another lie, crowding her in and lowering his voice to a murmur. "You didn't mind *anything* we did before."

She blinked. *That* had shaken her. "Oh? Are you saying that this Mademoiselle Servais was your . . . paramour?"

"Can you claim otherwise?"

As if she knew what he was about, she met his gaze coolly. "Of course not. I am not she. What do I care if you have ten paramours?"

He considered his choices. He could give up the fight for now. See what he could find out. Which might be difficult, given the fact that even the very respectable Beaumonde was obviously part of the plot.

Or he could do something that would throw her off her game entirely. Because if he pulled her into his arms and kissed her, the actress would not dare to call out for help from the guests—she wouldn't want to risk his voicing his suspicions before an audience. But she might lose her temper and give him what for. She hadn't liked him, after all. Besides, she'd been temperamental, easy to provoke. So if he could provoke her into a mistake—

Of course, if she really were the princess, what he was about to do could ruin him. But she was not—he'd never been so sure of anything in his life. And given that fact, *not* exposing her subterfuge could ruin him, too, if it came out later. He'd look the fool for not seeing through her disguise. His enemies would make mincemeat of his political aspirations.

He glanced around. The garden was empty now, everyone having drifted inside. And nothing else had provoked her into making a mistake. Unfortunately, until he could get her to admit her masquerade, he couldn't get her to tell him why there was a need for it.

"Now, sir," she began, "if you are quite done trying to make me out to be an impostor, I should like to return to—"

"Not yet," he said firmly. Once she rejoined her companions, he wouldn't have another chance at unraveling this deception. At least not tonight.

He snagged her about the waist, taking her by surprise, and pulled her into a nearby gazebo obviously kept dark for a reason. Then he murmured, "We should take up where we left off in Dieppe."

Find your next read at

XOXO *after* DARK

Join us for the best in romance,
ebook deals, free reads, and more!

Because the best conversations
happen after dark...

XOXOAfterDark.com
/ XOXOAfterDark
@ XOXOAfterDark